The Ayes
Have
It

The Ears Have It

Agents of the Convent
Book Two

Rebecca Connolly

Phase Publishing, LLC
Seattle

Cover art by Tugboat Design
http://www.tugboatdesign.net

Phase Publishing, LLC first paperback edition
July 2021

ISBN 978-1-952103-29-2
Library of Congress Control Number 2021913285
Cataloging-in-Publication Data on file.

Acknowledgements

To Addison, for being the best distraction from this project known to man. May I always be your favorite aunt, and may you always be as ridiculously fun as you are now.

And to chocolate. All of it. For everything. All the time.

Want to hear about future releases and upcoming events for Rebecca Connolly?

Sign up for the monthly Wit and Whimsy at:

www.rebeccaconnolly.com

A Proclamation

By Miss Leonora Masters
Headmistress of Miss Masters's Finishing School

Forasmuch as it has been thus Ordained by the powers that be that the Rearing of gently bred ladies requires some assistance, and in Keeping with traditions long established, It has been decreed that such rearing Needs proper establishment for training purposes, Given the span and scope of such development.

As it pleases the powers that be, Never forgetting the honor due to her subjects, Development and education of young ladies shall be Courteously and courageously given.

Owing to the need for such establishment, Unto the finishing of the female sex, Nobility shall be thus encouraged, Their patronage much desired, to Relinquish the education of such female persons as aforementioned Yet in their youthful and less informed state Into such qualified care.

Nevertheless, with charity and succor, females of a Lesser status shall be generously and Indubitably sponsored in their similar attendance herein For the purpose of gaining appropriate Education as befits needs and station.

Occupied thusly, this establishment shall henceforth Render such superior instruction and care, Defending the virtue and honor of her pupils, Engendering appropriate accomplishment upon all, Avowing to maintain the standards and Traditions of her forebears, and shall Henceforth fulfil all other obligations as so indicated.

Given under my Hand at Miss Masters's Finishing School in Kent, the 1st day of March, 1790, in the Thirtieth year of His Majesty's reign.

God save the King
Leonora Masters

Chapter One
London, 1826

*S*he wasn't going to make it.

It wasn't the first time she'd had that thought on a night such as this, but she was convinced she had never meant it more than she did now. Emmeline Bartlett was not going to get herself out of her scrape this time.

It would serve her right, of course. Young ladies of five and twenty did not gad about London's seedy side in the middle of the night to satiate their curiosity. And they did not do such a thing dressed in men's clothing. And they certainly did not steal from a gambling den when they did so.

Yet here she was, bolting down dark, dank, and cramped corridors in the heart of the Seven Dials. Her legs were encased in trousers, a padded jacket was fastened about her chest, her hair was tightly plaited beneath her cap, and her booted feet slipped on the damp cobblestone as she ran for her life.

In one hand, she had the list of names she had collected from that game of poker wherein young ladies of Society were being used as part of the ante. In the other... well, the other was gripping forty-seven pounds, three guineas, sixpence, and a ha'penny. That was her winnings—before the game had turned and the ladies started being used as chattel in a game they would only hear about in their nightmares.

But that had been her purpose in coming out to the Seven Dials tonight and the past three nights, attempting to find the correct gambling den. Her information had been vague at best, but there wasn't anything she could have done to improve her task except explore each option and rule them out. There were a dozen possibilities in the area of the Seven Dials she had isolated based on her information, and there was no simple way to remove oneself from such a place the moment it became clear it was not the correct locale. She'd managed two of them last night, but it had been a trial, and she understood completely why it was not a task that ought to be repeated.

Tonight, however, she had found the correct place. And now she was running for her life.

Oddly enough, it was not because she had been discovered as a woman but because she had cheated. Four others at the table had cheated as well, but she simply looked the least intimidating of the group. What she wouldn't give for some convincing facial hair and the stench of gin at moments like that.

She swiped an arm across her perspiration-dampened face, the carefully applied cosmetics smearing onto her sleeve. There was no point in keeping it on, given she had what she needed, and no amount of powder or shading would save her now.

It was as close to appearing masculine as she could get, and it sufficed for the intoxicated individuals she encountered in places like this. But it would not have passed any closer inspection. Despite her plain face and angular features, she was not as manly as she was ambiguous. A young chap in a thoroughly adult environment was all she could claim, and there were plenty of sots willing to take funds off such an individual. Admittance was rarely restricted to a certain membership, and if it was, she had made enough seedy connections to gain entrance.

She rounded a corner, her boots slipping again and nearly sending her crashing to the ground. She managed to catch her balance, and she turned to head down a new street in the exact direction she'd been coming from, which should, hopefully, confuse her pursuers.

Apparently, Mr. Markham was not keen on cheaters, and her tendency toward flight rather than fight had earned her a turn as the fox while two rather large, smelly blokes turned to hounds in this scenario.

A cramped alley to her right became rather appealing and she turned into it, desperate to find an additional burst of speed. But instead she found that she was growing more and more fatigued the more she ran.

She'd rain down a curse upon the head of whoever decided young ladies should not exert themselves. Emmeline would have been far better suited to her present chase had she been permitted to do more than the sedate exercise of taking a turn about the room.

Something to think about if she managed to escape this race of hers, but it was looking less and less likely.

Her heart lurched forward as she saw the alley open into a main thoroughfare. At this time of night, there hopefully wouldn't be anyone about. She was still not in any sort of polite section of London, but the closer she got to Covent Garden, the safer she would be, which was an ironic statement all things considered, but nevertheless…

She tore out into the main street, her feet carrying her farther out than she'd intended with her haste. She wrenched to her left, her arms flailing with the change in motion, and begged her legs to keep going, keep moving, keep propelling her away from danger.

Desperate to check the approaching threats, she glanced behind her, long having lost the sound of their paces behind her to the pounding in her own ears. She couldn't stop even if they had, not until she was back into more familiar territory.

Suddenly, she careened into a warm, lean body, falling to the side, and only just missing hitting her face against the cobblestone as a sharp pressure gripped her upper arm.

"*Cuidado te tengo,*" a deep, cultured voice rumbled in a language she didn't know.

She was righted before she could react, staring at the man in horror, fearing the worst. But he was not one of the men who had been chasing her, unless someone had found a shortcut she did not know. His complexion was dark, though not so dark as the man standing just behind his right shoulder. Both were of an imposing height, and the man before her was rather striking in his attractiveness.

Or would have been, had he not been gripping her arm. Neither were particularly well dressed, and both bore definite signs of scruff along their face. Fortunate men.

"Are you all right, *muchacho*?" he asked, his impossibly dark eyes searching hers, the word he used holding a twinge of curiosity to it.

Could he see that she was no man?

"Let go," Emmeline begged, lowering her voice as much as she could. "Please, sir. Please, let go."

He released her arm, nodding once. "*Sí insistes*. Take care of yourself." He nudged his head behind him in suggestion.

Emmeline did not need to be told twice. She dashed around them and used the size of the darker man to hide her retreat, staying as close to the buildings in the street as she could until she found another alley to cut back across. She would run back and forth all the way to Covent Garden if she had to. Whatever would hide her from the men from Markham's.

Some of these alleys would have smaller interior alleys that would hide her further still, and if she could find just one of them...

A jolt of victory and elation surged through her as she found such a one, and she slipped into its narrow depths. She could now continue to move rapidly, though not at the same pace from before, and her limbs thanked her for the change. Her feet, however, began to throb, tingle, and ache, each sensation in a different part, and she longed to get back into the soft slippers of a proper lady's attire. Perhaps there would still be a fire going in her room, and perhaps Bess would bring her a late tea if she were not already asleep.

Emmeline had more than enough practice with brewing her own cup of tea, so if her trusted maid had retired for the night, a cup of tea could still be possible. If the fire was still lit, of course. She could build up a fire that was already aflame, but starting one on her own... Well, she would do the best she could if there was no fire to be had.

Surely it couldn't be so difficult.

Scurrying as she was along the narrow alley, accompanied only by the occasional drip of the sewers, her heart began to slow its frantic pace. There were no sounds of pursuit, so unless Markham's thugs knew exactly where she was and how to circumvent her route, she ought to be safe.

Still, this was no leisurely stroll, and until she had reached her destination, she could not relax completely. Would not. This article was too important for that.

For three weeks, she had been trying to get this information and all its specifics, and now she had them. She could now expose the supposed gentlemen who took part and, hopefully, prevent the societal sacrifice of any other young ladies. How many had already been given up under such circumstances without any part of Society knowing the truth?

There wasn't much time to waste, so she might as well write the article tonight rather than sleep. She could claim a headache when she was done and earn herself a few hours of respite afterward. Her aunt's footman Declan would see the article was delivered as he always did, and she could enjoy watching the consequences of tonight's actions unfold when it came to print.

All of this would be worth it. She'd remind herself of that when she slept next, and when her body ached from tonight's adventure.

It would all be worth it.

Her small alley was about to open into another street, telling her if she were in any sort of danger or not. If she would have to keep running or not. If she would make it or not.

Weighing her options and examining the map of London's underbelly in her head, Emmeline held her breath before slipping around the corner and flattening herself against the wall. No steps sounded behind her, and none sounded around her.

Perhaps it was over, then. But...

She drummed her fingers against the cool brick wall at her back, then turned to her right and started toward the street at an easy stroll just as any London night dweller might have done. Her eyes darted back and forth, waiting for someone, anyone, to approach her from any direction.

None did, meaning it was safe to proceed to her actual destination, which would have surprised the men chasing her. Had they continued the chase, she had an alternate location in place, one that she would have to go to anyway, and one that was safer if she were being pursued. This place, however, was always her preferred first stop on nights like this.

She allowed herself to smile, moving almost silently along the streets, being free from any obstructions or distractions, free from any additional delays. Free to be a woman, in a manner of speaking. There was something beautiful about London in the middle of the night, and Emmeline was certainly the only one of her station—the only *woman* of her station—to understand that.

The stars were so bright, even though she couldn't see as many of them as she might when she was in Kent. At the Miss Masters's Finishing School, the stars were endless on clear nights. Though she was only a teacher on an occasional basis each term, being in Kent was a breath of much needed fresh, cleansing air. With such open space and brilliant scenery, the soul could not help but be lifted.

But, surprisingly, London at night almost felt like that. Almost. Although no one would believe her, should she have tried to explain those insights.

She passed a few familiar buildings, her heart seeming to burst within her with the heat of abject relief. Tonight had not been the most dangerous situation she had ever found herself in, but it had been the closest chase.

Emmeline moved down an unremarkable side alley, bemused as she found her present surroundings as comfortable as that of her aunt's home, though the level of elegance between the two could not be more different.

Aunt Hermione lived in relative luxury in Mayfair, though certainly not at the height of its fashionable extravagance. Covent Garden did not possess the same luxury. At least, not this side of it. Appearances where the wealthy *haute ton* might attend the theatre bore hints of finery, just enough to avoid offending its patrons. But this darker, reverse side was for the lesser creatures of London. And tonight, Emmeline was one of them.

Most of the time when she was here, she was one of them. She had only attended the theatre as a patron a handful of times in recent years. Turning into a spinster without much bother would do that to one's social calendar.

She tucked into a small side alley along a building, her fingers tracing the surface as she walked. The unobtrusive door she sought was then before her, and, as usual, it was unlocked for her. She slid into the building, latching the door firmly behind her before heading down the cramped corridor, releasing a heavy sigh and tugging her cap from her head. Scratching at her pinned up plaits, Emmeline moved farther into the building, the dim light in the place surprising. She had expected full darkness, as had been the case on previous evenings when she'd needed to return here. Still, there was no telling what the life of the theatre was like when the patrons departed.

She took care with her steps, not quite silently treading, but hardly stomping her feet to announce her presence. For all she knew, some of the actors might sleep here, and others might use the premises as living quarters—or for whatever else the space allowed.

Such as costuming a would-be journalist for London adventures.

She had her own collection by this time, of course, but she had only attained those articles of clothing by virtue of perhaps her greatest contact of all.

"What have you done to my pieces, Ears?"

Emmeline jumped at the sudden voice, turning toward the small room just off the main corridor where a woman, dark hair loosely plaited over a wrap-clad shoulder, stood watching her with a small smile on her lips. Her face was shockingly free of any of her usual cosmetics, which allowed the faintest lines on her face to be visible to the naked eye perhaps for the very first time. She'd called Emmeline by the pet name she'd had since childhood, yet it suited her activity in the streets too perfectly to ignore, and thus had become her self-declared code name. But as this woman knew Emmeline's complete identity, and was the only person on earth who did, the code name was irrelevant in this situation.

Which was likely why she had used it.

"Gracious, Tilda," Emmeline gasped, her heart barely managing to beat again. "I've had enough frights for the night, I hardly need you adding to them."

"Are you hurt?" Tilda asked at once, all teasing gone.

Shaking her head quickly, Emmeline came over to her, putting a hand on her friend's folded arms. "I am very well. Although my feet ache something abominable, and I may have turned an ankle, but all things considered, I am well."

Tilda seemed to take a breath at her account and nodded once. "And were you followed, dear?"

Emmeline hissed and nodded. "I was. I was caught cheating at Markham's club, and he doesn't take kindly to that. I had what I needed already, so I fled."

Now Tilda sighed heavily. "Oh, Ears. Darling, I've taught you better than that. How could you cheat so obviously? And to get caught? Emmeline, I can hardly keep my countenance."

The scolding made Emmeline laugh, which felt almost foreign after the night she'd had. "That is what perturbs you most about it?"

"I do have a reputation to consider." Tilda sniffed with some imperious air before winking as a corner of her lips curved. "Did you outrun them?"

"Barely," Emmeline admitted with another scratch to her hair. "I was not at all certain I would. I even ran into a man while I fled, but he caught me before I could fall down."

Tilda's eyes brightened in the dim light. "Did he indeed? My, my, Miss Emmeline Bartlett, perhaps you might find more than one victory in the events of this evening."

Emmeline rolled her eyes and leaned against the wall like she had seen many men do. "Not you as well. My aunt believes every day is a new opportunity for me to find a husband, and no lack of suitors can make her see otherwise."

"I'm a romantic, my dear. I cannot help myself." Tilda shrugged and grinned without shame. "What did the gentleman say when he caught you?"

"I doubt he was a gentleman with how he was dressed and how unshaven he was," Emmeline grumbled, lowering her eyes, and digging her toe into the ground. "And I was dressed in my disguise, so he would hardly show politeness."

"He was handsome, then. What did he say?"

Emmeline's head jerked up, and she gaped at her friend for a long moment. "Why would you think—"

Tilda waved a dismissive hand. "You became defensive rather than answer me. Simple enough, love. What did the handsome stranger say?"

With cheeks flaming, Emmeline thought back to the man and his silent companion. "I didn't understand the language, but he said something like, 'Qui dahdo teh tango.' I thought it might be Latin, but I didn't recognize the words."

"Sounds like a Spaniard," Tilda mused, still smiling before nodding in apparent approval. "Always a pleasant choice."

Emmeline snorted softly and straightened. "If your romantic sensibilities lead you to believe I will meet him again and be swept into amorous madness, so be it. I, on the other hand, would very much like a change of clothes and a bath. Do you think I might be able to acquire another set of clothing soon? And perhaps a greatcoat, as the evenings have been cold."

Tilda nodded again, this time firmly. "I can arrange that, yes. Would you consider cutting your hair? It would make your disguises much easier."

"Don't think I have not considered the idea," Emmeline told her on a heavy exhale. "But I believe it would send my aunt into a grave prematurely, to which the rest of my family might object. If you have suggestions to improve my appearance, I welcome them."

The skilled costumer narrowed her eyes as they traced over Emmeline's still-disguised figure. "I may have a few ideas. I shall send word when I need you to be fitted. Now do hurry home, love, or I shall worry."

"Here." Emmeline plucked fifteen pounds from her winnings and handed it over to Tilda. "For waiting so late for me, and for whatever efforts you need to lay out your ideas."

Tilda took the money and gave her a fond smile. "If only all my customers paid me on a whim as you do. You know I'd refuse it if I thought it would do any good, but I do so love additional funds."

Emmeline laughed and tipped an imaginary cap at the praise, as well as the admission. "If you find yourself in need of a good pot of chocolate, Aunt Hermione is hosting a bridge gathering on Thursday. You are always welcome."

"Is she accustomed to having actresses in the house?" Tilda inquired with mild interest.

"In her society, every woman is an actress." Emmeline grinned before curtseying playfully in her breeches. "Good night, Tilda."

"Good night, love. Jack will shadow you home. I insist."

It was typical for her to be seen home by the lad, and he was a rather pleasant ragamuffin. His tales of the streets were almost worthy of belief, but Emmeline could not quite extend her imagination that far. Still, he'd earn himself a decent wage for being sporting about the assignment.

And was given more for anything he could tell her about his true master, the Gent.

The Gent was a legend in the London streets, and Emmeline fancied herself a tiny bit in love with the idea of him, though she'd never met the man, nor would she ever. Doing so would lessen his appeal.

Emmeline made her way back out of the theatre and took perhaps a dozen paces before she stopped, glancing over her shoulder. "Come on up here, Jack. I'd rather a conversation than a shadow."

"Aw, miss, one o' these days, someone'll say sommat, and Gent won' let me work for Miss Tilda no more," Jack groaned as he trudged his way up to her side. "It's not worf da risk for a half a crown."

Smiling at the boy, Emmeline tilted her head. "What about two pounds sterling? I was a bit lucky tonight, and I can promise it to you for a story worth the walk."

There wasn't another word of complaint from Jack as he escorted her back to the elegance of Mayfair, and the look of adoration he gave the sterling was enough to make any story at all worth the giving.

Chapter Two

The coin in his pocket felt somehow heavier than a mere ha'penny, but nevertheless, he felt an odd sort of satisfaction in carrying it around. The young lady dressed as a lad had dropped it upon their collision the night before, and Teo had picked it up after nonchalantly directing her pursuers to go to their right instead of their left. Whatever she had done, she did not deserve to have thugs chasing her through the underside of London, particularly if she were attempting to impersonate a man.

She'd done a decent job of it, and had she not collided with Teo, allowing him to fully take in the padding of her coat and the distinctly feminine assets not quite as disguised as she might have wished, he might have believed it, too. He refused to give anyone else a chance to gain a similar understanding.

Picking up the ha'penny from the damp cobblestone after that had seemed a bit like a trick of fate, perhaps a signal for his own impending luck. Rafa had called him simple and foolish, but Teo didn't particularly care. He'd take any chance at increasing his luck and improving fate's opinion of him.

His first venture onto English soil, and his expectations were high in some respects, while being quite low in others. Simply put, business expectations were high, personal expectations were low. He'd been in harbor before, sat upon his ship while others saw to any necessary details, but for the most part, he and his company had avoided England for many years.

England could not be avoided now.

The pains of prosperity, he thought. He couldn't expect the company to grow and expand much more without bringing in British interests, no matter how much his uncle would have hated it. And his mother. And his grandfather. And his father.

Perhaps his father would have hated any connection to England at all. He had been English after all, by birth and by heritage, no matter how far he'd turned his back on it. Rightly so, as far as Teo knew from everything he had been told, but it did not follow that Teo should also have to avoid it.

Particularly now that his grandfather—that is, the father of his father—had died and named Teo his heir. That was not technically surprising, given there were no other grandchildren, but it also was rather surprising since there had been a rift of momentous proportion between father and son. The baronetcy's continuation had fallen into some question.

Teo hadn't even known there was a title in his family line, let alone anything to inherit, until he suddenly had done so. That is, should he choose to take it up. Apparently, that was an option.

His man of business, or whatever they were called in England, had insisted he could not make such a decision without seeing his estate and seat. In the interim, he would still retain the title.

Sir Teodoro de Vickers y Mendoza. That would turn some heads in the English ranks.

They'd have to call him Sir Teodoro Vickers, he supposed, though he did not care for it. In Spain, he had insisted on being referred to as Señor Mendoza, taking his mother's name rather than his father's, which his father had insisted upon.

Their life in Spain had been a strange one for Teo in that regard. His father was undeniably English, yet rare was the day that he spoke his native tongue. Teo had been instructed in it, but it was never spoken in their home. There was no discussion of England at any time, nor of his family. All questions Teo had ever asked had been brushed away without concern. He knew nothing about his family, his heritage, or England at all from his father. Only after his death had his mother given him any detail, and that had been just as lacking.

Sir Edwin Vickers, his grandfather, had not approved of his son's match with a Spanish lady, though her pedigree and station were of the highest degree. He had threatened to cut his only child off if he should marry her.

Apparently, that had not been enough of a threat. John Vickers became husband to Maria Graciela Isabella de Mendoza y Reynoso, and Sir Edwin had lost a son. His threat of cutting off his heir had proven to be unnecessary, as Teo's father had died before his sire so the estate would have fallen to Teo anyway.

Wherever Diehle House was, and whatever its condition, he'd have to see it soon and determine what he made of the things his father had turned his back on.

Luckily for Teo, that was not today's assignment. Today was simply business. Or so Rafa kept reminding him.

But heaven help him, Teo was curious. Curious about England, curious about his father, curious about the life his father could have led. He was curious about all of it. Though he could not claim such a curiosity for all his life, the moment he had stepped onto England's shores, everything he had ever wondered throughout his childhood had suddenly rushed upon him as though it had been an obsession.

Rafa had not been amused.

But then, Rafa was wholly Spanish to his core and still took some affront to England doing away with the Spanish Armada back in the reign of King Phillip. More recently, Rafa was more miffed he hadn't been invited personally to the Battle of Waterloo, or to supervise Napoleon's banishment on Elba so that he might do away with the man himself. He'd never forgiven the French for invading their beloved Catalonia, inserting their own puppet into Catalonia's leadership, and seeing Spain itself as a pawn in their greater game without considering her worth.

Only a step above England in his mind. Or a step below, in this case.

Still, he did see England as a decent enough opportunity for business, which diffused some of his resentment. Now there was only a determination to take advantage of their business and trade as much as possible.

"Kindly remember, *Capitán*," Rafa growled, his English practiced but not perfect, "these English are not our friends. We need their business, not their company."

Teo glanced at his partner, who had still not adjusted to the position, and raised a brow. "And you should remember, *compañero*, that in order for us to do business, they need to like us."

Rafa frowned fully, a truly impressive expression for his dark, angular features. "Like us? *¡Qué lata!* No one has ever liked me, *Capitán*, and you know that."

"True," Teo admitted as they walked up the cobblestones toward their destination, pretending to consider it. "Then we shall only attempt for them to find us agreeable. *¿Eso está mejor?*"

"*Sí, lo es.*" Rafa pretended to smile, then scowled in his usual way. "*Maldito* British. They own the world. We wouldn't need this if they did not."

"Also true." Teo yawned, scratching at his scruff.

Rafa gave him a disparaging look. "Did you not get enough sleep last night? Sleeping on a ship in port is not good for rest. You will always be uneasy."

Teo scoffed loudly. "I always sleep on the ship in port, *camarada*. Never bothered me before."

Rafa only shrugged his broad shoulders. "Bad luck of England is cursing you."

"*Disparates*," Teo insisted. "This might become my country, Rafa. *Mi hogar.*"

Now Rafa stopped and turned to him, expression severe. "*Tienes un hogar, Teo, y este no es.*"

As though he were being instructed, Teo nodded and gestured for his friend to continue. Rafa would never understand why Teo was even remotely interested in this place, so it was best not to agitate him further in that respect. He understood more than anyone what Teo's life had been, the situation he found himself in now, everything.

Rafa had been his closest friend for a decade—since the death of Teo's mother, which had led him to take up a position in his grandfather's company alongside his uncle. Rafa had already been with the company, and the two of them became fast friends. Things could have become difficult when Teo began to train for partnership despite Rafa being equally qualified and the senior of the two in the company. But never had his friend shared a single complaint on the issue.

And when Teo's uncle had retired to Valencia, there was no one that Teo would have wanted but Rafa by his side. As his uncle Jorge had only daughters and no sons, there were no familial complaints to contend with on that score.

And the business had prospered greatly with the pair of them at the helm. They'd expanded their trade to a dozen more ports, gone into partnership with fourteen new companies, and opened business in five additional nations. They were the third largest company with interests in the Indies and a good deal quieter than the other two, which both worked in their favor and against it.

They were becoming a particularly well-respected shipping company in Europe, and their influence and reputation would only continue to rise.

Partnering with merchants in England was the next logical step if they truly wished to reach impressive heights. Which, of course, they did. Teo did. This was his more certain legacy at this point, no matter how stable the investments of land were rumored to be.

His grandfather had an extensive estate in Spain, as befitted Don Alfredo Uribe de Mendoza y Araya, Duke of Albesanta, but the title had fallen to his mother's eldest brother, Rodrigo. His son would inherit afterward, and on it would continue to go. Uncle Jorge had taken Teo under his wing on the side of commerce, shipping, and the world of merchants, embracing the trade aspect of Don Alfredo's life. Thus, Teo did not feel himself particularly excluded from the grandeur afforded his titled cousins, as he had grown prosperous without one.

Now he had the shipping prosperity as well as a title. An English title, granted, but it was something.

He had not informed his uncle, Don Rodrigo, of his new English title, though he would have to do so soon. They had always been a close-knit family, raised less than a stone's throw from each other, and though Teo was half English, to them, he was full Spanish. He'd always considered himself Spanish. Still did, in fact.

But the letter from Sir Edwin's man of business, now Teo's, had brought in a hint of something else. A question. And it was a question that could not go unanswered.

"This place is not as exciting in the light of day," Rafa muttered, not bothering to use English at all now that there were more people milling about. All of them were occupied with one task or another, some looking rather industrious while others decidedly less so. These were not the fine types that would be found in ballrooms, but those that would certainly be ignored by those that were.

This did not make any sense to Teo, as surely some of them had business interests that relied on these very sorts. Did no one ever live in both worlds? His grandfather had seamlessly done so in Spain, and it did not follow that the way of life there should be so different than here.

"There are more characters about now," Teo pointed out, matching his friend by using their native tongue rather than that of their present host nation. "Does that not make it more exciting?"

"No," Rafa said simply, shaking his head. A corner of his mouth twitched in an almost smile. "There is no mystery without the dark."

Teo merely rolled his eyes and glanced up at the sign of the business they were approaching. "I believe this is it," he said in clear English.

Rafa nodded, tugging at his faded kerchief around his neck. "Let us pray they excuse *la moda* of sailors."

"Their man last night implied they would," Teo reminded him.

"You trust too much."

"You doubt too much."

They shared bemused glances, then started up the small set of stairs leading to the business entrance, pushing the door open without trouble and hearing the tinkling of a small bell over their heads.

"Be with you in a moment," a clear, English voice rang out from somewhere in the area.

The space was cramped and somehow caked in dark dust, despite there being neither dirt nor soil in the immediate vicinity of the building. A tall desk stacked with ledgers and diagrams took up most of the front space, and it would perfectly hide the person who had called out, but the voice had sounded somehow more distant than that.

"Strange setting to do business in," Rafa murmured in Spanish, his keen eyes taking in every aspect of their surroundings.

Teo nodded in return, taking careful stock himself. He did not imagine that all their prospective partners would be of the same

16

quality, nor that they would share their same priorities or views on the manner in which they conducted business. Some of their partners in other areas of the world operated in absolute squalor yet were more reliable in their business than those in more pristine offices. It was a balance between judgment and industry, and Teo prided himself on a keen sense of both.

A lad of no more than twenty appeared from the rear of the room, hurrying toward them. "Apologies, sirs. I was returning a ledger for Mr. Simms. How can I help?"

"Teo Mendoza and Rafa Teixidor to see Mr. Simms," Teo recited in his best English. "We represent *el Don Mendoza Compañía Naviera*, and we come with a business proposal."

The young man glanced at Rafa, who was undoubtedly a more imposing figure, then back at Teo. "Is he expecting you?"

"No, but I suspect if you inform him of the company I have just mentioned, he will find time to see us." Teo raised a brow in the exact manner he had seen his no-nonsense uncle do when questioned by employees of his partners.

It worked, for the lad nodded hastily. "You said it was…?"

"*El Don Mendoza Compañía Naviera*," Teo told him slowly and with great patience, as befitting any situation with one unfamiliar with the Spanish language. "I trust you may simply say Don Mendoza Shipping, and he will understand you."

The assistant dashed back toward the direction he had come, leaving Teo and Rafa alone again.

"Perhaps he does not know us," Rafa suggested in English. "Perhaps his interests lie in other avenues."

"This *Inglés*," Teo replied in an undertone, "was sniffing around Cadiz for interests last year. If he was sincere, he will have heard our name."

"Why Cadiz?" Rafa wondered aloud. "Why not Barcelona or Malaga? Or all of them?"

Teo smirked to himself. "Why indeed."

Rafa leaned closer. "Are you conducting business, *mi amigo*? *¿O una investigación?*"

"*Un poco de ambos.*" Teo quirked his brows, grinning now. "We must know our partners, so we must examine as well as talk business."

17

"*Inteligente, amigo. Muy inteligente.*" Rafa chuckled almost darkly. "Quite a game you play."

Teo tilted his head in consideration. "Business is a game, Rafa, is it not?"

"*Sí, señor,*" Rafa agreed, nodding sagely. "*Sí, lo es.*"

The assistant returned, countenance brighter. "Mr. Simms would be happy to see you. Follow me." He gestured and all but dashed ahead of them. Teo and Rafa followed him, in step with each other as they moved toward the offices.

One look at Simms told Teo the man had never been aboard a ship in his life, let alone gone to Spain. He was paunchy, robust, rosy-cheeked, and though his clothing appeared common on first look, it was carefully cultivated to appear so. Quite a game this was.

"Señor Mendoza," Mr. Simms said with no attempt at saying his name correctly. He focused on hoisting himself out of his chair, and after failing the first time, a successful second effort had him out of it. His thick double chin wobbled with the change in position. "Welcome to England, I suppose, eh? What brings you to the office of Simms and Simms?"

"*Gracias, Señor.*" Teo inclined his head, keeping a careful smile. "*Lo siento, ¿hablas español?*"

Mr. Simms's expression did not change, and he laughed as though Teo had said something witty. "I could not agree more, sir. Young Mr. Alter here mentioned you wish to discuss business?"

Rafa stifled a laugh with a cough but said nothing as Teo let his little game fall by the wayside.

"Yes, Mr. Simms," Teo said in clear English. "We wish to discuss your interests in Spain. I am sure you are aware that Don Mendoza has a reputation that would benefit your interests, particularly after the financial difficulties England suffered last year."

Mr. Simms chuckled and gestured for them all to take a seat, though Teo and Rafa remained standing. "Well, my nephew has been sticking his nose in various places around Spain to gauge interest in our operations, but we're establishing some very lucrative connections there. Of course, there will always be room for more parties willing to take a little additional risk with the port officials and customs officers."

Teo raised a brow at him. "Privateering? Smuggling?"

"Whatever helps you sleep more restfully, Señor Mendoza," Simms said without concern. "I assure you, our legitimate shipping interests are well enough, but if you are looking for a true partnership with the promise of something lucrative, I suggest we keep talking."

Something about the man's tone irked Teo, and he narrowed his eyes. "What's the cargo?"

Simms smiled unpleasantly. "Now, admitting such would be a trick indeed. The Trade has ended officially, but unofficially, there are several avenues: runaways, strays, even some that will pay to be taken away. Trust me, Mendoza, my contacts have enough access to keep everyone profitable for several years."

Teo ground his teeth, his lips pursing, not needing any further elucidation on the subject. "Don Mendoza Shipping does not ship humans, Mr. Simms. Nor do we have contracts with any that do."

The coolness in his tone had no effect on the man, and Simms only shrugged. "Just as you like, Mendoza. I trust you'll find other businesses more to your liking. England is full of the politer sort. Alter will see you out."

Teo nodded, turning to go but nearly colliding with Rafa who stood there staring at Simms as though his mother had just been insulted. "*Es hora de irse. Déjelo en paz*," he told his friend, taking his arm.

Rafa shook his head slowly. "*Yo podría matarlo.*"

"*Lo sé. Vamos.*" He nudged his head toward the door, and this time, Rafa followed. They made their way out of the building and moved up the street.

"Do you know anyone here to tell them about that?" Rafa asked in rapid Spanish as they continued away.

Teo shook his head, swallowing the disgust that had risen with Simms's admission. "Not by day, and certainly not officially. But once I do, he will be the first name I mention."

"And by night?" Rafa asked.

"We might find some more interesting options."

Chapter Three

"Miss Bartlett, would you mind checking my penmanship?"

Emmeline smiled across the room at one of her younger students. "Of course, Anna." She moved over to the desk where the girl sat, glancing over her very carefully penned page of sentences. "Lovely work. Your lines are straight, your letters connect, your pressure is even. Next, I would work on the spacing between each letter, as well as your diacritic placement. Do you remember what that means?"

The girl nodded quickly. "The dot of the *i* and the cross on the *t*, right?"

"Very good," Emmeline praised, her smile spreading. "You are making such excellent progress."

Anna beamed and went back to her work.

Emmeline watched her for a minute, all but shaking her head in amazement. Anna was one of the scholarship girls who came from the Rothchild Academy, a program specifically set up by Emmeline's cousin Lord Rothchild to help unfortunate girls receive an education. From there, they could then qualify for attendance at Miss Masters's Finishing School once they reached an acceptable mark so as not to be so far behind the other girls. Some of the scholarship girls had excelled so impressively that, even now, she could not recall that they had been in any way different from the other students.

Most of those girls would go on to become women of business, join the governess trade, or even make respectable, middle-class marriages. Seeing how they progressed from where they had come from, Emmeline had learned to never judge any girl by her birth.

Some of the students of a higher station, even with excellent governesses at an early age, did not complete their studies with comparable marks.

Being from a similar situation to those girls, Emmeline felt she could safely say such things. Of course, she herself had run rings around her governesses where her studies were concerned and had been called a hopeless bluestocking before the age of thirteen. But it had prepared her well to teach here.

Aunt Hermione did not find it particularly delightful that Emmeline had relegated herself to being a teacher rather than focus on becoming someone's wife, but she did not complain about the position often, as Emmeline was only in Kent at the school for a week or two every month or so.

Why Miss Bradford, the headmistress, continued to keep Emmeline on staff when she did not continuously live on site was beyond Emmeline's understanding, but there had never been any discussion of Emmeline leaving the post. She had continued to go back to London regularly under the guise of taking care of her aunt, and she returned to school when she claimed her aunt was improving, or that another family member could tend to her.

Aunt Hermione was healthy from the moment she was born, with never so much as a chill. But it was the best excuse for leaving Kent whenever she could to continue her excursions in London's less appealing side. The thrill of seeking out stories no one in Society wished to discuss, but had no issue reading about, was too much to ignore. Knowing she could gain access where no lady should—and could access stories she would never have heard otherwise—was a heady thing indeed. She could *tell* the stories she would never have heard otherwise.

For all the effort she put into the penmanship instruction of her students, her passion was in the composition course. She taught proper structure of sentences for the younger girls, using the writing of letters or even diary entries to help them comprehend format. For the older girls, she was able to expand their horizons a little, ask for imaginative compositions in either prose or verse, and enjoy the creativity so few ladies of station ever managed to explore.

She didn't flatter herself that her students found the subject or assignments as compelling as she did, but every now and then, she did come across extraordinary talent, and to see the joy fill those students with the same passion and drive she felt for the written word was well worth the inconvenience of making the journey from London to the school so often.

After all, her own love of writing and a perfect turn of phrase had spurred her present adventures, and she had no idea how exhilarating it would be to see her own words spread about London on the printed page.

Well, Emmett Barnes's words, which she had written. Emmeline Bartlett could not publish for the world. Emmett Barnes, however, was able to do so. And he was making quite a name for himself.

Even the printer had no idea his prized journalist on the secret side of London's news was a woman, and there was no reason to change that. Writing had opened up a world for the quiet, introspective Emmeline, and for the first time since she had lost her parents as a child, expressing herself came naturally. Her already voracious mind took the travel books from her aunt's library and wrote adventures for herself, and she began to plan how she might make them come true.

Though she had never been outside of England, which would have horrified the little girl who had made such plans, she had discovered that London had more than enough excitement to satisfy her once she uncovered it. Of course, along with that excitement came danger, and that was less appealing, but she'd come to accept it as part of the adventure. A required task for the stories she needed to tell. And now the danger was almost part of the fun. Almost.

The other night had been startling for her, given the speed of her pursuers. She had grown accustomed to burly men being slow and relatively easy to dodge, but these men had proven her wrong. She was fortunate to have escaped, and she was well aware of it. It had taken a few nights for her to not wake up with a start as she relived the chase in her dreams, but at least now she was restfully sleeping without seeing herself in the alleys of London.

The most damning part of her article was due to come out next week, which meant she would need to get back to London to watch the fallout. There was nothing more delicious than watching the effect her words had on the world around her, especially when her aunt raved about the revelations that the "marvelous writer Emmett Barnes" was sharing with the world.

There was no satisfaction greater than that. Well, other than the justice she felt was being served. She wasn't entirely self-serving.

"Miss Bartlett, I cannae remember how tae write a letter zed proper!"

Emmeline smiled as she returned to her present surroundings, turning to the adorable Scottish orphan who had joined Anna in the Miss Masters's school from the Rothchild Academy. "Properly, Jennie. Remember? Properly."

The little brunette wrinkled up her nose. "I dinna ken jus' what is properly done or no', Miss Bartlett, but I cannae write a zed like a lady."

Fighting a laugh, Emmeline nodded and came to her desk. "Show me how you're doing it, and I'll tell you what I think."

After a few minor corrections and a couple of suggestions for word usage, the class was dismissed for the day. She wouldn't have her older students for the class on rhetoric until much later in the day, which allowed her some time for herself. *Truly* for herself. A luxury she didn't often have.

In London, she had time that was unoccupied, and she had time for leisure, but it did not follow that any of that time would truly be her own. She would have to indulge her aunt or behave as a proper lady and do such activities as befitting them—such as embroidery or playing the pianoforte. She was dreadful at both, which was likely why she had been drawn to exploring London by night, besides the need for adventure. But she hadn't always wanted the adventure part of it. Just the quiet time. Out in the countryside of Kent, there was plenty of quiet, if she could sneak away for some time in it.

Or, on rainy days such as this, there was always the library. It was the most wonderful place in the entire sprawling estate-turned-school. It was massive—the largest library she had ever seen in her entire life—and if she would have had less restraint during her time here as a girl, her studies would have suffered immensely for having such an array of books at her disposal. Even now, she could lose herself in it.

She pulled out the pocket watch from the folds of her skirt where her pockets hid and checked the time. The girls would be enjoying their light luncheon, and if she decided to skip the meal herself, she could earn herself nearly two hours of uninterrupted library time. It was a temptation she was entirely incapable of resisting.

Emmeline all but skipped down the corridors in the way her younger students were prone to do.

"With grace like that, we should have you teaching dance with Annette."

Emmeline threw her head back with a laugh and turned to grin at Minerva Dalton, a fellow teacher and friend. "You should know better than that, Minerva. I only dance when forced, and even then, I'm hardly enthusiastic."

Minerva shared a smile, approaching with her usual enviable comportment. She was a mystery of a woman, not much older than Emmeline herself, who somehow blended in with the *beau monde* of Society, as well as the depths of its lowest class without truly belonging to any of them. But someone who did not know the woman might find her perfectly situated wherever she was.

It was the magic of Minerva.

"Having never seen you dance outside of the spring *fête*, I cannot comment on your abilities in earnest, Emmeline." Her smile spread, illuminating her complexion and crinkling her green eyes. "But someday, I hope to see it for myself."

Emmeline waited for Minerva to reach her side, then began walking with her toward the library. "Are you planning on coming to London anytime soon? There is plenty of room at my aunt's house, and you would be in nobody's way."

Minerva laughed softly. "Unfortunately, no, but thank you for your generous invitation. At any rate, I wouldn't wish to impose on your aunt when she is improving."

"What makes you believe she is improving?" Emmeline asked before she could stop herself, grateful her tone had managed to stay mild despite her shock. The lie regarding her aunt's health had become a trap in a way, though it did keep her from making additional excuses as to why she did not teach more frequently than she did. More than once, she had regretted ever saying her aunt was anything less than well enough.

"I apologize," Minerva said quickly, turning to her a little as her eyes widened, her face full of concern. "I presumed that because you are here at the school and not tending her, she is improving. If I am in error, I do beg your pardon."

Relief sank into Emmeline's limbs, and she offered a smile to her friend. "No apology needed. She does waver in her illness; I'll grant you that. I am not sure she will ever be fully well again, but I have a cousin who can relieve me of the burden of caring for her at times, which is when I am able to return here. My aunt does love to hear my accounts of our students when I come back."

"I am sure you are a great comfort to her," Minerva assured her, rubbing Emmeline's arm gently. Then her smile turned impudent. "You were going to the library just now, weren't you?"

"I was," Emmeline admitted without shame. "I have some time before my next class, and it is arguably the best part of this school."

Minerva gave a firm nod. "I'll concede that it is on the list of the school's best things, though not the top one for me. I was going there myself, but I fancied some luncheon as well. I'll go and fetch something and bring it back for the both of us."

Emmeline beamed at the woman who was likely the most wonderful person on earth. "You are an angel and a godsend, Minerva."

"One would hope to be both—perhaps after this life is concluded." Minerva winked and tilted her dark head in the direction of the library. "You go on, I'll be along shortly." She grinned quickly before turning and moving down the corridor with a light step.

No matter how many times she left for London or how long she stayed away, being back at the school always felt more like coming home than anything else. Even more than being in London most of the time. She adored London and all it had to offer, but Kent and the women at this school…

How could she continue to be so drawn to both? She would love to stay here with the other teachers, live in the teachers' quarters, instruct young students full time, and find true purpose in her life. She had such camaraderie with the other teachers when she was here, and that would only improve with a longer association.

Her aunt did not approve of her teaching here, wishing Emmeline would be more like the other ladies of her station. But as the school was so reputable, she couldn't exactly complain about impropriety. If Emmeline did not stay there constantly and spent enough time in Society to satisfy her aunt, she could continue teaching on occasion.

Of course, her aunt had no idea Emmeline was wandering London at night and writing articles for the gossip sheets, but that was neither here nor there.

Sighing happily to herself, Emmeline turned and started toward the library again. She hadn't really thought Minerva to be the library sort of woman, but she would welcome the company of someone else who could find a reprieve in that place, especially if that person also came with food. Perhaps there wouldn't be any need to return to London or to remove herself from such a lovely room and situation at all.

Alas, expectations existed, and Emmeline was constrained by them.

It was the unfair reality of the class in which she had been raised. Had she been born lower, even a half step, she could have done as she wished with less demands upon her life. She had no wish to be of the lowest station, given the hardships such people endured, but she would not have minded being able to mingle freely among them.

A small village would have suited her well, perhaps one where she might have owned a bookshop and taken lunch with the fine lady from the estate nearby. Not one with a title or a fortune so immense the distance between them would be too great for their association, but enough to allow Emmeline an occasional glimpse of a fine life to satisfy her dreams.

Not for her life, though. Finery did not guarantee happiness, and she knew that all too well. She wasn't unhappy per se, but she certainly had her moments over her life.

She arrived at the library, gleefully opening the door and striding in, her eyes immediately tracing along the nearest books. They stopped suddenly on a surprising figure at a table near the window, daylight streaming in from the courtyard.

A woman with fair hair pulled tightly back sat with a book open, the light in the room giving her a more youthful appearance than she'd have possessed without it. She was still a lovely woman, but her first bloom had faded, and only like this could she barely pass for being older than her students. Given how fatigued she looked at any given time, Emmeline took a moment to marvel at the new image of the woman she respected so much.

"It is your own time you are wasting standing there, Emmeline," the woman announced without looking up from the page. "Unless you would like to ask me to change seats so you may have this one, I suggest you get to it."

Emmeline chuckled and entered the room fully, moving toward the table rather than for her favorite section of shelves. "I'd never ask you to change seats, Miss Bradford. I think after all you do for this place you could sit on a throne in the center of it all."

The headmistress put a finger on her page and finally looked up at Emmeline with a smile. "I need no throne. Only a few unoccupied minutes to myself now and again." Her smile curved to one side in bemusement. "And in here, when it's just us, you may call me Pippa."

"Oh, I don't know about that," Emmeline blustered, shaking her head firmly. "You are my employer, and all due deference and respect applies."

Miss Bradford raised a brow, still smiling. "We're in the library to read for recreation, Emmeline, not in a public setting or among other teachers. Here, at least, I think you may let polite manners go."

"If you insist," Emmeline quipped with a bright grin. "What are you reading today, Pippa?"

The immediate shift in address made Pippa laugh, and she showed Emmeline the book. "*Robinson Crusoe.* My father used to read us passages before bed, and I've never lost my love for it."

Emmeline sighed in delight, nodding to herself. "I understand that all too well. I was in my aunt's library for hours on end when I discovered *Gulliver's Travels.* She despaired of me from that moment on."

"Probably appropriate." Pippa winked and pulled her book back. "How is your aunt?"

"Some days are better than others," Emmeline admitted, a twinge of guilt racing up her spine. "She has a stubborn constitution despite her frailty."

Pippa smiled thoughtfully, almost whimsical at the statement. "It's a blessing to have such a spirit despite hardship."

The guilt roared in the pit of Emmeline's stomach as she nodded. "Yes, I can only hope to possess some of the same myself when I reach her years."

"I have no doubt you will," Pippa assured her with an almost maternal look. "And I also have no doubt you will write several novels filled with that same spirit."

Emmeline stared at the headmistress, fear lashing at the previous guilt and filling its place. "Novels? I don't know that I would extend that far…"

Pippa's smile turned pointedly mischievous. "No? I remember when you were a student here, Emmeline. Your writing was extraordinary. And you teach writing and rhetoric better than anyone I've ever seen."

"Don't inform Miss Gallagher of your opinion," Emmeline said with a laugh, her conscience easing a little. "I believe she would take great offense to that statement."

"She would agree with me," Pippa insisted, still smiling. "She knew what talent you had. It was why she pushed you. What you did not see was how she would come to my office and show me your work, being as proud as if you had been her child. I knew then that if there was any way possible, I wanted you to teach here."

Had the sun shone from inside the room itself, it could not have been brighter in Emmeline's eyes. She could have floated away on an ocean of exhilaration and euphoria, despite the fact that she clearly remained on the solid ground. No floating, no sunshine, no heralding trumpets. But a vindication of her abilities to write…

That would deserve some sort of miraculous experience, would it not?

"Thank you, Pippa," Emmeline murmured, beaming at the woman who had given her this window into the most treasured part of her life. "That means a great deal to me."

Pippa winked and reached out a hand for Emmeline's, squeezing gently when she took it. "You don't need me to praise your work, Emmeline. I believe you know full well where your talents lie and that your heart leads you to the best avenues to fulfill them. I trust you to teach our young ladies here how they might endeavor to do the same."

Emmeline clamped her lips down on an almost hysterical peal of laughter. "Pippa, are you suggesting I encourage our students to become willful and headstrong? Defy the constraints of polite Society? Treat their hearts as something more than an impulse to be ignored?"

The wise, poised, and still beautiful headmistress only quirked a brow. "Well, I would hope you would advise them to keep some constraint on themselves, but in a general sense, that would all work very well, I think." She nudged her head toward the books. "You'll want to get to reading now, or we'll have used all of your precious spare time talking."

"Hmm," Emmeline quipped with a quick grin, "we can't have that now, can we?"

Chapter Four

"*I* hate England."

"You can't say that."

"I hate England. Shall I say it louder?"

"Rafa, so help me…"

"*Puedo decir lo que quiero decir, Teo.*" Rafa gave him a dark, pointed look. "*No puedo?*"

Teo exhaled shortly, muttering to himself in a blend of English and Spanish that no one would have a hope of hearing, let alone understanding. "I suppose. But only say it in Spanish, *te lo ruego.* I need someone in this country to like me."

"If they cannot deign to learn our language, why should we bother with theirs?" Rafa asked in plain English, not bothering to keep his voice down.

"Deign?" Teo repeated, grinning over at his friend. "Have you been studying English, *camarada?*"

Rafa grunted once. "If I must speak with the *tontos*, I shall at least do so without obvious error."

Teo laughed now, clapping Rafa on the back. "I will make a diplomat out of you yet, Rafa Teixidor."

"The devil you will," Rafa mumbled in near-perfect English, shrugging Teo's hand off. "This is business. Once business is done, we can be free of this place." He inhaled, making a face. "It stinks of fish and sweat."

"We're near the docks, *amigo*. Even in Barcelona, it smells the same."

"Barcelona has never reeked like this."

Teo rolled his eyes, shaking his head as he looked away.

The two of them continued their excursion to find potential partners and vendors. Their first day had soured after the distasteful interview with the human-smuggling Simms, and neither of them had felt much like continuing when the second interview had proved to be flimsy at best, even if it was entirely free of scandal.

So they'd walked around London by day, the same streets and alleys they had seen by night, and even that had not slaked Teo's curiosity for London. For all of England, really.

Their crew members were enjoying the time away from their assignments, no doubt growing fonder of England than Rafa was likely to do, which bode well for Teo's plans to stay. How long, he couldn't say, but he did not wish for undue influence taking him away from these shores. Not until he knew where his head and heart were with regard to his father's heritage. He owed it to his ancestors to examine his conscience with real honesty before returning to the country of his birth, the land from which he hailed, the part of the world his heart called home.

He owed it to his sisters living in Spain with their families, though they did not possess the same interest for England he did. They wanted answers to their questions and nothing more. He would do his utmost to bring that to them, but he wanted more.

He wanted a sense of what exactly his father had left behind in order to follow his heart and marry for love. What he had turned his back on. And, perhaps, to discover if he might have some regrets in doing so.

How he could assuage his mind there, he could not say, given his father's reluctance to discuss the subject while he was alive and his mother's determination to honor her husband's wishes after his death. He admired their mutual love and respect, but as he had grown into adulthood, he'd felt more and more driven to give himself and his sisters a more complete story of their lives. It was not only his father whose life had been changed by the decision to abandon England; it had changed the lives of his children as well.

Had there truly been no hope of reconciliation between his father and his grandfather as the years had gone on? Could he and his sisters have known their English family in childhood, had the connection been reforged? Was the bitterness of his grandfather enough that it would carry over to tenants and servants, rendering any attempt of Teo's to go among them fruitless? Should he abandon his own curiosity and return to the sea where he had been so satisfied and successful?

"*Capitán,*" Rafa murmured, nudging his shoulder a little.

Teo shook himself out of his sudden moment of reflection. "*¿Sí?*"

Rafa inclined his head toward the building outside of which they had stopped. "*¿Entramos?*"

Looking over the building and the sign, Teo nodded firmly. "*Sí.*"

Surely the business practices of Foster and Sons would be an improvement upon Simms's, and the property of this place alone should speak better for their influence. Entering the building, Teo glanced around the neat and tidy space with some satisfaction. Clean, orderly, fine without being ornate, and there were two clerks hard at work at raised desks in the open front room. With the opening of the door, both of their heads raised, polite smiles meeting their guests.

"Welcome to Foster and Sons," the one to Teo's right greeted. "Can I help you?"

"Is Mr. Foster in?" Teo asked, clasping his hands behind his back. "We would like to speak with him about expanding his opportunities."

"Mr. Jeremiah Foster Sr. is in meetings in Westminster," the same clerk explained with some apology. "Mr. Jeremiah Foster Jr. is out on the wharfs overseeing an incoming shipment, but Mr. Henry Foster is available, if you do not mind."

Teo maintained his smile despite being relegated to the second son. "Does Mr. Henry Foster possess the authority to make contract decisions? Or enough knowledge of the full ventures of the company to satisfy our questions?"

The clerks looked at each other, then back at him, the first speaking again. "I do not think he has the first, sir, but he most certainly has the second. And his recommendations are valued by his father and brother."

"That will suffice well enough." Teo nodded, letting his smile spread farther. "Teo Mendoza and Rafa Teixidor of Don Mendoza

Shipping would appreciate a few minutes of his time, if he has no objection."

The clerk who'd addressed them nodded and set down his pen, rising from his desk. "I'll be just a moment as I check with him, sirs. Please, make yourselves comfortable." He hurried out of their sight toward the offices, while his companion returned to his work.

Teo turned to Rafa, who was as impassive as he ever was in public. "What do you think?" he asked his friend in their native tongue, his voice low.

"If he can get us connections," Rafa replied in the same tone and language, "it will be worth it. If he has heard of us, even better."

"My thoughts exactly." Teo dipped his chin and moved toward the window, staring out at the London streets and watching the people move about. "It could open several doors for us, not just this one. If he is interested, we will need to explore the connections of the Fosters and see what possibilities might be on the horizon."

"And if he is not interested?" Rafa asked from his position beside him.

Teo shrugged, though his friend had not moved. "Then we will continue as we have done and seek for support elsewhere."

Rafa exhaled heavily and switched to English. "It would perhaps be helpful for you to make some connections of your own here, *Capitán*. For business."

Teo turned to Rafa in surprise, smiling broadly. "Are you telling me to associate with Englishmen outside of our attempts here, Rafa? Perhaps making myself available at social gatherings?"

"It would improve our business," Rafa mumbled, averting his gaze. "That has become abundantly clear."

"Doing so will undoubtedly extend our stay here," Teo pointed out with a quirked brow.

Rafa shook his head, muttering under his breath. "I realize that, Teo, and I will adjust my feelings accordingly."

There was nothing to do but laugh, and had they not been in public, Teo would have heartily done so until Rafa barked at him with some creative vulgarity. As they were before a clerk of the man they hoped to do business with, Teo managed to only chuckle to himself.

"*Cállate*," Rafa mumbled, frowning darkly.

Teo gestured a sort of bow in acknowledgement, curious as to how his friend would manage to withstand an even longer period of time in London when he was already so irritable. He would take great pleasure in reminding Rafa that the addition of social connections had been his idea, and not Teo's own. That alone would make lengthening their stay worthwhile.

"Señor Mendoza, Señor Teixidor, I am so sorry to have kept you waiting," a new voice announced, bringing both their attentions to the offices beyond. A man perhaps five years their senior, though no more, strode toward them, polite smile intact, appearance hale and strong. And he knew how to properly address them, which worked significantly in his favor.

"Not at all," Teo replied easily, inclining his head. "We have come without appointment, so we are at your mercy. Thank you for sparing us time."

"Of course!" Mr. Henry Foster grinned as he approached, shaking both of their hands without hesitation or reservation. "It's an honor, Señor Mendoza. My father greatly admired the business of your uncle and your grandfather. And Señor Teixidor, I understand you were trained up alongside Señor Mendoza through the ranks of the business. Tell me, did you start as a lowly seaman? A clerk in the business? What has your journey in this company been?"

Rafa appeared stunned to be addressed at all, particularly away from the office, and cleared his throat awkwardly. "Seaman, sir. I started as a boy learning every inch of a ship, and from there gained my education in the other areas of the business when I proved a willing student."

Mr. Foster shook his head in disbelief, his smile still fixed. "Remarkable. I'd have given anything that my youthful mind could dream up to be at sea. I was a clerk first, then eventually permitted to actually set foot on a ship rather than only read about them."

"My mother needed funds," Rafa explained in a controlled tone. "Starting as a clerk would have made me an apprentice, which would not have brought in as much funds. Necessity dictated my position." He managed to smile a little. "Not that I had any complaints about it."

Foster nodded, completely unruffled by Rafa's earlier correction of his assumption. "What young lad does not wish to go to the sea, eh?" He stepped back, gesturing toward the path from which he'd come. "Gentlemen, please."

Teo and Rafa started in that direction, letting Foster catch up and pass them to properly lead the way. It was not far to the office, and the space was even more tidy and structured than the front entrance had been. One might suspect that no work took place in this room at all, apart from the presently open ledger on Mr. Foster's desk, currently mid-entry, if Teo was any judge.

"Please, have a seat," Foster offered with a quick gesture to the chairs across from his desk as he moved to his own. When they sat, so did he, and his steady smile remained. "What can I do to assist the partners of Don Mendoza Shipping today?"

Teo raised a brow before looking at Rafa. "Not many people outside of our own company know of our partnership, sir. You are very well informed."

"We strive to be," Foster explained, sitting back a little in his chair. "Particularly with matters that most interest us. I can assure you, we've had our eye on the prospects of Don Mendoza for some years now, and we've rarely found a more impressive operation."

Foster was saying all the right things if he wished to enter a contract with them, but Teo was wary. Any time there was a situation that appeared too favorable, he could only doubt its prospects and search for the unspoken hindrance or caveat to the apparent perfection. What would it be here?

"What part of our operation would you say is the most impressive?" Teo inquired as mildly as he could. "Or of the most interest?"

Foster did not seem the least bit put off by the question. "I admire particularly how you have managed to stay relevant in the wool trade when Australia seems to be the heart of that particular commodity. You are still competitive in brandy, though the free traders of Cornwall cut off some companies at the knees. I understand Madrid has similar trouble with free trading?"

Rafa grumbled under his breath, shifting in his seat. "Yes, and they refuse to listen to the concerns of merchants who ask for change."

"Too many in power profit off of what should be restricted," Foster agreed with a firm nod. "I completely agree with you, sir." He eyed them both, a speculative light entering his expression. "I have heard some thoughts and predictions about Catalonia, where I believe you are based."

"Have you?" Teo mused, finding himself liking the man despite his reservations. "Regarding what?"

"Textiles." Foster grinned easily. "They say forward-thinking men will secure a grip on the market there before the rest of Europe and the world become wise to it. What would the pair of you say to that speculation?"

Well, well. That was an interesting insight for a prospective partner to bring up. Many businessmen with such information would hold it in reserve and take advantage of the market as it was rather than be in anticipation of what it could become. It would be easy enough to secure a lower rate of interest in the calm before the storm and leave none the wiser.

Yet Mr. Henry Foster had shown his cards to them rather than keep them to himself. Would his father and brother have done the same? Or would his actions jeopardize his standing with them?

Teo and Rafa exchanged a look, then Teo returned his attention to the man before them. "Forward-thinking ideas can open many doors," Teo said slowly, allowing himself to smile. "And the observant man might find several opportunities for himself that others fail to notice."

Foster nodded slowly. "As I suspected. And what might forward-thinking Spanish merchants expect in return for such opportunities?"

"Vessels," Rafa said simply, his tone warmer than Teo had heard it be in some time. "Connections. Access to the Spanish colonies, which our own nation's history has prevented us from having."

"All sounds very agreeable to me," Foster told them without hesitation. "I think we might be able to work out something or other that will be mutually beneficial for all of us, make no mistake." His eyes narrowed in thought as he rubbed his thumb against his fingers. "We should bring my father and brother into this conversation to give us all the full scope of possibilities. Depending on how things shake down from Westminster, alterations might be required for our regular way of doing business. Beyond that, my brother has been negotiating his own terms and contracts with interested parties, though none with any particular Spanish interest."

He trailed off, and Teo held his breath, a prickle of anticipation starting in his stomach. This much interest in what their company had to offer could only be promising, and while the Fosters examined their options and explored the possibilities with Don Mendoza, Teo and Rafa would set their own men to examine their operations in more depth. There could be no secrets in this partnership, especially when the stakes could be so high, and the prospect of a lengthy, long-lasting contract lay before them.

Foster suddenly met Teo's eyes, shook himself from his moment of reflection, and grinned openly. "Can I interest the pair of you in dinner and an evening with the Foster family? We could discuss business over port after the meal and see what brilliant ideas come to mind, then arrange details with solicitors in the days following."

It was all Teo could do not to exhale in a relieved rush of air. He managed to return the smile and nodded. "I won't speak for Rafa, but I am in agreement." He glanced over at his partner. "*Amigo?*"

Rafa's expression hadn't changed much, but as he did not look as though he had been paralyzed by boredom or on the verge of murder, Teo would consider it a success.

"Mr. Foster, with respect, would you consider your family to be part of the... *alta sociedad?*" Rafa asked.

Foster's brow furrowed at the change in language. "High Society?" he ventured.

"*Sí,*" Rafa said with a relieved nod.

The bemused grin on Foster's face eased any reservations Teo had. "I called upon my education in Latin for that, and I am pleased it did not fail me. *Señor,* my family are of good stock, well respected in all classes, but no peer wanted me or my brothers to marry their daughters. We do not stand on ceremony, nor will we expect you to be dressed for a ball at Almack's." He paused, chuckling softly and shaking his head. "Which likely will have little meaning for you, but believe me, it is a parade of puffery. You may come dressed as you are if it suits, and if you have something finer, you may wear that as well, but it will have no bearing on our treatment of you, nor our respect for your offer."

"He read you well, *amigo*," Teo laughed easily.

"Which only speaks of good taste," Rafa shot back. "I will be pleased to join you, Mr. Foster. *Gracias*."

Teo looked back at Foster with a bright smile. "*Excelente*. When would you like us to come?"

Chapter Five

"*E*mmeline, surely you are not wearing that for my card party."

"Why, Aunt? What's wrong with it?"

"It's… orange."

Emmeline glanced down at herself, then up at her aunt in disbelief. "It's saffron, Aunt. Sarah Millfield wore this exact shade at the Eatons' soiree a fortnight ago."

Aunt Hermione blustered in her usual way, her long fingers fluttering as though she could wash the color out herself. Her strings of pearls rattled against each other with the motions, and she sputtered in disgust. "Sarah Millfield is eighteen, my dear, and has a complexion far brighter than yours. She may wear whatever color she likes and still look lovely. At your age, you really must have a more selective taste in fashion. It will be far better for you."

"In what way?" Emmeline laughed. "I don't have any prospects, and I highly doubt my fashion has been the reason I am unmarried."

"We will never know," her aunt sniffed. She looked Emmeline over again, sighing in despair. "There is no time to change, so please make yourself as unobtrusive as possible. *If* that is possible." She quirked her brows in warning before turning from the landing and proceeding down the stairs as grandly as the Queen might have done for court.

Emmeline watched her go, then she could not help but throw her hands up in frustration and follow her aunt down with less grace.

It was destined to be another evening in the doldrums, just as was nearly every event her aunt hosted. Her teas and chocolate soirees were the exception, but the chocolate soiree only occurred once a

Season, and the teas came and went on her aunt's whims. Emmeline had few friends remaining in London, what with her age and natural inclination to be away from all social engagement as the years had passed, so any particular ball or party held little interest.

Perhaps that was why she had devoted herself to her writing and the investigations that led her to tell such compelling stories. She needed no friends, connections, or social activity to put pen to paper, and telling stories felt somehow bolder and braver than anything she could have done in a ballroom or on a promenade in the park.

It was her mask for the world. She had to be proper, poised, refined, polite, and a dozen other traits as Emmeline Bartlett.

But Emmett Barnes? He could write whatever he wanted, and no one would judge him for it.

And Ears? Ears could wander the London streets at will and discover the most glorious things.

That thought made Emmeline wonder why in the world she was going through with this charade in a gown her aunt would criticize the whole evening when her two more exciting and entertaining counterparts could find something better to do.

Her aunt turned then, giving her an expectant look and effectively ruining any chance of escape. Emmeline sighed and stepped to her side.

"All I ask," Aunt Hermione murmured, "is that you give me one hour and twenty minutes of time. One hour with a smile and pleasantries, then you may appear unwell for the last twenty. After that, you may make excuses, and I will concede to sending you to rest. Will that satisfy you?"

Emmeline looked at her aunt in joyous surprise, beaming with hope. "I love you, Aunt."

"Yes, yes, dear, I know." Hermione smiled smugly, her painted lips almost pursing as they drew to one side. "Try not to knock over any valuables in your illness."

There was nothing to do but smile and nod, which Emmeline was exceptionally good at, although in this case, she was sincere in both actions. She could happily agree to avoid knocking things over in her dramatics, and her smile was easy enough to maintain when she felt true joy and amusement in her aunt's company.

40

In lieu of laughing outright before they entered the drawing room, smiling seemed the best possible option.

It was not a constant, nor a given, that she enjoyed living with her aunt, but it certainly did have its advantages. Particularly when she recalled that her aunt was more like herself than she cared to admit. Not that she would ever be tempted to wander around London by night, but her aunt did have the same penchant for avoiding Society's events and demands, even if she did abide by its precepts. There was a careful balance to be maintained in such things. Emmeline did not care enough to do so. Her aunt, on the other hand, very much did.

Would it be so very dreadful if she were to completely throw the constraints of Society expectations off and be her own independent woman in truth, not just in secret?

She glanced sideways at her aunt, surveying her currently relaxed and easy demeanor. Such boldness would undoubtedly crush her or, at the very least, mortify her before Society and her friends. Though Emmeline did not care for such people and things herself, she did very much care for her aunt, and wounding her to serve her own purposes was not a sacrifice she was willing to make. Were her aunt truly as ill as she had led most of her associates to believe, she might have allowed herself the willfulness she felt burning inside. Given that Aunt Hermione was as hearty as a schoolgirl, however, Emmeline would have to continue playing the game until her circumstances changed.

What a discouraging idea.

"Will I like anyone you have invited this evening?" Emmeline asked of her aunt as they entered the drawing room to await their guests. "Or will I be a consummate actress the entire time?"

"How am I to know which of my friends and associates you enjoy being in company with?" Aunt Hermione shot back incredulously. "Your opinions, as free and uninhibited as they are, have never extended to actual persons with whom I frequently interact!"

Emmeline sighed, shaking her head. "That is because I do manage to maintain a modicum of politeness, Aunt, and I have no wish to give you offense by disliking the company you keep."

"And yet…" Her aunt's smile removed any sting from the conversation. "You must know, Emmeline, even I find the most adored company tiresome at times. I entertain because that is what women of my age, situation, and station do. When you marry, you will decide for yourself what sort of entertainment you will provide and among which branches of Society your attendees will be drawn from. Or you may defy expectation and convention by inviting all manner of people from wherever your interests lie. A married woman may do such things."

"So I must marry for my own independence of thought and taste?" Emmeline snorted softly. "You do see how backward that is."

Aunt Hermione answered with a low laugh. "Of course I see. We all see. That is simply the way of things, I fear. I could never invite some of my more colorful friends to afternoon teas were I unmarried. I would be expected to continue my aims toward marriage and courtship, at whatever age, and act accordingly. If you have no other reason to marry, my dear, freedom might be enough."

Guests began entering then, drawing her aunt's attention away from Emmeline for a moment, which was fortunate, as Emmeline's mind spun on the concept.

Entrap herself in marriage in order to be free to do as she pleased? Lose her identity and her dowry to a man so that she might be permitted independence from the continual monotony experienced by all women in Society? Bind herself to another person by law and in the eyes of God so that she might truly be herself?

She had heard of women marrying for love, for convenience, for connection, and for fortune, but she had never heard of a woman who had entered a marriage to allow herself to be more of herself. Would that sacrifice be worth it?

Emmeline forced herself to smile as the guests began to trickle in her direction, her face beyond any sensation as she did so. It was the standard response for all young ladies in public, and Emmeline had grown so accustomed to using it that sensation was no longer required. Her face did not need to show true expression to pass inspection. Only a smile. Always a smile.

A break in the arrivals allowed her to lean closer to her aunt. "Please tell me you did not invite eligible bachelors this evening."

"I did not," Aunt Hermione replied through smiling teeth. "If I had, I would insist you remain for three hours, not one hour and twenty minutes. And I would have sent you back to your rooms to change into something more fetching. Believe me, you would know if I had machinations for you this evening."

Emmeline swallowed a jolt of apprehension and nodded, suitably humbled. "Thank you, Aunt." She received a nod in response, then a gentle nudge to her side.

"Do greet Miss Allred, Emmeline. It is her first event since the end of her mourning for her mother, and her father will abandon her for his own devices."

"Miss who?" Emmeline glanced toward the doorway and felt an instant pang of sympathy.

A young woman of average height, a trim frame, and shockingly dark hair stared around the room with blatant hesitation, her wide eyes nearly as dark as her hair. The older gentleman with her, presumably her father—only slightly taller, though quite a bit older and rounder—paid her no mind as he pushed into the room, not quite jovial but certainly lacking her reserve. Miss Allred rubbed at her arm, just below where the mauve sleeve ended, seeming almost stiff in her nature, if not in her dress.

"Emmeline," Aunt whispered, her voice pleading with surprising earnestness.

"Yes, of course," Emmeline replied after a difficult swallow, starting toward the girl.

She remembered that vacant, hollow feeling, which ran rampant across Miss Allred's features. She remembered the sensation that being surrounded by people left her exposed in some way. She remembered walking about as though she were only a shell of herself, lighter than her company, yet weighed down by far more than she could relate. She remembered the fear that someone would ask after her, and the equal fear they would not.

It was a paralyzing, encompassing tumult that clawed at one's stomach, and nothing could settle it.

"Miss Allred?" she greeted as she approached the woman, keeping her tone gentle.

The round, dark eyes met hers, and a wavering smile spread full lips. "Good evening. I trust you are Miss Bartlett? My father said Mrs. Kirby had a niece staying with her."

"Yes, I am she." Emmeline smiled, curtseying. "Emmeline Bartlett. Please, feel free to call me Emmeline, if it will make you comfortable."

Miss Allred bobbed a quick curtsey, her smile not shifting in any way. "Thank you. I'm Lucy." She laced her fingers together in the appearance of a fine young lady patiently enduring conversation. "Have you been assigned to tend to me this evening?"

The question was kindly asked, but there was no hiding the hint of sharpness beneath it. Emmeline instantly liked her more.

"Yes," she admitted bluntly, feeling a woman in her state deserved the honesty. "And also no."

Lucy's pale brow wrinkled slightly. "How can it be both?"

"My aunt bade me to come and greet you," Emmeline explained, her own smile easier to manage now. "But once I saw you and understood, I needed no prodding." She shrugged slightly. "Both my parents passed away nearly ten years ago, and there are few people who comprehend the rawness of such a situation. We may speak of it or not speak of it. We may converse, or we may not converse. If I can make you more comfortable in being here this evening, I will aim to do so."

Lucy's dark eyes searched hers for a long moment, and Emmeline thought they might fill with tears, which could very easily have set her own tears flowing. This would have made her aunt both crossed and pleased—but would likely have been distressing for Lucy—given the presence of other guests. But thankfully, Lucy only exhaled a heavy sigh, which Emmeline understood all too well, and smiled a broad, genuine smile, which transformed her features into something of transcendent beauty.

"Thank you," Lucy said, her tone far less stiff and formal. "It is a terrible thing to be on display in this way, which will spread like wildfire, then everyone will speak of me, and of my mother, and of my looks, because I'm now out of mourning..." She shook her head, shuddering slightly. "I have spent the last two hours wishing my father would allow me to stay home in my most comfortable calico, curled up before the fire with a shawl and a book."

Emmeline gestured for them to move toward a set of chairs near a window. "I all but begged my aunt for the same. I do not have your excellent excuse; I simply cannot abide social engagements on someone else's terms."

Lucy walked with her, laughing as they reached the chairs. "I can honestly say I have never considered my true feelings regarding social engagement and interaction. It is what young ladies do, so it is what I did and what I would have continued to do before my mother died. I have no doubt my father would have had me continue to do so were it not for the constraints of traditional mourning." She leaned closer. "Apparently, it is imperative I make a good match." She widened her eyes meaningfully, then sat in the nearest chair.

"Isn't it always?" Emmeline asked, matching her pose in her own chair. "I haven't been considered a good prospect for some time now, despite my respectable fortune and connections, simply because it would no longer be fashionable to marry me. Yet the pressure of making a good match has not lessened." She looked around the room, shaking her head in disgust and resignation. "Oh, to be a man and be free to do as I liked no matter the age."

"I think my fortunes may be growing less respectable," Lucy murmured, her gaze casting over toward her father. "He will not confirm it, but I believe that to be the case. He is growing ever more insistent about my finding a match or entering into a courtship, and it had only ever been of a moderate focus before. And this is my only new gown, despite him being so insistent on me reentering Society and making the most of it. I am not to have any others, though the fashions have changed since I was last out."

Emmeline looked at the girl in sympathy. "Call upon me tomorrow. I have so many gowns I shall never wear again, and they would be easily made over. I'll pay for the alterations myself, and my aunt would heartily agree."

Lucy's head whipped around, staring at her in startled horror. "Oh, no, I could not! That was not my intent, Miss Bartlett, please–"

"Shh," Emmeline soothed, taking her hand. "I never suspected that as your intent. I am offering freely. You are in want, and I have surplus. Now, there is no assurance that your tastes will be the same as my own have been, so perhaps none of my gowns will be to your liking, but—"

"You will find I am rather accommodating," Lucy overrode without protestation. "I can see clearly where my father would have me blind, and any improvements would give me hope. Thank you for your generosity."

Emmeline chuckled softly and raised a brow. "Now, Lucy, kindly do not thank me before you have actually received something from me. I'll not have you playing desperate and taking what will not suit. Though my aunt would likely wish for you to have this gown I'm wearing, if her commentary before our guests arrived was any indication."

Lucy's eyes fell to Emmeline's skirts, her brow creasing again. "What is wrong with it? The color is fetching, and it brings a reddish hue to your hair that is quite becoming."

"Thank you." Emmeline beamed at her before plucking at a ruffle. "The trouble is that it is orange, which is apparently distasteful."

To Emmeline's delight, Lucy rolled her eyes. "Well, even if she would foist that off on me, it would not have nearly the same effect. I shall refuse it in advance, thank you, but only because it looks so very well on you, not because I too find it distasteful."

They shared a fond look, then fell silent, taking in their surroundings without participating in them. Other conversations took place around them, and it appeared a game of whist started in one corner, which was undoubtedly what her aunt wished, as she'd had the card table set out.

"If only there was a way for a young lady to earn some sort of funds without lowering her station," Lucy murmured. "Then I might feel some security in my position, even if my father does not."

A prickling of an idea started in Emmeline's mind, and she glanced at her new friend in speculation. "What is your age, Lucy?"

"One and twenty," Lucy replied easily. "According to my father, my age does not aid my prospects, and my mother's death came at a most inconvenient time for me."

Emmeline would ignore that, though it would take considerable restraint. "And you'll pardon my asking, but did you have a governess?"

"Oh, yes." She nodded fervently, an almost whimsical smile on her lips. "She despaired of me until the age of thirteen, at which point I seemed to have finally grasped her attempts at refining me. I begged my parents to send me to Miss Masters's Finishing School in Kent, but my father insisted it would cost too dearly."

Ah, she could not have planned a more perfect opening.

"I may have a solution for you, dear Lucy," Emmeline told her with a quick smile. "It would behoove us not to speak of it tonight in this company, but when you come to call tomorrow, we might find ourselves engaging in a far more interesting conversation."

Chapter Six

London at night was glorious.

Teo inhaled the strange combination of damp wood, salt, animal, and dirt—finding it oddly invigorating—wondering how the fragrance would change further from the Thames. What other scents would join the fold and what would leave? He had spent hours upon hours exploring places such as Barcelona, Valencia, and even Cadiz, and tended to do something of the sort in any port city in which he stayed for more than one night.

He blamed his grandfather. The man had told Teo stories of grand ideas, which came to him at night, of finding consolation in starlight and moonlight, of understanding the heart of a place only by moving about it in the still of night. Teo had never had the chance to explore any particular place with his grandfather in the night, but he remembered all too clearly when he had explored Tarragona by night, then told his bedridden grandfather about his experience. It had not come close to matching the stirring tales he had been told in his youth, but his grandfather had listened to every word as though he had taken the venture himself.

Therein had begun his tradition, and he'd seen most of the port towns of Europe in such a way, as well as a few ports in the Indies. But London...

Apart from their first night in port, when he and Rafa had simply wished to gain their bearings of the place before it was filled with workers and locals, he had not explored this place by night.

And with Rafa by his side, he would have had the place tarnished by his friend's opinions. Alone, he had a chance to indulge his curiosity, find pleasure in his discoveries, seek answers to questions he wasn't certain he could ask. Something about London had answers for him. Perhaps all of England would in a way, but London held a certain pull for him, which he could not quite explain.

And that was what brought him out here tonight, dressed in plain, simple clothing. Wandering the streets he did not know, trusting only in his natural sense of direction to guide him back to the ship when the time came. Until he oriented himself to the city, until he was familiar with his surroundings, he would have no map to guide him. By his own choice, he had not glanced at a map of the city yet.

There was an air of excitement about him on the first venture in a new place. Something eager and vibrant that hummed through him from his very core. A desire to unearth something yet undiscovered by him or perhaps anyone at all. An undeniable urge to find some delight in this country that he'd long to share with his late father. To wonder what sort of man he would be if this had been the country in which he was raised, not Spain.

It was as though there was half of him who had never truly lived, and tonight, he could finally start the exploration, as much of himself as the city.

There were a few other people out and about this late, though he could not claim to be fully alone. Some drunken sots stumbled along their way, some scowling creatures scuttled from one destination to the next without much concern for others. It occurred to him that his surroundings might lend him the necessity of intervening on behalf of unsuspecting women at the mercy of some villain belonging to the former categories of men, and he did not relish the thought. He would, of course, do all in his power to aid them, but his midnight walks were not intended to make a hero out of him. He could not bear unending gratitude for doing something that ought to have been unnecessary.

Yet he knew the ways of men without morals or goodness—he had come across several such beings in his travels—but he did not bring such men into his employ if he could help it. He and Rafa had set some hopefully imposing edicts about such things, and their employees abided by them. There had only been a handful of reports or complaints about comrades since they had brought those out, and such issues were resolved swiftly and without question.

There was enough prejudice against merchants and sailors in the world without adding to the stigma. They were not ruffians, nor pirates, and were not even privateers if they could help it. They aimed to live honorably when they were about their business. What a man did in his own home, Teo could not claim to know. Still, he had his resources for investigating such things had he any suspicions.

All in all, he was quite pleased with the state of his company, his workers, and his partner. He had no complaints about their business, their contracts, or what lay ahead for them. It was to be a time of growth and opportunity, and he would do right by his men and the legacy of his company.

But for himself…

It was strange, feeling as though he had gone through his life as somehow less than complete. There was nothing in particular he could put a finger on as to a reason, but knowing only one side of his heritage was an open wound to him. England had called to him from the moment he had learned of its place in his father's life. Even if he grew to hate the place—being able to see the heritage with the same disdain his father had done—at least it would have been earned. He refused to inherit prejudice.

After all, hadn't that been what Teo's father had railed against the most? His own father's prejudice against Spain and particularly Spanish women? The idea of sullying an unbroken family line? Was it not a similar crime to then blindly despise all English for the failings of one man? Teo had seen the beauty of English shores from time to time as he had sailed by, and he could not believe his father had been free of longing for the shores of his homeland for the entirety of his life. He would not believe it.

Being in London was adventurous enough for now, but he would be taking an opportunity to see the family lands and estate for himself. He could not refuse what he had not seen, and he could not abandon tenants and neighbors to a further unknown when he had power to alleviate concerns. Even his father would not have wanted that, and perhaps his sisters would understand that much as well. Surely they would.

A faint whistling sound brought his attention out of his reverie, and Teo slowed his step, watching a young lad leaning against the corner of a building up ahead. His cap was pulled down low, and he tossed a rock in his hand as though it were a coin he had just won. There wasn't another soul in the vicinity that he could see, yet this boy, no more than twelve, was content as could be in his place.

At this hour, how could that be? Did he not have a mother who would be concerned for his welfare? In lieu of such family connections, did he not have other lads in the same situation and of a near age with whom he might associate and form a sort of family with? Such children were not uncommon in any European city, but Teo had never seen them so solitary, especially at night.

Experience told him to leave the lad to his business, knowing that such boys were far older than their age would indicate. Sense told him to make simple inquiries as to his well-being. Humanity moved his feet forward.

"Evening, *muchacho*," he greeted easily as he neared the boy. "What brings you here this late?"

"Business, guv," the boy shot back defensively. "What's it to ya?" He looked up at Teo stubbornly. "And what'd you call me? I ain't no mooch—whatever you said."

"Easy, friend." Teo held up his hands in a gesture of surrender and soothing. "It means lad or boy, nothing more."

A suspicious expression replaced the one of defense. "What language be that? French?"

Teo fought a smile and shook his head. "Spanish, my friend."

To his surprise, the boy's face cleared and he immediately became easy. "Oi, yer alright, guv. Got no complaints wif Spaniards." He spit lightly to his left and shrugged.

"Glad to hear it." Teo took a position next to him, though far enough to avoid encroaching on his space. "So why are you here in the middle of the night? It's hardly a good spot for a young man."

The boy snorted softly. "I ain't typical in that sense, guv. I seen things that would make your skin crawl."

"I believe it," Teo answered with a nod, bemused by the boy's skillful evasion of the question at hand. "So?"

The question earned him a sidelong glance. "What's it to you?"

"Nothing. You're just the only boy I've seen out alone this late."

He shrugged as nonchalantly as his companion had, hoping it would settle his suspicions.

"I work for Gent, guv."

It meant nothing to Teo, but it clearly was supposed to have been answer enough. Teo shook his head. "I'm new to London. Who is Gent?"

"Who wants to know?" a deeper voice asked from the lad's other side.

They both turned, Teo with surprise, the boy more like a soldier. "Evening, Gent."

The newcomer, a tall fellow whose features lay mostly in shadow, leaned against the wall. "Dan. All well?"

"Boring as my mother's kin," Dan answered. "No show from the bloke, so I was making conversation with this guv. Spaniard. Seems decent enough, Gent."

Teo choked on a laugh, looking up at the man called Gent, who seemed to be having similar trouble. "Right, then, off you go. Same time tomorrow, if you're free."

Dan tapped the brim of his hat. "I'm always free, Gent. Best be off, Tilda won't hold supper." With that, he dashed off into the night, darting about the London streets as though he'd mastered them from birth.

"What sort of work does a boy his age do for a man this late at night?" Teo wondered aloud, keeping his voice free from disdain or darkness as he returned his attention to his new companion.

Gent was already watching him in return, his expression hidden. Teo's would have been easy enough to see, as he'd made no effort to obscure it, which could put him at a disadvantage. Still, he had nothing to hide, and no personal interests to protect.

"Nothing that would put either of us in prison or under holy damnation," Gent told him, his tone guarded. "And what interests you about this part of London so late, *señor? ¿Esfuerzos personales?*"

It took all Teo could muster to not gape in surprise. A British man of the streets educated in the Spanish language? It was unheard of.

"*¿Hablas español?*" he managed to ask without shame. He could almost see this Gent smile smugly.

"*Sí, cuando me conviene.*"

Well, it suited Teo to speak English with this stranger, just on the off chance he would need witnesses to whatever transpired. "I'm a merchant," Teo told him. "Newly arrived. After a day of business, I find nighttime exploration of my present destination restful and soothing."

"And beneficial to your business, I imagine," Gent added.

"It does not hurt," Teo agreed with a quick nod. "I saw the boy alone and merely wished to ascertain his well-being. Nothing more."

Gent grunted softly. "A humane wanderer of the night? Those are rare."

"And yet..." Teo trailed off waiting for further insight, hoping the so-called gentleman would oblige.

"*Entiendes bien el Inglés y lo hablas mejor,*" Gent praised, somehow without turning warm. "*Impresionante.*"

Teo switched to Spanish to continue the conversation, if for no other reason than to allay the man's concerns. "My father was English," he admitted freely. "I learned the language very young."

"Ah, that explains the perfect grasp," Gent replied, still in Spanish, his tone turning at last. "It is not an easy language."

"No, but I seem to manage. How did you come to master Spanish? It is not a particularly British interest."

Gent smiled fully now, and Teo could see it by the faint light of their surroundings. "No, but it is a personal one. Languages fascinate me and prove useful at times. I trust you know now they call me the Gent."

Teo nodded once. "I have no such name, but Teo will suffice. Or Mendoza, if you prefer surnames."

"Ah ha," Gent murmured, his Englishness making a grand appearance. "I know of your company well," he said in English.

Nothing could have surprised Teo more than that, including the man's use of Spanish. "Do you?"

Gent nodded. "I know a little of shipping in the region, and several associates know even more. All excellent, by the by, which is unusual in our line of inquiry. Your European influence is unrivaled. Are you seeking to spread into the English trade while you are here?"

"*Sí.* My partner and I are seeking contracts with some of your merchants here."

"Any luck?"

Teo shrugged a shoulder. "Perhaps. A few did not meet our standards."

"That does not surprise me. I could compile a list of potentially more promising candidates if you would like. But I understand if you prefer to make those decisions yourself. After all, I'm in no position to expect you to trust my opinion."

Gent chuckled to himself, which Teo found to be of interest. It was almost a sound of self-deprecation, and yet their conversation had been one of respectful business talk. The man who was dressed like any other man Teo had seen milling about the city at night spoke Spanish, recognized Teo's business, and had slipped into a tone of English speaking that did not fit a low station, yet could not be placed anywhere in particular as far as Teo recognized.

A man of mystery indeed, but hardly one to be suspicious of.

"On the contrary," Teo surprised himself by saying. "I would welcome your insight. My partner is less than thrilled by my interests here beyond that of profit, though he does share my moral concerns. The more efficient and expedient I can make our business, the more grateful he would be."

"Were I Rafa Teixidor," Gent murmured, "I'd find the British a trifle distasteful too."

Teo's eyes widened. "How the devil do you know his name?"

Gent laughed once. "I told you, Mendoza. I know of your company well. I also know Rafa's story. The rumor about how a British merchant mistook his father for a slave and sent him to England to be sold, how he then disappeared off the face of the earth..." He exhaled slowly, shaking his head. "If only the truth could be told. Rafa certainly deserves it."

What was he saying? Was there more to the story than Rafa or anyone else knew?

Before he could ask, Gent cleared his throat. "If you make a habit of wandering the night, I'll have the list delivered to you tomorrow. In the interim, I believe you may find Foster, as well as Baird, to be worth your time."

"I've met Foster," Teo told him, still reeling from the revelation.

"We have been invited to dinner to discuss prospects."

"Then you may not need my intervention at all." Gent looked Teo up and down. "Have you eveningwear?"

"Will I need it?"

Gent all but sighed. "Tomorrow, in daylight, perhaps wander to Covent Garden and ask for Tilda."

"Tilda who won't hold supper?" Teo asked, repeating Dan's earlier words.

"The very same." Gent nodded firmly. "Tell her Gent sent you, and she'll grant you what you need for a reasonable price."

"I was told I do not need to be trussed up," Teo insisted, feeling oddly defensive about his state and appearance.

"Not for the Mr. Fosters, no," Gent agreed. "But I can promise you all of the Mrs. Fosters will appreciate the effort. And to get the best business with any of the Mr. Fosters, you will want their wives to approve." Gent pushed off the wall and tipped his cap a little. "Well, the night calls. Pleasure to meet you, Mendoza. If I can be of any help, nighttime friends know where to find me."

Teo straightened. "Thank you, I think. Any suggestions as to where I might wander tonight to get to know London?"

Gent paused in his backing away. "Tonight? Try going west. See what comes of it." He tipped his cap again and disappeared into the night.

Teo pursed his lips in thought. "West." He considered his surroundings, pleased to find he was on a street running north to south. He moved to the end of the street, glancing to the left and to the right.

The only question was if he trusted Gent enough to believe he would suggest a worthwhile route for his evening or one that would be a complete waste. Then again, would anything truly be a waste when he knew nothing?

"West it is," he decided, turning to his left and starting down the street.

It was only a minute or two before he found himself whistling absently, just as Dan had been doing before Teo happened upon him. He couldn't help it; there was a sense of contentment that only settled upon him when he was exploring a city at night. He felt closer to his grandfather than at any other time, and a clarity settled on his mind. Why did he not find such feelings about his business during the day?

Thoughts of self-doubt began to creep in when he followed this line of thinking, and he did not need that clouding his experience tonight. He shook his head quickly, willing the troublesome, errant thoughts away as he might swat at a fly perturbing his peace. This was not the time for that. This was his own time, his own moment away from everything else in his life. Nothing would trouble or interfere with him here and now. Nothing could.

Sliding his hands into the pockets of his trousers, Teo glanced around the streets upon which he walked, taking in the buildings, the businesses, the signs of life that now lay dormant. The farther he got from the docks, the quieter the streets became. He did not expect that to remain the truth when he reached other parts of London, which bustled with activity no matter the time, but for now, the relative serenity of his present position was a welcome reprieve. Apart from his own whistling, of course.

A far more musical sound met his ears then, silencing his own whistling in favor of capturing the more pleasant sound in its entirety. Someone was humming, and they were humming well. The sound skipped and danced about like a blossom on the breeze and surprised him with its liveliness at this time of night. More than that, it was a song he recognized.

He glanced around, growing more curious the more he heard of the song. He wouldn't have necessarily called the vocalist musically gifted; such a thing was hard to judge by humming alone. But an energetic song he recognized in the middle of the London night.... . Now that was something he had to investigate.

His eyes fell on a lone figure on the other side of the street who was rather commonly dressed, though perfectly normal for the area and the setting, clearly humming what he was hearing, their steps nearly as light and agile as the melody.

Despite what he was seeing, there was one thing he could tell perfectly well. No matter how that person had dressed, there was no possibility they were a man. None at all.

Remembering the brief run-in he'd had with the young woman dressed in a man's clothing his first night in London, and the ha'penny he still carried in his pocket, Teo found himself smiling in her direction, more than half convinced she was that same woman.

Teo started whistling again, this time matching the tune of the song the woman was humming. It was from an opera that had opened a few years ago, one he had seen while on business in Lisbon, and he'd found it rather engaging and bright. The song she had chosen had been his favorite of the piece, and one of few he remembered, as it was easy enough to whistle along to.

As he'd hoped, after a moment or two, she looked around in confusion, eventually finding him. She stopped in her tracks, and he met her eyes, stopping as well.

The street parted them safely, and either of them could have continued without engaging with the other. He'd cross the street if for no other reason than to satiate his curiosity. But he would let her decide. At this time of night, in this part of London, he could do no less.

He watched as her fingers curled against themselves, then bit back a grin when she settled into her stance like a man, folding her arms and motioning with her head that he should cross over.

Without hesitation, Teo did so, taking care not to do so with haste. After all, she likely thought her disguise was undetectable, so his revealing otherwise upfront would not serve his cause.

"It's not often I meet a stranger humming *Zoraida di Granata* in London," Teo greeted in as friendly a voice as he could. "Excellent taste."

She did not react. "Well, *Vado a combattere* was my favorite number, and I was feeling rather at ease just then."

Was? Did she mean to say she was not feeling particularly at ease now, or was she simply offering an explanation? Whichever it was, she had lowered her voice to say so, masking her natural timbre, almost passing for a young man. Almost.

If he did not know otherwise, he might have doubted. If he had been drunk, he most certainly would have doubted. And perhaps that was the key to her disguise. Doubt.

"I do not mean to disturb, *muchacho*," Teo insisted, deciding to give her that doubt she clearly worked with.

Her eyes widened and looked him over for a quick moment.

"You're the man I crashed into the other night."

Ah, so she did remember him. It would appear one did not crash into a Spaniard every day in London. Or every night, rather. "*Sí, mi amigo.* I am glad I could prevent your fall while you fled your *cazadores.*"

What he could see of her brow beneath her cap furrowed. "*Cazadores?*" she repeated. "What's that?"

"Hunters," he recited. "Chasers, if you prefer. You were making great haste, as you say."

Her throat tightened. "Yes, I was. I trust those men were no trouble for you when they came across your path?"

Teo shook his head. "Not at all. I did give them rather roundabout directions when they inquired. Being a stranger to London, one does get so turned about, particularly at night. My mistake, I am sure."

She smiled at that, which warmed something in the pit of his stomach. "Undoubtedly. Imagine what might have happened if you'd had your bearings."

"Most troubling," Teo agreed. "I trust you are not being pursued tonight?"

"Tonight? No." She shook her head, looking around them with a smaller smile, which spoke of the same contentment he had been feeling all night. "No, this is purely a walk for pleasure. There is something wonderful about London at night." Her voice had shifted to less of a disguise, and she seemed aware of it, suddenly clearing her throat. "It helps me on nights when I struggle to sleep."

Teo let himself smile, truly amused. "I am the same way. Would you mind terribly showing me about London? Feel free to refuse me. We are strangers, after all."

"Only until we are introduced," she replied. "And someone who steps in to keep me from being caught in my hour of need is someone I may trust. Call me Ears."

"Ears? As in...?" He tapped the lobe of his right ear.

She nodded once, smiling. "The very same. If you're fortunate, you will come to understand why."

She was the second person of the evening who had an innocuous word rather than a name for an introduction. Did they know each other, or was this simply the way of London by night?

"I have no such moniker," Teo admitted with some reluctance. "If we are protecting our daylight identities, I have nothing to offer."

"Does no one call you anything but your given name?" she asked, her eyes narrowing.

Teo considered that. "Once in a while, I am called *Capitán.* Is that too revealing?"

She shook her head slowly. "Not at all, *Capitán.* Come on, let's introduce you to London."

"After you, Ears."

Chapter Seven

$\mathcal{W}$andering around London in the middle of the night with a man she did not know wasn't strange, was it?

It felt strange. That could have been because he was attractive, his voice made something tickle inside her chest, and he was under the impression that she was a young man.

Perhaps awkward was a better word than strange.

Except she didn't feel all that awkward. Things might get awkward for *Capitán* if he found out she was a woman, and he would probably treat her differently, perhaps apologize for his blindness and behavior. Then the easiness would fade into some strange battle of politeness. She hated those and experienced them far too often for her taste.

She had known *Capitán* all of ten minutes, and she wasn't ready for this to fade into the same staid interactions she always had with men. She just wanted to be herself and enjoy this walk. Whatever *Capitán* did after this was his business, and she wouldn't pretend to care. But right now, just in this moment, she was going to be herself and let *Capitán* be whoever he wanted to be with her. Even though he thought she was a man.

She hadn't bothered to shade her face in an appearance of facial hair or scruff, which could make her look even younger than her disguise already did. If he suspected anything unusual, he was not saying anything. Was not acting suspicious. Was not hinting at anything.

She had wondered if he had seen through her disguise when she had careened into him the other night. Something about his tone had seemed… curious. Suspicious wasn't the right word, but there was an air of bemusement that had made her wonder.

That was gone now.

So had he decided something? Or was he trying to figure something out? Why was this something she was fixated on when she was trying to find her way to somehow more exciting parts of London so that she could show off her knowledge to *Capitán?*

Heavens, she was awkward. It had nothing to do with the clothing she wore. It was simply who she was. It was why she had never had a courtship and would never marry. Aunt Hermione was right. Bless her stars, the woman was right. Emmeline was a hopeless candidate for marriage, despite her prospects.

No one wanted an awkward wife. No one.

Why was she thinking about marriage and courtship simply because she was feeling awkward? Because she was in the company of a man with whom she could talk freely? A man who made her want to look at him and had already offered her a service without asking anything in return?

And now she was out alone with him in the darkest parts of London without any protection. There were so many problems in this scenario, and she hadn't seen any of them until this moment. What in the world was wrong with her?

"Is it always this quiet so far from the river?" *Capitán* asked with real interest. "I've spent a few evenings wandering about since I arrived, but I've stayed fairly close to the docks and ports. There's a whole world down there, but here we are, mere streets away, and it is so quiet…"

"There are several worlds in London," Emmeline assured him, the irony in her statement certainly not lost on her. "Separate and distinct and sometimes occurring within the same house."

Capitán looked at her with interest. *"¿En serio?* That's an interesting thought, but I suppose I have seen the same at times in my own life."

"Have you?" Emmeline asked before she could stop herself.

Prying into a stranger's business would fall squarely under the category of awkwardness she had just been castigating herself over. Clearly, she was destined for doom.

He nodded in reply, his lips curving into some secret smile. "I have. My father was English, you see. At times, I would catch him in moments where he thought he was free from observation, and this pensive look would come over his face. Yet a few rooms away, my mother and sisters would be engaged in bright, cheerful music, which could not have been more different from wherever my father's thoughts took him."

"Was he cast off?" There was the prying yet again, and she was tempted to bite down into her tongue to keep herself from hastening the demise of her reputation.

Capitán shook his head. "I believe you would consider his state banishment rather than cast off, and it was self-imposed. He cast off his English family, although I believe he might have faced the same fate at their hands if he had not done so first."

"What for?" Oh, gracious, would no one stop her?

"Wishing to marry my mother." His smile turned a little bitter, but not entirely harsh. "I cannot blame him for that; she really was extraordinary. But he would not consider reconciliation, and he never returned to England, and I always wondered…" He shook his head, returning to his warmer self. "*Lo siento, muchacho.* A bit personal for our first true meeting, no?"

Emmeline didn't think so. She rather liked forgoing the polite discussion of the weather and the roads and anything else that no one truly cared about. But presuming they were of close enough acquaintance to be sharing secrets of their parents was, admittedly, a bit far. But only just.

"What does that word mean?" Emmeline asked him. "*Muchacho?*"

"Lad or boy."

Well, she couldn't have that. Much as she tried to protect her reputation and her person under the guise of being a man, she did not wish to maintain that facade with him. This was not an investigation on her part, and he did not appear to have nefarious intentions where she was concerned. Of course, that could change very shortly.

She might need to be prepared to run very fast and very far in a moment. Why had she not remembered her previous feelings with regard to footwear on nightly excursions? She had done well enough before, and if needed, she would do the same again. She must.

Pausing for a quick breath, Emmeline ventured, "Can I trust you, *Capitán?*"

He looked at her in surprise. "I would like to think so, *Orejas*. But I suppose it is not for me to say. Oh, and *orejas* means ears in Spanish. I trust you won't disapprove of the adjustment."

She waved a dismissive hand. "I don't, it's fine. Erm… about you calling me *muchacho*…"

Capitán stopped. "Yes?"

Emmeline winced, willing herself not to toy with her fingers in further awkwardness. "I'm not a lad, a boy, nor a man, you see. I'm a woman."

The soles of her feet and the pit of her stomach tingled in anticipation, preparing to flee just as she had the other night.

But *Capitán* surprised her and grinned widely. "I know."

Emmeline gaped. "You know? How could you know? I have it on very good authority that this is an excellent disguise."

"Oh, it is, *señorita*," he told her without hesitation. "I have no doubt it works well for you at times, but I highly doubt that the others you meet when disguised as such have the opportunity of colliding with you."

If her jaw could have dropped more, it would have. Her cheeks immediately began to heat, and she thanked her fortunes that it was night, and therefore the color of those heated cheeks would not be obvious.

"You…" she stammered, fighting to manage coherency amid the embarrassment accompanying her awkwardness. "You could determine my gender from that encounter?"

Whatever *Capitán* saw in her face clearly amused him, for his grin did not abate, and she would swear he was silently laughing at her. "No, but I was able to determine the padding of your coat as well as the smearing of your facial powder. It was not difficult to draw conclusions from the two, once I considered them after the fact. You do well with moderating your tone. I trust your natural speaking voice is considered low for a woman?"

"It is, actually," Emmeline replied in relief, allowing herself to speak in her natural tone now. "I had never considered that to be even remotely useful in my life—until I decided to gad about London by night in disguise—but it has proven to be quite an asset."

"I can imagine so. More than that, I can even fathom why you would go to such lengths to disguise yourself as such, given these excursions." He pointedly looked about them, causing her to do the same for effect. "It is not the place for a young woman, as it poses many more dangers for them."

Emmeline soured at his choice of words and folded her arms moodily, peering up at him. "Would you send me home, then? Treat me as a wayward child who cannot possibly fathom the risks?"

Again he surprised her. "Not at all. In disguising yourself, you clearly understand what is at stake and have weighed your options against them. I trust you to make your own decisions about your safety and that those who care about you have accepted the same."

The sharp sting of guilt lanced her lungs at that, and she bit her tongue this time. There was no sense in admitting no one who cared about her knew she did this, nor would they, unless something went terribly amiss.

Best not to reveal all her secrets in one night.

"And besides," *Capitán* continued, "now you find yourself in my company. I can give you several references as to my trustworthiness and bravery, my skills in fighting, and my ability to swiftly and neatly remove myself and others from dreadful situations."

Emmeline laughed at the sudden application to be her companion, or whatever he thought she might need. "I see. I must begin interviewing these references at once to determine your position, *Capitán*. But are they not all in your employ? Given the name you have provided me, am I to assume you are anything less?"

He made a face of consideration, then frowned. "Yes, I suppose that would be a slight complication to the arrangement. It would be considered some sort of betrayal or mutiny to have them go against me in anything, including this."

"And what is this exactly?" Emmeline demanded playfully but with some defiance behind it. "I have not had associates accompany me on my journeys, and I haven't intended for that to change. I need no guard over my person, and I hardly need a nanny with a knife to ensure I am well and whole."

He cocked his head at her, a bemused smile lighting his lips. "What tells you I am armed with a knife?"

"Please," Emmeline sputtered dubiously. "Allow me some intelligence in drawing my own conclusions. You hardly carry a pistol, and a rapier would be blatantly obvious. The only reasonable weapon for a man in your situation and of your persuasion is to be armed with at least two knives, if not three."

The widening of his eyes told her just how correct she was, and a jolt of satisfaction hit the center of her chest and radiated down to the tips of every finger. There was such delight in being correct in surprising assessments.

"Regardless," he said slowly, evidently still taken aback, "if we are both to be wandering the streets at night of our own volition, we might as well embark on those wanderings together. Or would you find my company so disagreeable as to ruin your experience?"

Emmeline snorted in derision, something she would never have felt comfortable enough or free enough to do were she back in Mayfair and surrounded by others of her station and situation. "Hardly. If you were not villain enough to find opportunity in the revelation of my true gender and had no qualms in redirecting the men who were after me on our first encounter, I hardly think your nature is sufficiently wicked enough to ruin what a night in London has to offer me."

"That is a relief, *Orejitas*," *Capitán* told her with a crooked smile that clenched her stomach in heated surprise, the sound of her name seeming slightly different. "If there is anything in this world I do not want, it is to ruin your night."

It was a flattering statement, but so inexperienced was Emmeline with such flattering statements that it fell hopelessly flat at her feet.

"Surely not," she protested in almost disgust. "There must be several other things in this world you do not want that rank far worse than the outcome of my night. Or any other time of my existence for that matter. Come now, do not turn overly complimentary simply because it is the way things are done. I grow so weary of people saying what they do not mean and wasting the breath they carry to say them."

"You prefer honesty and…" He frowned a moment. "What is

the word? Blunt?"

"We prefer the word frankness," Emmeline informed him with a faint sniff that would have made her aunt proud. "To be blunt is to be crass, and only the truly vile would dare be crass."

Capitán nodded as though he were suddenly a student under her instruction. "I shall make a note of that. Though I suppose I may be as crass as I please, so long as I do so *en Español.*"

"Yes, I suppose you may," Emmeline considered as they rounded a corner. "I had not thought of it that way, but there would certainly be a beauty and a freedom in using another language to disguise the true nature of your speech."

"But now you will know what I am doing," he pointed out with a light laugh. "Whenever you hear me switch over to Spanish, you will suspect me of being crass."

Emmeline chuckled herself, looking over at his dark, angled features. "Suspect, perhaps, but it is not as though I will know for certain, nor will I understand you. What does it matter what people suspect so long as you yourself know the truth?"

He smiled rather warmly, as though they had known each other far longer than simply one evening. "I see you do prefer frankness. You are quite open, are you not?"

"I am," she admitted with a heavy sigh and a shake of her head for the misery such a trait had brought her. "I wish to know things that no one should inquire about, to cast aside the polite restraints that are placed on conversation and topics of discussion and have all be revealed. I struggle with secrets, which is a delightful irony, given the massive secrets I live with and indulge in." She gestured faintly to her ensemble for effect.

"That does raise a question or two," *Capitán* agreed, though he did not seem particularly bothered by the idea. "But I can understand that."

She looked over at him again. "Can you?"

"Of course. We wish to be in control of the secrets of our lives, and by doing so, we are never harmed by them."

"Yes," she breathed, stunned he should so easily comprehend what she struggled to express. "Yes, exactly."

"Very well. Let this be such an opportunity. What is it you wish to know?" *Capitán* asked her, clasping his hands behind his back. "In particular."

Emmeline reared back a little at the direct question. "At this moment?"

"*Sí.*"

"What you are hoping to find in London by wandering at night," she confessed with an almost bashful smile. "I've never found someone else who chooses to do so without having some nefarious streak to indulge in."

Capitán looked up at the star-dotted sky partially obscured by the few clouds there. "If I knew what I hoped to find," he said slowly, "perhaps I might have found it by now."

"I thought you said you had only wandered London for a few nights," Emmeline pressed, stepping a little closer to hear better as his voice had softened with his admission. "How much searching can you have done?"

"Hours," he replied, mostly to himself. "Hours and hours. Not only of London, but of every city in which I dock. I explore every city by night, as though the night gives me a better understanding of the place, a truer sense of its heart. Yet London... London feels like it should mean something for me. I do not yet know what, but I have a sense it should."

There was a note of pain to his voice that made Emmeline hurt, some desperation she could sympathize with, even if she could not perfectly understand. She had never truly been desperate for answers, or meaning, or truth. She sought out stories, it was true, but that was adventure, not something personally significant. She did not need to risk herself in the London night to complete something in her soul. It filled her life with fullness, it was true, but she could hardly claim it had brought her life answers. That was far more noble than her excursions dared go.

She had spent more time exposing things of a shocking nature than she had finding meaning or purpose for herself. Was that something for which she ought to feel ashamed? Ought she to find a better use for her skills and talents than being a voyeur of the city's underworkings?

Memories of the stories she had written flashed through her

mind as she considered this. The woman who had been saved from a burning building by some mystery man known only as Rogue. The strict and overbearing governess who owned and operated a brothel in the deepest part of the Seven Dials. The disgraced peer who had made it a habit to turn his maids into mistresses and deposit them and their illegitimate babies in corners of London that ruined them from further employment. The quiet woman from the bakery who had endured so much in the French Revolution and still managed to feed the orphans of the streets without reservation or greed.

She had found remarkable stories—of good and of evil—and shared them with Society. She had learned more of the world from this one city than she could have imagined in a great deal of travel. She had opened eyes, which might have remained blind to all those that dwelled beneath them, and forced them to see and to acknowledge what they had missed. Was there not something noble in that?

"London does mean something," she heard herself say, wondering what she meant by it.

"For you?" *Capitán* asked, thankfully not inquiring after the long pause in conversation. "Or for me?"

"Both, I should hope." She blinked and smiled up at him. "It means something for me, certainly. It is the only home I have ever known, yet I feel as though I never truly saw it until I began to explore by night. There is a reason, or several of them, why young ladies are not intended to behave this way, but I'll never regret that I have. And for you... perhaps you will be able to appreciate what your father knew in his youth. Or what he did not speak of. Or complete his circle, if he was prevented from doing so. There are any number of things you can find here. Perhaps it is not simply one thing."

"You may be right, *Orejitas*," he murmured as he nodded, his smile still in place. "And perhaps I ought to let London speak to me rather than search for answers, no?"

It was such an unusual way to speak of their excursions, of their mutual searching, of the way of life itself, but Emmeline found that it made more sense to her than many other things she had heard her entire life. Perhaps she would find more meaning to her life from now on after all.

"I think that seems to be a very fine idea," she replied softly. "I hope you'll tell me if she does."

"Oh, I certainly will, *Orejitas*. Who else would understand my meaning?" He winked, which made Emmeline laugh outright. He looked around them, sighing softly. "I fear I have not learned much of the city and its aspects tonight, though I have certainly walked farther from the ship than I have done so far."

Emmeline wrinkled her nose. "I'm sorry for that. I should have been a better guide for you."

"On the contrary," he insisted, stopping their progress, and taking her arm. "It has been the most beneficial night I have had in quite some time. I have no regrets."

Something warm and soft wrapped about her heart, and there was nothing to do but smile at the man. "Nor do I, *Capitán*."

He returned her smile, and for a moment, the night grew quieter. "This seems a good spot," he suggested softly. "Shall we meet here tomorrow to walk again?"

There was no guarantee she could manage an escape tomorrow, but it would not be for want of trying.

"Yes," Emmeline said at once. "Yes, I would like that very much."

Chapter Eight

"You are insane, Teo. You are aware of this, yes?"

"Yes, Rafa, I have heard you say it many times."

"Yet you still proceed down idiotic paths."

Teo met his friend's eyes sardonically. "It is not idiotic to explore London."

"We have spent the entire day in London," Rafa reminded him harshly, his brow creasing with his frustration. "By your own account, you slept for four hours and no more. Are you trying to kill yourself?"

"You sleep on less whenever we are on the sea," Teo reminded him. "I never suggest you have less intelligence for it."

Rafa grumbled under his breath, some incoherent speech that wouldn't have done Teo any good to hear. "Will you at least consider sleeping in the boardinghouse rather than on the ship?"

"You know how I feel about sleeping on the ship."

"Yes, and I also know the amount of work that getting you back onto the ship is for the men who would much rather be sound asleep than be forced awake to cart their half-brained captain back on board in the middle of the night, and then secure the ship yet again despite having done so after he left." Rafa folded his muscular arms, giving Teo a challenging look.

Teo met it, feeling a slight twinge of guilt. "Have they complained?"

Rafa scoffed very low. "Of course not. They don't complain. But they have mentioned the efforts involved in your scurrying back and forth, and I inferred the rest."

This was an unusual tactic for Rafa to take to convince Teo not to live out of the ship while they tended to business ashore—to think of his men rather than himself and the inconvenience it was on them to cater to his requests.

"It doesn't seem to be a problem when we are in port elsewhere," Teo protested half-heartedly, knowing full well he would likely give in shortly.

His plaintive point had no effect on Rafa's demeanor. "Our usual stays are a few days at most, Teo. We've been here almost two weeks, with no sign that we will shortly be off again."

"That's because this is no ordinary stop," Teo reminded him. "We are not exchanging one load for another; we are attempting to expand the business, and such things take time."

"We know that," Rafa conceded with a firm nod. "But our men grow restless. They do not care so much about the business you or I or our clerks are about. They are seafaring men, Teo. And not being at sea makes them uncomfortable."

Teo frowned at that. There was no denying that, among his crew, there was hardly a man who had the same interests in England as he did. They had been curious, of course, but only as curious as they ever were when they reached a port that was new and unfamiliar to them. Nearly two weeks in the same place would have given them ample time to explore a new place to their heart's content.

The work he and Rafa had to do would not be completed for some time, depending on how many contracts they could secure and what details there would be to work out. He could hardly expect their entire crew to wait in readiness until all was resolved.

He sighed in thought, shaking his head. "You're right."

"I am?"

"If that surprises you—"

"No, I am well aware I am right. I just never expect to hear you say so." Rafa grinned quickly, then sobered. "We could keep a few men here with us and send the rest to Portugal. Dominguez is well respected; he could lead and supervise. The casks awaiting us can be inspected by our men, just as they would be if we were with them, and we can continue to do our usual business while you and I work to secure more."

It was a comfort to know Rafa had considered all the details and aspects of his plan before coming to Teo with it. More than that, it was exactly what Teo would have wanted and what he thought was the best course. Convenient to have a partner in the business who knew his preferences and shared his instincts.

"Agreed," Teo told him as he shrugged into his jacket, a darker, coarser one than what he had worn the night before but would suit better in the chillier night. "Ask Dominguez if he minds and see if he feels ready to take on such a responsibility. I believe he is, but he will need his own confidence to do so, not only our assurances."

"Yes, *Capitán*."

Teo smiled at the title, pausing slightly in the adjustment of his clothing.

Despite being in a position earning such a title, he would never again be able to hear it without thinking of Ears and her fascinating, open, and endearing ways. It wasn't the lateness of the hour that had rendered the quantity of his sleep so reduced. It was the recurring thoughts of his newfound companion continually preventing him from sleep.

He wasn't about to tell Rafa about her, nor about the way she remained on his mind even when he was focused on other tasks. If there was one thing that would make Rafa more irritated about Teo's interest in England, it would be involving a woman in the mix. Rafa was more a man of the world, in many respects, and did not expect to ever marry, settle down, or have a family. He preferred to visit certain establishments when he had the urge and leave them as free from entanglements as he had entered.

It wasn't quite as tasteful as what Teo would have liked, but Rafa was a good man, and it was better he behaved this way than to tarnish reputations of those who would never recover. He was simply not the sort to live the comfortable, respectable life. Even if he was respectable in his own way.

Teo, on the other hand...

If Rafa caught wind of Teo thinking about a woman he planned on spending a quantity of time with, he would begin to panic about Teo's eventual stepping back from business affairs. He knew, as Teo did, that it would happen someday when Teo found the right woman and the right situation for himself. He would always be part of the business, as it was part of his birthright and legacy, but when the time came, he would place his family as the priority over his own interests and business.

Rafa would simply prefer it not happen anytime soon.

That was not to say Ears could be such a woman, but Teo was not quite willing to rule her out, either. One night in her company had left him eager for more, and that was an encouraging sign.

Still, he knew nothing about her. She could be married. She could be a mother. She could be any number of things he had yet to discover, and it could be he was embarking on a scandal that would prevent him from truly securing answers or belonging from his more English side. He would simply have to hope and pray he would have the eyes to see such danger before it was too late.

"Will you at least tell me where you are going? Then I might at least send someone out in search of you, should you fail to return."

Teo blinked and gave Rafa a rueful look. "How would you know if I have failed to return? You stay at the boardinghouse, and I will return here until the crew has left port."

Rafa glowered darkly at him. "I would know, *amigo*. Tell me."

"I imagine I'll end up somewhere around Covent Garden tonight," Teo told him evasively, raising his chin a touch in defiance. "It attracted me today, and I'd like to see more of it."

Just as he'd hoped, Rafa scowled further, which was always impressive. "That woman is a menace. I don't know where you got her name from, but you should burn that place to the ground."

"Her theatre?" Teo asked with all innocence. "Or the lodgings of my informant?"

"I'd not complain about either. Or both."

Teo chuckled, pulling the kerchief from his neck, and folding it loosely. "She has the ability to make both of us look better than merely presentable for our dinner with the Fosters tomorrow, and to find that in so short a time is extraordinary. Particularly at the price she quoted."

"If I recall, Mr. Foster did not seem to think we would need to be fully trussed up," Rafa mused sarcastically. "Now, I could be imagining such a statement, but I have never been particularly imaginative in that sense."

"We have been invited to a family dinner," Teo reminded him, firmly emphasizing the word family. "As in there will be others present besides Mr. Foster and his father and brother. I know you consider women to be moderately useless where your time is concerned, but these married men are undoubtedly influenced by their wives. Perhaps even heavily so. Now, do you recollect the expressions my sisters wore when we would arrive at their homes dressed in our simple attire, even if it was clean?"

It was comedic how churlish his friend became at the mention of it. "Elena and Catalina are rather free with their opinions. English women would never be so."

Oh, if his friend only knew how incorrect such a statement was.

"Not to our faces, perhaps," Teo allowed, "but I can promise you their opinions would be made known to their husbands once we were away. So, for the sake of our business prospects with them, we will make an effort and let Miss Tilda have her way with us."

Rafa raised a brow. "I've never let any woman have her way with me, and I am not about to start now."

Teo rolled his eyes and turned away to finish getting ready. "Behave yourself, Rafa. If her efforts on our attire can improve our chances of securing promising contracts, it will be worth the suffering you endured, will it not?"

"It would have to be an astonishingly promising contract."

"Then let us hope you impress the wives of the Fosters creditably." Teo looked over his shoulder at his friend, daring him to continue this argument. Though he was a larger and stronger man, though he was far more imposing, and though he could have continued to press the complaint until Teo grew weary of the battle, Rafa only shrugged and folded his arms more tightly against himself.

"Is that acceptance?" Teo demanded.

"It is a decision to let things proceed and see what comes of all our efforts," Rafa replied in a surprisingly flat tone. "Including that harridan with too many pins and a wagging tongue."

That was as good as Teo was going to get from the man, and he nodded in acknowledgement. "Very good. Now, unless you wish to detain me further, I will go."

Rafa stepped back and mockingly gestured the way to the door.

"As you wish, *Capitán*. I bid you a good evening and safe wanderings."

There was nothing to do but ignore his friend's surly petulance and his mockery, and it was easy enough to do so knowing Ears would be waiting for him just a few streets away from the docks. It was astonishing how such a thought could bring a smile to his face, even if he did need to hide that smile for now to keep Rafa from guessing his true motivation.

It did not take long for him to be once again strolling along the cobblestone in the dark, whistling to himself the selfsame tune Ears had selected the night before. It was a jaunty, engaging song, and it would never again fail to be anything but joyous.

He needed no guide nor map to lead him to their arranged meeting place, his feet knowing the way with more certainty than they could have walked the path to his family home in Albesanta. Though he could not have recited to anyone the buildings he was passing on his way, he knew without a doubt he was on the right course and would soon begin his hours of entertainment, enlightenment, and enjoyment. It was a wonder he had managed to do anything even remotely productive this morning with such an evening ahead of him.

A familiar figure stood easily at the corner he was headed toward, and he noticed her hair was not so tightly tucked beneath her cap tonight. A few curling tendrils escaped out the back, and Teo's eyes focused on those curls as though a lifeline.

What color were they? Did they naturally curl, or was it simply how her hair had been styled during the day? Were they long when unbound? When had hair become so interesting?

She turned, no doubt catching his whistling, and her quick, easy smile in his direction shuttered up all thoughts of hair. She could light the world's darkness with such a smile. He could barely tell the color of her hair or her eyes, the shade of her skin, or if she bore freckles, but he could see that smile. It was quite simply the loveliest smile he had ever seen.

"Good evening, *Orejitas*," he greeted, tipping the brim of his hat in precisely the same way he had seen Gent do the night before.

She delighted him by repeating the gesture back to him. "Evening, *Capitán*. Have you had a good day?"

"A busy one, certainly," he admitted with a weary exhale, the events of the day rushing back on him as he considered it. "Whether it was good or not will have to wait for the consequences to determine."

"That sounds promising," she replied, peering up at him as he approached. "An active day is surely better than a stagnant one, is it not?"

A young woman who wished to be busy and active in her life, not just relegated to finer things? She was a rare creature indeed. But then, did not women of the middle and lower classes need to work more than those in the higher positions? Perhaps she belonged to that class of women and was putting on a finer accent as part of her disguise. He would not put her at the height of Society, not that he knew much of it, but he had some difficulty imagining her as a washer woman who lived two streets away and collected a passel of children during her life.

Still, his sisters were technically of a higher class in Spain, and they appreciated more in life than leisure. It would bode well for Ears and her future if she felt the same.

"Undoubtedly," Teo told her, smiling fondly. "It is appreciated, however, to know a day's outcome before it has ended."

Ears nodded in agreement. "I concede to that. Unless, of course, one's day was entirely filled with active boredom, and the outcome can be determined before one has left one's bed."

He laughed at the sour note her voice had taken on. "Was that how your day has been, *Orejitas*? Active boredom?"

"In excess," she groaned, looking up at the sky before closing her eyes. "I am exhausted but have not done anything that should have fatigued me so. It was all sitting and chattering, or listening, in my case. I could not have gotten a word in edgewise even if I wanted to, and I can assure you I did not want to."

Her answer did not give him much guidance on her position in life, or what exactly she might have done to earn such a description.

"And why could you not refuse to spend your day in such a manner?" Teo asked with real curiosity. "Find some other activity to engage in that might better suit your preferences."

"I am not my own mistress," Ears told him after a moment's

hesitation. "Despite being five and twenty, I do not have the authority or freedom to make such determinations."

Five and twenty? He would not have put her above twenty years in age based on her appearance even in the limited light of night. The lamplighters had been along in this part of the city, but without the finery to render streetlamps at frequent intervals and no interior light to aid them, there was not enough light to determine the finer aspects of one's appearance.

Five and twenty. No wonder she had firm opinions and decisive thoughts. She'd had enough experience to find likes and dislikes in almost any societal aspect.

"Is there no one to whom you might appeal for improvements to your day?" Teo inquired tentatively, wondering just how open she would be with him tonight, particularly when he had very many questions. And more kept coming the better he knew her.

Ears laughed one very soft, very derisive laugh. "I'm a woman, *Capitán*. And an unmarried one. What I want to do and what I am able to do very seldom converge."

There was no helping the thrill of elation that shot through both of his legs as he heard that blessed word from her lips. Unmarried. Ideas and fears of scandal fell away, and all he was left with was anticipation. What exactly he was anticipating did not have words or, indeed, boundaries, but there it was all the same.

Before he could offer any other questions, sympathies, or suggestions, Ears brightened and turned to face him, propping her hands on her slender hips.

How he had missed they were slender before, he would chalk up to her disguise. He had to.

"Well, *Capitán*," she began in a formal—albeit eager—tone, "what would you like to see tonight?"

"Are you truly able to wander the city at my leisure?" He shook his head in disbelief, no matter how he loved that she was offering. "Given your day was entirely at the leisure of others, would you not prefer to have it all your own way now?"

Her grin became something remarkably cheeky, which prompted an appreciative smile of his own. "My own nighttime wanderings are usually investigative and occasionally quite dull in the process. Not so dull as the days I spend, grant you, but hardly something I would subject a friend to. Besides, I am presently not investigating anything at all, so my leisure is your leisure."

A friend, was he? On so short an acquaintance? There was no match for this night, in his estimation. None at all.

"Covent Garden," he managed to suggest around a congested throat.

"Excellent choice," Ears praised. She pointed up the street behind her. "Right this way, sir. Covent Garden and all its wonders."

She turned to start walking, and he followed, nearly skipping to her side in his eagerness. "Are there many wonders in Covent Garden?" he inquired in bemusement. "Or is that your own embellishment for my benefit?"

Ears laughed in earnest, a delightful, warm, throaty sort of laugh, which seemed to radiate from her core. "I suppose that depends on who you ask. I find wonders there every time I go to the theatre. Have you seen any part of Covent Garden yet?"

"I was there earlier today, as it happens," Teo confessed with an abashed smile. "Business, in a way. But I was with Rafa, so it was not something I could explore at my leisure."

"Drat Rafa for preventing you," Ears shot back, swinging her arms almost like a man as she walked in her fitted trousers. "Rafa is…?"

Teo winced at the revelation he'd unwittingly made. "My business partner and friend."

Thankfully she only nodded primly. "Well, should I ever meet the man, I will scold him for you."

He would pay a great sum of money to see the almost diminutive Ears give the tall and intimidating Rafa a tongue-lashing. The outcome would be entirely unpredictable, and he was delighted imagining the possibilities.

"I have no doubt you would." Teo cleared his throat, desperate to change the subject quickly. "Tell me about Covent Garden, then. What should I know that I might have missed today?"

"Well," Ears said on an exhale, "once, it was an open-air fruit and vegetable market. Then the coffee houses, theatres, taverns, and brothels began to come in…"

Teo coughed at her easy mention of brothels, giving her a sidelong look. "You are aware of these places?"

She did not even blink. "Of course. I once investigated a situation involving three of the brothels in Covent Garden, and I found some delightful ladies who have been very helpful to me in the years since."

Investigate? She kept using that word, but it was without any context that would give him understanding. As a young woman, what could she possibly be investigating for? Or for whom?

Would she begin investigating him if he proved mysterious or interesting enough?

He hated even thinking the question, but it was a natural progression of thought from his previous ones.

"Does the market continue even with all the additions?" he asked, trying to think back on the morning as he shifted the conversation back to Covent Garden itself rather than the ladies one might find there at all hours.

"In a word, yes." Ears hummed an almost-laugh. "It is complete and utter chaos, given everything else. One wonders if the area will finally give way to one direction of Society or another, but it seems to hover precariously in some sort of undetermined state."

Teo felt his lips curve further as he listened to Ears, though she wasn't looking at him presently. "You describe it so eloquently. Poetic, even."

"Thank you." She looked away, sighing as she took in their surroundings. "I fancy myself a writer sometimes, and the more I write, the more words seem powerful and simple—more than I ever imagined. And nothing gives me satisfaction quite like a good turn of phrase."

A writer who investigates? What a curious creature Ears was! What a puzzle! He was going to rather like continuing to meet with her, and he would endeavor to properly appreciate every facet she revealed.

"You've been to the theatre here?" Teo gestured toward their destination.

"Oh, yes. And the Royal Opera." Ears glanced up at him now, almost speculatively. "What sort of business did you have in Covent

Garden today? You didn't see the market, or do not recall it, so you must have been at one end or the other, not the center."

She was witty and intelligent, he'd grant her that, and she had no qualms in asking the direct questions. Which was well, as he had no qualms answering them.

"A fitting," he said simply. "Rafa and I are to dine with new associates tomorrow, and it is a family dinner. I am to understand a finer impression than we were previously told would benefit our chances of success."

"Oh, most assuredly," Ears insisted, making him chuckle. "Men have no notion of such things. You were quite right. But what tailor did you go to? I don't know of any in this area."

Teo's chuckle turned to a full laugh. "I'm not certain I would call her a tailor, but I received Señora Tilda's name from a reputable source."

Ears barked a loud burst of laughter, clamping her hand over her mouth. "You went to Tilda? You must have high connections indeed, *Capitán*. She almost never takes private clientele."

"You know her?" Teo all but gaped at her while she continued to laugh. "Truly?"

"I am quite certain," she said between breathless giggles, "that there is only one Tilda who deals with clothing. She was, and still is, a famed costumer for the theatres in London. She is the one who tends to my disguises and helps me travel about London undetected. I don't know very many people who have worked with her personally besides myself. What in the world did you think visiting her at a theatre?"

"We didn't," Teo protested, becoming a little confused. "She had a storefront. Just there." He pointed toward a darkened building on the corner they presently passed.

Ears hummed to herself, the sound still filled with laughter. "I see Tilda is up to some games. No business has succeeded on that premises for twenty years or so. Last year, it was for rare books and antiquities. There's no telling what it truly is this year, but I can assure you I have only ever met Tilda in the back rooms of the theatre."

"She is an impressive woman," Teo recalled, amusing himself by thinking of Rafa's discomfort throughout the whole of the appointment. "She made Rafa bristle with such skill."

"Yes, she would." Ears shook her head, smiling still. "She is strict, witty, sharp, generous, conniving. Truly, Tilda is unlike any other woman in the world."

Teo bit the inside of his cheek for a moment, then ventured, "I may not have quite the scope to say such a thing, but I believe you are as well, *Orejitas.*"

Her brow creased as she looked up at him. "I am what?"

Venturing further still, Teo reached out and took her hand in his. "Unlike any other woman in the world."

Her lips parted, her eyes widened, and just when he thought she might bolt for fear, Ears's lips curved into the most precious smile he had ever witnessed in his entire life, and her hand squeezed his.

Nothing more needed to be said.

Chapter Nine

Her head had not ached this much since the Gable ball, where she had been so bored, she had been reduced to sampling punch the whole night. The Gable family apparently preferred spirits in their punch, and a hefty dose of them.

Today, however, spirits were not the trouble. Inadequate sleep was.

It would not have been such a problem had her aunt permitted her to continue sleeping, as any young lady of Society would have done after a late night of activity. But as her aunt had no idea of her spending a late night in activity, Emmeline could not very well beg for the traditional remedy for such a headache.

So she would just sit here and silently sip tea, which did nothing to ebb away at her pain, listening to puffed up ladies come up with ridiculous ideas for helping the poor. Her aunt was on the committee for a charity organization, and Emmeline had been dragged to every meeting possible. She knew Aunt Hermione had the best of intentions and likely would do whatever she could to help the less fortunate, but the others who claimed to have an interest… well, it would take a catastrophic episode and a hefty threat of Christian damnation to make any of them even blink over the contents of their change purses.

"What about books?" one of the ladies said as though it were a bright idea. "Surely, we all have books in our individual libraries we might donate to the poor."

"Wonderful idea, Sara," another interjected, clapping her hands. "My Stephen has so many books he never reads, and it would be no trouble to secure several of them to give away."

"Indeed," a younger woman with shockingly pale hair added. "I am in no way against the lower classes being educated. I do believe it has been said that education is the first step on the road to success."

Emmeline barely restrained a dubious snort as she sipped her lukewarm tea again. Her aunt, sitting beside her, hummed very low in some sort of disapproval.

What did she object to exactly, Emmeline wondered? The idea of educating the poor, or the glaring inanity of the entire argument?

"I think, ladies, you might be missing the point," the woman from Emmeline's left broke in, her voice sounding very tense.

All attention turned to her, and Emmeline, caught in the woman's periphery, turned to face her as well. There was a tension in her expression that perfectly matched the tension in her voice, which made Emmeline rather interested in what exactly she was going to say. Any woman who felt tense throughout this meeting and its discussion would say something worth hearing, no matter which side of the argument she took.

She was a stout woman, though she wasn't especially large in any places. Her hair was dark but streaked with grey, and her gown was neat, fashionable, and flattering. Simple, but certainly fitting all the necessary marks of a lady of Society. Perhaps only just so, but that was entirely to her credit insofar as Emmeline was concerned.

"The idea of donating books to the poor," the woman said carefully, her eyes pointedly meeting those of the others in turn, "is a good one. Education is important for progression. But it fails as a solution for our aims in this organization. We are not, if I understand correctly, seeking to help the poor progress, but to survive. To educate the poor, they must have the funds and abilities to receive such an education. Giving them our books will not put bread on their table, nor will it put meat into the mouths of their children. It will not clothe their backs, nor will it keep them warm in the winter."

"But," the pale-haired woman broke in, looking truly bewildered, "we must start somewhere, Mrs. Foster."

Mrs. Foster turned her stern gaze on her. "We must start with survival, Mrs. Aimes. Books are no good to those who cannot read."

Mrs. Aimes's eyes widened, and she looked around in horror.

"They... cannot read?"

"Oh, good heavens," Aunt Hermione muttered from Emmeline's right. "Who let this cricket into the room?"

Emmeline coughed delicately, bringing her napkin to her mouth to cover the smile she could not suppress. Sometimes her aunt was truly delightful.

An auburn-haired woman in the room sighed heavily. "Well, does anyone know how we might better understand the conditions of the poor? We must know what they suffer so that we might provide relief."

It was the start of a worthwhile conversation; Emmeline would grant her that. A weak start, a stupid start, but a start.

"We could visit," Emmeline muttered to the ladies beside her as she picked up her tea once more. "See for ourselves, perhaps."

"Don't shock them into swooning," Aunt Hermione murmured with a quirk of her lips.

"Yes," Mrs. Foster added in an undertone. "There are not enough smelling salts to revive them all."

The three of them silently shook with their laughter while the members with less awareness of the world beneath them continued to bandy about with naive, evasive, and cheap ideas of how to better pretend to be good, charitable, Christian women who actually cared about their fellow creatures.

"What about that man who writes such shocking tales from that part of London?" someone suddenly exclaimed. "Emmett something or other."

Emmeline froze, her lips touching the porcelain of her teacup, her eyes flicking toward the voice.

"Oh, dear," someone else groaned. "What about him? I do so hate those stories, why must we be subjected to hearing such secrets?"

"You read every word of them, Sophia—voraciously so, and you know it!"

"Emmett Barnes, that's it. He is clearly aware of the poor and less fortunate just as much as the villains in that part of the city," the first voice chimed again. "Would he not be able to enlighten us as to their state?"

This suggestion was met with silence from every quarter of the room, Emmeline included.

The truth of it was that Emmett Barnes *would* be able to provide them some insight and valuable insight at that. What's more, he would love such a noble enterprise as a reprieve from the shocking stories he was so used to sending about. Not that the shocking stories would cease, for there were some noble moments in those as well, but the chance to share the truth of what the majority of London's populace endured... would be a calling worth interrupting even the most shocking of stories.

But, of course, she could not be the one to add to this conversation or, indeed, make suggestions that would improve her own secret favor.

"I suppose it would be rather neat and tidy to have someone else look into such matters," one of the other women said, her tone unconvincing. "Then we would not have to stoop—that is, lower..."

"Yes, yes, we quite understand your distaste, Ellen. Do not trouble yourself to find polite words where there are none," Aunt Hermione snapped, waving her hand dismissively.

Emmeline could have hugged her aunt enthusiastically for such a barb, but it was hardly called for, so she merely set her tea back down as gently as possible.

"But how does one communicate with a man such as Mr. Barnes?" Mrs. Aimes asked, looking just as clueless as she had been three minutes prior. "None of us know him."

Well, that was not entirely true, but Emmeline would allow the inaccuracy to pass.

"His publisher, surely," someone else said. "Apply to the publisher, who will certainly see the message delivered accordingly. All will be well and good, and we might understand the most pressing needs. Then, finally, we may do something rather than simply talk of doing something."

If it were not impolite to do so, Emmeline would have toasted this suggestion with her teacup. So, in tribute, she sipped again. Her cup was empty, which was awkward, but she could pretend all the same for the time being. She could make herself another shortly if it would be possible amid the conversations of others.

How many cups had she had so far? Two? Three? Would another

give rise to unfavorable comments? She could have slapped herself for being so silly. Comments over an excess of tea? More than half of Society would be commented on for doing so if that were the case. One could hardly be considered British if they were judged for the number of cups of tea they consumed in a day. Or a sitting.

More tea it was.

Emmeline rose as gracefully as she could from her chair and moved to the tea tray to one side of the room.

Mrs. Tremball didn't live in the nicest home in London, but her drawing room was particularly large, which did make it a perfect location for their meetings. More than that, she always had an excellent tea for them. Even if she added nothing of value to any conversation they'd ever had. Ever.

While the women discussed the options of what they could ask Emmett Barnes to specifically write about, Emmeline poured a good amount of tea into her cup, more than she usually did. She glanced over at the clock on the mantle of the room, hiding a groan that there was still another half hour left in their scheduled meeting time.

Had she really told *Capitán* last night that her day had been filled with boredom? Today had the potential to be far worse, but her aunt was usually more accommodating after these meetings. A foul mood made her rather amenable to Emmeline's rather reasonable requests, and there was never any doubt Aunt Hermione would leave the meetings with a foul mood.

Poor soul. Her good heart and sincere motives were never matched by the others in her circles. If only she would defy expectations and seek out friends of other classes and stations, ones that might raise a brow from her more Society-obsessed acquaintances. Mrs. Foster was a bit unconventional for the circles, being the wife of a merchant, but their fortunes were such that they could not fashionably be excluded from events and gatherings. She seemed to have a decent grasp on the reality of the world rather than the perfect picture Society wanted to paint.

It would do her aunt some good if Emmeline were to encourage that connection.

Dropping one too many sugar cubes into her tea, she drowned them in a quick splash of milk, then turned back toward the group, stirring almost too vigorously to be considered genteel.

"Very well, I will write to the publisher," the one her aunt had called Ellen announced with some disgust, throwing her hands up. "For pity's sake, this is worse than getting my eldest daughter married off."

Emmeline bit her lip, both wanting the details of that story and very much not wanting them as well. She resumed her seat cautiously, sipping the still hot liquid gently to avoid burning herself.

"I think now would be the perfect time for a brief respite," her aunt announced, somehow managing a smile that ought to console any number of them. "We will reconvene in five minutes or so."

Heads nodded around them, and private conversations struck up around the group. Emmeline shook her head, sipping more tea.

"Is it just me, or are they more insipid than usual today?" Aunt Hermione asked in a very low voice.

"Oh, thank you for saying so," Mrs. Foster gushed, turning to face them both. "I thought for certain I was in the wrong meeting for most of that discussion. They are not paragons of wisdom, intelligence, or humanity at any given time, but this…"

Emmeline swallowed her tea and looked between the two. "If the pair of you feel this way, you ought to start a separate group devoted to true interests and action. Let this organization be all superficial and insincere, something for appearances. But if you truly wish to do something…"

Mrs. Foster gave Emmeline an assessing look, then turned her attention to Aunt Hermione. "She is quite an intelligent, well-spoken young woman, Mrs. Kirby. I'm quite impressed."

Aunt gave Emmeline a fond smile. "Thank you. I've always found her to be outspoken, but she certainly does it well."

"Where did I learn that, I wonder?" Emmeline asked, returning her aunt's look.

"No idea," came the cool reply, accompanied by a wink.

"I can see a real fondness between you," Mrs. Foster commented, still smiling at them both. "You are fortunate. My daughter-in-law Charlotte lived with her aunt for several years before marrying my son, and it was a dreadful situation."

Hermione tutted softly in sympathy. "The poor thing. I find it hard to believe, or forgive, a relative taking up guardianship of an innocent ward and somehow finding themselves inconvenienced or imposed upon for doing so. It should be no hardship to take in a little one whose loving parents are no longer on this earth to care for them."

"I quite agree," Mrs. Foster echoed. "I have tried my best, from the day of their wedding, to treat her as I would my own daughter and not simply the woman who married my son. To care for her as a daughter and shower her with all the love and respect she did not receive from her aunt."

Emmeline felt a sudden rush of love and affection for Aunt Hermione, finding it difficult to swallow as she did so. Her aunt had taken her in when her parents had died, though her guardianship was technically in the hands of Emmeline's cousin. Her aunt had insisted that, since her own children had grown, it would make more sense for Emmeline to reside with her than with anyone else. Emmeline had been too numb at the time to make any such decision for herself, and when she had felt emotionally stable enough, she'd gotten so accustomed to her aunt's home that it had become her home as well.

And nothing had changed since then.

She might sneak out of her home to venture out into the city, she might escape every month to do some teaching in Kent, and she might dream of adventures she would never experience, but she adored living with her aunt. She adored the relationship they shared. She adored knowing that she was loved and valued, even understood at times.

It was the best substitute for her own parents that she could have hoped for. Had Aunt Hermione known that when she'd offered to take Emmeline in?

"That is a beautiful thing," Aunt Hermione offered, bringing Emmeline out of her wistful reminiscence. "You are to be much commended, Mrs. Foster."

Mrs. Foster blushed a little, her smile soft. "She is an easy woman to love, so it was not difficult. And she and my son have the most delightful little children, and they do adore them so."

"Grandchildren are the delight of our lives, are they not?" Aunt Hermione echoed with her own smile.

Emmeline sipped her tea, praying no one would ask her about marriage or children as part of this conversation.

"What would you say to taking an interest in orphanages and foundling homes, Mrs. Kirby?" Mrs. Foster suddenly suggested, her eyes bright.

Aunt Hermione shifted in her seat, canting forward a little. "I'd be very interested. Those poor, deprived children, and one hears such stories about parish nurses and the like."

"One even hears of private establishments offering money for abandoned children," Emmeline broke in, setting her teacup down. The older women looked at her in surprised silence. Oh dear.

"Hears of what, Emmeline?" her aunt inquired stiffly.

"Money?" Mrs. Foster echoed, looking slightly green and grey in the face.

If it was possible for one's insides to wince, Emmeline's did then. How had she heard about those horrid places? In which capacity? How could she relate what she intended without betraying herself? Her mind spun with a rapidity that left her dizzy.

"There was an article some time ago," Emmeline stammered, looking between the ladies in turn. "That writer they spoke of earlier. He discovered a woman in Cheapside selling unwanted or stolen babies. Surely you read it…" She held her breath, waiting for the shock and disbelief to fade.

"I read that story!" a nearby woman broke in, looking at Emmeline with some interest, tuning in to their conversation. "Absolutely horrifying. I told my husband about it. He works for Bow Street, and he contacted authorities to shut the woman down. We took all the babies to the Foundling Hospital. Imagine what might have continued to happen without Mr. Barnes shedding a light on it!"

Despite her present state of near-paralyzing fear, Emmeline did manage to find some satisfaction and pride in the words of praise for what she had written.

It had been a harrowing experience, that particular piece. What had failed to make it into the article, out of necessity, was that the woman in charge had taken the babies of her two unmarried daughters and sold them for a profit, despite her daughters wishing to raise their children.

The entire episode had left Emmeline feeling rather ill, and she'd been unwell for days after several of her investigations into it. At least it had ended well, and she was grateful to hear that action had taken place to improve the situation. She rarely had information about remedies to the situations she revealed, and no influence to bring such change about herself.

Aunt Hermione swallowed with some difficulty and finally looked at the other woman who had spoken. "Bless you for intervening there, Ruth. And bless your husband for his actions."

Mrs. Foster shook her head. "What mother would sell her child? Abandonment at all must surely come out of desperation, but to be paid for it…"

"A different desperation perhaps," Emmeline suggested softly, gingerly venturing back into the conversation.

"I cannot abide it," Mrs. Foster whispered. "Any mother worth much ought to feel her heart break as she chooses to give up her child. She should not be rewarded for doing so. She should go on with her life and feel the pain of it daily."

Emmeline bit her lip, wishing she had never brought the subject up. "And what if the child did not come by means the woman had a choice in?"

Mrs. Foster closed her eyes, her throat tightening. "Bless those sweet girls, I know there must be many out there. That is different. I pray those angels are blessed with peace in knowing they have done right by that equally innocent babe in giving them a future." She shook her head, exhaling roughly. "I should not generalize such tragic things. One does not know the circumstances, and judgments should not be made."

"Leave the judgments to the Almighty, I say," Aunt Hermione murmured. "Only He can truly do so." She reached out to put a hand over Mrs. Foster's. "Perhaps in our efforts, we might also do something for the unfortunate mothers. References for good employment or something."

Ruth pulled her chair closer and nodded fervently. "I've heard stories, Mrs. Kirby, and that could do a great deal for improving the state of affairs."

Mrs. Foster nodded, sniffing back apparent tears. "We must see that the children are truly cared for, not merely tended to. And the mothers should never feel the sting of the same judgment that I have just made."

"Mrs. Foster," Emmeline protested as gently as she could. "No one views you as some great sinner for what you have said. You clearly have the heart of a mother—a truly sincere one. You cannot see how anyone could give up a child and not want to die from doing so. It is how anyone might wish their mother would be."

She sniffed again and offered Emmeline a watery smile. "Bless you, my dear, for saying so. I am quite ashamed of myself in spite of your kind words. I must take a better interest in these women and these babies. I must learn of situations and understand for myself just how perilous their circumstances are." Her smile turned a little rueful. "Perhaps I should not judge our companions so harshly for their ignorance of the condition of the poor. A lack of understanding can be cured by willingness to learn."

"Hear, hear," Ruth chimed in.

Aunt Hermione looked around the room for a moment, her face scrunching up slightly. "Yes, but how many actually have that willingness to learn, I wonder?"

That was a question Emmeline wondered as well. The entire conversation was spinning in her mind, completely adjusting her opinion of her day, of this meeting, of these women, of everything she had associated with Society and its inhabitants.

How could she have known there were women like these in circles so close? She had known her aunt was in possession of a well-meaning heart and had more intelligence than she liked other people to think. But Emmeline had always assumed that they were an aberration from the rest.

She knew her fellow teachers at Miss Masters's in Kent would feel the same as this group she presently found herself in. They'd had some rather in-depth conversations on difficult subjects as they had interacted with some of the scholarship girls from the Rothchild Academy and had spoken on what interventional options were available to them in order to make a difference. But she could hardly consider her fellow teachers to be of equal station. Most of them taught because they had no other options in their lives, and teaching was their means of living.

High Society had very few angels, in her experience, and very few willing to try and become such. But here there were at least a few. And if she did her bit as Ears to help them in the ladies' missions, she might feel she was making a more significant contribution than simply taking part in the conversations.

Emmett Barnes could do his part; Ears could do hers. Emmeline could guide them both and find herself giving new life and meaning to her adventures.

Now she had a task to perform at the request of others. They did not know they were asking her, of course, but they had asked all the same. Some might have asked insincerely, but others had not.

It did not matter. She could write a series of articles about the circumstances on the streets of London beneath the observation of the high and mighty. She could force the willfully ignorant to see what they avoided. She could start the uncomfortable conversations that would need to take place if there was any hope of circumstances improving. It wasn't a scandal to uncover; it did not save any reputations or the like. This was different. This was deeper in some ways.

A different angle for Mr. Barnes and different interviews for Ears. Different clues, different feelings, different in nearly every possible way. Hopefully different in risk of dangers as well.

Perhaps best of all, this was something different enough that she could include *Capitán* in the activity, if he had an interest in it. She prayed he would. This would be a remarkable adventure for the pair of them and would give them even more reason to walk London at night. It would bypass the distance that existed in any degree of conversation before intimacy of connection came into play and allow them to find a depth that could take years to develop under other circumstances.

What an opportunity that would be. Oh, if only she could meet him tonight, they could get started right away! But he had his business dinner tonight, for which Tilda had fitted him so appropriately, and, for his sake, she hoped it would come out perfectly.

Perhaps she could spend her evening planning the next escapade and provide him with an exact structure to their time together. And if he did not wish to join her, he could walk away freely, and she would not have to wonder any further about him.

But if she knew *Capitán* at all from their brief time together, she suspected he would find the task as exciting as she. And it would become something they could share.

Chapter Ten

"Would you stop pacing?" Teo all but barked at Rafa in Spanish.

Rafa glared and continued to pace. "Why aren't they down to greet us yet?" he replied in their native tongue. "We arrived at the requested time, dressed beyond what they will expect, and they are not down here to welcome us! Something is wrong, Teo. We should go and save our time and energy for potential partners with more respect."

"Shut up!" Teo barely avoided putting his head into his hands as he sat in the chair he'd taken up in the drawing room of the Foster home. They'd been here nearly ten minutes, and he had not thought either of them particularly anxious about the evening, but here they were, snapping at each other like bickering spouses, and something small and irritating clawed at his stomach the longer they waited.

Was this what they could expect from supposedly polite Society in England? Yet how could any respectable business discussions happen if potential partners were forced to linger in drawing rooms beyond what patience could endure?

A dark, calculating thought darted across his mind, stealing his breath. Was it because they were Spanish? His grandfather had, by all accounts, been prejudiced against the Spanish, and he knew full well a man like Rafa would have been sent into the slave trade not so long ago had he fallen into the wrong situation. Teo was fair enough in complexion that he would not be obviously suspect to such things, but after months on the open sea, he developed such a brown shade of his own skin, it could raise questions. It was a disgusting, ruthless business, yet it still ran across the face of the earth as a plague in some places.

Were they being subjected to similar feelings in this place?

He hadn't felt in any way patronized by Mr. Foster when they had met at his office, no hint he was in any way uncomfortable in their presence or in their discussion. Perhaps his parents, who would have belonged to a different generation, might have a certain bias.

He didn't like thinking and feeling this way. He wanted to believe the best in people, believe that a man was judged by his character and abilities, not any mislaid beliefs about the land of his birth or the shade of his complexion.

If nothing else, he and Rafa had a fortune enough that any person on any shore should be eager to listen to a business proposition. Money washed away a great many perceived sins, he had learned, and surely it could do so here—were they being perceived as sinful in any way.

There was no proof that was the case here.

Footsteps sounded in the corridor just beyond the room, and Teo stood, tugging at his new, pristine evening jacket in anticipation.

It was only the same wiry butler from before, and he bowed as he entered, revealing a perfectly round patch of baldness at the crown of his head.

"Sirs, Mr. Foster bids me to extend an apology to you for their tardiness," he said with an actual hint of feeling. "Master Thomas, the son of Mr. Henry, and Master John, the son of Mr. Jeremiah, took a fall while at play shortly before your arrival, and they are being comforted and tended. As this is a family home, they pray you will understand their wishing to set them both to rights before returning them to the nursery. They anticipate a few minutes more delay and ask for your indulgence in this matter."

Teo paused at this revelation, unsure if his uneasy state at present would allow him to believe this so easily. He would never suggest to a servant that his masters were offering convenient excuses, particularly when he did not know them well, but when left to his own suspicious devices, and Rafa's support of them…

"Are the boys of the rambunctious sort?" Rafa asked, his accent on full display as he did so, which may have been intentional.

The butler's mouth quirked in a slight smile, yet another unusual revelation. "Yes, sir. Only yesterday, they set up a challenge for sliding down the railing of the family stairs. It is, admittedly, a very long railing and at such an angle... Well, I am told it makes for most excellent sliding if one is prone to such things. At any rate, they both ended the event with holes in their trousers and abrasions on their knees. They are of an age and rather behave more as brothers than cousins, which, I can assure you, gives their mothers some agitation."

Teo watched Rafa's reaction, curious about the inquiry his friend made but finding this tale an easier one to take after hearing the first.

Rafa smiled almost whimsically, which would have startled everyone who had ever met him. "Who won?"

The butler seemed just as surprised by the question as Teo. "I believe it was decided Master Thomas did, sir, though I cannot say how the judging of such a contest was carried out. If you will excuse me, I will see to ensuring that dinner will be served hot and promptly upon request." He bowed again, then departed the room, leaving them alone again.

Teo still watched his friend, curious and now managing a smile of his own. "Thinking of Pablo?" he asked in Spanish.

Rafa looked at him, the smile fading into his usual blank expression, though the warmth still lingered in his eyes. "Yes. If he fell, I got a scratch. If I was ill, he got a fever. I perfectly comprehend the situation above us, and I think we might be at ease now as we wait." To emphasize the point, Rafa took a pointed step to his left and sat upon the chair.

It was the first time he had stopped pacing since they had been asked to wait for their hosts.

Teo shook his head in bemusement, feeling his own irritation fading in the face of Rafa's comfort.

It had been entirely unnecessary for his thoughts to take the turn they had, and he felt a little ashamed they had done so without provocation. He did not know the Fosters well enough to presume they had any prejudices whatsoever, let alone they should be laid so squarely at his and Rafa's feet.

If he could avoid casting aspersions against their hosts for the rest of the evening, aloud or in private, perhaps something could be salvaged for their business.

"As simple as that, eh?" he asked Rafa as he resumed his seat as well. "All suspicions gone; all irritation fled?"

Rafa glanced at him coolly. "If you had a brother, Teo, you might understand such things. Your male cousins, fine men though they are, were not raised in the same household as you, and were never quite the rambunctious sort. This is a family home, as they said, and I think we may think better of the family for rallying around their young rascals."

Teo narrowed his eyes at his friend. "Are you turning soft, Rafa?"

"Hardly," came the terse reply. "Simply allowing for favorable explanations rather than poor ones."

"Who are you, and what have you done with Rafa Teixidor?"

Rafa ignored the question and Teo entirely, his eyes fixed on a point on the wall in front of him.

That was well enough, and Teo allowed himself to take a slow, consoling breath for himself as they sat in silence now.

All would be well. The evening would proceed when the family felt comfortable enough for it to do so, and they would be able to engage in profitable business discussions once the meal was over. He highly doubted it was in good taste to discuss such matters at the meal itself, but he would follow the lead of their host in this.

The home was tidy and clean, though as he understood, not located in the more wealthy or fashionable part of London. Cheapside, it was called, though he failed to see what could be cheap about such establishments when they were fine enough to still be impressive. The furnishings were elegant, if not a trifle rustic, and he found the arrangement of this room to be perfectly comfortable. He did not feel as though he would soil the furniture by sitting on it, yet he was glad Gent had suggested they meet with Tilda for clothing. They were far better suited to their surroundings dressed as they were now than what they would have been had they worn their usual attire.

It was an intriguing idea, this family in trade being so respectable and wealthy. He'd made some inquiries once this meal had been set for them, and it was well known that the Fosters were doing well for themselves. Their status was rising ever higher, and their circles were broadening at an alarming rate. They had never been destitute, he understood, but the sons had brought an increased visibility and profitability to their father's business. The partnership between the three Foster men seemed to be working rather well, and Teo had yet to hear a disagreeable word said about any of the men or their business practices. Don Mendoza Shipping could be fortunate indeed to go into business with such men.

Silence reigned for some minutes more, the ticking of a mantle clock giving them the only indication time was passing in any way. That, and the slow loss of feeling in Teo's left leg. Minor details.

Again, footsteps were heard, and the pair of them slowly rose, sensation returning to Teo's limb with an aching, wave-like roll. An older gentleman who somehow still seemed to be in his prime appeared, flanked by two younger men who could have been reflections of the other. All were dressed in dark evening wear, broken up only by the glimpse of linen shirts beneath simply tied cravats. The elder gentleman bore a gold chain linked to a pocket of his weskit, but they were nearly identically dressed in every other sense.

Teo and Rafa matched them well in style, and Teo sent up a silent prayer of thanks to the Gent for his intervention.

"Señor Mendoza, Señor Teixidor," the older gentleman began, his faintly lined face wreathed in concern. "A thousand apologies for your long wait. I trust Edmonds explained the situation adequately for you?"

"He did, sir," Teo replied with a polite smile. "How are the boys?"

"Well enough, sir, well enough." He clapped his hands together, rubbing slightly. "Now, I have slightly breached etiquette, but I trust you will not hold that against me. Jeremiah Foster, gentlemen, at your service." He inclined his head in a brief attempt at a bow.

Teo and Rafa did the same. "Teodoro Mendoza, sir, and my partner, Rafael Teixidor."

"Ah, I was wondering which was which," the grinning Mr. Foster answered without shame. "Pleased, charmed, and all that. My sons, gentlemen. Jeremiah Foster Jr., my eldest. He prefers to be called Jem." He indicated to the man over his left shoulder, who did a better job of bowing, his smile slight, but present. "And Henry, I believe, you met at the offices." He gestured over his right shoulder, where Mr. Henry Foster inclined his head in his father's interpretation of a bow.

"We did, sir," Teo replied with a nod. "It is good to see you again."

"And you as well," Mr. Henry Foster replied. "We are eager to discuss business, but I think we might appease our hunger first."

"And we apologize in advance," Mr. Jem Foster broke in, his reserved expression clearly no indication of his opinion, "for the curious looks, questions, and remarks of our wives, sister, and cousin."

Mr. Foster chuckled heartily. "Yes, yes, they have never met anyone of the Spanish persuasion, you see. Well, not officially, at any rate."

"Officially?" Rafa asked, his brow creasing with the curiosity of his question.

Mr. Foster only waved his hand to follow them. "You will see, sir. Come, let us go up. The ladies will start without us otherwise."

With a bewildered look at each other, Teo and Rafa followed their hosts out of the room and up the stairs.

"*¿De verdad empezarían a comer sin nosotros?*" Rafa asked Teo in an undertone as they ascended.

Teo could only shrug in his confusion. He had no idea what the ways of the English were in this regard, let alone what a family not squarely in the upper class might do.

"*Nunca entenderé a los Británicos,*" Rafa muttered, shaking his head.

Truth be told, Teo was not sure he would ever understand the British either, even if he did try to move more freely among them. It was entirely possible that it would take a lifetime of exposure, if not training, to accomplish such understanding. He wasn't sure he wanted to give that much time to the effort.

The dining room was conveniently located just off the stairs to the next floor of the house, and the ladies stood within, staring at the door in anticipation.

"Ah, charming picture, are they not?" Mr. Foster chuckled and patted his pocket where, presumably, a pocket watch sat. "Allow me to make some introductions before we sit. Here we have my daughter

Alice, Mrs. Jennings. Her husband could not be with us this evening, as he is part of His Majesty's Royal Navy and currently at sea."

A pleasant-looking young woman with hair that could only be described as a pale brown curtseyed, a suspicious swelling in her abdomen giving perfect explanation for the youthful fullness of her face and the warmth in her eyes. "*Señores.*"

Someone had taught the lady how to greet them, and it was a mark of respect that would not go unnoticed. Teo smiled and bowed slightly, as did Rafa.

"Charlotte, my daughter-in-law, who is wife to Jem," Mr. Foster went on. The auburn-haired woman shared her husband's penchant for slight smiles and curtseyed without a word.

"My wife, Martha, goddess divine and paragon of perfection," he said without any hint of hesitation.

Mrs. Foster, situated just opposite them on the far head of the table, had started to curtsey, then stared at her husband in embarrassed mortification, her eyes wide. "Jeremiah, for shame!"

"I have none, madam, where you are concerned," her husband replied easily. "And there is Anna, Henry's wife."

She curtseyed in an almost bright bob of a movement, her smile wide. "*Señores.*"

"And here," Mr. Foster finished, gesturing almost grandly to the remaining woman just to the right of his own chair, "is my brother's daughter, Mary Foster."

Mary Foster was a stunningly beautiful young woman. Her hair held shades of brown and gold, curled of its own accord, and her skin held just enough of an olive tone to it that Teo had to look twice. Her eyes were the palest green he had ever seen, and her smile was perfectly shy in the most becoming way. "*Señores,*" she murmured, curtseying even as her eyes darted between Rafa and Teo almost eagerly.

"Mary's mother was Spanish," Mr. Foster told them, his voice ringing with pride. "The poor woman died in childbirth and had no family of her own, so Mary came back to live with us. My brother has passed on now, but Mary is very much a daughter to us." He glanced at Teo and Rafa with a smile. "So you see, 'not officially' is an apt description. We never met Estella, and without Spanish relations for

Mary to know and love—"

"*He estudiado español, señores, para comprender mejor mi herencia,*" Mary broke in as though she could not help herself. "*Sé muy poco, pero lo estoy intentando.*" Her accent was not perfect, but it was certainly better than they heard from most attempts.

Rafa had not moved from Teo's side, and for a moment, Teo could not be sure his friend was even breathing. But then he spoke, his voice unlike anything Teo had ever heard from him.

"*Lo está haciendo bien, señorita. Muy bien.*"

Teo could have choked on the warm softness he heard in Rafa's tone but settled for glancing at Mary Foster's face just in time to see a pleased blush rise in her cheeks.

Well, well. Perhaps they had better do business with the Foster family regardless of how this meal proceeded. Rafa's soul could depend upon it.

"Well, I will not pretend I understand the Spanish language," Mr. Foster blustered with a laugh, "but I believe I do know what *muy bien* means. Very good indeed. Let us eat! *Señores*, please sit where you like, we have no ceremony here."

Biting the inside of his cheek, Teo looked at Rafa who was staring at him in a sort of panic. Poor man.

"After you, Rafa," he said simply, gesturing, very faintly, to the seat beside Mrs. Jennings. It would be a safer place for the overcome man, and yet it would allow him to continue gazing at the fair Señorita Foster without being rude or raising suspicions.

Rafa exhaled briefly, relief evident in his eyes, and moved to the seat indicated.

Teo, on the other hand, moved around the table to sit between Mr. Henry's wife and Señorita Foster, feeling safe enough from her charms, given Rafa's reaction.

And there was the small matter of the image of the ever-delightful Ears flicking through his mind every few seconds, giving him more warmth in his chest than even the sight of Señorita Foster's beauty could match.

Curious thing, that.

The rest took their seats as well, and soon the meal was underway, conversation and chattering occurring down the table, across it, and in every conceivable direction. Even the more reserved pair of Mr. Jem and his wife were fully engaged in the discussions, only slightly less animated than the others.

It was the noisiest family dinner Teo had ever attended in his life, possibly including his own. Though when all the extended Spanish relations joined in, the volume did tend to increase exponentially.

"So is this your first time to England, Señor Mendoza?" Mrs. Anna Foster inquired, turning to face him a little.

"It is, Mrs. Foster," he replied with all politeness.

She smiled as she set her cup down. "Please, call me Anna. It is not a familiarity, only a matter of convenience. You dine with three Mrs. Fosters and three Mr. Fosters. We all listen to each other's conversations at dinner, so it can be very confusing. Save the mister and missus distinction for my father and mother-in-law. But for the rest of us..." She gestured around at the younger Foster family members. "Charlotte, Jem, Henry, and Anna. We will all insist."

One glance at the others told Teo she was correct, and though it bristled slightly against his politeness, he nodded. "Very well, Anna, if you are certain."

"I am," she quipped, nodding firmly. "And do you intend to stay long in England, or will you return to Spain when your business is concluded?"

Teo pursed his lips slightly, unsure how to answer. He glanced at Rafa, who had heard the question and was watching him. After a moment between the two, Rafa lifted a shoulder and returned to his meal. That was likely as close to permission as he would get.

"I cannot say, Anna," Teo admitted, his throat going dry. "Because I do not know myself. You see, my father was an Englishman."

"Was he indeed?" Mr. Foster interjected from the head of the table. "By heavens."

Teo swallowed rather than nod. "I introduce myself as Teodoro Mendoza, and the world knows me by that name through my grandfather's business. But in truth, my name is Teodoro Vickers. In my culture, one would say Teodoro de Vickers y Mendoza."

"There's more," Rafa rumbled from his seat, still not looking at him.

"Is there?" Charlotte asked, her eyes wide as she looked at Teo. "What?"

"My English grandfather," Teo told her, hesitating, and feeling a little queasy at this revelation, "was a baronet. My father perished some years ago, and as I understand it, I am the heir."

Silence reigned over the table for a long moment.

"Well, well," Mr. Foster said after a moment, smiling at him in surprise. He raised his glass and cleared his throat. "To our esteemed guest, Sir Teodoro de Vickers y Mendoza."

The others raised their glasses, including Rafa, and echoed the toast.

Teo could have evaporated on the spot without any trouble. "Please," he begged, looking at his host, "I am not accustomed to such things. I would not wish for my English position to affect our business. I know nothing of my holdings, only that it lies somewhere in a place called the Midlands."

A scattered bit of chuckling sounded from the table at that, but Mr. Foster continued to watch Teo without altering his expression. "I can assure you, sir, I intend to do business with Señor Mendoza of Don Mendoza Shipping just as I intended at the start of this meal. If Sir Teodoro wishes to ask anything else of me, he is at liberty to do so. The affairs of the British peerages, inheritances, and all else give even those who are accustomed to them moments of pause and headaches. If he should require any assistance in the details there, I am happy to oblige him." His smile deepened, a light of mischief entering his eyes. "Though I have never been plagued with such lofty matters myself. Lowly people are we, sir, and not likely to ever be anything more."

Relief washed over Teo as the speech concluded, and he smiled at the self-deprecation of his host. "I can see nothing lowly here, sir. I believe Rafa and I dine with the best tonight."

Rafa nodded firmly and raised his own glass. "*Salud*," he intoned.

Delighted, the Fosters lifted their glasses and echoed him. "*Salud.*"

"Somewhere in the Midlands," Henry Foster repeated, snickering aloud. "By Jove, Mendoza, I've never heard anything so perfectly vague in my entire life!"

Teo laughed, as did the rest of the table. "I have yet to truly identify the place," he protested, "let alone see it!"

"There's your first lesson, Father," Jem suggested, glancing down the table. "Show Sir Teodoro a good map of England and help him find the Midlands. Give him a place to start."

"I'm not sure even you could find the Midlands, son," his father replied with a smile. "Tricky thing, the Midlands."

Teo grinned at the easy family banter and found that, oddly enough, he was in no hurry to get to the business discussions after all.

Chapter Eleven

It was agony waiting on the corner for *Capitán* to arrive. She'd barely been able to sit still all day as she worked to continue planning the course of action she had started the night before. Short of drawing them a map herself, everything else was prepared.

Except for his arrival.

Emmeline shifted her position, adjusting her feet in the new footwear she had acquired that morning. They were not quite masculine, but they would allow her to walk farther and longer than she might have done in her usual shoes for the disguise, and she would need to walk several streets several times in the next few days or so to get the job done.

Where was he? Waiting was the absolute worst of all things, particularly when one is anxious to be gone.

A few days. That was all she had before she would have to return to the school for a week, and it would be the perfect time to see all the articles published.

She had arranged for Declan to go to the printer's tomorrow on the off chance the ladies had managed to form coherent thoughts enough to send the note so soon, and also to collect the pay that was due to her for the sale of her column.

She could use the funds to help in bribing new informants when she came across any. Bribery was always worth saving for.

Sighing with her natural impatience, Emmeline hid herself more fully in the shadows the building behind her permitted, propping herself against the wall to continue her waiting. She watched as three children darted by in their own little cohort, each of them silent in their motions as they moved. She waited to see if they were being pursued, but no one followed them.

Curious thing that such young children roamed about London so late, but their clothing had securely lumped them in with any other beggar of the streets. There was no polite hour, no schedule that could be adhered to in those worlds. There was only need and opportunity. One must work from a very young age if one were to survive.

Her contacts in these parts had told her that time and again, but she had never found cause to interview any of the children that occasionally darted here and there. Perhaps this new task, a series on understanding the state of the poor, might give her such a reason and cause. Speaking with children would add a tenderness to the articles that could resonate with the more family-oriented members of Society.

But on the other hand, it could also appear as an obvious ploy by the writer to toy with the emotions of the more sensitive hearts reading it. She would not need such criticism that could detract from the truth she would be trying to relate.

It had been some time since she had simply stood and waited on a night where she had a task before her. Occasionally, her stories had involved her needing to watch a location to track movements, or wait for certain individuals to come or go, or for certain individuals to feel brave enough to speak with her about the situation at hand. Waiting around to learn more about the mysterious fellow known as Rogue had been one of those times. It had been a project that took several months and had often been pushed aside for more pressing stories, but she always came back to it.

What a marvelous day it had been when she had found someone who could recall the man's appearance enough to describe him to an artist. What exactly the outcome of such revelations had been, she did not know, of course, but she hoped the man received some of the credit he deserved, especially for saving the lives of the woman and her child from the building that had caught fire.

There were other names she had occasionally heard tossed about the streets she wandered so, but none of them had been attached to particular stories of her interest. Everyone in this area knew the name

Gent, but as far as she could tell, he had never done anything particularly heroic or worthy of note. There were some rumors he looked after a group of children, but as none of the children had apparently been saved from dying a horrible death or on the brink of starvation, it was simply not a story of interest.

She'd heard of a Mr. Turner some years ago down in the dock region, but whoever he was and whatever he'd done had vanished, and no one could confirm any of the stories attributed to him.

There was another world down in these lower parts of the city, people and places not visible to the naked eye, and transactions that took place without an obvious manner of currency. The truth of it was Emmeline could have lived down here for six years as some imagined character observing all and never truly write a full and complete account of what took place, how life was, who deserved their fate, and who had just been unlucky. There were all sorts, and that needed to be told as well.

"Who are you hiding from, and how can I help?"

Emmeline stiffened for a moment, then sighed as the sound in her ears registered as one she trusted and enjoyed. She looked up at the dark figure of *Capitán,* the streetlight doing no favors for her, as his hat cast most of his face in shadow. But, bless him, he had not shaved today, so his jaw was lined with stubble, and it added handsomely to his dark appearance.

"No one, and I'm not sure," she answered with a smile.

He paused, staring at her, his eyes perfectly black within the shadow of his face.

"What?" she asked him, tilting her head.

He shook his head. "It's just… the light caught more of your face than I expected when you looked at me, and…" He reached out tentatively, and his fingers brushed the side of her face just along her cheek.

His touch was gentle, though the tips of his fingers were rough and callused. Still, the feel of them sent a shiver down her spine and across her arms. "What did you see?" she breathed, hypnotized by the sensation of his fingers against her skin.

"*Belleza y luz,*" he whispered, his fingers passing down the curve of her cheek to the line of her jaw. "*Calor. Demasiado y no lo suficiente.*"

Emmeline's legs began to shake beneath her, though her back still pressed against the wall. "You're speaking in Spanish," she murmured, her eyes fluttering as his hand traced back up her cheek.

He chuckled softly, his breath warm and inviting. "I know, *cariño*. It is safer for us both if I do."

"Why?" she demanded. She opened her eyes and met his gaze as squarely as darkness allowed. "I don't understand the language. How can that be safer?"

He cupped her cheek and leaned closer as his thumb brushed her skin. "Because I said too much, and in English that would have frightened you."

Emmeline's breath caught in her throat, but fear was the farthest thing from her mind. "How do you know?"

His mouth curved to one side. "Because it frightens me, *cariño*. And I don't know what to do about it."

Lands, that was a perilous thought.

Well, she was very nearly on fire here, and having him closer was both better and worse for such feelings. Ridiculous—this man she had met three times in her life was stirring up all sorts of sensations and peculiar thoughts in her, but that was the truth of it. His fingers on her face were heavenly, and the idea of gloves in polite Society was suddenly of much greater understanding to her. People did need to have sanity, she supposed.

"You are turning so warm," *Capitán* murmured, his thumb brushing her cheek once more. "What thoughts can be bringing that about, I wonder?"

Emmeline blinked, knowing the burst of heat in her face would make that worse for them both. "Do you expect me to answer that, or…?"

He laughed fully and backed away, his hand dropping from her face and leaving her surprisingly chilled. But she could breathe freely once more, which was a marked improvement.

"No, *Orejitas*, I would prefer you not answer the question," he assured her with a quick and easy grin. "Particularly if we wish to accomplish anything at all tonight."

Gracious. What *was* he imagining there? What was she even doing here, besides burning to ash? A faint whistle a few blocks away seemed to snap her from the heated stupor she found herself encased in.

Right. Assignment.

"I have a proposition for you," Emmeline announced, finally feeling able to straighten fully and remove herself from the aid of the wall behind her.

Capitán folded his arms and cocked his head. "I'm listening."

How could that answer positively make her knees ricochet against the air itself? Swallowing, Emmeline focused her gaze on a tuft of his hair hanging just over his right ear. "I need to investigate the real conditions of the poor in London. The streets they live on, the businesses about, treatment they face, conditions of their homes, and the like. Whatever we can find."

"Why do you need to do this?" he asked without rancor, ridicule, or distaste. Just a simple, easy, honest question.

A woman he had known for almost no time at all, who dressed in men's clothing to avoid detection, had told him she needed to go into worse conditions than they already walked in during the middle of the night in London, and all he wanted to know was the reason. What kind of man was he anyway?

"I write," she said simply, not sure what else to say. She heard him laugh, and her eyes darted to his mouth, the fascinating aspect of his person that it was.

"Yes, so you've said."

Right, she had said that, hadn't she?

"I mean I write for publication," she elaborated, her ears burning as she shared the most private part of her entire secret. "For the papers. They don't know it's me, of course, I write under a man's name, but what I write gets published, and the public reads it."

Capitán stared at her, and she could almost feel the blinking in disbelief. "That's remarkable, *Orejitas!* It's a shame you cannot use your own name, but to see your words printed for the world to read... You must be more brilliant than I gave you credit for, and I already considered you in the highest terms."

Flattery would get him everywhere and nowhere with her, so there was no cause for the burst of heat somewhere below her throat. "Thank you. I don't know about brilliance or the like, but I do have some success with a few of the stories."

"Humility becomes you, *Orejitas*, but it is not necessary with me." He grinned and shook his head. "Remarkable woman. So, you are to write about the poor?"

"Yes," Emmeline said quickly, moving the conversation along with relief. "There are a few ladies of my acquaintance who have expressed their wish to help the poor in some way, but in their particular circles, they only know of their own situations. In my own unconventional way, I can provide them with a better, clearer picture of what is suffered, and then perhaps they might know where to begin."

"Adventuress, scholar, and patron of the downtrodden," *Capitán* said softly, his admiration unmistakable even to her. "What can she not do?"

"Secure a husband, according to my aunt," she muttered before she could help herself. Her cheeks flamed the moment the words escaped her mouth. "I should not have said that. We've not given each other any identifying details, and now—"

"*Orejitas*," he overrode, "*todo está bien*. I'll not be able to identify you by your stating you have an aunt who wishes you would take a husband. Just as you will not be able to identify me by my saying I have a sister who repeatedly orders me to take a wife. Do you know what that makes us?"

Emmeline wrinkled her nose. "Hopeless?" she ventured.

"Human." He smiled, immediately putting her at ease. "Although my sister would certainly consider me hopeless as well."

"I've been hopeless since I was fifteen," Emmeline told him, smiling sheepishly. "I never wanted to conform to the expectations of a lady in the way my aunt wished. I wanted adventure and freedom; I wanted to see the world. So, I spent nearly all of my time in the library, losing myself in stories and in the atlases, imagining great wonders and travels for myself. But I've never left England, you see. All of my adventures remained in my head."

"Until this," *Capitán* pointed out, gesturing to their surroundings. "Do you not think all of this is an adventure?"

Emmeline nodded, rubbing her arms against a sudden chill that had nothing to do with the air around her. "It is, sometimes more than others. The first night I snuck out of my aunt's home, I was tormented by my feelings and desperate to escape. I was missing my parents so dreadfully, and no matter how good my aunt was, she could not replace my mother. I don't know what I intended by leaving the house, and I was certainly not dressed as you see me tonight. I just knew that the house that was not my home had grown stifling, and I needed air."

She shook her head, lost in the memories, echoes of her pain flicking their fingers against her heart. "I don't remember how far I walked, but I remember wondering how the air in London, which I had never enjoyed before, could suddenly feel like a cool glass of water on a hot summer's day. How I could feel free and new in a place I had lived most of my life. How I could find things of captivating interest that I had passed earlier that day without even the briefest glance."

Looking around her now, Emmeline found herself sighing, the joy of that first night racing back over her, filling her with an exuberance that never entirely faded. "London became the world to me. I could explore it without restriction, uncover its mysteries, find treasures. I recorded all of it, every single detail I could recall, and those early diaries are locked in a truck in my aunt's attic. I may never see the world, but I have seen London in a way that very few can claim and with a completeness that almost no one will ever know."

There was no reply from her companion, prompting her to look back at him in hesitation, afraid he would find her excessive rambling ridiculous, and see her for the hopeless case that everyone else seemed to. But she ought to have known better.

Capitán stood exactly where he had been standing, his eyes trained on her, his hands in the pockets of his jacket. She watched as his shoulders moved on an inhale, followed by the accompanying exhale. He said nothing.

"Too much?" she asked with a wince, managing a weak laugh. "My aunt always tells me I say too much and ought to moderate my choice of words. Rambling is a sign of an unhinged mind, she says, and no relation of hers can be unhinged."

"With all deference to your aunt," *Capitán* said in a low voice she almost couldn't catch, "I believe she should say less and pay attention more."

Emmeline blinked at this response and turned more fully to him. "What?"

"I mean no disrespect," he insisted, holding his palms up gently. "I simply think she is unaware of the true, incomparable nature of the woman entrusted to her care."

She stared at him in silence as he lowered his hands. Words tried to form, but her lips refused to accommodate them.

"You are extraordinary, *Orejitas*," he went on, something raw entering his voice that frightened Emmeline, just as he'd warned. "I hardly know what to make of you, yet the more I see, the more you make me feel, the better I understand. I don't know your name or even the exact details of your face, but you have become the most important person I have met in England. Perhaps even a wider world than that, but it is surely too soon for such thoughts."

It was likely too soon for this entire conversation, and yet Emmeline felt as though she had been waiting an eternity just to hear these exact words. She'd call it flattery, but it was too serious for that. She'd call it exaggeration, but it felt too personal. She'd call it a bluff, but even her skill at detecting such lies was failing her spectacularly.

"I don't feel extraordinary," she replied, her voice barely above a breath, feeling she must make some response to him in this moment. "I only feel like me."

"That," he said firmly, "is the most extraordinary part."

Now he was making little sense, but how delicious the senselessness was!

"I think you may already know me better than any person on earth," Emmeline admitted, unable to hold back the confession, which had barely reached her mind before it came tumbling forth. "I don't know if that is because of my reserve or because there is something different between us. I don't know anything, *Capitán*. But I think you do."

"*Podría amarte, lo sabes,*" he murmured, his voice rippling across to her in the dark. "*Tan pronto y tan fácilmente.*"

Something about his words set her ablaze yet again, and the incineration was most welcome.

"Spanish again," she reminded him with a playful smile. "Saying something crass, *Capitán?*"

His smile lit her kneecaps once more. "That all depends on the feelings of the hearer, *Orejitas*. So." He clapped his hands together, rubbing slightly, which made her laugh. "You mentioned your proposition. What am I to expect in return for going along with you to investigate the poor?"

That caught her off guard. "In return?"

"Indeed," he replied in a near-perfect English pronunciation. "Propositions must be mutually beneficial to all involved, else it is just a favor, no?"

Drat, he was right, and she hadn't considered offering him something in return for this. She just wanted to take back her own selfish interests in the night but did not want to do so alone. She wanted to investigate *with* him and to see what he might see that she might miss. She wanted to spend more time with him, and the night was all they had. She had to do this task, and she could not bear the thought of missing more moments with him, but they all must occur at the same time by necessity.

"I fear I have nothing to offer in return," Emmeline confessed weakly. "Perhaps this is a favor after all. Would you come with me, *Capitán?*"

Slowly, he closed the distance between them. Emmeline's heart pounded furiously, riotously within her, perishing to know what he intended, what he would say… what he would do.

"I need nothing in return, *cariño*," he said as he reached out and laced his fingers through hers, the gentle abrading of skin lighting various parts of her on fire. "To be with you, to learn more of you, to see your London and not someone else's, and to have your hand in mine is repayment tenfold of anything you ask of me." He dragged their joined hands up and pressed his lips softly to the back of her hand.

Gracious. A Spaniard in the night was a dangerous thing. Why was there no warning about such things? Somehow, parched though she was, Emmeline managed to smile, though her heart was still bounding within her chest enough to choke her once or twice.

"*Gracias, Capitán*," she sighed, too befuddled to even manage embarrassment at how pathetic she sounded.

His eyes widened and a quick grin made her laugh. "*¿Qué fue eso? ¡Hablaste español!*"

Emmeline freed one hand and patted his chest, still laughing at his eager expression. "Steady, I only know one word! Well, three, I suppose, since I know your name and your name for me. But one new word of Spanish is hardly enough for me to understand anything else!"

"It's enough that you've learned that!" He cupped her face playfully, somehow still containing heat in his fingers. "To hear my language from your lips is a beautiful thing, no matter how limited. I will teach you more!" His hands fell away before her mind could spin, thankfully, and he took her hand, pulling her from the corner and down the street. "First, a greeting—"

"Wait, *Capitán*," she begged with a laugh. "We are not walking about London so that I might learn Spanish. Remember my task?"

He nodded fervently. "*Sí, sí, lo sé.* See the poor, take notes, write the truth. We can still learn Spanish as we go."

"You don't know where we are going," she reminded him, tugging against the hand he held. "And you're trying to lead."

He immediately stopped and held their joined hands away from him. "True, and I can only claim my extreme elation on your choice of words. Please, *Orejitas*, lead the way."

Emmeline smiled and turned down a street to their left, keeping her hand firmly connected to his, pulling him along when he playfully resisted. He was soon back at her side, and, though he said nothing, the energy exuding from him was palpable.

After perhaps a minute of complete silence, Emmeline grinned at him. "You were really excited that I used a Spanish word, weren't you?"

"I was," he said in a rush, no hesitation in his tone or demeanor. "You have no idea, *Orejitas*. It was the greatest surprise."

Chapter Twelve

Five minutes into a darker part of London than he'd ever known, and already he felt himself stripped of joy. How did anyone live in such a place as this? How did anyone escape this? How did they survive it?

He'd already looked at *Orejitas* several times to make sure she was not overcome, but she was perfectly composed, her face a mask of unflappable determination. She had likely seen such streets before in her years of exploring London, but that had been for the other stories she wrote. This was specifically aimed at these exact surroundings, which meant she would have to, in some way, embrace the horror so that she could more perfectly relate it to others.

Bold, fearless woman. She could have no equal in the world.

It was not that he had never seen poor people and poor situations before. On the contrary, he had seen a great deal of them in a great many cities and ports around the world. The questions he found himself asking were not new ones, nor was it the first time they had been asked, even by himself. It was simply the first time he had seen them in London, and such things ought never to become commonplace in one's eyes.

He found himself grateful most of the children would be asleep at this time of night so he would not hear their cries, and he found himself wondering how the dark, dank, cramped streets he walked along now would change when the light returned in the morning.

"Where will you begin?" Teo asked *Orejitas* in a low voice, fearing that speaking too loudly might somehow disrupt the scene of wretchedness around them. "With the hour being so late, surely you will not find a variety of subjects to speak with."

"You're right," she replied, her voice equally subdued. "Some things truly do require the light of day to explore with the depth I prefer. Tonight, we may only be able to see the areas for ourselves. We will see fewer beggars, as even they must sleep if they can, but there can be no hiding the filth."

As though on cue, he stepped into a puddle of some sort in their path, though there had been no rain that day, and they were not particularly close to the river. He frowned down at his foot, raising his leg to shake the mysterious moisture from the leather of his boot.

"I do not want to know what that is," he muttered.

Orejitas, much to his surprise, dropped to a squat beside him, eying the puddle. "I don't think you will need to be overly concerned." She leaned closer and sniffed carefully. "I believe that is washing water. Perhaps laundry day for one of the locals."

There was some comfort in that, admittedly, but it so easily could have been something else. Yet his brave, curious *Orejitas* had no hesitation in inspecting it, and no sign of disgust had appeared on her face.

"You've seen all of this before, haven't you?" he inquired as they continued to walk again, taking her hand.

Her hold on him tightened perceptibly. "Many times. I can never really come down here during the day, as my aunt has such a hold on my schedule and my doings. But I have made some contacts over the years who venture into these parts, and they bring me information that is often of use."

"Often?" Teo repeated, giving her a curious look. "Not always?"

She shook her head. "They do not always know what it is I am seeking, so it cannot always be of use. I very rarely give my contacts the whole of the picture or all the details of what I am looking for. I found that, if I do so, they only relay what they think is relevant to my aims. And more often than not, it is something seemingly innocuous that tells more of the story."

"Innocuous?" He stumbled over the word a little. "What does that mean?"

Orejitas scrunched her face in an adorable sort of pucker as she thought. "Dull, I suppose. Ordinary might be a better word."

"Ah." He nodded. "That makes sense. Do you offer them more if something proves particularly useful?"

"I have in the past," she answered with a light shrug as she stepped around a more unsavory patch of something on the cobblestone. "Sometimes I still do, but my usual band no longer requires the additional incentive. They know how I work, and we have a sort of mutual respect, which protects all involved."

"And they all know you as Ears?" he pressed, fascinated by her story, by her activity, by her motivations. Fascinated by her, really, in all her wonderful, captivating, mysterious facets.

She nodded, a small smile lighting her face. The darkness of the night was more complete here than it had been in the other streets they had walked, so features were less certain, but as his eyes had adjusted, he could see her smile clearly.

"Yes. Some of them likely suspect I am a woman, but they have never said anything. Nor have they tried to take advantage of that if they do suspect."

A million and three scenarios, which could end in varying degrees of ruin or harm, flashed through his mind, each of them leaving him more chilled than the next.

Recórcholis, how was he going to sleep at night knowing she was wandering about in dangerous paths and intentionally, at times, putting herself in harm's way? He wandered about dangerously himself at times, but he had the means to defend himself. They had yet to discuss it, but he had no idea if she was equally equipped to do so.

"Forgive me if this does not sound flattering to your ears," he began slowly, struggling to think of English words when his mind was spinning in frantic Spanish. "But are you... able to appropriately cope with such a situation, should it arise?"

Orejitas frowned a little before glancing up at him. "You mean, can I defend myself?"

"*Sí*," he replied on a relieved breath. "I did not want to imply you could not, I simply... do not know."

"It's a fair question, given our surroundings," she assured him with a quick wave of her free hand. "The truth of it is, I'm not sure."

¡Santo cielo! He could only shake his head as he fought for control.

"*Ay qué miedo*," he grumbled. "Please, explain."

Thankfully, *Orejitas* did not laugh at his exasperation. "I carry a knife on my person," she admitted without reservation, "but I have never had to use it. I have occasionally been in a spot of trouble, as I was the other night when I crashed into you…"

A spot of trouble. He might not know much of the particular phrases the English use, which make little sense to foreign speakers, but he had a sense that anything being "a spot of" was relatively minor in the accepted scheme of things. That being said, a woman of her stature and relative defenselessness fleeing two large, thick, physically imposing men with some degree of anger to aid them did not seem to be a minor situation that could be relegated to "a spot of" anything.

"But experience has taught me," she went on, "I am quick on my feet, so I have thus far been able to escape the more perilous situations without having to test myself in any physical sense."

Teo inhaled and exhaled slowly, and as silently as he could so she might not be alerted to his present distress. "Would you, perhaps, have interest in learning some defensive skills? Should the need arise, of course."

Suddenly, *Orejitas* was quietly laughing beside him. "It's rather killing you that I don't know anything, isn't it?"

All of his breath came out in a rush of air, and he wanted to sweep her into his arms but resisted the urge. "*¡Qué susto!* You cannot imagine. I am ready to bind myself to your side simply to assure myself of your safety. I recall you saying you needed no guard over your person, but I am fully ready to be just that."

"I was blustering for effect at the time," *Orejitas* admitted, her thumb rubbing against the skin of his hand. "I have never needed a guard in the sense of opportunity, though I daresay if I thought about it too much, I might reconsider in the apprehensive sense."

Please reconsider, he nearly begged, though he managed to bite his tongue adequately. They turned a corner down another street, which was less imposing, though just as dark.

"Heavens," *Orejitas* breathed. "Look."

Teo was looking but was not sure what she meant until a movement caught his eye. A small figure moved almost haltingly along the street several meters from them, wrapped in some fabric that might have been a blanket or a shawl once, but not one of cleanliness or quality. Teo could see one of the holes in the material from where he stood.

Was this person old? Injured? Both? They did not look around, did not appear to search for anything, which likely meant they knew their surroundings well. It was too late for matters of business to be going on, and a lone figure of such apparent weakness was certainly not commonplace.

"Let's go to them," *Orejitas* murmured. "See what help we can offer."

"*Cuidado, Orejitas,*" he replied in a low tone.

She squeezed his hand. "Does *cuidado* mean careful?"

"*Sí.*"

She nodded once. "Come with me, and we will be safe."

As if he would let her venture off alone right now. The woman was mad if she even considered the thought. Still, her certainty of the statement settled his stomach, and no doubt would have given him the warmth of comfort had they been in a situation that permitted such feelings.

They moved forward cautiously, not exactly hiding their steps, but also not giving them any particular haste. The figure did not move with any additional speed themselves and, in fact, seemed to struggle more with every step. Then suddenly the figure collapsed to the ground and did not move.

"*¡Diablo!*" Teo hissed, running toward the poor thing, *Orejitas* just behind him.

He reached the shrouded creature, quickly pulling the coarse, tattered fabric away from them. A girl of no more than eight years old lay there, more frail than anything he'd ever seen, her hair matted and filthy, and dark bruises marred her cheek and the portion of her arm he could see through a gaping hole in her too-small gown.

"Oh, sweet girl," *Orejitas* murmured softly, pushing some of the hair out of the girl's face. "Is she breathing?"

Teo leaned close, then nodded as relief hit his throat. "A little." He exhaled and gingerly lifted the girl into his arms. "Is there a place we can take her?"

Orejitas nodded at once. "Yes, I know a place. It is not too far, if you can manage her."

He gave her a look. "She weighs nothing. I can manage."

"Of course." She smiled at something that must have amused her and waved for him to follow. "We must hurry, for her sake. Come on."

They moved as fast as he dared, careful not to jostle the tiny girl for whom every breath seemed a struggle. He lost track of the turns they took, the number of streets they walked, but *Orejitas* moved with such certainty, such clarity, even in these darker parts of the city. He trusted her implicitly, and that seemed to be all he needed at this moment. He'd have followed her anywhere, he realized, without question. What could that mean?

The streets were growing wider and were better lit, though he could hardly have called the neighborhood a fine one. Nor could he have necessarily said it was safer, but it was better than the place from which they had plucked this child and undoubtedly better than what she might be returned to.

Orejitas turned down one more street and stopped at the first door she reached. The windows were filthy, and no light shone from within. Given the lateness of the hour, that was not in the least surprising. Would whoever lived within be easily roused by them? What aid could they offer this girl, and what hope could be given?

She knocked firmly, though Teo would have been more tempted to kick the door in and bellow for assistance. Still, she knew the person, or persons, within, and he did not. Perhaps hers was the better way.

"Did they hear you?" Teo could not help but ask, keeping his voice low.

A light suddenly flickered in the window, and she pointed at it, nodding once.

He should have known. She always seemed to know. Not only could he trust in her, but he could trust in her experience and knowledge, her skills and instincts. He was a sailor and a merchant who had seen much of the world, but she knew this place and these people as well as he knew any corner of his ship or his crew. She was the captain here, not him.

The door in front of them creaked open, and an elderly man with tufts of white hair peered out at them in the darkness, a candle held aloft in one hand. His eyes widened when he saw them. "Ears? Pity's sake, gel, it's later than hell. A man needs sleep to be as beautiful as me."

Teo reared back in bewilderment, glancing at *Orejitas* in confusion. This was the man who was going to help them? With what? Gaining an appreciation of their youth?

"I know, Suds," *Orejitas* said. "I would not have come at this hour if I had a choice." She turned and waved Teo over. "We found this girl in the street in Stepney just now. She collapsed before our eyes and seems both injured and starved."

Suds's eyes moved to the girl in Teo's arms immediately, and Teo's opinion of him shifted at once as he saw an alert intelligence that surveyed her frame with lightning speed. "Bring her inside, then, chap. Mind your head. Shorter blokes than you have walked away with a crown of bruises." He turned back into the house, pushing the door open wider.

Teo entered, ducking just as he had been warned, and looked about the shockingly crowded room. Piles of belongings and paper took up almost every portion of the floor, and what limited furniture there was in the room bore an equal load to the rest of it.

Where in the world was he supposed to lay this child?

Thankfully, the old man continued to wave them through. "Not in here, lad, we'd never find a soul we set down. Here in the back where I've space."

Teo nodded, following as *Orejitas* stepped in front of him to lead.

"He intentionally crowds the front of his house," she informed him in a whisper. "Makes people less likely to stay when they call or ask for a favor."

"I can see why," he shot back, making a face.

She giggled softly and continued after their eccentric host, passing through another doorway, this one equally as low as the first.

When Teo stepped through, he breathed a deep sigh of relief. This was a far better space for their needs, no hint of the hoard of clutter the front room had borne so proudly. A sturdy wooden table sat prominently in the room, and Suds waved him over to it.

"Here, my man, lay her here." He plucked a folded sheet from nearby and spread it over the table, then took a faded pillow from an armchair, setting it at the head.

Teo did so, gently placing her head as fully on the pillow as he could manage. He pulled aside the ends of the fabric he had carried her in and winced at the sight of several angry scratches on her arms.

"Hmm," Suds grunted, seeing them as well. "Likely an alley cat. See the small, yet equal striations in the marks? Shouldn't be an issue, though it could raise an infection." He moved his attention to the girl's face, brushing her bushy, dark hair from her face. "Poor lamb. This bruise is fresh enough to worsen, and her eye will likely blacken too."

Teo found himself staring down at the unfortunate girl in a new kind of horror, never having seen such marks on one so young. A slender hand slipped into his as it hung limply at his side, and his fingers curved instinctively around them, grasping for the warmth within them.

Orejitas leaned her head against his arm, curling into his side as though for comfort, which he wondered how to give under the circumstances. They stood there together, watching Suds survey the injuries and condition of the child, barely moving, neither of them speaking themselves.

Suds took hold of the girl's tiny wrist, his fingers encircling it easily, finding a particular spot. His eyes narrowed as he waited, then his lips pursed in a wrinkled knot of sorts. "Weak, but steady." He looked up at them, his eyes much younger than his years. "You say she collapsed. What was her condition prior to the collapse?"

"Halting," *Orejitas* told him. "Perhaps limping. We could not tell if she was young or old by her movements."

"I suspect she is likely both, if you take my meaning." He quirked his brows knowingly, his expression filled with sympathy and concern. "Let's see to her legs and feet, perhaps that will enlighten us as to her gait."

Teo thought to interrupt, to beg for privacy and respect for the girl, but then saw it was unnecessary when Suds picked up a blanket and laid it over the girl's torso and thighs.

"Ears, love," he murmured, crooking his fingers. "Would you kindly come and divest the child of her tattered stockings? She wears no shoes, poor thing, and the stockings may be burned for all the use they are."

Orejitas nodded, coming around the table to the opposite side of Suds. She reached gingerly under the blanket and had the too-worn stockings removed in short order. "May I wash her hair, Suds?" she asked softly, her voice cracking at the end.

"Yes, love," the old man replied. "Check for cuts and scratches, though I don't suspect any. And watch for lice."

If anything he had said shocked her, *Orejitas* gave no hint of it. She nodded and turned to the fire near them, swinging a kettle over the weak flames. With an expert touch, she stoked the fire, filling the room with light and warmth.

Teo watched her move and work with as much interest as he did Suds, marveling at her self-sufficiency when, by all accounts, she belonged to a higher class than one which would tend their own fires. She had no airs, no qualms, no barriers to her abilities, no hesitation in doing whatever was needed, or whatever she sought to do. She had an active hold on her life, despite having such restrictions as any woman of her circumstance. What a wonder she was, and what a picture.

A picture of perfection, Mr. Foster had said of his wife the night before. Yet the phrase seemed more apt for this woman before him, much as he respected the woman to whom it had been applied.

Perfection in every respect, and yet he did not know her name and had not studied her face.

"*Capitán*," she said softly, her eyes raising to his, "would you bring me the large basin by the window, please?"

Startled at being addressed, given his private reverie, he nearly jumped at the request, turning to do as she asked. He brought the bowl to her, swallowing his sudden nerves.

"Now, would you hold it while I pour?" she asked.

"*Sí, cariño*," he answered, gesturing gently with his chin. When the basin was full of steaming water, he carried it to the table while she brought soap, toweling, a cup, and another basin, this one empty.

Without a word, the two of them set to work on the girl's hair,

Teo assisting without being asked, working alongside his perfect *Orejitas* as she gently dampened and washed the dark, matted mass of hair, her fingers working through the tresses with the tenderness of a mother. Every knot within was cleared, and every pass of fresh, clean water brought forth more dirt, crumbs, and a few insects. Only when the water from her hair ran clean and clear did *Orejitas* cease her washing, ending the moving ministrations that Teo counted himself fortunate to witness.

Suds had concluded his investigation of her legs and feet, citing a bad sprain of an ankle to be the cause of her staggering, though the collapse, he said, was entirely due to starvation. He'd set about making a broth while they had continued with her hair, and while the broth boiled, he'd procured a small, clean nightgown from his rooms above.

Once Teo and *Orejitas* had toweled the girl's hair enough that it would not drip, Suds had pulled over a screen so that *Orejitas* could change the girl into dry, clean clothing.

"She's ready," he heard her call from behind the screen, sounding exhausted.

He rounded the screen, his heart aching at the difference in the little girl's appearance as he looked on her. She might have belonged to a wealthy family in the highest circles, but for the bruising she still bore. Yet she had been suffering so, and apparently without someone to care that she was. If he'd had any doubts about the articles *Orejitas* wanted to write about the poor, they were gone now.

Someone had to tell the world of her. And someone would.

Teo picked the girl up as gently as he had done before, bringing her around the screen to the faded couch near the fire. Suds had made a sort of bed for her, the bowl of broth sitting nearby, the old man himself waiting on them.

"Bring her here, then, lad," he encouraged. "I'll try to get some of this into her and watch her a while."

It was on Teo's lips to argue, but he caught sight of *Orejitas* leaning against the table, almost slumping in her posture, and nodded. They needed to rest, and he would watch over her if Suds would watch the girl.

Once the little one was settled, Teo moved to *Orejitas*, taking her by the arm. "Come, *cariño*. You need to rest."

She came without resistance. "So do you, love."

His heart lurched at the term, though he had heard Suds use the same with her without any romantic meaning. He refused to consider her use of the word the same, given she had never used it before. And he had to hope.

He moved them to a divan nearby, sitting himself nearest the head and leaned against it, opening his arm for *Orejitas* to lean against him. She did so, removing her hat with a weary sigh, and gripping the back of her neck with a soft groan.

Unable to resist, Teo reached for her face and gently turned it toward him. The light had never been so bright when they had been together, and the chance to see her face in light, just this once, was too much to ignore.

She looked at him with tired eyes, no less stirring for such a state, and their dark, cognac depths searched his face as though just realizing the opportunity herself. Her hair was a rich mahogany, streaks of a reddish hue highlighting parts of it, and the curls he had noticed before still sat in their place without alteration. Natural curls, then.

He ran a hand over that blessed hair, still plaited and bound in the style of her disguise. His eyes darted from freckle to freckle across the bridge of her nose and cheeks, also catching the faint dimple in her cheek as she sleepily smiled into his touch.

Her natural, unadorned appearance unmanned him, robbing him of breath and words in a way he had never experienced in his life, including earlier that evening. A glimpse of her fair skin had been all he'd seen then, but this…

"*Hermosa, cariño*," he breathed, returning his gaze to hers. "*Muy hermosa.*"

She hummed a small laugh and touched his jaw. "Safer in Spanish again, *Capitán?*"

"*Sí,*" he whispered as he gently pulled her against him, cradling her against his side. "*Mucho más seguro.*"

"Hmm," she sighed, nestling against him. "Well, I find you particularly attractive, too."

He choked on nothing, glancing down at the top of her head. "I thought you did not understand Spanish."

She yawned, one hand resting against his chest. "I don't. But it's what I hoped you said about me, so I pretended you did."

Cielos, she had no idea what she did to him, or how close she was to the truth.

Feeling her weight against him grow heavier as she drifted off, Teo turned to gently press his lips against her hair. "*Duerme bien mi ángel. Voy a estar aquí.*"

Chapter Thirteen

Sleeping against a Spaniard was marvelously good for the constitution. Not that Emmeline had extensive experience with such things, but the hour or two she had from the night before certainly put some rosiness into her cheeks today. The additional hours she had slept safely in her own bed had nothing to do with that, she was certain.

It had been very early in the morning, just before dawn, when she had stirred from such delicious slumber. Curled up as she had been against *Capitán* on the faded divan Suds had pulled out for them, waking had been a trial. Such comfort and respite she had never known, and to be held against *Capitán* so securely, yet so tenderly…

It made her shiver now in recollection when she thought of that moment before they had slept, when he had studied her face as though he would never see it again. When his eyes had traced every feature and every freckle. When she had committed the exact shade of his eyes to memory and could draw the angle of his jaw with her eyes closed. When she had witnessed the perfect unison between movement of his lips and the corners of his eyes. When her heart had cried out that this man was what she wanted.

Such a thought had never occurred to her, and in the morning upon that particular recollection… Well, she had never sprung to her feet so rapidly in her entire life, denial racing through every portion of her body on wings of lightning. Even now, she felt queasy at admitting it had been one of her sleepy, dreamlike admissions to herself.

The very idea of such a realization was laughable. Impossible.

Unimaginable.

How could *Capitán* have such a profound hold on her when they barely knew each other? Surely she must have been delirious with fatigue. Yet after several hours of sleep and several conversations with herself, she settled on this one truth: the statement had not been entirely incorrect.

More than that, she refused to fully admit. But it was not a lie. And for that reason, she could not help but smile today, which, unfortunately, meant her aunt continued to give her curious looks.

As she was doing at this moment.

"Are you sure you are well, Emmeline?" Aunt Hermione pressed for what had to be the fourth time that morning.

"Yes, Aunt," Emmeline replied without looking up from her book. "As I have said."

She heard more than saw her aunt rustle in her seat. "Yes, dear, I know you have but... you are just so flushed, and you have a queer little curve to your mouth."

Emmeline laughed softly. "It is a smile, Aunt. Not a symptom of fever."

"Perhaps we should bring in Doctor Banks to examine you, to be certain all is well."

"It would be a useless expense, Aunt. And you do so hate extravagance."

"Where health is concerned, Emmeline, there can be no extravagance."

Emmeline paused, placing a finger in the place she had read last, and peered over at her aunt with bemused interest. "Truly? Remind me to make the same argument when you refuse to have the doctor summoned after the next whist and gin night."

Aunt Hermione straightened in her chair, a slight flush entering her cheeks. "I haven't the faintest idea what you mean."

"Don't you?" Emmeline raised a brow, smirking at the older woman. "How often have I tended your feverish, aching head and helped peel your soft-boiled eggs on such mornings?"

"Then you can understand why I wish to extend the same courtesy," her aunt pressed, turning more fully in her chair, her faintly wrinkled brow creasing more deeply. "You slept so very late, and you always rise so early."

It was touching how concerned Aunt Hermione was—even amusing beyond belief—but Emmeline wondered how her aunt would react if she knew what series of events had caused each of the curious symptoms she mentioned. Such as a man.

Emmeline sighed and tried for a sympathetic smile. "Would it set you at ease if I went out for a walk? Took some air?"

"Yes," her aunt said at once, nodding fervently. "Yes, it would. Take a servant with you, should weakness overtake you or you feel unwell."

"I will take Declan, if you agree," Emmeline suggested as she closed her book completely and rose. "He has walked with me before and knows my favorite paths."

Aunt Hermione continued to nod as though she could not stop. "Yes, I agree. He is a sturdy fellow and could carry you if your strength should fail you."

Now Emmeline rolled her eyes. "Aunt—"

"It is possible," she insisted. "Jane Halston was struck down with a sudden fever last year and was bedridden for the entire Season!"

"Jane Halston has consumption," Emmeline reminded her with a pitying look. "She is struck down at least every other year, and the doctors have wondered about the strength of her heart since she was a child. I am, and always have been, hale and whole, Aunt."

Aunt Hermione bit her lip, looking as though tears could be called upon. "Perhaps I should keep you at home, dear. What if you should be overcome and must be confined to your bed? I will blame myself entirely."

"Aunt," Emmeline all but barked, "I will go for a walk because I feel strong. The cool air will settle the color in my cheeks. I will eat my usual amount at dinner and at supper. Tonight, I will retire early so that tomorrow, I may rise at my usual time. Will all of that satisfy you?"

Her aunt stared at her, eyes wide, clamping down hard on her lips and making a strange, muffled chirping noise. But then she nodded, just once.

"Very well, then." With a final warning look, Emmeline turned from the room and started down the corridor, hiding a smile. If only it were always so easy to escape her aunt's observations and schedule.

She moved toward the kitchens—where the housekeeper would likely be conferring with the cook about the day's meals—and smiled when she passed Declan on the way down.

"Declan, would you be able to escort me on a walk into Town? I must go out on an errand."

He paused, his brows rising. "Of course, Miss Bartlett. Are you certain this is not an errand I can do on your behalf?"

"I am certain," she replied, answering the hidden question within the obvious one. "Though perhaps we might see to that other arrangement we've discussed before in the same outing."

True to his nature, Declan's smile was only in his eyes. He nodded with due deference. "Very good, Miss Bartlett. Would you like the carriage or to walk it in its entirety?"

"Walk it in its entirety, please. My aunt would like me to stretch my legs and get fresh air in my lungs." Emmeline smiled at the irony, which only Declan would comprehend.

"Yes, miss."

"Thank you, Declan. I will just let Mrs. Harvey know what we are about and see if Cook can spare any morsels for the poor. Then I should be almost ready." She nodded, more to herself than to him, and turned to continue down to the kitchens.

She hadn't planned on bringing a basket of food originally, but in realizing that walking about London by day would limit her usual activity, and indeed, her route, it seemed the best alternative. She could visit the poorer sections of London with a charity basket, and no one would think anything even remotely amiss. Indeed, she would likely find herself, or her aunt, praised for such Christian impulses.

And she had one destination in mind where the basket would most certainly be of good use.

She would return to Suds's home and visit the precious little girl from the night before and see how she was getting on. The girl had not woken before she had left, and she thought it highly unlikely she would have done so before *Capitán* departed, either. He had still been sleeping when she took her leave, and she thought now, as she did then, it was undoubtedly safer for them to part separately.

She did wonder how he had reacted to her disappearance,

though. Madly so.

Suds would be able to tell her, and he would have a particularly interesting take on the entire situation. He usually had a great deal to say regardless of the circumstances, so seeing the interaction between the two of them and how they slept would have provided numerous thoughts for commentary.

It might also be the perfect opportunity to ask the man for his advice or any suggestions on the subject. Not that she thought *Capitán* would confide in another total stranger, but Suds would have a better idea of the ways of men in such things. He could tell her if she were being ridiculous, or if she had reason for concern, or if she ought to run for her life. She did not suspect the latter was likely, but one could never know for sure. Could they?

Once changed into an appropriate walking ensemble and armed with a basket of food and preserves, Emmeline left the house with Declan a dutiful seven paces behind her. It took some adjustment walking this direction and in this manner, considering she knew the path by heart when she was in the dark and dressed in attire where she was able to move freely and with haste. She had even run the path before simply because she could, wanting to feel the night air rushing against her face.

But dressed as a woman and portraying a fine impression of a lady, the well-trod route felt unfamiliar and strange.

Ladies were sedate; Ears had no need to be. Ladies were graceful; Ears did not care to be. Ladies were fashionable; Ears was functional. When push came to shove, Emmeline Bartlett would much rather be Ears than a lady. But, alas, only a lady could be seen to move by daylight.

Ears was a creature of the night alone.

Still, no one questioned a lady walking toward Cheapside and beyond carrying a basket of charity. That, at least, was convenient and something she would do well to continue in the future, should she need to.

She wouldn't be able to do quite as many things when appearing as Emmeline Bartlett, but she knew full well that smugglers who were also polite members of their local society had inventive means of disguising their wares. She could easily arrange for outings to the poorer parts of London if she continued to extend charity. Or if she found a church she could frequent for appearances of piety. One would never question those outings if she appeared circumspect in the undertaking.

She would have to take even more care than she did at night, given the chances of being seen, but it might be worth such a risk.

There were only a few contacts that knew the secret of her gender, and only they would be trusted with her daytime locations. Most of the business would simply be the sharing of information, but she would be amenable to bringing along monetary incentives. Perhaps some of her aunt's gin if it would improve matters. In her experience, it rarely did.

Declan did not say anything as they walked, which was fairly usual. Even when he was engaging in the secret work that Emmeline had asked of him, words were at a minimum. It was part of what made her choose him as her assistant with the printer in the first place. He was discreet, he was loyal, and he did not ask questions… anymore.

Upon her first asking him, he asked a great many questions, yet as time went on and as he became more aware of her actions, the questions faded into understanding. He was an educated man for a footman, which wasn't common, and it did allow him to read any information he was presented with at the printer and relay such things to Emmeline when he returned home.

The printer knew Declan was not Emmett Barnes, or, at least, he refused to claim to be, so no decisions were ever made on the spot. It had proven challenging for the impatient man at first, but when Emmeline's articles as Emmett Barnes became ever more popular and the demand for them increased, he too stopped asking questions.

It had been a smooth system for all of them in the last year especially, and it had opened Emmeline's eyes to several possibilities for the future. Provided she—or Emmett—ever truly made it out of London.

She could not write anything about Kent or Miss Masters's school. Not if she truly wished to protect her identity, and not if she truly cared about her students. It would not be fair to them to be subjected to the gossip sheets before they even had reputations to protect. No, the school was hallowed ground in Emmeline's eyes, and while it was no secret Emmeline Bartlett was a teacher there, no one would ever know Emmett Barnes also knew every inch of the estate and the grounds.

"Miss Bartlett?"

Emmeline jerked her head up, the sound of her own name startling her, as she could not recall under what circumstances she was traipsing about or, indeed, as whom.

She looked around, catching Declan's impassive expression, the tilt of his head the only sign of expectation. "Yes?" she asked with a confused blink.

He gestured very faintly with his left hand. "Is this your desired destination?"

Oh. That. She had entirely forgotten she had been moving toward something, not just moving for the sake of it. Luckily, as she took in her surroundings, her feet had not been so mindless. They were indeed at her desired location, and in the light of day, Suds's residence looked somehow more cheerful and less welcoming all at once.

"Yes," she replied, this time with unmistakable firmness, should he have any question about the location himself. He had never ventured here for her sake, after all. He would not be surprised by the location, but neither would he recognize it. Only she could do that.

She knocked with less energy than she had the night before, adjusting the basket on her arm as a strange bout of nerves began to run their way through her frame. It was an utterly ridiculous sensation at a time like this. She had met Suds dozens of times over the years and had been teased, scolded, and advised by him in various capacities.

She had simply never done so dressed as Emmeline Bartlett. He would not have known her name had they been introduced publicly. Her eyes widened at that thought, and she turned to Declan. "Do not address me by name," she hissed quickly.

His brow furrowed. "Miss?"

"Perfect," she grunted before whirling back around as the door opened.

Suds looked far more crotchety than she had ever seen him, and the dark, stain-streaked apron he wore over his simple clothing was clearly meant to identify him as some tradesman, but for the life of her, she had no idea what it was.

His expression cleared of all irritation once his eyes took her in. "Ears? Are ye bleeding mad?"

"Not yet," Emmeline quipped. "I fancied a walk, and I wanted to see if the girl was well." She lifted the basket in suggestion.

Suds chuckled, shaking his head. "You are incorrigible, gel, you know that?"

"So I've been told." Emmeline batted her lashes. "May we come in?"

He stepped back, gesturing simply. "Aye, mind your head, lad."

Emmeline did not watch to see if Declan ducked as she entered the house herself, stripping her gloves from her hands. "How is she, Suds?"

"Fair enough," he replied, thankfully not bothering to insult either of their intelligences by pretending he did not know. "She slept longer'n you or your cap'n, and she's showing a fair appetite today."

"Did she talk?" she asked him, moving through to the back of the place. "Did she give you a name?"

Suds smiled in a rather paternal fashion. "She did, Ears. Amy," he called as they rounded into the room, "got someone who wants to see you."

The change in the little girl now from how she had been in the night was startling. Her head of dark curls was the same, though it was far cleaner than it had been when they'd found her. Her bruises were still clear as day, but her pallor had faded, and her eyes were bright in the light of day. She did not smile as she stared at them, fear clearly etched in every fiber of her tiny being.

Emmeline smiled in what she hoped was a warm and comforting manner. "Good day, Amy. Don't be afraid, we are friends."

Amy did not look so certain, a stuffed bear in her hold being drawn closer and closer to her chest. "Mr. Suds?"

"Nothing to fret, dearie," he assured her, coming to sit on the couch beside her. "Miss E here is one of the ones who brought you here last night. She saved you. And that bloke's jus' here to keep her safe. Which means he'll keep you safe, too. Isn't that right?"

"Yes, sir," Declan replied without a hint of pause. "Miss Amy." He bowed, just as he might have done had Aunt Hermione asked for tea.

Amy smiled a little at the gesture, and Emmeline could have hugged the footman for his intuition. She held up the basket a little. "I brought you a bit of food, Amy. I know Mr. Suds has probably fed you some good things today, but perhaps something in here might be a favorite?"

If there had been any doubts about Amy's starvation prior to their bringing her here, the way in which she stared at the basket of food would have erased them all. At once, the too-frail girl became somehow angelic as well as feral, though she did not move from her place. It had to be a sustained deprivation of food and sustenance to engender that sort of transformation, and for it to happen in one so young…

Emmeline moved to sit beside the girl, wondering if she might leap over her to tear the basket apart. Thankfully, Amy seemed to have more restraint than that. They looked through the basket together, and, as Emmeline had hoped, Cook had packed something Amy would enjoy: marzipan.

Cook had fashioned some into little horse figurines, and Amy gnawed at one while playacting some sort of game with the others. The play horses frolicked and cantered rather delicately and made no play sound, but there was something very deliberate in their motions, something innocent in each turn they made.

Of all the items in the basket, the girl had found marzipan most to her liking. Marzipan was not uncommon for any of the people of London, regardless of their station. More elaborate designs might have been made by the cooks of high Society, but just as much marzipan was consumed by the lower orders as the rest. Perhaps it was a comforting, familiar treat for her. A simple thing that reminded her of home. If she had a home.

"Amy, who hurt you?" Emmeline ventured to ask, careful not to touch the bruises on the girl's face as she gently ran a hand over the girl's unruly hair.

"Mr. Blaine," came the unconcerned reply. "It's 'appened afore. I shoulda known. 'E don't like beggars. Or gels. Or chil'ren."

Emmeline looked over Amy's head at Suds whose jaw had tightened. He nodded once, his eyes darting back down to his new ward.

"Do you live with Mr. Blaine?" Emmeline went on.

Amy snorted softly. "No' im. 'E'd never 'ouse a cat. I live on me own now. Since Mam died and I been 'iding from the overseers."

Avoiding the workhouse would not have been difficult, being her size and canny as to the nature and ways of the streets, but it certainly could have gotten her into a deal of trouble. If she had been placed in one of the more generous facilities, they might have given her the promise of more in her life, but as for the rest...

She'd have been better alone in the streets, even with the likes of Mr. Blaine to contend with.

Emmeline watched her play with the horses a bit more, smiling at Amy's single-minded focus. "You seem fond of horses, Amy. Do you like them?"

She nodded without smiling. "I see 'orses in the streets sometimes. Not down there, but in the upper streets. They pull coaches and fings. Sometimes people ride 'em. I ain't never seen one close before. Never seen one run."

Such a sweet, soft statement of regret. In that moment, Emmeline would have given anything to take the girl to Hyde Park so she might see one close and perhaps watch one gallop. But such an outing would have been so foreign to girls like Amy. So unfathomable.

And Emmeline Bartlett could not walk into the poorer parts of London without a child and return to Mayfair with one in tow. It could not happen.

She looked at Suds, tormented by the predicament. He seemed to understand and nudged his head toward the far side of the room. She rose and followed him, wringing her fingers in distress.

"What can I do?" she whispered when they were apart from Amy and Declan.

Suds smiled and put a hand over hers. "Never you mind, Ears. I'm sure by now you've heard of a bloke on the streets called Gent?"

She nodded quickly. "Of course I have. One can't walk down Brick Lane without hearing his name a dozen times. I've spent four years trying to meet the man, but he's more elusive than a Cornish smuggler's punishment."

"He's got an eye out for tots in London," Suds told her, chuckling at the reference she made without directly acknowledging it. "Keeps 'em in line and safe. I'll get word to him about Amy here, and I have no doubt he'll adopt her into his street family, same as he's done with others."

Emmeline wasn't certain how to feel about that. Suds might have known the Gent, but she did not. A man with a particular interest in children who did not take them off the streets? Was that really the best option for them?

Seeing her hesitation, Suds gave her a look. "She can't go home with you, Ears."

"I know that," she replied stubbornly, though her mind spun on unlikely scenarios where it might have been possible. "I just don't like the idea of sending her with someone even I cannot track down."

The older man narrowed his eyes at her. "Do you trust me, Ears?"

That was not fair. Of course she trusted this man. He had been one of her very first contacts when she had started exploring London, and while he had never had to intervene on her behalf in a time of trouble, he had certainly been a safe haven for her as she maneuvered throughout this secret life of hers. She trusted him with her secrets and her life.

Sullenly, she nodded. "Yes..."

"I trust the Gent," he told her in as firm a tone as she'd heard from anyone alive. "He will take care of her. I promise."

It was impossible to doubt the man when he spoke like that, and though she still had personal misgivings, Emmeline felt a few of the knots leave her stomach.

She nodded, swallowing with some difficulty. "All right. I'll leave her to you, then."

Suds smiled at her, patting her hand gently before turning to watch Declan quietly interact with Amy. "I must say, Ears, you are a surprising one. First the Spaniard, now this bloke? Does the cap'n know about him?"

"Declan is not... he's not like..." Her cheeks flamed as her heart seemed to ignite as well, the image of *Capitán* softly smiling as he touched her face searing the insides of her wrists and the soles of her feet. "It's not the same."

The knowing chuckle from the man beside her did nothing for her state of incineration. "Oh, I think that is clear, Ears, my gel. Very clear indeed."

Chapter Fourteen

"I've told you already, Mendoza, I did not suggest this meeting. It was requested."

Teo shook his head firmly, grinding his teeth. "I haven't taken any meetings without Rafa present, Henry. It is not right."

"It's an introduction, not a business discussion." Henry shook his head, exhaling shortly. "My father insists some of the men we are meeting with will respect your title more than your expertise. For the best chance of success, as we are looking for additional financiers, we must play to the Society's hierarchical views. Surely you understand that."

No, Teo did not understand it. His title was minor, barely worth retaining, and he didn't know a thing about the estate he was supposed to be master of. He had no plans for enhancing estate farms, no comprehension of the commerce in the Midlands, no notion of his nearest relative, and could not recite any members of his English family tree beyond his late grandfather. And he'd only known his name from the papers his solicitor had sent upon his inheritance.

He had nothing to offer the Society hierarchy, and any sort of introductory conversation among them would require some topic on which they could all contribute. Unless these gentlemen knew something of the quality of cotton or wool from the newer English mills, Teo could not see how it would be possible.

"I do not like it," Teo grumbled darkly. "And this linen is a noose."

Henry snorted once as they moved toward the home in

Whitehall where they were expected. "That is a cravat, Mendoza, and gentlemen wear them."

"I don't." Teo sniffed, shaking his head in disgust for the ridiculous signs of status.

"When you are Teo Mendoza, you don't," Henry pointed out, nodding to a passerby briskly. "But I can assure you when you are Sir Teodoro, you will."

Teo did not like that idea, nor did he appreciate the reminder. Social gatherings for the sake of socially gathering was not his idea of time well spent, especially when there was work to be done elsewhere that he particularly enjoyed. But while Teo Mendoza could work for his living and work himself to the bone alongside his crew and employees, Sir Teodoro de Vickers y Mendoza was an enigma who had yet to present himself or make his preferences known.

"Will he?" Teo muttered as he jammed a finger beneath the folds of linen in an attempt to loosen their hold on his throat.

"Don't disrupt it, I beg you," Henry asked before Teo could work the fabric too much. "I'm not a valet, and recreating the style for the sake of your respectability is not something I am capable of."

It was an amusing statement, given Henry's cravat looked well enough in its place. Not as fine as Teo's, which was irritating, but clean and crisp as apparently all cravats must be. It did not seem particularly likely the Fosters had valets, but perhaps Mr. Foster had one who could assist the others when finer apparel was required.

Teo did not have a valet either, but since moving into the boardinghouse, Mrs. Jones had been particularly attentive to Teo and Rafa. One of her servants had come up to help Teo with his clothing this morning as a note from Mr. Foster had arrived to encourage the more elegant garments, and the lad hadn't appreciated Teo's utter cluelessness as to his wishes for such things.

Would he need a valet if he remained in England and took up his rightful place? He would need a home, that was certain, but were lodgings easier to acquire than servants? He'd never really tried to attain either, as he'd simply taken up the family rooms by the business in Spain, but here...

Did he even wish to remain?

The image of his sweet, beautiful, impetuous *Orejitas* came to mind, and he could not help but smile at the picture she presented. At the warmth that spread throughout his frame. At the sudden light he could feel swirling about in his chest. Ears was in England, and he adored her.

Could he stay for one incomparable woman? When the rest of his life was elsewhere, was she enough to stay?

Holding her in his arms as they'd slept a few hours had been so perfect, so right. Seeing her face in the light had filled him with completeness, a fulfillment he had been waiting eons for and never known it. There was nothing more to wish for in that moment. Nothing more to seek. She was the perfect answer to so very many questions, yet his knowledge of her, of the details that made up her life and her being, all were lacking in many respects. And yet in spite of all that lacked, he knew her. Understood her. Loved her.

The impression stole the breath from his lungs, his eyes widening. That wasn't possible, was it? To love someone so quickly and yet so entirely? He did not even know her name. He did not know her family, her situation, her place in the world. He did not know if she preferred jam on her toast or if she could sing or if she arose early or late. He did not know how long her hair was or the taste of her lips or the way she took her tea. He didn't know so many things about her, things that would have built her up and created the striking picture of her identity.

But he loved her. Or, at the very least, he nearly did. He'd known this was coming. He had said as much to her the other evening, though admitting his feelings in his natural language was easier and safer. Less vulnerable. Less perplexing.

Could she feel it? Could she know he felt so much he could barely speak of it?

Suddenly, he longed to be away from here. To fly to the darker sides of London and wait for his sweet girl to arrive. He wanted to hold her in his arms, just to assure himself he hadn't imagined her to be as wondrous as she seemed. To feel how she made his heart race and pound and thunder, how she filled his life with light and direction and laughter. How she completed him.

The part of him that had always felt missing—what he thought was England—could it have been her all this time? His soul crying out for its final, brilliant, best part that lived somewhere beyond his own shores and without knowing he existed?

Yes. Yes, that was her. That could only be her. And that… she… was everything. *Cielos*, what a revelation!

"Turn here."

Teo shook himself, the blissful fog of his heart's epiphany fading into the stale, damp streets they traversed in broad daylight. Far from *Orejitas,* far from their world, far from anything he found enjoyable. The sour taste in his mouth at the sudden change was not welcome.

"I don't like this any more than you do," Henry uttered from beside him as they turned and started down the next street. "Believe me, I would prefer to be down at the docks offloading cargo. But my father insisted this is important, and these men requested the meeting once he went to them for investment. You cannot blame them for not wanting to invest blindly, can you?"

"I can when it must be done with such finery." Teo groaned, craning his neck. "For men who can look down on tradesmen, they certainly demand a lot of us, do they not?"

Henry raised a brow, gesturing faintly with one hand. "And I thought you did not understand the way of British business. I see you grasp it entirely."

It would have been amusing had it been so very not amusing.

The days following their dinner with the Fosters had been a whirl for their business. Not only had each of the Foster men been in favor of joining forces with them, but they had formed a plan for a very specific partnership, which gave them significant influence over the shipping in the Spanish colonies in the Americas. The Fosters had business connections scattered around the globe, and with a bit more investment from other significant men, the combination of their two businesses in partnership could become something rather extraordinary.

They would continue their individual ventures, naturally, but partnering in other avenues would guarantee that both companies gained access to supplies and contacts of which few could boast. And in one fell swoop, Rafa and Teo had been nearly adopted into the fold of the entire Foster family.

Of course, Rafa was particularly interested in the charms of Miss

Mary Foster, and she seemed keen on improving her grasp of the Spanish language under his excellent tutelage. If any of the other members of the Foster family had concerns about a potential union there, they were neither speaking of it, nor acting in any way to prevent it.

At any rate, it now appeared Teo, as the head and face of the Don Mendoza Shipping company, would have to face the potential investors without actually speaking of their potential investment. Business meetings came naturally to Teo, were something he had grown up with and grown into. But standing around with fine men making polite conversation and drinking port? Surely there were better things to do.

"Will your father and Jem be here?" Teo asked as they crossed the street. "Or were you sent to collect me and accompany me?"

"They'd better be here," Henry retorted without shame. "With Jem fussing over the state of my clothing last night, it would only be fair to see him trussed up."

Teo grunted once. "Rafa wasn't disappointed to miss this outing, especially when he saw what I was wearing. He, I am told, will be meeting with Mr. Baird and his company down on the docks at their invitation to inspect their most recent cargo."

"Fortunate man." Henry sighed with a hint of longing. "You'll enjoy working with Baird. The man has principles and unrivaled expectations of quality. His grandfather was a privateer, you know, and the Crown's favorite one. Bit of a favor, given when he wanted to establish a base of operations here, but the son and grandson do very well. They certainly keep us alert in a business sense."

"Does it bother you," Teo cleared his throat, craning his neck once more at the annoying brush of linen, "that we are also negotiating with Baird?"

Henry shook his head without hesitation. "Not at all. As I said, Baird is a good man. You are wise to seek out multiple contracts and various connections. Besides, they have better connections to the Indies, though do not tell my father or Jem I admitted it." He laughed easily, tipping his head toward a building that looked identical to the ones on either side of it. "Here we are."

"And who is our host again?" Teo inquired, finding his mouth and lips suddenly dry with nerves.

"A man named Pratt. Bit of a featherbrain, but his wife is rather sharp. And they are extremely well connected." Henry exhaled a slow breath, as though he was preparing himself for the event himself. "Within, you will find a few members of Parliament, a smattering of the peerage, and a few who are simply gentlemen in search of a worthy investment."

Teo stared at the door they approached as though all those men stood in a line at it, waiting to speak with him. "I had no idea your father was so well connected."

"I don't know about well connected," Henry admitted as he rang the bell to the place, "but he certainly is well respected, as far as trade goes. And word spreads when opportunity knocks."

"*Tenía miedo de eso*," Teo muttered under his breath, forcing his hands to remain at his sides rather than tug on the linen strangling him.

Henry snorted softly. "I don't know what you just said, but I have a feeling I agree with you."

Teo nodded, not feeling particularly inclined to elaborate on his feelings or translate his words. It would serve no purpose, at any rate.

The door opened before them, and they presented their cards, which seemed a ridiculous waste yet again, but at least no one could claim the pair of them were not proper. A murmur of voices was heard from above them as they entered, drawing Teo's attention upward, though there was not much to see on the plaster ceiling itself. A few details admirably done, but nothing he had not seen before. Interesting that a home of simple elegance was to be their meeting place rather than a home of extravagance that would impress.

Had that been a strategy on the part of the men above? The simple tradesmen would do better in a less auspicious space? Or best not to overwhelm the Spaniard? Clearly, he had been spending too much time with Rafa. He was suddenly suspicious of everyone and everything.

"Right this way, please, sirs," the stony-faced butler intoned, turning for the stairs and leading them up.

It was unfortunate that Rafa was not walking beside him now, as it would have been the perfect time to converse in Spanish to put himself at ease about the situation. As it was, Teo could only stew in his own anticipation without relief. An idea occurred to him, and he looked at Henry with interest. "Would it serve my purposes today to be more English or more Spanish?"

Henry returned his look in surprise. "You mean... pretend to be less Spanish or pretend to comprehend English less?"

"Exactly so," Teo replied in his best imitation of the English accent. His own natural accent was present, but much less pronounced.

"I'll leave that to your own judgment," Henry replied with a chuckle. "Some will like your Spanish side, others are only here because of your English heritage. Pair them against each other at your will. I think you'll know soon enough who appreciates particular aspects."

Well, if Teo could turn the forthcoming interlude into a strategy himself, he might find it all the more interesting. After all, he was the one they wished to meet. Yes, he needed to impress, and yes, his business surely needed investors if they were to accomplish the lofty goals they and the Fosters had set for themselves, but he was also preparing to make his mark as Sir Teodoro Vickers. There had to be some power in that.

Not a great amount, given he was not a duke or any such thing, but he did have a fair fortune himself, if he could bring Diehle House into his interests. Which would mean becoming Sir Teodoro. That was something to consider.

The conversations in the room silenced as he and Henry entered the room. The butler inclined his head to the attention of the others. "Mr. Henry Foster and Sir Theodore Vickers." With a snap of his heels, the butler left, leaving the pair of them standing there in a room full of strangers.

Teo nearly choked on the egregious English pronunciation of his name, his world turning off-kilter for a moment or two. He had never been called Theodore in his life, and he was not about to start now.

A slender man with a ridiculous smile and an elaborate weskit approached, hand outstretched. "Apologies, my dear fellow. Chipman is dreadful with foreign names. Please excuse his error." He turned at once to the rest. "Gents, this is Sir Teodoro Vickers, baronet. Also known as Teo Mendoza of the Don Mendoza Shipping company."

The correction was welcome, but the embarrassment remained as the discussion in the room started again as he was briefly examined by the others, then, it seemed, dismissed by a few. Others seemed to wait in expectation, expressions unreadable.

"There," the slender man said, turning back to them with a much less ridiculous smile and a more natural expression. "That should weed them out, eh, Henry?"

Teo stared at the man in shock. "Your butler did that on purpose."

"I pray you'll forgive the little trick at your expense, Vickers," came the unconcerned reply, though there was a sort of apology in his eyes. "Or do you prefer Mendoza? I'll call you whatever you prefer, despite what others might choose."

"This is our host, Mendoza," Henry interjected. "Jeremy Pratt."

Teo shook the man's hand, curious by the sudden shift in the man's personality, as well as his trick. "You said he was a featherbrain," Teo protested half-heartedly.

Pratt chuckled easily. "Oh, I am to most people. It serves my ends, rather like that little twist on your name. I don't mind it; my true friends know of my substance." He clapped Teo on the shoulder and turned to face the room. "Now, I believe Mr. Foster Sr. and Jr. are in talks with Gilbert just there. Good fellow, bit of a cheat at cards. Wharton in the corner is a surly sort, but there's a keen eye for business, if you can look past it. Montgomery there is your token earl with too much money and in need of a place to put it…"

He continued around the room, giving Teo the names, as well as very brief descriptions, of each man present. It would be interesting to see if his personal impressions aligned with Pratt's, or if the bias he was unintentionally giving was to put himself in greater favor with Teo himself.

"And that should sum it up," Pratt finished with a sigh, patting Teo's shoulder once more. "Kindly spend a moment or two talking with my father-in-law. He won't be an investor, but when he heard I was hosting this little soiree, he demanded an invitation. He spent ten years in Spain in his youth, so if he remembers, he may try and converse in your native tongue. I apologize in advance for the experience and any offense given in his hash of words."

Teo had to laugh at that, nodding at the explanation. "It may be the brightest part of this whole endeavor."

"No, dear chap, that would be me." Pratt laughed at his own stupid joke and swung away, returning to the featherbrain character he apparently wore so well, and moved to another group of men to talk.

"Where should I start?" Teo asked Henry, who had watched and listened to the whole introductory speech with interest if not outright amusement.

Henry glanced around, eyes narrowing. "Why not there? Mr. Jackson is a member of Parliament. I believe from Bristol, and it could be worth a discussion, particularly if he has access there."

Teo nodded and strode in that direction, taking a note from Pratt's behavior and pretending to have more confidence than he truly owned at the moment.

"Gentlemen," he greeted when he reached the group.

"Vickers," the tallest man greeted, his voice deeper than anticipated. "I am Edward Jackson, and here you find Sir Pierce Tomkins, Arthur Adlam, and Byron Felix. How do you do?"

It was on the tip of Teo's tongue to answer the question before recollecting that in England, the phrase was more of a greeting than a question to be answered. He bowed rather than reply directly, and it seemed to be the appropriate choice.

"I understand your father was English, Vickers," Sir Pierce began, his tone rather stuffy, though not entirely disapproving. "From what part did he hail?"

"The Midlands, sir," Teo told him, praying he would not ask more questions. "My grandfather was Sir Edwin Vickers of Diehle House."

"Ah, I do recognize the name. A distinguished family, you must be rather pleased." There was a slight frown for a moment, then the gentleman's brows cleared. "Diehle House, did you say? I thought that place had been laid to rot."

Teo kept his face clear from emotion, though a gnawing sensation pulled at the back of his stomach. "I cannot say, sir. I have not yet seen the place. My father and grandfather did not part well. I was not aware of my inheritance until recently."

"Fortunate man," Mr. Adlam said with a shake of his head. "To make your own way of things without the influence of ancestors weighing down on you is fortunate indeed. You want my advice? Tear the place down and make it your own."

"Oh, I don't know," Mr. Jackson broke in. "Sir Teodoro might find treasures in the old place and particular ties to his most ancient and distinguished family line." He toasted Teo faintly with a glass, something almost hard in his glance.

Teo felt on edge at once. "I understand you represent Bristol in Parliament, sir. Fine shipping tradition there."

"And I feel that tradition in every bill that crosses my path," Mr. Jackson told him, nodding firmly. "We've cracked down hard on smuggling in the last several years, but still they manage to get goods and trade past our men and into the hands of blackguards on shore. I've got merchants barking down my neck about securing the waterways and borders with more force to keep the legitimate businesses prospering, but a number of MPs continue to fight against such sanctions and restrictions."

"Would such sanctions be a deterrent for foreign trade?" Teo wondered aloud, keeping his tone easy and cursory.

Jackson shook his head hard. "I have conferred with several of my foreign associates, who believe an orderly system would actually help the shipping trade flourish all over Europe. Might even spread to other countries and ports, not only British ones. With the appropriate papers, any ship carrying legitimate trade and cargo would be free to do just as they have done. Only the ones without papers would be suspect."

"I imagine inspections would be in order from time to time," Teo added, something about the scenario not sitting quite right in his mind. "To guarantee the cargo is legitimate. After all, one must not allow forgeries of papers to let the smugglers sneak through."

Mr. Jackson smiled an almost cool smile. "I see you understand my meaning, sir. And mind yourself, sir. I fear you are being watched." He gestured faintly over Teo's shoulder.

Teo pretended to search the room in the opposite direction,

letting his eyes fall on the men to whom Jackson pointed. There were, indeed, a group of men chatting amongst themselves, and one or two flicked their gazes in his direction, their meaning unclear.

"You will want to surround yourself with friends and allies, *amigo*," Mr. Jackson murmured behind him. "London can be a dangerous place for a man of business."

Teo nodded to himself and turned back to his own group, smiling now. "Thank you for the warning, Mr. Jackson. I shall take it into consideration. Now, can you tell me the most profitable shipping companies in Bristol?"

Chapter Fifteen

*H*er article on Amy had taken London by storm.

Well, so her aunt had said the day before at breakfast, and she hadn't specifically said it had been Emmeline's article. But she *had* praised Emmett Barnes for his work, and how heartbreaking the story of the little girl was, and how she was pleased he had been so keen to heed their request that he'd written it so soon after asking.

Emmeline took that to be praise for herself, despite her aunt's ignorance. And for her next article, she wanted to focus on those who exploited the poor.

Tonight, they would be finding Mr. Blaine and learning everything they could about him, provided *Capitán* came. He hadn't the night before.

She had tried not to be too upset by his absence and had started looking for clues and inspiration on her own, but the night did not hold the same charm to it without him. She'd have gone to find him, but she had no idea where he lived. She'd have sent for him, but she had no name or direction to give. She'd have felt betrayed, except they had never said they would be together every night. She had no right to expect anything of him. No reason to, even though her heart cried out that she needed him.

Still, walking out into London tonight, she hoped desperately he would come. She had stopped by Suds's home before truly starting out, and he relayed the entire story of getting Amy into Gent's care. How Gent had stooped down to her level to talk with her, then had taken the girl by the hand and led her away to another group of children, all of whom had been as warm and welcoming as anyone could wish for.

Suds had checked with Amy before she'd left to make sure she knew how to find his home again should she ever wish to see him. When she'd recited his location with perfection, he said he'd never felt quite so proud of a young'un.

In a way, Emmeline was sad Amy had found a better place to stay. She was a little attached to the girl and would have loved to see her frequently. But Suds had reminded her that he was an old man without a wife, and a child needed more care than that. Which begged the question as to the Gent's status in life, as well as any woman with whom he might share that life with.

But Suds was not going to get into details of another friend's life, especially when he was as secret as Emmeline in many respects. She longed to tell *Capitán* about the day she had given the marzipan horses to Amy, how childlike she had been, and yet how aged she was by what she had seen and experienced in life. She wanted to tell him where Amy was now, and what she had relayed about the life she'd led in London before they'd found her.

There were so many things she wanted to say, and yet a greater part of her just wanted to feel his hand in hers. His arms around her.

There were so many barriers in Society and in her life as Emmeline Bartlett. Until *Capitán* had taken her hand that night, she had not touched a man's bare hand since she had been a child, unless she considered the handshakes she had given as Ears. She'd not known a caring embrace from a man since the passing of her father, and even then, the last hug had come from her cousin. He was her guardian, despite her age, and they were rarely so familiar as to embrace.

She did not want barriers with *Capitán*. She did not want restrictions. She did not want...

What did it matter what she wanted? There would be barriers between them regardless, and no matter how she might adore him, the reality of life was that they could not continue to meet in the dark of night without names and without ties for the rest of their lives. Especially not if her feelings continued to be what they were. She would long for more, and what if she brought herself into ruin by a moment of weakness? What would she do then?

Her aunt could not bear a scandal and did not deserve to be so subjected to one. Who *Capitán* was in the light of day would become important sooner or later, and until she knew that much, she could not continue to hope for anything. She could not bear to.

Perhaps it would be better if he did not appear anymore. Then she could return to her usual activities and safety, the anonymity of disguise and darkness allowing her the freedom nothing else did. This was what she needed to focus on, not the impossibly attractive, breath-stealing, heart-snatching, laughter-engaging, incomprehensibly perfect specimen of a Spanish man whom she was only too keen to dwell on.

Oh, heavens, did she love to dwell on him.

It wasn't even an intentional thing now. Her mind simply leapt to his image whenever it had a breath otherwise unaccounted for, and sometimes, even when it didn't. The laughing edge to his smile, the tempting depths in his eyes, the rumbling sweetness in his voice, the curl of his tantalizing accent…

Her palms itched to run along the rough stubble of his jaw, and her fingers yearned to claw into his hair, though she had yet to see him with his cap off. Should he appear tonight, could they not take a romantic walk along the Thames? Find some unoccupied fire and sit beside it curled together? Anything would do, anything that had no other purpose other than for them to just be together.

She longed to be his and his alone, just for one night. Not Emmett Barnes preparing a story. Not Ears investigating this or that. Not Miss Bartlett yearning to fly away. Just Emmeline. Just a woman. Just his.

Would that really be so impossible?

But he didn't know Emmeline. He only knew Ears. Or *Orejitas*, as he called her, and she knew it was similar to what he had told her was the Spanish word for ears, but not exact. She'd not asked him what his adaptation meant, or why he had changed it, but she was constantly wondering. She didn't mind; it was a lovely sounding word, and her heart leapt whenever he used it. Was there anything to be done about the effect he had on her? Did she want there to be?

She heard approaching steps and felt a trembling start in her legs. It rolled up the length of her until it seemed the hairs on her head quivered as well. So much for his effect.

"I wasn't sure you'd come," she announced softly, turning to smile at his approach, but her smile died.

He was there, but he was not alone.

Emmeline pushed off the wall, ready to bolt from both, her entire body going cold even as her heart pounded fire in her chest.

"What is this?" she demanded in a lower, more aggressive tone.

Capitán said something to the man beside him, who was of a similar height but a stockier build, then continued toward her alone. "Easy, *cariño*. Let me explain."

"You brought someone else," she hissed when he was close enough. "Do you not understand the precarious position I put myself in with you being alone? And to have another stranger with me?"

"I do understand," *Capitán* insisted, his voice as gentle as one might have used on a wild horse. "Which is why I have brought him. I wanted... I hoped you would allow him to teach you to fight."

Emmeline stared at him for a long moment without blinking. "To what?"

"Fight," he said again, his brow creasing. "*La lucha. La defensa.* Um, protect yourself."

"Oh." She frowned slightly. "You want me to learn how to defend myself."

"*Sí, cariño. Por favor.*" He placed his palms together in a praying motion, his eyes locked on her.

Her agitation began to ebb away, and she swallowed, finding her lips curving into a smile. "Is that Spanish for please?"

He nodded once. "*Sí.* I need to know you will be safe no matter what. That you can fight if you need to. That I... that you..." He exhaled roughly, his eyes falling to the ground at her feet. "Please, *cariño*. I need this."

"And you think I need this," she murmured, anything remotely resembling irritation fleeing in the face of complete adoration for the sweetness of this man before her.

"I don't know if you need it," *Capitán* admitted. His eyes raised to hers, almost hesitant in their action. "But I will know you are equipped by the time we are done, which will help me to be less afraid for you."

Emmeline's eyes widened, her heart dropping into her stomach. "You're afraid for me?"

He nodded without hesitation. "I know how capable you are. How brilliant. How daring. How adaptable. And I have seen you fleeing danger before. I know you have escaped other dangers long before I ever crossed your path, *Orejitas*. I simply ask that you allow me a chance to see you escape from all the rest, because I will not stop you from doing any of this. Yet I need to know you are safe at all times."

She'd have run into his arms had they been alone. She'd have knocked the hat from his head and pressed her lips to his in an untutored fervor that would have consumed her. She'd have taken full advantage of wearing trousers and wrapped her legs about his hips as she clung to his neck with pathetic desperation and eternal devotion. Any number of those things she would have done—had they been alone.

How did one relay such a message without doing such things?

Feeling her pulse pound in her throat, Emmeline started slowly toward him, closing the distance. She stopped just before him, close enough she could feel his clothing brush hers with every breath he took. His eyes searched hers, darker than she had ever seen them, something tender in his expression.

Reaching down, she took his hand in hers, lacing their fingers. The brush of skin sent her pulse shooting down her limbs, and she caught how his eyes widened at the contact. She exhaled slowly, bringing their joined hand to her lips to kiss the back of his.

"All right," she breathed against the skin, loving the friction of his hand against her lips. "Teach me."

She felt, and heard, a groan from his chest, and her eyes fluttered as he leaned forward, pressing his lips to her brow, knocking her hat askew. She gripped his hand more tightly, holding it to her as though it held his heart. His free hand cupped her cheek, and they stood there for a long moment, closer than they had ever been, yet somehow...

"*Gracias, amada mía*," he murmured against her brow. "*Significa el mundo. Gracias, gracias, siempre gracias.*"

Emmeline breathed in the fragrance of him, the feeling of his warmth seeping into her skin and her lungs, the taste of his hand on her lips as she brushed against them again and again. Gads, was there any moment more transcendent to a being than this?

Whatever the barriers, whatever the challenges, whatever stood between them, she did not care. She was his, and she wanted him or no one. That was it. This was it. Only him.

She felt him breathe against her and knew he was ending this breathless respite, likely due to their guest, who might have found their interlude rather uncomfortable. But if she were to learn to fight and actually earn the beauty of the moment, it needed to happen now.

He pulled back, smiling down at her, and brushed his thumb over the fullness of her cheek in one lingering stroke. He dropped his hand and turned to his companion. "*Santiago, ven aquí por favor.*"

The man came forward with almost abrupt movements. He nodded his head at Emmeline. "*Señorita.*"

She nodded in return. "Santiago." She looked at *Capitán*. "Has he ever taught a woman to fight before?"

"He has," *Capitán* confirmed. "Feels very strongly about it. And he is the best fighter I know."

"Does he speak English?"

He smiled and asked Santiago a question, presumably the one she had just asked.

Santiago grunted once. "Some. Enough."

Emmeline smiled at the brusqueness, oddly more at ease with such a thing than with overly attentive warmth. "Can't argue with that." She stepped back from *Capitán* and looked around. "Will we learn here?"

"Down the road," Santiago answered. "Alley is much better."

That made sense, though it ought to have frightened her a little. Alleys were traps in London, as she had learned early on. But alleys were also the best places to avoid being discovered. Most of her informants preferred to give her their findings in alleys.

Santiago led their trio down the street, away from the nearest streetlamp, and turned into a surprisingly wide alleyway, cleared of debris, rubbish, and any additional clutter that might have prevented them from having enough space.

He turned to face Emmeline and his master, gesturing to the middle of the alley.

"*Señorita, que vengas al centro, por favor,*" he said with another emphasis on his gesture.

She did not need a translation to understand and left *Capitán's* side with a final squeeze to his hand. Standing before Santiago, she felt a slight trickle of apprehension. Not that this man would harm her, but that she might disappoint and prove incapable of defending herself. What would *Capitán* think of her then? What would he do?

Santiago said something to her, his expression earnest.

"He says, 'I am going to pretend to be an attacker,'" *Capitán* translated from the side. "'If I do anything that frightens you, anything that offends, you need only say stop.' Um, that is *pare* in Spanish."

Emmeline nodded. "*Pare*," she recited. "*Gracias*."

Santiago smiled a little at her Spanish. He put his hands on her arms, lining them up almost evenly. He was a good hand's width taller than her and certainly larger in stature, and a scar across his jaw proved his experience in a fight. He reached out, patting her leg, and mimicked widening her stance. She followed suit, giving him a questioning look.

"*Bueno*," he grunted. He showed her the heel of his hand, then began rambling again.

"'When an attacker comes at you from the front, you may punch him in the nose or throat. Using the heel of your hand like this brings about a great deal of force. More than you might expect. Those sensitive areas cannot take such force, and you will have time to escape.'"

Emmeline nodded at the translation and mimicked his motions with her hand. Santiago stepped back, then started coming at her in a menacing way. At once, Emmeline jammed the heel of her hand toward his nose, though he caught it easily.

"'You will need to move much more quickly, or he can stop you,'" *Capitán* said for him.

Santiago backed up again, then came at her once more. This time, Emmeline's hand shot out, and he barely dodged it.

She frowned. "You still avoided it."

"I watched for it," Santiago said in broken English, chuckling. "Attacker won't know."

Slightly mollified, Emmeline went through the exercise three more times, learning to recoil her hand as quickly as she lashed out, to better use the force and avoid being caught herself. Then Santiago pulled her closer to him, bending his elbows and gently tapping it at her jaw, speaking in rapid Spanish.

"'In closer fights, your elbow can be a very effective weapon. Shift your weight to the foot of the same side as you lay the blow. This will allow you more force than simple arm strength.'"

He tapped his chin, his neck, his temple, and his jaw, then stepped back and slowly came forward, allowing her time to master the motion.

"'Yes, that is good. Don't be afraid to throw your might into it. Once the attacker is stumbling, you can escape.'"

Emmeline nodded, narrowing her eyes, and craning her neck as a suspicious thrill of excitement began to tense along her back.

Santiago came at her again much faster, and though her pulse jolted with fear, she landed a glancing blow at best along his jaw.

"*Bravo, señorita*," he told her with a gentle pat to her elbow. "Again."

Twice more, she rammed her elbow at his face, then he showed her how to adjust the motion if the attacker were behind her. With his hands at her hips, he helped her master the rotation without losing her force, and she glanced over at *Capitán*, who had stopped translating. He watched them with narrowed eyes, his frame taut. Even in the darkness, she could see that. She bit back a laugh, which only made him shake his head, no smile appearing.

Santiago tapped her elbow, reminding her of the task at hand, and she brought the back of it up to his face, just as he'd shown her. Then suddenly, his arms were around her waist. Not tightly, but he secured his hands at the front of her.

"If like this," he grunted, apparently aware his master was no longer interpreting for him, "things difficult."

Emmeline nodded, feeling far more alert now.

"Best trick," her teacher went on, "is to get low and make space. So." He emphasized his hands where they were, still loose. "Bend at hands, send arm back to face."

Face flaming, Emmeline did as he bid, bending slightly at the waist.

"Use legs," he insisted. "Whole body lower, *sí?*"

She unlocked her knees and crouched while she bent.

"Arm to my face."

Almost blindly, she thrust her elbow back and up, catching his ear.

"Other arm next."

She obeyed.

"Many times each arm until release."

She jammed her elbows back once more each until he released her. He remained in a curved stance while she got free.

He looked up at her. "Now, elbow down on back of neck, knock down."

She did the motion, and he obliged by lowering himself to the ground. He looked up at her, his face against the stone. "*¿Entiendes tú?*"

Guessing at what he meant, Emmeline nodded. More than that, she suddenly saw the need and the usefulness of what he was teaching her, and she was determined to master it. "Again."

He nodded, springing back up and gesturing for her to stand in front of him.

She looked over at *Capitán* again, no longer wanting to laugh, and she found him watching her with as much seriousness as she was feeling at the moment. She nodded at him, a newfound confidence nudging its way into her chest.

Capitán returned the nod, his lips now curving ever so slightly. He saw what she felt, and it pleased him. This was what he wanted. How could she know that from only a look?

Santiago's arms were suddenly around her a little tighter than before, but not greatly. She went through the motions fluidly, her blows behind making no contact with him, but the speed was one that allowed him ease of avoidance. Thrice more, and she landed a blow on his jaw, which broke her concentration.

"Oh no!" she yelped, springing away from him, and covering her mouth. "I'm so sorry, Santiago, are you hurt?"

He rubbed at his jaw a moment, wincing, then began to chuckle, smiling at her. He rambled something quickly in Spanish, which made

Capitán laugh as well.

Emmeline propped her hands on her hips and looked between the two. "What?"

"He said, *'Ella es una cosita poderosa, ¿no es así?',* and I agreed," *Capitán* replied simply, still laughing to himself.

"Which means?" Emmeline demanded with minimal patience.

Capitán met her eyes squarely. "'She is a powerful little thing, isn't she?'"

Oh.

"Have you had enough for one night?" he asked when she said nothing more. "We can continue tomorrow."

Startled and slightly embarrassed, Emmeline nodded, turning to Santiago. *"Gracias, Santiago."*

He bowed a little, still smiling at her. *"De nada, señorita."* He walked over to *Capitán* and shook his hand, then left the alley without another word to either of them.

Emmeline stood in the center of her makeshift fighting ring, her fingers rubbing together.

"Orejitas? Is all well?"

She swallowed and looked over at *Capitán*. "Thank you. For wanting me to learn, for bringing Santiago, for caring enough to want this for me."

Capitán's shoulders dropped on an exhale, and he came to her, cupping her face in his hands, tender and fervent all at once. "I want everything for you, *cariño*. You must know that."

Emmeline stared up at him, her heart rocking back and forth within her. "You said that in English," she whispered. "Are you no longer frightened?"

His lips curved and his thumbs brushed against her cheeks, waves of a ticklish sensation screeching down to her toes. "I am now more frightened of you not understanding, *cariño*, than I am of you knowing."

Sighing, she closed her eyes, and Emmeline leaned forward, pressing her brow against his chest. His hands immediately fell from her face as his arms wrapped around her, pressing her firmly against him, holding her perfectly close. She slid her arms around him, letting her fingers dig into the fabric of his clothing, feeling the power of him and the heat of his being.

Nothing had ever felt more like home in her entire life. There could be no obstacles to this. No barriers. No complications. This had to be right. This had to be all.

And if she had anything to say about it, that is exactly what it would be.

Chapter Sixteen

*W*atching *Orejitas* learn to fight was a complicated experience. He was amused, he was pleased, he was proud, and he was outside of his mind with jealousy. It had never occurred to him to kill one of his own men, but last night, he had been sorely tempted.

Tonight, it was little better. He knew full well Santiago had no intentions toward Ears, that he was devoted to his wife back in Albesanta, but it did not mean Teo was particularly comfortable with the man putting his hands on her hips or around her waist or anywhere else.

It was fortunate that Ears was delightfully quick at learning these skills, or Teo would have been in trouble. There could be no more lessons, not until he found control over his jealousy, and he had no notion of how long that would take.

The night before, after the fighting was done, he had held her for what felt like hours, reveling in the feel of her and the way she clung to him. The beauty in their closeness. The perfection in being together. They'd eventually left the alley and gone about their usual evening business, exploring the poor streets, and looking for any information about the famed Mr. Blaine young Amy had told Ears about in Teo's absence. They met with several of Ears's local contacts, none of whom struck Teo as being particularly trustworthy by appearances, but all of whom agreed to bring information to the pair of them the following night.

Which was tonight.

With Ears being so determined to discover as much as possible about the man as soon as possible, she had wanted to start the evening earlier than normal. It was no trouble for him. He had no calls upon his time or person, but the challenge lay with her and her ability to get out of her home without incident or discovery before the place was darkened with sleep.

Still, she had managed it well enough, and now, watching her fight with Santiago, Teo felt more and more impressed by her. He had not found the time to tell her yet, but he had discovered the article she had written after they had rescued Amy. He hadn't been quite sure at first, given the name of the author and some relevant specifics being left out, but once the story unfolded, he was quite certain Emmett Barnes was his sweet Ears. And she was a masterful writer.

The piece was evocative, powerful, cutting, and intelligent. It held enough description to bring reality into the story without being bogged down by the details. The conditions described would have harrowed any mind capable of imagining it, and any charitable souls with true hearts of goodness would have been struck by the tale the writer told. It was a captivating article, and Teo had no doubt more articles relating to the condition of the poor would be demanded.

If he moved about in any kind of society, he might have heard the article discussed, but his business meetings had no interest in the poor, and a sole interest in money. Or connections, profit, expansion, and opportunity.

He had met some cunning men of business, and some men he wished were in business, and other men he was particularly grateful to not be in business with. These meetings he now had Rafa in with him, as the official introductions had been made and impressions had been formed. And where Teo might not be up to asking difficult and pressing questions, Rafa always was.

If only Teo could manage to talk Ears into doing some investigating as to the secret dealings of his potential partners while doing her own work. He'd trust anything she brought to his attention, and he had no doubt the proof would be irrefutable.

A loud thump on the ground brought his attention around, and he was stunned to see Santiago flat on his back and Ears standing nearby, looking bewildered herself.

"*¿Estás bien, Santiago?*" Teo asked with minimal concern, more shocked than anything else.

162

"*Dáme un momento.*" Santiago raised a finger, breathing slowly.

Teo looked at Ears, who was gaping at him. "I am so sorry," she mouthed.

He had to grin at that. "I do not believe an apology is needed, *cariño*. I think you did exactly as you were told."

"Yes," Santiago coughed from his place on the ground. "*Muy bien.*"

"It doesn't feel *muy bien*," Orejitas grumbled, folding her arms. "I have a lot of guilt, as a matter of fact."

Santiago sat up, rubbing the back of his neck. "*La culpa?*" he asked.

"*Sí,*" Teo replied, by way of translation. "Guilt *es la culpa en Inglés.*"

"*No bueno,*" Santiago grunted as he heaved himself from the ground. He moved to *Orejitas* and took her hands, unfolding her arms to do so. "No guilt, *Orejas. Lo hiciste bien. Bien,* hmm?"

Reluctantly, *Orejitas* nodded, gripping his hands with her own. "*Bien, Santiago. Gracias.*"

Santiago smiled and patted her cheek, then turned to come to Teo. Brushing at his arms, he began muttering in Spanish. "That girl is one of a kind, Captain. You make something of her, or so help me, I will curse your family line until the end of time."

Teo cleared his throat, feeling the threat down to his bones. "Thank you, Santiago," he said in rapid Spanish. "You can go now."

His friend nodded, then turned to *Orejitas*. "*Buenas noches señorita.* Good night."

She beamed at the new phrase. "*Buenas noches.*"

With a wave for her and a glare for Teo, Santiago left them, muttering in Spanish still. Teo didn't catch most of it, but that was undoubtedly for his own good. He'd hate to have to mark Santiago down as insubordinate when he was doing him such a great favor.

Orejitas came over to Teo, smiling more than she had all night. "Do you feel better about my defenses now, *Capitán?*"

He placed his hands on her arms, smiling fondly. "I do. Don't you?"

"Marginally." She wrinkled her nose in an almost laugh and moved to pick up her jacket and cap from where they'd been set down. "We'd better hurry. I haven't got much time before I need to

meet Skips and Bert. Do you think they'll have found anything out
for us?"

"Who can say?" Teo replied as he gestured for her to lead the
way out of the alley. "If the man is protected, information could be
difficult. But if he is beating children, then Amy will not be the only
one to have felt it."

Orejitas frowned. "I wish I knew more children in the area to ask.
I am rarely about when they are, except for a few stragglers, and they
are usually hurrying home, so I don't get to speak with them."

Teo hesitated a moment, then said, "I may know how to find
one or two."

She jerked to look up at him in shock. "You do? How?"

"The night I met you, I met a young lad all alone. He was not
hurt, nor was he unwell, and we had a brief conversation. I believe I
may be able to meet him again. Possibly." He winced, wondering if it
might have been better not to speak of it at all.

"Truly?" *Orejitas* cried, gripping his arm. "Oh, love, that would
be marvelous! Imagine the other children he must know, and surely
they would speak to us after what happened to Amy."

"They may not," he told her, ignoring how his heart burst at the
endearment. "They might be more afraid and less willing. If he is a
danger, what happened to Amy could be something they all fear."

She hadn't considered that; he could tell by the way her
expression fell and how she bit her lip. But then her brow wrinkled,
and her eyes darted a little as she thought.

"What are you thinking?" he asked when she said nothing else.

Her eyes rose to his. "I think we have to try. But there's not
much time. Will you go try to meet him while I meet Skips and Bert?
Then we can both go see Flincher and Wash."

Teo nodded, feeling rather comfortable with the arrangement, as
the first two informants were fairly harmless, and the latter two were
the ones he mistrusted most. "*Sí, cariño.* Be careful."

She smiled a little. "How do you say it in Spanish?"

"*Ten cuidado,*" he rumbled, drawing closer to her.

Now her smile spread. "*Ten cuidado, cariño,*" she whispered.

Both of his knees buckled at her words. "*Santo cielo,*" he breathed,
feeling almost drugged by the sensation. "Do you know what you

said?"

"Be careful," she quipped with a wink. "And some kind of endearment I've probably got the tense incorrect on, but I think you'll accept it anyway, given you use it for me."

"I'll accept it," he insisted with a swallow. "*Gracias.*"

She rose on her toes and kissed his cheek, nuzzling against him for just a moment before darting off, giving him no chance to take her in his arms or kiss her senseless or even recall what his name was.

Santo cielo. He was a doomed man.

Swallowing once more against an arid throat, Teo found his knees in place and started in the opposite direction, wondering how he could possibly accomplish what he'd claimed and bring something useful to *Orejitas*. Still, an idea was worth something, wasn't it?

He whistled the short, piercing sound he'd heard Dan use the night he met him, then listened in silence as he walked. Nothing happened. That was promising.

Sighing with irritation at himself, he whistled again. This time, there was a whistle in return.

Teo stopped in his tracks, waiting. The area was right, if Dan kept to the same area, and the same time of night.

What was he thinking? Anyone could repeat a whistle. This was a dark area of London, and there was no telling what he was signaling with his whistle. He was not from the streets of London, and he had no connections he could call upon at a moment's notice. He could have just whistled for his own robbery. Or horribly violent death. Perhaps both.

"You called?"

Teo whirled on the spot, stunned to hear a deep voice rather than the impudent, young one of Dan. To his relief, the approaching figure, once the streetlight caught him, turned out to be none other than the Gent. He'd take that as an alternative.

"*Maldita sea,*" Teo said on a relieved exhale, rubbing at his chest.

Gent chuckled, inclining his head. "*Lo siento, compadre.* I take it you were not expecting me?"

Teo shook his head, still willing his heart to resume a more normal pace. "I was looking for your *muchacho* from the other night. Dan."

"He's around here somewhere." Gent leaned against the nearest building, apparently in no hurry to fetch the lad. "Why do you need Dan?"

"I am helping a friend," Teo hedged, folding his arms in what he hoped was a show of confidence. "We are looking for information."

"On?"

Teo pressed his tongue to his teeth, hesitating. He didn't mind Gent, nor did he think the man was a villain, but this was not his project, and the less people that knew about it, the better.

"Mendoza, if there is anybody who knows the London streets, it is me," Gent told him, the words impatient, the tone less so. "Tell me what your friend is looking for."

Praying he would not offend *Orejitas* by revealing anything, Teo uncrossed his arms and slid them into his trouser pockets. "You may have heard the story of young Amy, the new girl in your charge."

Gent straightened slowly, and while it had never occurred to Teo before how dangerous the man could possibly be, the coiled tension in the man's frame just then told him everything.

"How do you know about Amy?"

"I was one of the people to find her," Teo said simply, not bothering to elaborate further or to try for reassurance. If the man could not see that much about Teo, he was not nearly as insightful as he thought himself.

Gent frowned at that. "My contact told me it was Ears who found her."

"I was with Ears." Teo smiled flatly. "Suds would tell you so, if you asked."

"I believe you, don't worry," Gent told him with a wave, as though Teo had somehow risen from his position. "You're friends with Ears?"

Teo nodded, feeling proud at being able to admit that. "Yes. Have you met?"

Gent shook his head. "Haven't had the pleasure, though I've heard his name everywhere."

Hearing the pronoun Gent used, Teo felt right in keeping some of the information back from the man. "Amy told Ears a man named Mr. Blaine was the one who beat her. So Ears wishes to investigate him and see if there are other children who have received the same."

"Blaine, eh?" Gent glowered, his jaw tightening. "I've heard his name floated about as well, but nothing of significance. Give me five minutes, I'll have half a dozen children here for you. Take them to Ears, if you'd like. I'll see what I can discover about the blackguard as well. Don't worry, I'll see that Ears gets everything. If someone is beating children, even the riffraff will take offense."

He didn't wait for Teo to reply and strode off into the night as though it were his own mission to discover what he could about Mr. Blaine rather than the task someone else had taken up.

It was a trifle strange to be standing in the dark, dank London street alone without a purpose for himself. Waiting had never been one of his strong suits, particularly when there was something else he wanted to be doing. It was not difficult to imagine the sort of troubles *Orejitas* could be having on her own on a night like this, and knowing she was better prepared defensively, while helpful, did not exactly assuage his fears.

She had gotten through nights on the streets without him before, he reminded himself. Years of them. He did not even know the other investigations she had done before they had met, so there was no way of knowing how bad it could have been. But she had never suffered a major injury, at least as far as he knew, and she was not afraid, despite knowing what was out there.

He had to trust her, had to believe she could take care of herself no matter what happened. He knew that in his mind. He could tell himself the same things over and over, all logical and factual and true. It did not stop him from worrying, from fearing, from doubting. Not because he didn't trust or believe in her. Not because he thought she was weak or incapable.

But because he loved her. It was entirely emotional, hopelessly illogical, and completely nonsensical. Which meant there was no hope for it.

He'd accept that so long as she would. He could not turn into a nanny with a knife; he'd promised her from the first he would not. But neither could he let her go alone if he could help it. Two nights ago, he hadn't been able to get away. Not with the new associates he'd met and their desire to do business with him. There had been no way to get a message to her, so he'd had to hope she would be there the next night as well. He'd been fully prepared to offer an apology, but she hadn't asked for one.

And if their embrace that night had been anything to go by, she hadn't needed one. Was that a good thing or a bad?

A quick whistle met his ears, and he turned, eyes widening when he saw Gent with the promised half dozen plus one: a familiar little girl with dark curls.

Teo gaped at seeing her. "Amy?"

She broke free from the rest and ran for him, giving him no alternative but to scoop her up. She surprised him by hugging him tightly, searing his heart with the sweetness of the embrace.

"Mr. Gent told me you saved me," she said as she hugged him. "I couldn't remember, then I saw you, and I did! I remembered! Thank you for saving me."

Teo hugged her back, his throat closing briefly. "I am so glad you are well, Amy." He pulled back and smiled at her, taking the liberty of touching her hair, just as he'd done that night. "You had me very scared at first."

She nodded somberly. "Mr. Suds said I was lucky you found me when you did. Mr. Blaine beat me bad, and Janie says he did her too." She pointed to another girl, this one a little older and a little taller, but with the same expression of being aged beyond her years.

Teo felt something crack within him, looking at each of these children in turn, and wondered what they had suffered. He returned his attention to Gent, who did not seem surprised by what he saw in Teo's face.

"You wanted children," Gent told him softly. "These are a few who can tell you what you need to know."

"Will you all come with me to speak with my friend about Mr. Blaine?" Teo asked them. "I don't want any of you to be afraid. Ears and I want to help, not hurt, and Mr. Blaine should not be allowed to continue harming anyone."

"We ain't afeared, sir," one of the boys announced stubbornly. "Gent won' let a fing happen to us. Afore Gent, we might've been afeared o' Blaine an' the like, but no more. Down wif Blaine and his bleeding frog friends!"

Teo frowned at that, unsure of the meaning, but Gent stiffened, drawing his eyes.

Gent stooped just a little, putting a hand on the boy's shoulder. "Jack, does Mr. Blaine have foreign friends? Or are you just calling toffs frogs?"

"Naw, Gent, he keeps comp'ny with the French!" Jack announced without shame. "Always 'as done. Sometimes 'is French friends beat us, particularly if they's in a foul mood."

Why French associates ought to be significant was beyond Teo, but so long as no one was maligning the Spanish, he could accept it. Gent, on the other hand, straightened slowly, his face a careful mask.

"Mendoza," he said in a low voice, as though they were the only two in the street, "can I trust you to take the children to Ears on your own? I'll have an associate meet you here later to fetch them home." At Teo's quick nod, he turned to the little ones. "Children, you are not to go anywhere unless it is in the company of Mr. Mendoza, Ears, or Toby. Understood?" He looked around for confirmation from them all, his eyes falling on Amy. "You do exactly what the other children say, Amy. You don't know Toby yet, but they do. No one else, all right?"

"Yes, Gent," the children all replied in a chorus.

Gent nodded again, meeting eyes with Teo and exchanging some mantle of guardianship, which suddenly sunk deep into Teo's chest. The man turned and seemed to disappear into the night, leaving Teo to stare around at his new charges.

Orejitas was going to be stunned to see this many children, let alone to see Amy again, and she was going to curse someone or something when she discovered she had missed the opportunity to meet Gent at last.

"Well, shall we go see Ears, then?" he asked in what he hoped was a relatively cheery voice, though with these sorts of children, he suspected such niceties were unnecessary.

A few nodded while others shrugged, and Teo led them all down the streets, back the way he had come, Amy still snug in his arms.

He'd never given much thought to being a father, or anything remotely resembling parenthood, but it was impossible to keep the thought from his mind at this moment. A child in his arms and others

169

at his feet, leading them all through possible danger as their sole means of protection... Without knowing a single one of them, he'd have given his life to protect them, each and every one. Was that simple humanity, or was he feeling something significant?

He'd been a fine enough uncle in his life, as far as he could tell, to his sisters' children, and they all seemed fond of and attached to him. He'd always been told once he'd found the right partner in life, he would want a family and children with her. When he thought of things in that context, and with *Orejitas* as his partner...

If he let himself think it, he could imagine little Amy in his arms as their daughter, and he was simply out for an evening stroll with his girl. They'd be returning to her mother shortly, and he would get a gentle scolding for spoiling her too much, but all would be said with such love and pride. He would know such joy and love in seeing her, knowing the daughter in his arms was as adored by her mother as she was by him. No imagined future had ever been so sweet as that.

"How will we know Ears when we see 'im?" one of the children asked him.

"Like this," Teo quipped. He began whistling the tune of *Vado a combattere* from *Zoraida di Granata* just as *Orejitas* had done the night he'd truly met her.

The children giggled at the jaunty tune, then gasped in surprise when they heard it echoed back from ahead of them.

"Is that Miss E?" Amy whispered in Teo's ear. "Mr. Suds told me not to tell anyone about her, especially that she's a lady."

"Yes, *mi hija*," Teo replied with a smile as the beloved figure appeared around a corner. "That's her."

Orejitas froze as she saw the gathering of children, then stared at Teo in shock. "I thought you said one."

He grinned at her. "And you said there would be more. So, here are more."

Her smile was sweet, reminding him of his imagined scene and making him yearn for it fiercely. She glanced at the girl in his arms and gasped in delight. "Amy!"

Amy wriggled free from Teo's arms and darted to her, hugging her tightly around the waist. "Mr. Gent said we're going to talk about mean Mr. Blaine. All of us have sommat to say 'bout him."

"Gent?" *Orejitas* repeated, looking at Teo again. "They came from Gent?"

"I didn't know..." Teo began, not quite knowing how to finish the statement. He didn't know what? Didn't know Gent would be there? Didn't know Gent had so many children in his care? Didn't know his plan would actually work?

All of them were true, just as it was true seeing *Orejitas* with Amy again, seeing the tenderness between the two of them, told him everything he needed to know about the mother *Orejitas* would be one day. The mother of his children, he hoped.

She continued to watch him, clearly at a loss.

He cleared his throat. "We have them for as long as you need. Gent said we could return them to the street I've just come from and deliver them to an associate named Toby. They all know him." He moved over to her, taking her gently by the arm. "One of the boys said something about Frenchmen with Blaine to Gent, and he left straightaway. Seemed rather agitated and became very concerned about the safety of the children. This seems bigger than exploiting the poor, *cariño*."

She nodded, and he watched her throat work on a swallow. "Then we will be exceedingly careful and go someplace quiet and safe to have our discussion. After which, we will return our young friends to Mr. Toby and continue this investigation, no matter how big it gets."

"Are you sure?" he asked her gently, squeezing her arm.

She met his gaze squarely, her chin lifting. "Absolutely, *cariño*. Are you?"

As if he could be anything less than sure with her.

"*Absolutamente.*"

Chapter Seventeen

The very last thing Emmeline wanted to do after an exhausting night of interviewing and investigating was prepare for a ball. There wasn't anything to be done about it, as she had already sent her acceptance, and her aunt was beside herself in anticipation of the event.

Why, Emmeline couldn't be sure, given she had been to many, many balls and dances and parties over the years, and none of them stuck out in her mind as being particularly exciting.

Surely her aunt was not still thinking Emmeline might catch the eye of a particularly fine bachelor who begged for courtship. At the age of five and twenty, with several London Seasons behind her, Emmeline was hardly what eligible men were looking for in a wife. As there really was no other reason to go to balls and parties, given she did not enjoy dancing, the whole evening was destined to be pointless.

She would get home very late, or very early, depending on one's interpretation of the thing, and she would not be able to go out to see *Capitán* tonight.

That was the deepest cut of all.

Yes, she wanted to continue her investigation, which was capturing so much of her time and thoughts. Yes, she wanted to discover more about the darkness that even she had not anticipated discovering in London. Yes, she wanted to see that the sweet children they had met last night received justice for the neglect and brutality they had faced. But was it so selfish for her to want, most of all, to be with him?

It was more than she could bear, thinking of him and missing him when she could not do anything about it. Their anonymity was their safety, but it was also a marked detriment to their progress in this relationship of theirs. She was in love with him, and she was more than half convinced he was tending in that direction himself, yet they did not meet or connect in the light. Never by day, only by night. Could any sort of relationship truly be worth anything with such restraints?

He had been a godsend last evening, bringing those children for her to talk to and talking with them himself. He had gone with her to meet Flincher and Wash after they had seen the children safely returned to Toby, and his presence beside her with those two was a comfort. She had no concerns about her safety where they were concerned, but the information they gave her…

Mr. Blaine was an evil man, there was no doubt of it. His brutality toward children and women extended everywhere, and his finances were so tightly secured, he could not be ruined. How and why they were so, she had yet to discover, but *Capitán* said he would find out. It seemed he had been making new contacts in whatever business he worked in, and somehow, there would be information he could obtain through those contacts. Emmeline did not think to ask further questions, and simply trusted he would see it done.

There were brothels Blaine had been barred from, given his violent reputation, and there were several ladies whose injuries at his hand prevented them from continuing their work in such establishments. A few had been reduced to working on the streets themselves rather than in establishments, and there were fewer protections available to them in doing so.

As for Blaine himself, he left his home consistently once a day, always at the same time—just at dusk. He would walk down his street, turn left, continue toward the piers, stop off to visit some of those unfortunate women reduced to offering themselves for scraps, then he would visit one of the warehouses. His visits could last from twenty minutes to almost an hour, but so far, he had yet to exceed that hour. Then he returned home without a single stop.

Then there were the comings and goings from his own house. Men were continuously entering his house while others left, sometimes in the early morning hours, sometimes midday, and other times just before he took his nightly walk to the warehouse. No one had ever seen servants about, which could explain the state of the windows in his home, and yet with so many men entering and in some cases staying, one would have to assume there was at least a cook.

And one would hope he did not have any maids about.

Emmeline asked Wash to keep her informed as to the movements of the house and had asked Flincher to look further into the warehouse, but she did not expect to have more information from them. Neither seemed particularly keen on continuing to look.

Skips and Bert, on the other hand, had their own network of informants, and they had promised to continue their digging in whatever ways they could. If she knew Bert, that would mean talking with the prostitutes in detail, which would be useful in some ways but also occupy his own interests for far too long. Skips was more of a street man, keeping his band of pickpockets busy, selling information and trinkets to whomever they could. He did not blackmail Emmeline the way she knew he did others, but she suspected that was because she constantly paid him and paid him well. And because she was asking him to do what he already wanted to do. It was a convenience for them both.

It had been all she could do to get as much information down as possible when she returned home, and still her mind swam with it. Her dreams had been of her endlessly scouring the darkest parts of London for answers, and while no danger had specifically come to her in her dreams, the threat of it was always there. She had not dreamed of her excursions for years.

Emmeline blinked, sitting at the writing desk in her parlor, and tried to recall what her thoughts had been prior to her exhausted distraction. She had been recording additional details in her diary, just as she always did after an eventful night, and her mind had wandered of its own accord. What had she even been writing?

She glanced down at the diary, frowning a little. Her coherent thought and clean hand had changed to a wandering hand of indistinguishable whirls and swoops, effectively making whatever she thought she had been writing irrelevant. She could only hope it truly had been.

Closing her diary, Emmeline put her face in her hands, sighing heavily. Sleep had not been kind to her, and though she had been awake now for several hours, she did not feel in any way improved.

She pressed her fingers into her brow, trying desperately to soothe away the ache that was pounding there. If only she could avoid the ball entirely, claim to being ill, and retire early with a cup of warm milk. That would surely set her to rights. But she had made the argument at breakfast, and she had made the argument at luncheon, and her aunt was having none of it.

According to Aunt Hermione, Emmeline had been well enough yesterday without any aggravating activities that would have made her unwell so there was no need for her to miss the ball. She had gone so far as to suggest a cup of tea and a bit of smelling salts. Emmeline had conceded to the tea, but utterly refused the smelling salts. She wished to improve her headache, not enhance it.

But one could only make so many cups of tea before it became redundant, and sitting here beside her fourth serving, Emmeline was certain she had taken in all of the restorative properties tea had to offer her. And if the clock on the mantle was any indication, she truly needed to go and get ready for the ball.

"Emmeline!" her aunt's voice bellowed from somewhere in the house, nearly shrill now. "I will *not* be late for Mrs. Halsey's ball. Do cease your scribbling and come ready yourself!"

There was nothing to do but faintly groan at being screeched at, particularly when Emmeline was fully aware of the time and had a ghastly headache that would not abate, but it was her aunt's house, and if she wished to screech in it…

She rose from her chair, folding her shawl around her as though it could somehow ward off her aunt's demands, and left the parlor. She caught sight of her aunt's maid hurrying up the stairs, no doubt to set her aunt's hair, and felt a pang of sympathy for her. Every ball was exciting for Aunt Hermione, though she was long past being concerned about marriage for herself or her daughters, and she did not dance. But all had to be perfect for a ball, as much for herself as for any young ladies in her charge, which meant Emmeline would also be expected to be perfect, which meant she would be fully inspected before they could leave.

No orange gowns would be acceptable this evening. Not that she wished to wear one. If she knew her aunt, the gown she would wear to the ball had already been selected, pressed, and laid out for her. It would suit her, she had no doubt, and she would look well enough.

When it came to her hair, however…

"Oh, good, you heard me," her aunt said on a dramatic sigh as Emmeline passed her room.

"I believe they heard you in Whitehall, Aunt," Emmeline replied with a tight smile, pausing to look in.

Aunt Hermione's eyes narrowed. "If you are well enough to banter, you are well enough to go."

Blast. She hadn't suspected a trick in her aunt's actions. Why had she not been sullen, drawn, and listless?

"I will go get changed," Emmeline grumbled, turning to go.

"Please don't be downcast," her aunt begged, losing the crisp edge in her voice. "You leave for Kent tomorrow, and I don't wish us to part poorly."

Emmeline froze, her body going cold. "I what?" she half whispered.

"Let us enjoy our evening together," her aunt pleaded from behind her, "before you return to school. I know it is just a week you spend there, but I do so enjoy your company, even when you vex me."

Her words could barely be heard over the sound of Emmeline's own thoughts whirling in her sluggish mind. She flipped the pages of an imaginary calendar, dates and events flying this way and that as she tried to recollect the schedule she had adhered to for months now. Surely she hadn't forgotten her teaching. Surely she had more time.

But, of course, her aunt was correct. She would be leaving on the morrow, shortly after breakfast, making the journey out to Kent. She would remain for a week, perhaps a day more, then return after seeing to the work of her students and setting the next lessons for them. It was the way things had been for years, and the way they would undoubtedly continue.

She had simply forgotten.

In all her time spent with *Capitán*, she had forgotten she would leave, that they would be parted for a time, incapable of communicating at all for a week.

How could a man who had only been in her life a month—even less than that—become so crucial to her life, previous duties and responsibilities became inconsequential? How could she love a man so soon and yet with such depth? How could her life have altered so suddenly without her noticing?

She left in the morning. How was she going to tell him? How could she get word to him?

Suds. She could send a note to Suds when they returned from the ball, and he could find him. He could see that *Capitán* knew she had not abandoned him, given up, run away, or been in any kind of danger. There was no telling what he might imagine when she failed to arrive night after night, but she could not bear to think he might imagine her indifferent.

That would be worse than danger. She was anything but indifferent.

"Emmeline?"

She turned slowly, belatedly reminding her lips to smile at her aunt, who had unknowingly made her evening far worse yet given her time to remedy it. "I will not be downcast, Aunt," she forced herself to say. "No more than usual, at any rate. You know how I feel about balls and dancing."

Aunt Hermione smiled, apparently believing her attempt. "I do, dear. But there is to be a marvelous supper, you know. Mrs. Halsey does not scrimp on such things. And Mrs. Foster has promised to attend, so perhaps we may continue our conversation about the poor. I know you are taking an interest there. Will that not make the evening more appealing to you?"

On a usual evening, yes. At a typical ball, yes. Had she not fallen in love with a man she desperately needed to see right away, yes.

But this ball? On this night? Having fallen in love with a man she needed to see before she left in the morning?

No. No, it would not.

"Yes, Aunt," Emmeline lied with a kind smile, even as her chest began to tighten with anxiety, fear, and anticipation. "I think it might."

Without waiting to see if her answer placated her aunt,

Emmeline turned once more and hurried to her room. There was no time now, and she could not imagine she would manage to slip away from the Halseys, let alone from their home. Mrs. Halsey had a keen interest in Emmeline helping her daughter with her penmanship—the girl was hopeless, but her mother was undeterred—and if Emmeline was unoccupied for any length of time...

She could suffer an accident at the ball. Punch spilled all the time so it would be easy enough to manage. And if she managed to spill punch on the right portion of her skirts, it should not leave them permanently stained. If her aunt had selected something heavily embroidered, it might make things difficult, but certainly not impossible. But the spill would have to be obvious enough no one would question her needing to leave. And she needed to be clumsy enough no one would be surprised.

Emmeline might not be naturally graceful, but she certainly was not clumsy. Still, she would see that an opportunity presented itself. That would have to do. It was the only way to feasibly escape the evening and get to *Capitán*. Or get a note to Suds to meet him. Or do anything. She would take anything at this point.

Once in her rooms, she stripped her day dress off and tugged the pins from her hair. She would only have a few minutes before one of the maids would come in to assist her, and if she wanted any hope of accomplishing something tonight, she needed access to storage. She tugged off her chemise and moved to the bureau for a fresh one, something cut a little better for a ball gown and a little more convenient for her. One must never underestimate the convenience of ladies' pockets.

Just as she'd gotten the new chemise on and tugged into proper place, her maid Bess entered the room, calm as ever, with curling tongs in her hand. "Good evening, miss. Have you seen the gown your aunt selected for you?"

Emmeline turned to the bed, glancing at the gown for the first time. "I hadn't noticed, but it seems lovely."

"Oh, it will be quite fashionable, Miss Bartlett." She set the curling tongs down and moved to the bed herself, picking up the gown and giving it the slightest shake. "White silk and gauze, miss. And Indian-blue silk flowers on the shoulders and hem. And here?

These white and blue silk folds on your bodice will be exquisite. I've some pearl hair pins and small flowers to set in your hair, if you find that agreeable."

Bess was clearly an admirer of fashion, and the prospect of going to a ball dressed in such finery would have been a dream for her. In her attempts to write about the poor, she mustn't forget those who were servants. They had gainful employment, but things such as balls, which Emmeline detested, would have been unimaginable for them. Proper perspective was everything.

"Whatever you think would suit, Bess," Emmeline told her, smiling as she raised her arms to have the gown placed. "I have no doubt you will make me as beautiful as lies within your power."

"I will do my best, miss, though I believe you are more than halfway there naturally. And with this gown alone."

Emmeline smiled to herself at the compliments, both of herself and of the gown, and, for a moment, forgot about her panic and her distress. But only for a moment.

When she had been trussed up enough to pass her aunt's inspection, Emmeline was rambling up the streets of London in the coach, her eyes scanning every possible corner and person to see if her beloved *Capitán* might have wandered further than his usual routes. But of course, it could not be that simple, and before long, they were at the Halsey home without a single sign of him.

She would have to go ahead with one of the other plans, then. Simple enough.

She glanced down at her gown, frowning. With the gauze layer over silk, it would be difficult to manage a decent stain that would not actually ruin the garment. She wanted to escape, yes, but she did not wish to permanently ruin the beautiful garment.

Opportunity would have to knock and let her know what it wanted.

Mr. and Mrs. Halsey were effusive in their greetings, of course, and Tom Halsey, their son, pretended to be interested in what Emmeline said, likely at his mother's prodding. He must have been told it was time to secure a wife, and no young lady was to be ignored, not even a spinster like Emmeline.

Once she and her aunt had entered the ballroom, however,

everything settled into the familiar rhythm of Society events, and she found herself in safer territory—in a manner of speaking.

She would not be permitted to sit for at least an hour, giving time for the old ladies to do so and for dancing to begin. It was not fashionable for a young woman to sit unless it was clear she would not be asked for a dance. Until that time, Emmeline would have to remain standing and attempt to look remotely interested in the events surrounding her. Aunt Hermione, however, could sit whenever she liked. Surprisingly, she came and stood at Emmeline's side.

"Thankfully, the event is not a crush. I would have thought Mrs. Halsey desperate for Tom to marry anyone, yet I only see half of the eligible young ladies here. Curious."

"If they are that desperate, why invite me?" Emmeline wondered aloud. "Surely I am no candidate for the puppy."

Aunt Hermione coughed a delicate laugh. "One would hope not, dear, but all connections are worth something or other, and Mrs. Halsey would not dare slight you when she so desperately needs you to help her daughter grow legible."

"I doubt even I have the skills for that," Emmeline mumbled, shaking her head. She looked at her aunt curiously. "Why are you not sitting? Surely you don't mean to stand with me the whole of the evening."

"Of course not," her aunt huffed. "I will stand with you a few moments, then find a seat. Solidarity, my dear."

Emmeline hummed in amusement. "Thank you, I believe."

Her aunt gave a prim nod in response, keeping her gaze wandering freely about the room. "A pity. There does not appear to be punch set out."

If anything was going to make Emmeline sour further that night, surely such a statement was it.

"Of course not," she muttered to herself, scratching that potential plan off her imagined list. "So, who do the gossips say is the catch of the Season, hmm? Should I make a play for him?"

"You would only be so fortunate," her aunt shot back without sympathy. "Mr. Mortimer is apparently redeeming himself in his exile, but despite the rumors of his return, I cannot think so. The scandal was so widely known."

"Indeed," Emmeline murmured, not particularly listening.

"Mr. Robinson would make a good catch, particularly as his uncle is poorly," Aunt Hermione continued, despite Emmeline's lack of interest. "The Earl of Rausten has a lovely ring to it for a young man, don't you agree?"

Emmeline only shrugged. "Perhaps."

Undeterred, her aunt continued to rattle on, not even pausing to sit a few minutes later as she had claimed she would. But the constant speech did have an odd way of setting Emmeline at ease when everything else within her seemed in turmoil.

How was she going to get through this night? Standing here for hours when she had far better things to do was maddening beyond belief. Her aunt was not one to retire early from a Society function, and Emmeline would not be able to get away herself. She would have to settle for sending the note to Suds as she'd originally thought, though it was the least satisfying option.

Without speaking to *Capitán* herself, she would not have the satisfaction of seeing his reaction, hearing his voice, feeling his touch. She would simply have to trust her feelings were in some way reciprocated. Trust in him more than she ever had, somehow.

And she was not very good at trusting so.

"Oh, bless them, they've invited Lucy Allred. Doesn't she look well? Poor thing, it would be lovely for her to make an advantageous match."

Emmeline nodded absently, desperate to find some better feeling than despair filling her chest.

"Mrs. Kirby, Miss Bartlett, I had hoped I would see you both this evening!"

The voice was familiar, but in her present haze, Emmeline could not place it. Still, she turned toward the sound with trained obedience, her eyes absently on the dance.

"Mrs. Foster! We were just saying the same of you as we came in," Aunt Hermione gushed, her fan moving rapidly enough that Emmeline felt the breeze of it.

"Marvelous article from Mr. Barnes, don't you think? Exactly what was needed, and I cannot wait to see what he does next. We should meet soon to discuss our plans," Mrs. Foster said earnestly, her words nearly as rushed as her thoughts must have been. "But I do forget myself. I spoke to you, Mrs. Kirby, about our new friend, the Spanish baronet."

The word Spanish lit into Emmeline's ear like fire, and she found herself looking at Mrs. Foster with more interest.

"Indeed, yes," Aunt Hermione was saying, nodding eagerly. "I wondered if he might attend tonight. Do you think he will?"

Mrs. Foster smiled widely, creating deep dimples in her cheeks. "I think he has, Mrs. Kirby." She turned and waved a little. "Let me just fetch him over, he is so attentive to us all. And dear Señor Teixidor, of course, will not leave our Mary's side. We expect an engagement any day, and perhaps I might make that introduction on a more intimate occasion. He does not enjoy social gatherings. Ah, here is Sir Teodoro now."

Emmeline's eyes darted to where she indicated, and her heart stopped dead in her chest at the sight of the man walking toward them.

Capitán.

He was dressed in perfectly elegant attire, his dark hair perfectly in place, though a trifle longer than the current fashion. He was perfectly handsome, perfectly smiling, and perfectly *there*. He saw her then, and his smile faded into outright gaping, his eyes widening as he slowed a step.

Her eyes filled with tears she could not help, her throat clenching and unclenching the way her fingers might have done.

"Sir Teodoro de Vickers y Mendoza," Mrs. Foster intoned through some strange fog, "might I present my friends? Mrs. Kirby, and her niece, Emmeline Bartlett."

Emmeline was beyond words, beyond feeling, beyond existence as she stared at his glorious form before her, and his eyes looked nowhere else but her.

"Charmed," he murmured, his voice as familiar and warm as her own skin. He bowed, his eyes steady on Emmeline, speeches and heavenly choruses and poetry filling their depths.

It was all she could do to curtsey, and even that was far less than steady. Her lips moved in some formation of a word, though the word itself was lost on her.

He extended his gloved hand, palm up, fingers shaking ever so slightly. "Miss Bartlett, do you waltz?"

"Yes," she breathed, taking his hand and moving with him before she had finished saying so.

Her aunt and Mrs. Foster said something behind her, but she heard nothing of it. She heard nothing but the sound of her own heart and breath, racing and pounding through her ears.

He was here, and she was here, both in their natural place and station, and yet…

"*Santo cielos,*" he breathed beside her, his hand clenching hers almost painfully. "Of all the women to see…"

"I cannot breathe," Emmeline interrupted, gasping through her unshed tears. "I cannot think. I—You… you're a baronet?"

"*Sí, cariño,*" he replied, his delicious accent sending a shudder through her chest. Or perhaps that was the hand he set at her waist as they assumed position for the waltz. Or perhaps it was his eyes on her, the closeness of their bodies, the brilliant light by which they could see one another.

Perhaps it was just him.

"Your name, *cariño,*" he murmured as they began to move to the music. "Say it again."

Emmeline was entirely unaware of her body's movements, of the steps she took, of the motions of the dance. She could only feel his hand on her, the heat of his arm, the pounding of his heart.

"My name is Emmeline," she told him, the simple introduction feeling more like a confession of love than anything else. "And you?"

"Teodoro," he whispered. "Teo."

His name echoed through her body, as though carrying light with it, and she pulled herself closer to him, unable to resist. "Teo," she repeated.

She felt the groan rise up within him and felt the headiness of it in herself. "My name from your lips is the sweetest sound, *cariño.* By what providence are we dancing together now?"

"I don't know," she murmured, blinking away her tears and swallowing hard. "I did not even dare to pray for this. But I…" She bit her lip, shaking her head. "I feel as though I am dancing in the heavens and not on earth at all."

"I thought you were beautiful by the light of the moon," he told her, nothing but adoration in his expression, "but *mi querida*, nothing compares to this."

Emmeline felt herself smile, albeit dreamily, the tears not quite gone. "English again. You spoil me, *Capitán*."

His smile could have rivaled the glory of the sun. "Teo, *mi querida*. Now we have no secrets."

"I don't want secrets anymore," Emmeline insisted. "Not from you."

He shook his head, his breathing not quite steady. "*Te adoro, mi amor. Soy todo tuyo. Eternamente tuyo.*"

"Frightened, Teo?" she murmured, even as shivers of delight raced up her spine.

"No, Emmeline," he told her, the sound of her name music to her own ears. "Overcome. Entirely."

Oh, this was madness, and she was going to expire where she stood. "I must see you," she whispered in a raw, almost hoarse tone. "Away from this. I must see you alone, as we always are."

"*Lo sé amada*," he replied, his voice a caress when his hands could not be. "Can you find your way to the garden? When the dance is completed, can we meet there?"

"Yes." She nodded emphatically. "I will find a way. But I have never been in there. I do not know the grounds or where—"

"We have found each other in more difficult settings," Teo overrode gently, his smile curving crookedly in a way that numbed her left leg. "I will find you."

Emmeline could barely nod, barely think, let alone reply. It was astonishing she had not caught fire in his arms, so alight was she. So flickering. So feverish. So overcome, as he'd said. And so wild to be away from this crowd and this place, from Society and from politeness, from everything keeping them apart, despite being so maddeningly close at this moment.

Lord, would this dance never end?

Minutes, which felt like the length of hours, passed, and the dance finally ended. Teo returned Emmeline to her aunt with a kiss to her hand, and if that did not set her aflame...

"Charming fellow, from appearances," her aunt mused when

Teo had gone. "Was he an amiable partner?"

"Forgive me, Aunt," Emmeline burst out, her breath rushing with painful weight. "I must take some air, please, excuse me." She turned and made her way to the garden doors, barely restraining herself from running headlong toward them.

Almost... almost...

The night air was cool and fresh, but she barely noticed as she took the stone path into the darkness. Away from the windows, away from the doors, away from any onlookers, and as close to the darkness as possible.

They would find each other, he'd said. But how? And when?

The whistling of a tune stopped her, and she whirled, beaming at the night itself. She whistled in return, matching the tune, her tears returning with a vengeance she had never known, her heart aching with each pound against her ribs.

Then he was there, rounding the tall hedge and striding toward her with a smile she would carry with her until her dying day. With a rush of emotion that caught a sigh, a sob, and a groan all at once, Emmeline ran to him without hesitation, unable to find even a modicum of restraint.

He caught her in his arms, and his lips found hers in an instant. She folded her arms about his neck, her fingers clawing into his hair as though they had done so dozens of times, her lips opening to his kiss and desperate for every pass of his mouth over hers. He devoured her with a fervent intensity, over and over again, searing her soul and stealing the breath from her lungs. She had never been so consumed by only feeling, so captivated by sensations, so restless in her own being, and every taste of him drove her wild for more.

He cupped her face with one hand, his fingers gripping against her hair and scorching the skin beneath. He kissed her with the same beautiful passion she'd seen in him from the very first moment, and without reservation. Though this was their first time, though it was *her* first time, this was natural and easy, familiar and comfortable, yet she felt dragged against hot coals in the most delicious manner. She could not recall where she ended and he began, could not find the ground beneath her feet, could not imagine...

She was dying here in his arms, among his kisses, and yet she felt as though she had never lived.

His lips moved from hers, nipping and dusting along her cheek, at her ear, along her jaw. Heated caresses that breathed new life into her once-aching heart. Emmeline cradled his head against her, wishing she had words to beg him to continue, to thank him for this, to wish aloud for the night to never end, to know how to share with him what he was sharing with her.

But she was a novice, and so he must lead. And how delightfully did he lead!

Through the frantic sounds of her own breath, she heard him speak, whispering against her skin as he layered her throat with kisses. Rambling sweet sounds of Spanish, which sank deep within her, despite having no translation. She knew what he said, what he felt, what he meant. She knew the sounds of his adoration and felt the preciousness of the moment down to her core.

Should the dawn ever come, she would not recognize it. Or herself. Not anymore.

Teo stilled against her, his mouth at the juncture of her neck and her shoulder. His breathing was unsteady, hers all-out panting, and her fingers in his hair had turned to gentle caresses. The frenzy was ending, fading into a contented beauty only the quiet could illuminate.

All she could do was slowly, shakily, almost silently sigh.

"*Te amo, querida,*" he whispered, pressing his lips against her neck before drawing back up and kissing her lips slowly, lingering with a tenderness that shook her knees.

"I know," she replied as she slid her hands to cup his jaw, her fingers brushing the skin gently through her gloves.

He grinned, nudging his nose along hers. "How can you know, *querida*? You have no Spanish."

"I have some Latin and Italian," she assured him with a brush of her lips at his chin. "And surely the word for love could not be so different between the three languages."

"You know," he murmured, shaking his head in disbelief. He captured her lips again, humming a little as he did so. "Of course you know, beloved Emmeline. Divine Emmeline. Brilliant, bold, *perfecta* Emmeline."

She all but whimpered, her palms stroking his jaw and reaching for his hair once more. "Gads, it sounds so good to hear my name." She huffed at not feeling his skin on her bare hands, and paused to strip her gloves from her hands, tossing them behind him. "What I wouldn't give to be in our usual place right now."

He bit the tip of one of his own gloves, tugging it off easily before returning his hand to her face, making her sigh with the loveliness of its touch. "Not I, *querida*. I want to be nowhere else but here with you."

Emmeline rested her brow at his chin, smiling as he brushed kisses against her. "Oh, Teo, I was desperate to somehow get to you tonight, and I was terrified it wouldn't happen. I'm leaving tomorrow, I'll be gone for a week. I didn't want you to think... I was afraid that..."

"*Callada, amor,*" he said gently, his thumb sliding over to touch her lips. "I'd have waited every night for you until you returned and held you closer when you did." He touched his mouth to her brow, his arms gently folding about her in a comfortable embrace. "Where are you going?"

"I teach at a school in Kent for a week every month," she admitted as she ran her fingers along the back of his neck, the confessions falling from her lips now, unable to bear the secrets any longer. "I teach writing and penmanship and rhetoric. My aunt wouldn't let me teach all the time when I started, since I must be a fine lady—"

"I find you to be a very fine lady indeed," Teo praised with a soft laugh.

Emmeline snickered softly, gripping his neck briefly in appreciation. "But I really must go. I cannot stay, not even for you."

"I thank you for wanting to," he told her, the friction of his lips against her brow tightening something in the soles of her feet. "But this may be opportune. I have yet to see the estate I inherited from my grandfather in the Midlands. If you will not be in London, I might as well not be in London. Perhaps I should go to the estate and see what I think."

She pulled back, looking up at him and searching his eyes for a moment. "You aren't sure about it?"

"I am not sure of anything, *mi amor*, except you." He touched his brow to hers, holding her close. "But now we know each other by name, so I may write to you. Tell you all about myself, if you wish. Continue to be with you, in a way."

"Yes, please," Emmeline begged, nodding against him. "I will write to you as well. Every day, likely multiple times. I cannot bear to be parted from you, Teo. Particularly now—"

He kissed her softly, silencing her words. "It is enough, *mi amor*. One week, and we will be together once more. I will hold you to my heart until you cannot forget the sound of it."

"Can you not do so now?" she whispered, running locks of his dark hair through her fingers.

"*Cielos*, Emmeline." Teo laughed a little, nuzzling against her cheek. "You will make me insane. But we will be missed soon and must get back. Unless you wish to be a scandal?"

Emmeline frowned, groaning a little. "I wouldn't mind it, but I could not shame my aunt."

"Nor I." With a steadying breath, Teo stepped back just far enough to take Emmeline's hands and no more. "Let us set ourselves to rights, then return. But before we do, let me make one thing perfectly clear."

She tilted her head curiously. "Yes?"

"I love you," he said firmly. "Emmeline Bartlett, my sweet *Orejitas*, I love you."

Emmeline clamped down on her lips hard, her lungs shaking with the desire to sob in relief, in delight, in any number of feelings. "I love you, Teo Vickers Mendoza. Or however you say your full name."

Teo tossed his head back on a laugh and drew her to him for a sweet embrace. "I'll teach you, *amor*. If you will dance with me again this evening, I'll teach you all I can."

"I'll always dance with you, love. Always."

Chapter Eighteen

Lincolnshire was, without a doubt, the most beautiful piece of land Teo had ever seen. Lush, rolling hills of green, coastlines that rivaled his favorite places in Catalonia, and a wildness that excited one's soul and lifted the spirits. It was both impressive and simple, natural and cultivated, familiar and foreign, all from just his first glimpse. It was as if he had come home. And now he had been here two full days, he was only surer of it.

Diehle House was an immaculate place, stirring in its majesty, yet easy in its nature. Neither ostentatious, nor simple, free from creeping vines, yet overwhelmed with wildflowers, and from the moment he'd entered its doors, he'd found hints of the family heritage he had never known.

Portraits hung on every wall, not just in the gallery, and there was little guidance to their identities. But he could see the resemblance to his father and, at times, to himself. It was a strange thing, feeling as though one belonged, yet did not. The place held a heaviness within its walls that spoke of misery and strife, of memories long held, of secrets never revealed. He half expected to see his grandfather descend the stairs one morning after breakfast, if not encounter his ghost in the orangery.

The first day, he had explored the house from top to bottom. Only a cursory exploration to familiarize himself with the place rather than to learn its history. The in-depth discoveries would come as he spent more time in the place, which might not occur on a one-week venture. Particularly not his first one. He might explore his grandfather's study, if not his room, but perhaps not the family attics.

The place had minimal servants, which was not surprising after all these years, and none of them required his presence in any way, shape, or form. They all performed their tasks simply to keep Diehle House functional, if not running smoothly. His appearance the other day did not surprise them, nor did it disrupt them, unless he was to consider his meals in the dining room or the footman who had become his valet for the time being.

There was no place for him in the running of the house, he had realized, and there was a strange comfort in that. Sir Teo did not make Diehle House what it was. That was one less thing for him to worry about.

Yesterday, he met with the estate agent, who had been delighted to see Teo, and he had taken him across every inch of the estate grounds. He'd met any available tenants, examined their farms, listened to their concerns about the lands and the crops and the harvest in the distant future. He'd learned about the nearest village of Kirton, the significant members of local society, the history of the region, and the troubles the area had faced.

His head swam with all of the information, but he had also felt exhilarated by it. Rather like he did with his shipping company.

He felt called to it, called by it, and, more than that, equal to it. Which was not to say he would ultimately succeed in it, that it—or he—was incapable of failure, but he felt that he could at least do some good. That he was not wasting his time here. That he just might find his place here, as he had done with the shipping company. The only question he had was if he would do it.

And Rafa was not helping him there.

They were sitting in his grandfather's study, left unchanged since the day his grandfather died. Rafa sat in a chair beside the desk, poring over business ledgers the estate agent had left for them. It was apparently very interesting, as Rafa traced the words with a finger, flipping back and forth between pages, nodding to himself.

"Something interesting, *amigo?*" Teo asked from his seat behind the desk.

"I could ask you the same," Rafa replied in careful, practiced English. "You have been staring."

Teo frowned at the accusation, feeling a little surly. "What do you make of this place?"

"Ah." Rafa closed the ledger, turning in the chair to face him. "You think I will disapprove?"

Teo switched to Spanish, finding rambling in his native tongue easier than his adopted one. "You haven't been fond of the idea of my taking on the English position I've inherited, and I haven't been sure of it myself. I've grown fonder of England than I ever imagined before I arrived, and now that I am here…" He shook his head, shrugging a little. "I don't want to leave, Rafa. I adore Spain, it will always be home, but here—"

"You don't have to do what I say or approve of, Teo," Rafa interrupted brusquely. "I am not your parent, nor am I any kind of authority."

"But you are someone who I respect," Teo pointed out with a serious look. "I take your opinion into consideration."

Rafa snorted softly. "That is your fault, not mine."

Teo groaned, leaning his head back on his chair, his friend's surly nature not helping the issue he was facing. As per usual, his thoughts turned to Emmeline, to their last night together and the tender passion they had shared. He had told Rafa all about her on their travels to Lincolnshire, and Rafa had reacted with surprise, then with teasing, and then, surprisingly, with understanding.

When he thought about taking up life in Diehle House, he could only imagine truly doing so with Emmeline by his side. With her being the lady of the house. Working with him. Bettering life with him and for him.

He'd received another letter from her this morning, just as he had every day since they'd parted. Somehow, she'd managed to have a letter waiting for him at Diehle House when he'd arrived. He had devoured every word of it, longing for the touch of her hand or the whisper of her lips.

It had been a beautiful introduction of herself, the details they hadn't yet shared but which created the fullness of the picture he held in his mind of her. Even in her letters, her command of language was astonishing and her descriptions vivid. She was witty, she was clever, she was impossibly sweet.

He missed her more through her letters than he'd ever thought he could miss another living soul.

The letter he'd read this morning had spoken of her life at the school in Kent. The students she taught, her fellow instructors, the strangeness in living so apart from London when so much of her life was centered there. She told him how she claimed to everyone there that her aunt was ill to explain why she must leave, though she wondered if the teachers might actually understand her nighttime excursions more than she'd previously thought.

I hadn't thought anyone would understand my love of exploring by night, Teo, until I met you, she'd written. *I sought adventure in the only means available to me, and in doing so, I found the greatest adventure I could have known. I had given up on ever finding love, let alone finding understanding, and yet I find both in you.*

I have never felt less alone in my life, my love, even though we presently are apart. I carry your love with me daily. I pray you might do the same with mine.

He'd been without words and breath so long after finishing her letter, he'd wondered if he might have suffered some sudden illness. But no, all had returned to him shortly following. It was only love he suffered from, not illness, proving there could indeed be joy in suffering.

"Emmeline has changed everything for me, Rafa," Teo admitted aloud with raw honesty, his throat nearly closing on the words. "Everything."

"That is no secret. Before I even knew about her, I could see that." Rafa shook his head, a small smile on his own lips.

Rafa did not smile, usually, and Teo stared at him with wide eyes. "And I may safely say Mary Foster has done the same for you."

"Undoubtedly," Rafa replied easily. "She is loveliness itself. I did not know a woman like her could exist in the world, let alone that she did exist. Her beauty is incomparable, her sweetness is pure, her goodness… I feel human when I am with her, and more than that, I feel worth something. I've never felt less than that, but the impact of being in her presence is something I cannot shake. And I don't want to."

"So you will marry her," Teo said without hesitation and without question.

Rafa's smile spread. "Perhaps. Her uncle is pleased to have me away for a week, not because he disapproves, but because it will tell us all what the truth of our feelings are. Wise fellow, Mr. Foster."

"The truth of our feelings," Teo repeated, more to himself than anything else. "Yes, perhaps that's it."

"Did you finish your letter to her this morning?" Rafa asked with a would-be innocent air. "Don't deny it, I know you've been writing to each other daily."

"I did," Teo shot back. "And it was an excellent letter. Did you finish yours to Mary?"

Rafa's mouth curved slightly. "My Maria," his said pointedly, using the Spanish version of her name, "has several letters from me, and she will open one each day until I return. Unless I am feeling the need to add something more, I will not write while I am here. Anymore."

"My heavens," Teo murmured, stunned into near silence. "You're a romantic."

His friend scowled. "I am not."

"You are!" Teo laughed, looking up at the ceiling of his grandfather's study in delight. "Rafa Teixidor is a romantic. The world will never know another wonder. You wrote Mary a separate letter for every day you will be gone so she might be reminded of you. And you've sent at least one letter, I saw it being sent when we arrived. I never thought I would say such a thing, but you are a fine appreciator of romance."

"I simply wish to make her happy," Rafa grumbled, shifting in his chair to look away from Teo. "She has a particular way of smiling when she is pleased, which is rather fetching. I like to imagine she is smiling that smile when she reads them."

"Romantic," Teo quipped with another laugh. "Embrace it, my friend. Your Maria will love it."

True to his nature, Rafa grumbled incoherently to himself, likely using some foul words. Teo didn't mind. It was good to have the familiar banter with his friend once more and to see he was as moved by a woman as Teo was. Perhaps that was the great wonder of the world.

"But as for your question about your estate," Rafa announced from his seat, no longer sounding quite so surly, "I think it is a fine place. Plenty of promise. Close enough to the coast that you could open an office for us there. I think this place suits you, Teo. As your grandfather always said, land is safe, shipping is risky. Why else do you think he spent so much time cultivating his estate when he was not with us at the shipyards?"

That was true, and Teo had not forgotten the lesson from all those years ago. His uncles had decided to divide their father's interests among themselves, and it had worked very well. Don Rodrigo managed the estate as the current Duke of Albesanta, while Uncle Jorge had been the owner of the shipping company. He still owned several shares but had decided to enjoy retirement from the business itself. Would it offend either of them if Teo stepped back from the company himself?

He did not want to abandon it, as he still loved the work and the thrill of being at sea, but neither did he wish to abandon this estate and the people. Though he had not been here long, he did feel drawn in, fond of the place, and attached to the people. There was a sense of responsibility he could not shake off, and he felt he owed it to his father to try and make this place what it could have been, had he inherited it.

What he would not give to have a word with his English grandfather about what happened between the two of them. To hear his reasons for forbidding the match. To understand how such drastic steps came to be taken. And who had made them first.

Teo frowned up at the ceiling, his eyes focusing on the painting there. It was an unusual work of artistry, some sort of battle on the sea being portrayed, yet the men were in small boats, separate from the frigates in the distance. He turned his head to examine the next panel, which showed the coast and the boats being dragged in, as well as some caves. But the panel did not complete itself, as the wall was there, and that did not make sense.

Why would the artist choose to do a part of a painting that did not properly resolve? He examined the other panels, but everything followed the same pattern, flowing toward the wall without resolution.

He frowned. "Rafa."

"Hmm?"

"You explored the house, yes?"

"Yes. Why?"

"What is in the room next to us? Just there." He indicated the wall to his right.

Rafa did not even look up. "The library, Teo. You remember, you referenced the English texts of Shakespeare to quote something to your Emmeline."

He had done no such thing, and Rafa knew it. But he would not be put off by the jab, now that he thought about the layout of the house, and the corridors he'd explored. The library was the next door down the corridor, but the dimensions were wrong for it to be the room adjacent to this.

Teo rose slowly, looking over the wall carefully. There was a shelf of books, but it did not match the shelves on the opposite wall. There was a window behind the desk, but it did not sit equal distance from each wall. If there was anything Teo had learned from the layout and structure of Diehle House, it was that everything was orderly.

Something was not right here.

"Rafa." Teo nudged his head toward the wall. "That wall is not original to the house. There must be another door."

"Now you are imagining things, my friend," Rafa said with a groan, but he arose in spite of his words and began surveying the wall himself.

They went to the bookcase, tested its mobility, and determined it was not attached to the wall, ruling it out as an access point. They examined the faded wallpaper of the room but found no obvious disturbance in it. There were no hinges to indicate a door, no loose floorboards, no indication that any part of the room was anything but what it appeared.

Giving up, Rafa resumed his place in the chair, muttering once more. Teo moved to the window of the study, staring out at the grounds behind the house. None of this made sense, but he could not rid himself of the thought that there were more secrets to this house than just what had occurred between father and son within the walls.

He turned, leaning his back against the window, thinking harder. What would Emmeline have done? As Ears, in the darkest parts of London, what would she have done?

Her voice suddenly rang in his mind. *More often than not, it is something seemingly innocuous that tells more of the story.*

Dull and ordinary—she had said that's what innocuous meant. Something that would not draw attention. Teo turned his head to the right, looking at the corner of the room where the walls touched. Nothing was there. Nothing.

Why was nothing there?

Something should have been there. A sideboard, a shelf, a chair. Having nothing in that space wasted it, and nothing was wasted in Diehle House.

Eyes narrowing, Teo pushed off the window and moved to the corner, looking over every inch for whatever it was he was missing. He reached out and ran his hand over the wall, feeling for any difference beneath the surface of the wallpaper or even atop it. Then there was a dip.

His eyes widened, and he moved his fingers over the surface again. Dug into the wall, perfectly hidden in an identical pattern to the wallpaper, were indentations, spaced and aligned like the tips of three fingers, and Teo's fingers fit very neatly into the space.

Small mercies in family likenesses.

"Rafa," Teo called, his back to his friend.

"Hmm?"

Teo pressed against the indentations, and the wall shifted, swinging away from him with a resounding creak of disuse. "I think I've found it."

Rafa shot to his feet and came up behind him. "Go in," he urged.

"Do not pressure me," Teo ordered, though he was close to laughing at his friend's eagerness, mostly because it matched his own.

He pushed the door open fully, having to duck through the low-hanging frame, finding himself in a small, narrow room. A window sat in the wall, perfectly spaced with the one in the study, which would explain the perfect and unremarkable layout of the house facade from that side. On the window ledge sat a single candle in its holder, cobwebs extending from it.

There was nothing else in the room. No furniture, no portraits, not even curtains for the windows. It was, for all intents and purposes, an empty, useless space.

"That was uneventful," Rafa mused as though commenting on the weather. "Ah, well."

Teo refused to believe his grandfather had built a false wall in his study to hide nothing. He frowned up at the ceiling where the artwork continued, showing men within the caves continuing down tunnels toward a house where a single light sat in a window.

What did it all mean?

Teo walked about the room, his eyes casting over everything.

Something innocuous… something innocuous.

Floorboards beneath his feet groaned, and he stopped, glancing down. A faded, dusty rug lay there, almost lost amid the dirt and general dingey feeling of the room. Stooping down, Teo tossed it aside, coughing in the cloud of dust he became momentarily encased in. When the cloud cleared, he glanced down at the floor.

A trapdoor. Simple, straightforward, and perfectly hidden in a secret room.

Was Diehle House once used for smuggling, then? Were they about to stumble upon a cache of goods still in need of having its duty paid?

Teo worked his fingers under the edge and pried the trapdoor open. He could not see a thing at first, the depths of the makeshift cellar completely dark, and he had no candle at hand. But the underside of the trapdoor had words carved into it, and he tilted his head to read it from the proper angle.

"*J'ai vécu*," he read aloud. "French, yes?"

"I lived," Rafa translated, coming over to crouch beside him. "Was your grandfather of French descent?"

Teo shook his head. "I haven't the faintest idea, but this does not seem like a family motto."

They stared into the cellar again, the only thing making itself known in the darkness a sturdy, large wooden ladder.

Rafa whistled softly, just once. "What in the world have you stumbled upon, Teo?"

Again, Teo could only shake his head. "I don't know. But I may know someone we can ask."

Chapter Nineteen

"Another letter for you, Miss Bartlett."

"My, my, aren't we the popular one this week?"

Emmeline blushed as she took the letter from the maid who bobbed and left without waiting for thanks or acknowledgement. "Is it so very obvious?"

Minerva Dalton chuckled warmly, her head falling back as they sat in the warm sun of the courtyard. "Perhaps not to everyone, but I have been with you for the last four you have received. Either someone is unwell and you are receiving news, or you have a secret. Care to share, Em?"

No, she did not want to share, not even with someone she admired and trusted as much as Minerva, especially since she had several secrets for which she had been receiving letters.

If this letter was from Teo, she could tell her friend a little.

If it was from Tilda... well, Tilda was the only one in her secret London life who knew her identity, so she was the only person who could be entrusted to pass information on when Emmeline was away. If Tilda were sending her letters, it was of utmost importance.

Tilda had written nearly as many letters as Teo in the last few days while Emmeline had been at the school, which was both encouraging and terrifying, particularly in light of Teo's last letter to her.

Discovering the secrets of his grandfather's estate had shaken the man, particularly when he had relayed the information to a contact in London who had then sent a reply that asked Teo not to touch anything, not to move anything, and to allow connections of this particular contact to investigate the possibilities surrounding the mystery. It could have been enough reason for Teo to wash his hands of Diehle House entirely, to remove himself back to London, and to give up his claim to the baronetcy. But it had not.

I want to start a life here, he'd written. *I feel there is much good I can do and many I could help. Whatever strife occurred between my father and grandfather, the people on the estate did not feel it. I would like to maintain that care, and somehow breathe new life into everything.*

That was just like her Teo. Despite a shocking, potentially unsettling secret of his family home, he was not put off by it. He wanted to take what had been and transform it into something better, something brighter. Would nothing ever cloud his optimism?

His outlook brightened Emmeline's own thoughts, though she'd not experienced the same thing, and made her wish to be better herself. Learning more about this man she already adored was filling her life and her days with light and laughter, making her yearn to return to London and to his arms. He told her all about his family— everything she had wished to know and had not known to ask.

He wrote of his beloved grandfather in Spain, who had been a wealthy duke of substantial influence; his sweet mother, who'd never had a harsh word for England, despite the displeasure of her father-in-law; his uncles, who had become second fathers when his own had died; his two sisters, who clearly filled his life with joy and laughter.

She could see each one of them in her mind's eye through his descriptions and his stories. She felt she could embrace each of them without having met a single one, would be welcomed by each of them—should they meet—and might find her own life enriched for having them play a part in it. They were beautiful and vibrant on the page, brought to life by Teo's love and affection for them and their significance in his life.

He praised her way with words, her writing, but in his words, she found solace and beauty and benevolence. She found magic and wonder and whimsy, romance and mischief and tender regard. He made her smile, made her laugh, made her swoon and sigh. He'd found a connection to her through these letters that might have been missing otherwise. He found how to speak to her soul. Not that he needed the additional means of making her love him.

She was fully in love with the man, and the more she learned, the more she loved. Soon, she would feel nothing else in her life but love for him, she was certain. She would wake up and feel love for him. She would walk the grounds of the school and feel love for him. Write a letter and feel love for him. Drink tea and feel love for him. Play a song poorly and feel love for him. Lay her head on her pillow and feel love for him. Breathe in and out and feel love for him.

It was a ridiculous cacophony of love in every waking moment and at least half of her sleeping ones. It was stifling. Freeing, but congesting. Liberating, yet confining. Exhilarating, and soul-shattering.

Perhaps the cacophony wasn't from the love itself but from her. Perhaps she was the cacophony. Or she was simply naive, inexperienced, overemotional, and entirely too willful to enjoy a sedate, peaceful, composed sort of romance, which so many others seemed to have mastered. No one else seemed to be driven into insanity by love of another, and certainly no one in Society would have been. How could something so fierce and so potent come on so suddenly?

Her aunt would never believe it. Then again, her aunt would rejoice and force them to the altar of the nearest church simply for their liking the way the other person smelled.

Having only truly smelled Teo once, Emmeline could not say for certain she did enjoy his fragrance. And she shuddered to think what he might feel about her scent, given their meetings usually took place in the dark parts of London among the soot and filth. It was a miracle he loved her at all, in fact.

"Aren't you going to read it?"

Emmeline exhaled slowly, bringing herself back to her surroundings, and looked at Minerva as she reclined so elegantly on the blanket they had brought outside. "Will you question me about it if I do?"

"I will not," Minerva vowed in her finest crisp voice. Then she smiled a sly grin of sorts. "Your emotions will be written across your face as it is, so there will be no need for questions."

The relieved sigh Emmeline had been in the process of releasing suddenly snagged in her chest, and she glared at her friend. "Rude and impudent, Miss Dalton."

"Factual and intuitive, Miss Bartlett," she shot back without shame. "Now, go on and read your letter while I lay here and look elegant." To emphasize the notion, she propped herself back on her elbows and crossed her feet at the ankles.

Emmeline raised a brow at her, even as her fingers fumbled with the wax seal of her letter. "Very elegant. Natural, too."

"I thought so."

Shaking her head, Emmeline returned her attention to the letter, doing her best to ignore Minerva beside her, as she now knew her every expression would be studied.

Tilda had more information for her, and it was not good. There had been an increased number of people going into Mr. Blaine's home in London, both men and women of all stations and walks in life. Coaches came and went with frequency, and the locals were beginning to comment. Mr. Blaine himself was leaving his house more and more, and the men tailing him for Skips reported his travels as far as Mayfair and Whitehall rather than his usual walks toward the docks. The addresses were listed, and in each case, he had been permitted entrance without any question and remained for over an hour.

What in the world would a bottom-dweller such as Blaine be doing on the finer side of London? What connections could he possibly have there? She was not so innocent as to believe there were not villains in Mayfair and Whitehall—having uncovered quite a few of them herself over the years—but recent information had identified Mr. Blaine as a money lender, and that was all. No family, no decent reputation, no holdings but the grime-laden home she had seen herself, and no ties to any clubs the fashionable members of Society might have frequented.

Who was this man in truth?

She returned her focus to the letter, her eyes skimming the neatly penned lines. Tilda was offering to place one of her actresses within the house as a scullery maid, insisting this man was a crook, and that the only way they could catch him would be from within.

Emmeline could not allow that. Not with the way this man treated women who had been within his walls before, and not without knowing who or what he truly was and the risk he posed. He could easily have been a purveyor of the occult, or a distributor of opium, or the secret head of a smuggling armada that lay in wait beyond the channel.

Whatever he truly was, he used violence as a means of communication, and no one was going to risk their lives for information that might be nothing.

Yet how could they determine if it *was* nothing? What if it was something? What if everything was in plain sight, and she was too occupied with looking for the hidden message to notice? What was innocuous about this man and his routine?

She shuffled the pages, looking at the notes Tilda had included from the contacts: a schedule from Bert on Blaine's own comings and goings, rough sketches of individuals who had arrived at Blaine's home, accounts from neighbors as to his dealings and interactions prior to this week, and reports of a delivery of groceries and the removal of laundry.

Emmeline stared at that particular item on the notes. If a bachelor had his laundry sent out for cleaning, to whom did it go? And when did it come back?

"Minerva," Emmeline said aloud, trying for a calm, cool tone, "do you know anything about laundry services in London?"

"I beg your pardon?"

Emmeline forced a coy smile on her lips and glanced over at her. "Not the sort of question you were expecting?"

Minerva was frowning at her in a surprisingly dark way. "No, and I find your reaction to the letter itself highly disappointing."

"It is not my fault you built it up into something grand," Emmeline retorted.

"Clearly, my life is starved for entertainment." Minerva sputtered softly, her brow creasing in thought. "Laundry in London. Well, it has been some time since I lived there, and it was not exactly a situation of my own establishment, but I believe there were businesses of a sort set up for such things. I knew a woman who worked as a laundress, and her children ran from house to house collecting the bundles."

Emmeline smiled at the idea. "What a charming notion. No

doubt they hoped to receive a farthing or two for their efficiency?"

"Undoubtedly. And occasionally, they succeeded." She flashed a quick grin, then twisted her lips as she thought further. "I cannot remember much beyond that. Why not ask Mr. Adkins? I believe he had a London residence before coming here, and he is unmarried. Someone would have had to do his laundry, and he did not do so himself."

"Heaven forbid," Emmeline muttered, trying desperately not to imagine the hulking, yet gentle Mr. Adkins acting the laundress for his own linens.

"But why the question, Em?" Minerva pressed, venturing where Emmeline had prayed she would not. "Your aunt has servants to do that, surely."

Emmeline forced a smile of what she hoped appeared to be resignation. "With the cost of my aunt's physician being so frequently called upon, and all my earnings here going to her care, I'm afraid there is not much left to use for servants. My cousin and I are looking for other ways we might maintain our aunt's standard of living and care without compromising so much financially. We will likely have to retrench from London entirely if she—" Realizing what she had been about to suggest, she clamped down on her lips hard and looked away.

Had she truly been about to say it would be too expensive to remain in London if her aunt continued to live? Oh, one day, when heaven was her home and all was known, her aunt was going to curse her name for making her not only an invalid, but an expensive one. Somehow, Emmeline wanted to laugh at the very idea.

"I am so sorry, Em," Minerva soothed, sitting up and taking her gently by the arms. "It must be so very hard to see your aunt suffer and want for means to care for her."

A burst of giggles threatened to well up, and Emmeline nodded her answer, keeping her face turned away. Forget being cursed by her aunt in heaven, there was no possible way Emmeline would be receiving a heavenly reward after all the lies she had told, especially after laughing about it.

"Try Mr. Adkins about the laundry," Minerva urged gently. She rubbed Emmeline's arms a little. "I am sure he will have some ideas for you."

"Thank you," Emmeline squeaked and hurried to her feet, dashing out of the courtyard and back into the school before she could lose her composure in a way she would have a hard time explaining.

Safely ensconced in the school, Emmeline found an empty corridor and released the breath she had been holding, along with a rush of laughter even she failed to understand. Danger lurked in London, a plan was forming in her mind, and she was laughing about her aunt being an expensive invalid.

Something was wrong with her, and sooner or later, Teo would see that as well. So much for love.

Once she had managed to regain some control of her senses and recollect the proper priority of things, Emmeline strode down the corridor back to the main of the school, her mind beginning to work on options.

She had an hour before her next class of the day, and depending on what Mr. Adkins had to say, she might need that time to send a few missives to London. Or she might only need to retire to her room and record her thoughts and plans in her diary and then, once back in London, talk to Teo about the details. He had a fine head on his shoulders and trusted her well enough to not question the general idea. There would be several parts of the plan to see to, and she would need all the help she could get. But there was no point in venturing into a wide scheme before she knew if any part of her plan would work.

The only question that mattered at this moment was of Mr. Adkins's location during the luncheon portion of the day at this school.

She moved toward the school's entrance, knowing it would likely not be so easy, but feeling it a decent enough place to start. A few of the students passed her on her way, greeting her politely and ducking their chins as they did so. She waved to some of the older students, all of whom waved back, though few of them were in class with her now.

It gave her some reassurance that she might have been a decent instructor for these ladies and perhaps did some good.

Rounding the corner, toward the foyer and grand entrance, she began peering into rooms in the hopes of finding him greeting a student's parents or arranging a carriage for prospective sponsors or any of the other hundreds of details a butler would have to see to in a place this size and with this many inhabitants. Who knew what else Miss Bradford—Pippa—had him overseeing here?

"It is marvelous to see you here again, Your Grace. We have very much missed having you, if you'll allow me to confess it."

"I have missed being here, Adkins," a low, natural, familiar-sounding feminine voice answered. "I often say as much to His Grace, don't I, Hawk?"

"Almost daily, as it happens," a masculine voice replied, his tone rife with amusement. "I tend to wonder why she married me at all."

Emmeline exhaled slowly, belatedly recollecting to whom the voices belonged.

The Duke and Duchess of Kirklin.

Her Grace, formerly known as Clara Harlow, had been a teacher at the school up until the late autumn, at which time she had been arrested for some dreadful misunderstanding, and the duke had seen to her release and thereafter married her. It was entirely unsuitable for a duchess to teach at a finishing school, so naturally, her position had to be given up. Emmeline had always considered Clara to be a friend and ally, and she had missed her.

But Emmeline had never been one to associate with a duchess. They would never stoop so low and could not be bothered to feign an interest. Or so she had always presumed in the past.

The trio appeared then from the entrance, the duchess looking almost resplendent, despite her relative simplicity, and the duke, as handsome as she remembered, looked at his wife as one might hope he would.

Adkins, on the other hand, nearly tripped over himself in his delight over the visitors.

"To what do we owe the pleasure of your visit, Your Graces?" he asked them, somehow walking sideways and forward at the same time. "The fête is not for some weeks yet, and I was not aware of Lady Adrianna expecting visitors."

"No, Adrianna would be quite miffed at my arriving so

unannounced," the duke replied. "No matter how she adores my wife."

The duchess laughed at his statement. "Ignore him, Adkins. We've come to see Miss Bradford. We've settled in at Kirkleigh again for a time, so we thought to pay her a call."

"Excellent, excellent, most excellent," Adkins bumbled in his jovial way. "Marvelously good of you." He finally looked ahead of him and spotted Emmeline. "Ah, Miss Bartlett! Do you see who has come back to our hallowed halls?"

Emmeline smiled with real delight, despite her inner turmoil at the moment. "If only it were to stay, though I suspect His Grace would have some objections to the idea."

"Only a few," he quipped easily. "Miss Bartlett, pleasure to see you again." He bowed smartly, which was good of him.

"Your Grace," Emmeline murmured with a curtsey, wondering if she ought not to have curbed her tongue before him. She turned slightly to the duchess, offering another curtsey. "Your Grace."

She curtseyed as well, then came forward to take her hands. "Emmeline, I do hope you might forgo the titles and call me Clara again. I am the same as I ever was, you know."

"Well, almost," her husband added, still grinning.

Emmeline liked the duke immensely she decided, despite only having met him a handful of times. "Is he always like that?" she asked Clara, pleased to be reminded of her friend beneath the finery.

"Always," Clara assured her, eyes widening for emphasis. "Maddening man."

"I heard that."

"And I said that," she shot back, raising a brow. "Behave yourself, Your Grace, or I will send for your sister."

Emmeline snorted a soft laugh, which made the duke chuckle.

"I see Adrianna's reputation is well founded. Ah, well." He sighed, clasping his hands behind his back. "I suppose I must find my way to the library or some such while you ladies talk."

"Actually," Emmeline interjected, wincing, "I must speak with Mr. Adkins here first. If I may, Your Graces."

"Of course," Clara responded without malice. "Please do. And I would much rather not keep Miss Bradford waiting, with all she has to do. But I would like to speak with you, Emmeline, before I leave. Tea?"

Emmeline nodded, grateful for her understanding and for her offer. It was so wonderful to be reminded of friends and to see those friendships rekindled. While she might never ask Clara for favors or patronage, she would occasionally very much like to take tea with her.

Clara squeezed her hands, then took her husband's arm to continue down the corridor toward Miss Bradford's offices.

"What can I do for you, Miss Bartlett?" Adkins asked, losing none of his congenial nature in the question.

"It is an odd question, Mr. Adkins," Emmeline admitted. She laughed in spite of herself, twisting her fingers together. "I wondered what you might be able to tell me about laundry in London."

His eyes widened, and his smile faded with his shock. "Laundry, Miss Bartlett?"

"Yes." She cleared her throat, trying to recall what she had related to Minerva. "My aunt is unwell, you know, and her finances cannot support a staff such as she has. My cousin and I thought of trying for a laundry service in London rather than using the maids that will remain after we must let some go."

Adkins did not seem entirely convinced, his brow puckering at her story, but he nodded all the same. "Ah, I see. Well, I cannot say much about Mayfair, Miss Bartlett, which is where I understand your aunt to live—"

"We don't mind Cheapside," Emmeline insisted before he had finished, flashing what she hoped was an eager smile. "We've also decided we cannot afford high opinions, so…"

"Just so," the butler murmured. "Well, when I was a young man and living in London, I placed my laundry in a canvas bag, and the housekeeper, or landlady, would stack all the canvas bags together on the back stoop. The service would then fetch the bags from the building, take them to their wash house, and return them two or three days later."

Emmeline nodded like the rapt student she was. "And was this just weekly? Or biweekly?"

"Biweekly, if you had not the linens for weekly, and only weekly if your linens were plentiful." He shrugged, which seemed a strange motion for the formal man.

"I appreciate your candor, Adkins," Emmeline told him, smiling politely. "I know it is not a delicate question, but would you happen to know the cost of such services?"

He smiled back at her. "If I only answered delicate questions, Miss Bartlett, I'd rarely answer questions at all. I cannot remember plainly, but I may have some record of it in my quarters. Will you permit me to fetch it?"

"Of course, though I don't wish to put you to any trouble." She bit her lip, hoping it would convey the innocence it ought to have were the situation truthful.

"Not a bother, Miss Bartlett," he assured her. "Won't be a moment. Ah, and if you'll be so good as to go to the console table there, I believe you have a letter. I'd have brought it straight to you, but Their Graces arrived, and—"

"Not a bother, Mr. Adkins," Emmeline overrode with a fond wink. "I am perfectly capable of fetching my letter. Thank you."

They parted, he to his quarters and she to the table, though her step was a deal livelier than his. If she already had a letter from Tilda, that would mean...

There was no helping the squeal from her lips as she recognized the hand of the letter. *Teo.*

She broke the seal quickly, her eyes darting over the words as though hungry for them.

Mi querida Emmeline,

Last night, I dreamed of you. We danced in a ballroom together, just the two of us, waltzing to the strains of our beloved Zoraida di Granata, *and when I awoke, I ached for your touch as never before...*

Chapter Twenty

$\mathscr{W}$aiting was intolerable.

He had paced for an hour, he was sure, waiting for Emmeline to appear. They had arranged everything perfectly, from the place they would meet, to the time, and to the way she would wear her hair, of all things. It had been a silly game between them, as though it had been months apart rather than a single week.

A lifetime had been in that week, and one of agony, of longing, of brief and blinding moments of joyous light. Now it would all be forgotten, and forever could begin. Provided she appeared at all.

He'd arrived in London that morning, the journey from Lincolnshire seeming interminable in length compared to days before. Rafa had given up on communicating with him and had resorted to dozing like an infant, despite the confined space and rough terrain, or else he was laughing at some private joke he was not sharing with Teo.

The joke likely *was* Teo, but he was not saying that, either.

It was entirely unclear how Rafa could be so calm about the length of their travel, given he had been parted from the woman he adored most in the world for a week as well, yet he was as calm and serene as the dawn.

The reversal of their natures was not amusing.

Thankfully, things moved at a far more agreeable pace once they were out of the carriage and able to move about in London. Teo had met with his solicitors, all of whom had been delighted he was taking up the baronetcy and Diehle House and offered immediate advice as to the tenant farms and running the place. But Teo was a tradesman and a merchant by training, and his swift, informative replies to their well-meaning suggestions startled a few of them. To their credit, none had seemed particularly upset by his ideas and proposals, and he suspected they would work well together once they all adjusted to the new tone of things.

The greatest thing to come out of the meeting was the revelation of a town house in London that was presently lying unoccupied and untended but was rightfully his.

Why he had not been notified of such a place upon his first arrival did not have an explanation, but it seemed a small thing now. Teo, Rafa, and the men of their company who had remained behind moved into the place and had spent the day doing their best to clean and tidy without the aid of servants, as none had been secured as yet. It seemed that Sir Edwin had come into London infrequently while he lived, but he refused to give up the place, should his son ever return to English shores.

There was a sad sense of hopelessness in such a thing, and Teo wondered if his father ever knew. Nothing he had found in Diehle House had spoken of Teo's father, or of their disagreement, or, indeed, of any opinions at all. Nothing but the secret room and the hidden door leading down into tunnels that extended far from the house. He'd not explored the length of them in their entirety, but the men that Gent had sent up to investigate had done so.

It had seemed the most obvious choice to notify Gent when he'd discovered the strange painting and French phrase carved into wood. Gent might not fully comprehend its significance, but surely he would know others that might. And, as Teo had hoped, contacts of his most mysterious friend had appeared with shocking speed once his note had been received. They had begged his pardon for not divulging much information but assured him repeatedly that Gent would see him fully debriefed when able.

Teo didn't mind the wait for that; after all, his grandfather was dead, and what harm were the secrets of a dead man?

He ought to search the town house for any similar secrets. He was not so concerned about tunnels and passageways in Lincolnshire, especially given the distance Diehle House was from any other significant establishment or structure, but London was entirely different. London had its own horrors, secrets, and dangers, and he did not want any of them to infringe upon his home and his life.

Once he was certain his house was secure, he would need to hire servants to clean it up, renovate where needed, and breathe new life into an admittedly gloomy place, though it was in a rather tidy corner of Mayfair near St. James's Square. The exterior certainly matched the majesty of its neighbors, but upon stepping inside, one might feel a loss of light beyond expectation.

He could not have that in his home. Not if he wished for Emmeline to live there. Not if he wanted her to marry him. And he desperately wanted her to marry him.

He'd first considered the idea the second day he had been in Lincolnshire but had not truly made the decision until the fifth day. A letter had come from Emmeline, just as it had every day, and he'd smiled the whole course of its reading. He'd laughed at her wit, marveled at her intellect, and felt the strangest sense of home simply in reading words she had written for him.

Emmeline was home. His sweet *Orejitas*—the vibrant, fiery woman who had shown London to him in a way he would have never seen—made every day not only worth living, but exciting to live. She made him delighted to even exist. Having never been anything less than content to exist, the idea of suddenly being delighted by it was strange and bewildering. Yet it was a wondrous thing!

He only wanted to delight in living if she were doing so with him. Contentment with life was satisfactory, and delight with life was extraordinary.

Only Emmeline did that for him, and he did not wish to return to mere contentment. It would be the stars of life for him, or else all would become darkness. She had to say yes. He could not imagine anything else.

He frowned to himself now as he stood in their designated place, still waiting. Was there an uncle he should be applying to for her hand in marriage? A guardian? Her aunt, perhaps? He would ask Emmeline herself first, of course, as there would be no need to apply elsewhere if she happened to refuse, but when that was done, did anyone else need to become involved?

How did he still know so little when he felt he knew her so well?

But it was no matter, he supposed. She would tell him if there was anything else to do, anyone else to see. If she wished to be with him, she would see it done. There was simply no stopping Emmeline Bartlett when her mind was set on a course, and heaven help him, he adored that part of her perhaps most of all.

A faint whistling reached his ears, and he immediately perked up, looking around him for the source, whose tone and inflection, even in this form, he knew better than the sound of his own heart.

The melody was theirs, crying out to him in joyous strains even in its simplicity, and never would he hear that song without searching for her. Then she was there, reaching the edge of his vision in the weak light of the night, and his heart stopped fully.

Cielos, even like this, she was the most beautiful creature on earth.

He couldn't wait; he strode toward her with eager strides, and she hurried for him. He shook his head as he reached her, his feelings in his throat, and batted the cap from her head as his lips came crashing down on hers. The long, luxurious length of her curling hair tumbled free, catching in his fingers as he cradled her in his hands and brushing against his already sensitive skin. Her mouth held a fire within it, much like her soul, and it threatened to consume him, consume them both. Her fingers gripped at his jaw, at his neck, pulling him closer to her with every pass of lips and brush of skin. There was no restraint, no hesitation, no reluctance to be found between them as they kissed again, again, and again.

Never enough, and yet far too much. Too bright, too breathtaking, too stirring an embrace to dream possible, yet here it was in his arms, sinking deep into his very core and unravelling every sense and thought he'd ever known. Birth and death in one glorious illumination, and he had never quite breathed until this shared breath with her.

She whimpered against his mouth, an almost desperate sound that clawed at him, made him ache, and was followed by a sigh that robbed him of strength.

He could never let her go. Never.

"*Mi amor*," he rasped against the perfect, soft lips his own had so worshiped. "*Mi hermosa, amada, impresionante ángel. Te extrañé. Te adoro. No puedo respirar sin ti. Maldición, cómo te extrañé.*"

"I know," she whispered, nuzzling against his lips as they brushed her cheeks, her lips, her brow. "Whatever you said, my love, I feel it too."

He chuckled softly against her ear, kissing the tender skin and rendering a shiver from her that only brought her further into his arms. "*Sé que lo haces, mi amor. Puedo sentirlo.*"

Emmeline's sigh rippled across the skin of his neck, and he ducked his face into her shoulder, fighting for control. His fingers found her hair, wandering along the length of it and stroking absently within. "You said you would wear plaits," he reminded her with a teasing nip of his lips against her jaw.

"I had intended to," she replied, digging her fingers pointedly into the back of his neck in return, earning herself a growl from the depth of his chest. "But I found I wanted to feel your fingers in my hair, should the opportunity present itself. Brilliant man that you are, you accommodated my wishes beautifully."

He laughed fully now, cupping her lovely face in his hands. "Delighted to have served you, madam." He leaned down to kiss her again, slowly and softly, lingering with tender caresses.

"Will you always welcome me this way when we've been apart?" Emmeline asked him dreamily, arching further into him and locking her hands securely together behind his neck.

"If we are ever to be apart again," he quipped with a quirked brow, "then yes, I am sure I shall. But I don't intend to part from you, *cariño*, so we must find another occasion."

She stilled in his arms, her eyes widening. "What did you say?"

He hadn't intended to approach the subject so casually, but now he had led them there, he might as well move forward with the idea. After all, she was clasped within his arms and fully agreeable to his attentions.

"I don't wish to be parted from you, Emmeline," he told her with all seriousness, looking deeply into her eyes. "Ever. One week away from you has been more than enough to assure me that I will love you for the rest of my existence. I cannot continue to be with you only in the dark of night. I want mornings and afternoons, sunrise and sunset, the heat of summer and the chill of winter. *Cariño*, I want everything with you."

Her breathing had grown the slightest bit unsteady, and her stunned expression had not changed. It was not entirely encouraging.

"Say that you love me," he pleaded as he suddenly felt the cold grip of fear clutching at his chest.

"I do love you," she whispered, though her lips barely moved. *Cielos...* it sounded like a farewell rather than a declaration.

"Then why do I think you wish me to be silent rather than go on?" he pressed as gently as he could, though he could not help the sting of bitterness that edged in.

Slowly, her hands unlocked from around him, and slid down his chest, resting against his heart.

"*Por favor,*" he breathed. "*Cariño, por favor...*"

He watched as her slender throat moved, struggling for a swallow, felt the trembling of her fingers against his chest. She wasn't pushing away, wasn't fleeing, wasn't moving.

"I do love you," she said again, her voice firmer than before, which only sufficed to return sensation to one of his legs. "More than I am able to express. It terrifies me to feel so much. I am not afraid of being with you, but I am afraid..."

Her voice broke, and though he could barely feel his own breath, he reached for her face, tenderly stroking it. "*¿Miedo de qué, querida?*"

"Of leaping," she whispered, her body quivering in his hold. "Of giving in to this madness we've felt. Of becoming a lady in a country house who never goes anywhere."

"Emmeline—"

"Of resigning myself to the quiet life," she went on, apparently not hearing him. "Of never feeling free again, never finding my place, of constantly wishing my life were something else." Her eyes raised to his, and she laid trembling fingers alongside his cheek. "Of making you despise me when the woman you think I am disappears."

He closed his eyes in agony, turning his face just enough to kiss her fingers and palm, a pained dance against the cold, tender flesh. "*Nunca podría despreciarte,*" he vowed.

Emmeline turned his face back to hers, forcing him to meet her eyes. "You would, my love. And I am not brave enough to endure that."

How she could understand that when she could not understand

214

the depth of his love was astounding. Infuriating, and yet he felt no rage rising. He only felt cold and empty. Lost. Desolate.

"Is this farewell, then?" he forced himself to ask, praying the ground beneath his feet would not fall away entirely.

Blessedly, her hold on his face tightened. "No," she told him, a new light entering her eyes. "No. Because I love you, Teo de Vickers y Mendoza."

The perfection in her pronunciation of his name drew a smile from his lips, which seemed a miracle in the midst of his torment.

Her thumb brushed his smile, her expression softening. "I love you. And I don't want to be afraid. But, darling... I am not ready. Not yet. I know you think I am brave and bold and fearless, but I am not. In truth, I am a woman who has been hiding for years. Not because it was better, not because I wanted to, but because I was lost. You have found me, my love. But *I* haven't found me."

The ice that had threatened to seize his chest began to ebb back into warmth just enough that he could breathe once more. He was still cold, but at least he could breathe.

"I must find myself," Emmeline insisted, her hand dropping back to his chest, pressing against his heart. "I cannot give myself to you until I do. I cannot give what I do not know."

Teo covered her hand with his own. "I know you. And I love you."

The smallest smile known to man graced her lips. "And I must trust in that until I am ready. Can you bear with me, Teo? Can you wait with me? Can you still love me if I cannot leap?"

If he had known before this moment that she would not agree to marry him, he might have wondered about his feelings for her. He might have stormed off, avoided meeting her, taken their entire relationship apart as he searched for his misunderstanding. He might have railed against the heavens for making him love someone who could not give him what he asked for, who refused to make him happy, who had brought him to the gates of heaven and then barred him entrance.

But standing here with her, feeling how his heart pounded beneath her hand, breathing in the air about her, surrounded by her light, he could not do any of those things. He would never be able to do those things. He was hers. He would always be hers.

"*Sí, mi amor,*" he heard himself say, nodding as his thumb stroked along her hand. "*Sí,* I can wait. And bear with you. And love you. *Siempre.* When you decide you are ready, I will go on."

The mighty exhale of her relief shook them both, and she leaned against him, her brow replacing her hands on his chest. Her body shook as with sobs, yet there were no tears, and her arms weakly wrapped around him.

"Thank you," she murmured against him, her voice muffled but audible. "Believe me, I do love you. I do. I love you, I love you."

He closed his eyes against the war of feelings tearing at him, the sweet agony of her words, and the weight of her touch. He pressed his lips against her hair, holding her close but without the same desperation he had known only moments before.

In her wildness, her independence, her bold brilliance, she had hidden a fragility he hadn't expected, and it humbled him now to have such a precious secret revealed to him. He had been entrusted with the delicacy of her spirit, and he felt anchorless in its revelation. How could he have known her heart was so tender? How could he *not* have known?

For all his love of her, he had failed to see this sweetness of which she was so ashamed. This beautiful, exquisite, gentle piece of her heart that she was so afraid of breaking.

Que el cielo lo ayude, it only made him love her more. Love her better. Love her sweeter.

"I love you," she whispered again, almost rambling in his arms now. "I love you."

"*Silencio ahora, dulce,*" he told her with another kiss to her hair. "*Todo saldrá bien. Te tengo. Te amo. Ahora fácil.*"

The more he spoke, the less she trembled, his fingers weaving in and out of her hair in what he prayed was a soothing pattern. She rested her cheek against his chest, breathing deeply as though she might sleep in his arms. Her frantic pulse pounding against his own chest soon quieted, steadied, began to match his own.

He spoke softly to her, uttering gentle reassurances one after the other all in his native tongue to quiet her mind as well as her heart. He felt himself soothed by holding her, by the very words he spoke, and marveled at the change in him from one moment to the next.

Such extremes had taken hold, and yet one thing remained steady. He loved her. And in loving her, he could wait.

Eventually, she stirred in his arms, and he slowly broke his hold around her. He waited until she raised her gaze to his, then stroked the underside of her jaw. "*¿Mejor, cariño?*"

"Does that mean better?" she asked, her voice as soft as that of a child.

He nodded slowly, his mouth curving. "*Sí.*"

"A little," she replied with her own nod. "Less afraid."

He leaned in to kiss her brow tenderly. "Then that is enough."

Emmeline exhaled slowly, swallowing once, a new composure falling over her face. "I need to meet my contacts. Will you come with me?"

"*Por supuesto,*" he assured her as he held out a hand, wondering if she would take it.

She moved away for a moment, fetching her cap from the ground where he'd flung it. She twisted her hair into a semblance of a knot, then placed her cap there to encase the lot of it.

Then, and only then, did she take his hand.

Orejitas once more on the streets and in control. Mostly.

Her grip on his hand told him she was not so steady as she might have wished. He would offer her whatever strength and support he could, but even he could not walk this journey for her.

"What do we know?" he asked her, though he knew much of the details already from their letters.

"Mr. Blaine is not what he appears," she recited as if she'd memorized her response. "He lends money but spends almost nothing. He lives among the poor and the dissolute but is removed from it, too. He moves in circles too high for his circumstances and too low for his practiced manners. He is cruel to children, to women, and to animals, yet he has never been arrested for a crime. He has neither friends nor family, yet there are near-constant visitors to his home."

"He is a paradox, then," Teo mused, piecing together an image of the man he had never seen. "In every respect."

Emmeline exhaled harshly through her nose. "Something is not right, Teo. And I will discover what it is."

He glanced down at her in surprise. "How?"

She hesitated a moment, her brow furrowing. "I am going to insert myself into his day-to-day activity and life somehow. Get into his house. See with my own eyes—"

"No," Teo interrupted with surprising harshness. "No, Emmeline. *¡En absoluto! No puedes acercarte a él. ¡No harás tal cosa!*"

"It does no good to argue with me, Teo," she shot back, pulling them to a stop, glaring up at him with no hint of cowering or hesitation in her voice. "This is what I do and what I have done. I will do it, so you can either help me, or you can let me be."

He stared at her, heart thundering in his ears and heat rising to their tips as fear and fury battled.

She lifted her chin, daring him to say anything further.

He could only exhale slowly and mutter, "*Eres la mujer más enloquecedora de toda la creación.*"

Her eyes narrowed. "That does not sound flattering, *cariño.*"

He managed an almost sincere laugh. "It's not."

"And will you let me be?" she asked him, the fire returning to her eyes and her expression.

Cielos, it was madness to love this woman!

"If I could let you be," he told her, grumbling even as his fear for her swiped at his heart, "I would have done so by now."

"It must be a trial to love me."

"*Eso depende del día.*"

"Frightened or overwhelmed?"

"Wise," he admitted simply. "Very, very wise."

Chapter Twenty-One

There were worse plans she had set into motion. She couldn't think of any at the moment, but she was sure there were. This would simply be somewhere near the top of the list of poor ideas in her life.

Still, Emmeline did not have any better ideas, particularly ones that she could implement quickly and without much fuss or bother. She had done enough research to organize a strategy and was as prepared as any person could be, under the circumstances. She had involved as limited a number of people as possible and had taken great pains that no one should suffer for her actions.

Which is why she was walking into East London at sundown rather than when it was full dark.

It had been easy enough to convince her aunt that she was unwell and ought to retire early. Her nerves had prevented her from eating much, and her distracted nature made her seem more lethargic in her responses to questions. She'd been more reserved in the days following her reunion with Teo, as might be expected, given the circumstances. One did not hear such confessions regularly, and finding herself unable to be swept up in his fervor, she'd felt an enormous amount of guilt.

He'd been as sweet as ever, as charming and as gracious, though perhaps a trifle less playful. He held her when she asked yet maintained a distance that frightened her. Was this a show of respect for her hesitation, or was he reconsidering the idea of her altogether?

She'd told him she loved him. Repeatedly. Excessively. Pathetically. Had that been what had changed him?

Whatever it was, her thoughts were consumed by him as much

as they were by her plan, so there was not much room for conversation or banter. Her silence worried Aunt Hermione to such an extent that she had insisted Emmeline retire early, and if she were still unwell in the morning, the doctor would be fetched. If Emmeline survived the night, she would happily subject herself to the doctor's examination in the morning.

It had been simple enough to sneak out of the house when forced to retire early. She had drawn all of the curtains in the room, leaving it too dark to examine the bed closely, and—barring her aunt actually seeking for Emmeline's body among the bedsheets—her absence would not be discovered despite leaving hours before her usual time.

Then there was the simple matter of Teo. He would not be joining her tonight, having some sort of business gathering at his new home, which was one of the main reasons she had selected this night for the plan in the first place. If he would not be there to prevent her from her actions, there would be no detriment to them. In an ideal world, he would have been engaged in these activities with her, but given his reaction to her suggestion the other night...

She had never seen Teo in a temper before that moment, and she was not keen to repeat the experience, particularly when there was no other course but the one she had suggested.

It *had* to be this way. She would not risk anyone else, and she would not make any reports or accusations without proof. She was a journalist, not a gossipmonger. If this was nothing more than an illicit fighting ring or smuggling operation, she would not go so far as to give Mr. Blaine the title of murderer or the like. He did beat children, which was deplorable, and if that was the extent of his villainy, she would shout it from the rooftops.

But she would not label him merely a child beater if his sins were of greater extent.

Perhaps this was some cruel obsession in her mind and not a search for truth. After all, she had not known of Mr. Blaine before Amy had told Emmeline her beating was at his hands, and she might never have heard of him otherwise. She had been investigating the conditions of the poor and preparing to write on them. She had wanted to write on those who exploited the poor, and somehow that had led to a fixation with Mr. Blaine and the strange sort of life he lived.

Was this what she had reduced herself to? Track one man and his strangeness rather than focus on a plot and unravel it?

No, she reminded herself. Had not the gambling ring started with an investigation into Marcus Coyle and how he'd arranged a match for his sister with Peter Lane? Had not the discovery of Rogue begun with an interest in the whereabouts of Charles Orkney? Did she not begin investigating the downfall of Ann Sanders when she'd discovered the fate of maids from an entire neighborhood?

Tonight was not about Mr. Blaine, except for the information he could provide them. He was the key to a bigger story, and that bigger story was what she wanted. Oh, there would be hell to pay for the beating he gave Amy and Jane and Charlie and all the rest, hopefully each in their turn, but this was no fixation for the sake of it. This was uncovering secrets in a dark part of London that affected many lives, and as of yet, no one else was intervening.

Emmeline could do so. And she would.

She had dressed a mite differently tonight, using less padding than she normally did to fill out her figure and none at all through the shoulders. Her bindings were all the same, her hair was in its usual arrangement, and she had smudged powder in places on her face and neck to hide the feminine softness. The result had her looking like a lad of twelve who was shortly to grow a great deal and did a fair amount of scowling. Which, as she understood, boys of twelve tended to do as it was, so that might have been the most convincing part of her disguise this evening.

She slowed her step as she neared the juncture of the two roads by the abandoned mews, exactly where the boy said she would. She'd paid an exorbitant amount to take his place in delivering, but as he'd said he did not like delivering to the gentleman, it was not much of a sacrifice. The additional money was for his silence.

It would all be worth it if this worked.

Tucking the brim of her cap down a notch further, she rounded the corner and came to the inner door of a tunnel, which was propped open by a middle-aged woman wearing a damp and stained apron, and a scowling expression amidst straggling hair streaming from her cap.

"Yer late," she hollered at Emmeline, waving her over. "That'll cost ye."

Emmeline hastened to her, grumbling an apology.

"Eh, yer not 'im," the woman accused, grabbing Emmeline's jacket. "Where's the boy?"

"Don't like the gentleman," Emmeline grunted in an imitation of the boy's accent. She shrugged as if she did not care. "Said I could take it."

The woman sputtered and shook her head. "As if I make enough money to be particular about me customers. Bloody airs of 'im. Fine, take it, and be quick about it! Don't like to be kept waiting, this 'un; paid me extra to have 'is timing. Don't you ruin me business's reputation!"

"Yes'm," Emmeline murmured, gripping the canvas bag and hauling it over a shoulder, taking off at a near run, though the weight of the laundry wasn't enough to truly make haste. So long as she appeared to do so, it should suffice.

"You tell 'em next pickup is Tuesday!" the laundress hollered after her.

Emmeline didn't respond, praying she was not supposed to under the circumstances. Once she'd rounded the corner again, she stopped her attempts at speed and walked at an easier pace.

The first part was done without much ado. Now all she had to do was convince whoever answered the servants' door that she should bring the laundry inside rather than leave it there.

And accept her fee, of course. She might as well get something out of the evening besides information.

It was only three blocks to Blaine's house, and the servants' entrance was on the west face of the house, accessed by a narrow alley. She had been told, in no uncertain terms, that she could not deliver the laundry to the main entrance unless she wished to receive a beating. As she had no interest in entering through the front, or to receive a beating, the west face entrance was perfect for her aims.

The sun had gone down completely now, giving the alley a more ominous feeling that seemed oddly fitting for the evening. The decrease in light would benefit her disguise, and, if Mr. Blaine had the guests he was expected to, the limited number of servants would not have much time to spend seeing to the laundry she delivered, leaving the perfect opportunity for her.

His house was the last in its row, and she reached it shortly, noting it was far more poorly kept than his neighbors'. Was that intentional or coincidence? It would not surprise her if the man simply could not be bothered to care about appearances. Or much of anything else.

She rounded the corner of the house, pausing at the unremarkable door set almost exactly at the corner. Her heart skipped in agitation, and her throat burned, making swallowing impossible. But there was no time for hesitation.

Emmeline exhaled roughly, forcing a bit of a growl to lower her voice even more, then knocked firmly.

For a moment, nothing happened but the uneven pounding of her heart.

A scuffling sound followed, and she held her breath as the sound drew nearer. The door swung open, and a haggard-looking footman in need of a shave stood there. "What do you want?" he barked.

"Laundry for the gentleman," Emmeline replied in a surly tone, shrugging the bag for emphasis. "Madam said 'twas special request."

The footman glowered. "'Course it was." He glanced behind him, then down at Emmeline. "Can you take it to his rooms? Got guests at the moment, and he gets in a mighty fury when I leave 'em."

Emmeline squinted up at him. "How much?"

"Look here, you little imp—" He paused, listening to something within, then hissed and returned his focus to Emmeline. "I'll give you a shilling to carry it up plus the shilling for delivery."

She opened her hand, crooking her fingers.

Whatever the man uttered, she couldn't make out, but it sounded very foul indeed. Still, two coins dropped into her palm. She nodded, clasping her fingers about them and tucked them safely into her pocket.

"Up two flights, third door to the left," the footman ordered, still glaring. "Don't make a sound, and don't hang about. You won't get more than you've got." He stepped back and ushered her in quickly, then pushed her toward the stairs before shutting the door soundly behind them.

Emmeline started up the stairs, looking closely after the man to better track his movements. She could deposit the laundry easily enough in the room, but it would be finding whatever gathering was taking place afterward, situating herself safely out of sight, and listening to the conversations that would pose a problem. Perhaps getting the laundry and getting into the house were the easiest parts of the mission.

The stairs were creaky and dusty but for a particular path that was cleared enough, and it was all she could do to ascend them without making too much noise. It would be easier to move in silence once she was relieved of the bundle on her back, and if she could time it right…

She reached the top of the second landing and hurried to her left, counting out to the third door. "Ah ha," she breathed, pushing the door open and peering in.

It was the most unremarkable bedchamber she had ever seen in her entire life. A simple bureau to one side, a four-poster bed with tattered hangings, and a writing desk that was so ancient and outdated, it might have belonged to the valet of Queen Anne herself. It was as though the room were ready for arrangement rather than already arranged. Still, there was no accounting for taste.

She moved to the bureau and dropped the canvas bag beside it, taking a moment to open the doors and peer inside. Unremarkable jackets, simple linen shirts, no discerning details in any respect. He could have been every man and no man all at once. No one would ever identify him by attire or style, unless one could quite simply say "plain and ordinary."

Her eyes fell to the bottom of the bureau, which was shockingly clean compared to the rest of the place. Why should that be?

She stooped to get a better look and peer toward the back, and found a button sitting against the floor, threads still attached from the garment it had once clung to. She scooped the button up, marveling at the clean, cool metal of it and at its engraved surface. She squinted at it as the writing was impossible to make out in the dim light of the room.

Shoving the button in the same pocket as her coins, she felt around the base of the bureau for any other surprises and felt the boards shift.

She stilled, staring at the surface breathlessly. She pressed again, and the entire base moved from its setting. Beneath the boards sat a box of sorts, open to her view but difficult to explore without more light. Her eyes had adjusted some, but there was not time to see much. She pulled out a map, setting it to the side. It was followed by a list of names. This she pocketed, hoping to steal a glimpse in better light and return it later. Everything else seemed to be letters, though there were a few sheets of music within.

A musical villain? That was more amusing than it ought to have been.

She replaced the map and the boards, then closed the bureau and left the room, her steps much softer and easier now. She hurried down the stairs, shortly returning to the main floor of the house.

Now. Where would the host and his guests be? And where would the irritable footman go?

A hum of voices drew her toward the front of the house, and she crept forward, praying Mr. Blaine had not added more servants to his household that might spot her. The dining room appeared to be to the right, and light shone from beneath the door. The voices seemed to be coming from within, so Emmeline tucked herself beneath the console table beside the door, wincing as the space proved far more inconvenient to her back and knees than she'd anticipated. But it was an excellent space for hiding in the dim light of the corridor, and no hastening footman would pause to check there.

The moment she'd completed that thought, the door swung open, and crisp steps all but stomped away, a man muttering something about dismissal and duty.

She could only spot him as he turned toward the back of the house, and the sight made her grin. The footman, it seemed, was no longer needed at dinner. Hers would be the only ears to overhear conversation at the table, then. Marvelous.

"Enough of this," a voice sounded clearly from within. "I am tired of waiting. When will all be ready?"

A rumble of seemingly approving replies sounded, and

Emmeline closed her eyes to focus her hearing as much as possible.

"Everything will be in place on Thursday, Faust," a deep, harsh voice replied. "Do not tell me about the need for haste; you have no idea the moving parts we have had to arrange."

"Eight is not good enough," a new voice insisted. "There are ten halting the bill, and two more besides who might lean. A dozen was what we needed, yet you've only arranged for eight to fall."

Someone growled and slammed the table. "Do you really believe I would do less than is needed, Abel? The eight were selected because of their stalwartness, not for convenience. Our sources say that two have been called away and will not return for the vote, and the death of the others will sway the wavering two into submission, particularly when our pieces apply their additional pressure."

Emmeline turned cold where she sat crammed between the legs of the console table.

Death? Eight would die for whatever cause the room within had planned? Who were they? Thursday was the day after tomorrow; she had no time at all.

She fumbled for the paper in her pocket, leaning toward the light from the door as she unfolded it. More than a dozen names were on the list, though the letters were arranged in some hidden way. Six had been crossed off, but the rest… The list had to be the potential victims. More than eight names remained, but at least this would be a start.

She had to go. Now. There was no time to waste listening further, and no other details important enough to wait for. Eight lives were at stake.

Though she was desperate to bolt from her hiding spot and tear from the house, though she wanted to knock the console table over and flee, she could not lose her composure. She could not be discovered. She could not be caught.

Listening for any approaching footsteps and hearing none, she awkwardly slid from her hiding place and back out into the freedom of the corridor. She crept toward the back of the house, barely breathing and too afraid to even return the page of names to her pocket for fear of the sound it would make. She forced her breathing to slow, to remain steady, to remain as silent as possible, though each inhale seemed thunderous to her ears.

Somehow, she reached the servants' entrance undetected, which prompted a rush of relief to hit her chest.

Not yet, she thought viciously. *Not yet.*

She had to get away first. The footman could have been standing outside the door at this moment and would have been only too pleased to have her in his clutches.

Gingerly, she opened the door, glancing out at the dark London streets.

No one was there.

She exhaled slowly, pausing only to collect her thoughts. Only one occurred to her. *Run.*

She tore from the house, shoving the list into her pocket, and sprinted up the street. There were no sounds of pursuit, but that did not settle her in the least. She raced through the darkness, turning onto any street that would lead her out of East London. Any route that would separate her from the conspiring men. Any alley that would guide her farther toward the only destination possible, under the circumstances.

Teo.

She had yet to visit him there, but she knew the address well enough. He had been curious about its location and what that could imply, and her reassurance that St. James's Square was sufficiently respectable and adequately fine had delighted him. Now she wished it had been a bit closer to her present location.

Tearing toward St. James's as she was would be a sight, particularly if any in the neighborhood were entertaining guests, but at least her disguise was in place. She might as well be an errand boy, so perhaps she would not even garner a second glance. One could only hope.

Her feet ached already with their pounding against the ground and the unforgiving pace she forced upon them. She had fled danger before, but hiding and dodging had been the game then, not all-out speed, and never had she been forced to run such a great distance. No amount of ladylike walking, even if eagerly engaged in, could have prepared her for this.

At least she knew London enough to be well-oriented. The city spread out before her like a map in her mind, and she raced toward St. James's Square without any difficulty beyond the physical aspect of doing so. There was no time for doubts, for reserve, for any questions about his feelings for her when she'd refused the question he had not asked. He was the only person she could trust with this, and he would trust every word she said.

Everything else could wait.

The streets became cleaner and better lit, the buildings more immaculate, and her instincts to behave with propriety licked at her heels. Mayfair's finery could not have had more of an impact to her evening than this, and still she ran recklessly through it. Houses were alight with activities in various parts, and others were dark and silent. She ignored them all.

St. James's Square was suddenly before her, and her legs renewed their energy and power at being so near their destination. She leapt the few steps to the door and pounded furiously, no thought for decorum, discretion, or any form of restraint.

Her lungs caught flame and her limbs began to shake now that her frantic race was done, while her throat seemed to throb in time with her pulse.

Why wasn't he answering?

She thumped the door again, a pained whimper ripping from her in distress. As she slammed her fist against the surface once more, the door swung open, and a young man in plainclothes stared at her without emotion.

"Yes?" he asked in a thick Spanish accent, only mildly concerned by her state.

"I need to see Sir Teo," Emmeline gasped, finding speaking at all to be rather difficult. "Immediately."

His brow furrowed. "Sir Teo not... *disponible*."

Emmeline's stomach dropped. "He's not here?" she cried, ready to sink against the doorstep.

"He is inside," the young man said, shaking his head. "With men."

Her kneecaps nearly gave way with relief. "Get him. Please. Please, get him."

"No," he told her simply but firmly. "Tomorrow."

"This cannot wait!" Emmeline insisted, trying to force her way in despite his blocking her.

He rambled at her in Spanish, clearly trying for politeness.

"*Juan, deja pasar al chico,*" a familiar gravelly voice said from behind him.

Emmeline gasped as Juan stepped aside to argue the point, revealing Santiago standing there, his expression showing no surprise at seeing her. She did not wait for the men to settle things and ran to Santiago herself.

His eyes widened at the state of her. "*¿Orejas? ¿Qué está mal?* Problem?"

"Yes," she told him firmly, grabbing his arms, her mind spinning on the very limited number of Spanish words she had learned. "*¿Dónde está Teo?*"

He winced a little at her poor accent, but he patted her arms all the same and pointed at a set of double doors to her left. "*Allí.* Go."

"His meeting?" she asked, finally feeling hesitant about bursting in when there would be others present.

"Important?" Santiago returned with a raised brow.

She nodded, feeling a wave of panicked tears rising. "*Sí. Mucho.*"

Something about her choice of words made Santiago smile. "*¿Entonces que estás esperando?*" he asked, nudging his head toward the doors.

What exactly he said was lost on her, but the meaning was clear.

Emmeline turned on the spot and ran for the doors, throwing them open without caution. "Teo! Help!"

She skidded to a stop at the sight of six men within the room, all of whom now stared at her in shock.

Teo leapt to his feet. "*Orejitas,* what is it?" Without a word to the others, he strode over to her, eyes full of concern. "What's happened?" He looked her over, his eyes raising to hers knowingly. "You did something."

Her eyes filled with tears, and she gripped his forearms as her body shook with fear. "I've heard something... something dreadful, and I didn't know where else to go."

He put a hand to her arm immediately. "Tell me. Whatever it is, we will see to it."

She searched his eyes, despair washing over and through her. "Even if it's a matter of life and death and possibly the fate of England?"

A few of the men slowly rose behind Teo, seeming to be on alert now, but she only had eyes for him. For his response. For his love.

"Blaine?" he asked simply.

She nodded once.

To her surprise, he grinned. "Well, you have just stumbled into a meeting including several secret operatives, *cariño*. So you really have come to the right place."

Emmeline blinked. "What? You're a spy?"

"Not yet," someone quipped with a laugh.

"Oh, Sir Teo, you have to be more gentle when you tell people these things," said another who was shaking his head. "Frankness only brings problems."

Somehow, Emmeline swallowed and looked beyond Teo to the others. "I'm not shocked. You would not believe some of the secrets I have heard in Society's higher circles," she said with a wave of her hand.

A strikingly handsome, somehow familiar man leaned on an armchair with interest. "Oh, really?"

"No, Pratt," Teo called over his shoulder without looking.

The man frowned grumpily and groaned like a child.

Teo smiled at Emmeline. "Perhaps later, then," he amended. "No, I am not a spy. But I am being recruited to be a set of eyes and ears for the rest of these men and some others who really are spies."

He gestured to the men behind him, one of whom Emmeline hadn't noticed and who was the most familiar face of all. Her beloved guardian.

She gaped at seeing him. "Fritz?"

He grinned without shame. "Evening, Ears."

Teo turned and gaped as well. "You know her name?"

Fritz shrugged. "I gave it to her when she was a child. Always eavesdropping. Always." He chuckled at the memory, though no one else did.

"You are supposed to be a dignitary who doesn't really do anything," Emmeline pointed out, only relaxing slightly.

"And you're supposed to be a fine lady who teaches girls how to write," he shot back.

She winced. "Don't tell Aunt Hermione."

"Same to you." He turned to the others. "Gentlemen, meet my lovely cousin and ward, Emmeline Bartlett."

Emmeline looked around the room, pursing her lips. "Right, this is awkward. Am I supposed to curtsey in breeches?"

The one Teo called Pratt shrugged. "I've seen stranger things."

Teo took Emmeline's arm and led her to a chair, then crouched before her. "What did you hear, *cariño?*"

Quickly, she relayed everything she knew, and everything she had heard. She pulled out the list of names and handed them to Fritz, who then passed it around to the others.

"I didn't know what else to do," Emmeline told them all, her audience completely rapt at her words. "I don't even know why they want to kill whoever is on that list, or who these men were, but I couldn't…" She paused, recollecting her other find of the night. "Wait, I forgot…"

Her fingers latched onto the button in her pocket, and she pulled it out, squinting at the letters that were now much clearer than before.

"*Un lointain rivage,*" she read aloud with a frown. "Foreign shore in French? What could that mean?"

The silence of the room spoke volumes, and she looked up at five startled faces, with only Teo and a darker man looking equally confused.

"What?" Emmeline asked again.

Her cousin shook his head slowly. "Ears, I think you may have uncovered your greatest plot yet. But don't have Barnes write about this one, eh?"

It was all she could do not to fall out of her chair. "You knew?" she gasped.

Fritz snorted softly. "Of course I knew. I'm still your guardian, and when I hear that you are leaving your position at the school to take care of an ailing relative, knowing you don't have an ailing relative, I investigate. Did you ever wonder why you were never caught before?"

"Because I'm careful."

"Because you are constantly tailed," he corrected.

Emmeline scowled at him. "Name one time I needed help."

"August, 1824," Fritz recited. "You came out of a gaming den and two blokes followed you. Your shadow took care of them."

So that was how she got away. She'd been uninterested in the gaming itself at the time, which was ironic, considering the more recent chase from a gambling den. "Name another time," she demanded.

His eyes narrowed and his lips quirked as though he fought a smile. "All right, so you're careful, but there's a reason you were not pulled into my world of operatives, despite your obvious talents. It's because I knew exactly what was at stake, and my little cousin was not getting involved."

"Fat lot of help that did in the end, eh?" They shared a true smile now, and, somehow, Emmeline found comfort in the night after all.

"Excuse me," Pratt said with a raised hand. "Did you say her name was Ears?"

"Yes."

"Ears, as in the name we have been hearing from our contacts for some years now?"

"Again, yes."

"Then I have a couple of questions."

Fritz rolled his eyes, heaving a sigh. "Go on, then."

Pratt cleared his throat. "One, I had no idea Ears was a she, not a he. No judgment, just acknowledging. Two, how in the world has Ears not been an actual operative? Thirdly, and slightly similar to question two, *why* is she not an operative? And finally—" He paused, grinning mischievously. "Would it be impolite to thank her for making Rogue the most popular man in the London League?"

Emmeline's eyes widened. "He's one of you?"

"He's right here," one of the men announced, smiling a little wryly and waving. His hair bore the slightest bit of curly dishevelment, and his eyes were the palest blue she had ever seen in her life. He looked almost exactly like the sketch she'd had done.

"I am so sorry," she whispered, horrified at having exposed one of Britain's secret operatives in such a way. "I'd never have done such a thing had I known."

He shocked her by chuckling. "Quite all right. It was a nuisance for a while, but I did meet my wife because of it, so one day, I may thank you. Not tonight, but one day. Now, shall we discuss the mass assassination plot that is forthcoming?"

They all nodded, but Emmeline felt the weight of the evening suddenly press down on her. Teo rubbed her hands and moved to sit beside her, tucking her against him.

"There, *cariño*," he murmured. "Take some rest."

She shook her head against him. "I want to be involved. I want to stop this."

"You will," he assured her. "You will help, I promise, but nothing is going to be done tonight. You need to rest. I am not going to argue on this."

"Don't be worried," she said sleepily, more than willing to lose herself in the comfort he provided. "The dangerous part is done already. I should have told you, I'm sorry."

He laughed softly, his arms encircling her. "We can argue about that later, too. You rest, I'll listen, and when we have a plan, I'll make sure you're a part of it."

"Wake me when there is one," she insisted, though her words had no force to them. "If I fall asleep. I might not."

"*Serás amado*," he said softly, kissing her dirty, smudged forehead tenderly. "*Solo dormir.*"

As though he had commanded her in some spell, Emmeline's eyes closed, her breathing deepened, and soon, all she knew was the warmth of the arms around her.

Chapter Twenty-Two

The last day and a half had been complete and utter chaos, with minimal sleep, endless meetings, and so many code names that Teo could barely keep his own name in mind. Rafa was far less confused.

From the moment the men of the London League had taken over, Rafa had been particularly invested. He could strategize with the best of them and had no hesitation or reluctance in being fully involved with their plan to countermand what Emmeline had uncovered in her investigation. An investigation that, he had to admit, he was still slightly queasy about when he considered what it had entailed.

She had been so close to disaster at so many points throughout the evening. Could have been captured, could have been harmed, could have been beyond saving. Learning what they had from the London League about this group of Frenchmen and their British supporters, everything became more important and infinitely more terrifying.

His grandfather had been part of this plot. That was what the phrase on the trap door had told Gent, and why so many of his contacts had come out to Diehle House to investigate further. The smuggling in of Faction operatives into England was being portrayed on the ceiling, and the tunnels extended out to the coastline for that very purpose. They had then used Diehle House as a transition point for those operatives as they were relayed to their specific assignments.

Teo had been ashamed of his grandfather for years, purely based on the fallout from his father's marriage, but learning of this had shattered his hopes of finding a good man beneath the darkened image.

The local connections were being thoroughly investigated to ascertain their loyalties and to prevent any addition of French Faction pressure to Teo's life once he officially took up residence. He'd already felt the pressures from Mr. Jackson and his friends, who, he now believed, were supporters of this faction, if not key members. He'd leave the details to the actual operatives, but he felt certain about his own course.

He would undo what his grandfather had done. He would use Diehle House for British operatives and contacts. Would make his house a refuge for them without question or judgment. Would do all in his power to see that good prevailed, that England was protected, and that those fighting against evil and tyranny would have a friend and ally in him.

That was going to be the legacy of the Vickers line. At least, the one that would come through him. And he had a feeling his wife would support him in this. Once she was his wife, of course. They had yet to return to the subject.

She'd slept in his embrace for much of that first meeting and allowed him to carry her up to one of the rooms when those among the group who were operatives dispersed to begin their work. Her cousin, Lord Rothchild, had watched Teo's interaction with her with some amusement but gave no indication that he would interfere, which seemed a great victory. He'd insisted on returning a few hours later to fetch his cousin and see her returned to their aunt's home so her disappearance would not be discovered.

When Teo had asked him how they would manage to get inside undetected, Lord Rothchild had only grinned and assured him that, between Emmeline and himself, they had many ways. It was still unclear if the statement had been meant as encouraging, intimidating, or frightening.

Teo had not slept much while Emmeline had done so, though he had spent some time at her bedside, watching her sleep and pondering over his feelings for her. And what plans he might venture to hope for.

Once all of this was settled, and the plot she'd uncovered was foiled, he would try again to propose matrimony. He might not succeed, or even get the words out, but he needed to try. Needed to link them together. Needed to remain with her. Needed to protect her.

A nanny with knives, she had once said. Well, he'd be that for the rest of her life if she didn't marry him. Perhaps that should be his convincing point.

They'd been apart for nearly a full day now, each safe in their respective homes and only awaiting news and their assignments. The only orders they had were to be dressed in plain clothing.

Teo, for one, was going mad with the waiting. Rafa had been pacing in the drawing room, having sharpened his knives and loaded his two pistols at least twice over. They had been repeatedly assured that several operatives would be involved, and there would be many parts to play in the events forthcoming, yet no specifics had been given to them since the day before.

Were new operatives verifying the information that Emmeline had gathered? Were they assessing the situation from different angles? Had they discovered new details and were even now piecing them together to make the plan more infallible?

Teo would have, at this point, taken any information. Any sort of a resolution of the whole thing entirely. He did wish to be part of the thing. And Emmeline, for one, would be furious if she were excluded. Her cousin would need to mind his step if he were foolish enough to do that to her.

There was a knock then at the door, and Teo bolted for the door before recollecting that, in his position, a gentleman did not answer his own door.

"Rafa," he barked, jerking his head to the door.

"Yes, sir," Rafa grumbled sullenly as he strode past, shaking his head in irritation. He swung open the door, his stance defensive. Then he stepped back without a word as Mr. Pratt—whose code name was Rook, Teo recalled—strode in wearing very common apparel.

"Good day, *amigos*," he greeted in an almost cheery tone, though there was a hardness there that had Teo on alert. "Ready to vanquish our foes?"

"Is it time?" Teo asked at once, a sharp jolt of anticipation striking his chest.

Pratt nodded, his smile tight. "Shortly, yes. Rafa, you're with me. I'll explain on the way what we're about. Teo, you're to go to Bond Street. Outside of Hartley's, you will meet Ears. The pair of you will proceed down Bond Street until you reach Burlington Gardens. At the corner, Gent will meet you both. Understood?"

Both men nodded, though questions swirled in Teo's mind. It was not yet one in the afternoon, far too early for ladies to be promenading about Bond Street. The area would still belong almost strictly to gentlemen about their business. Was Emmeline to be dressed accordingly?

There was no time for those sorts of questions, particularly when Pratt was already turning out of the house with Rafa, ordering Teo to either wait five minutes, or take another exit of the house.

Teo was done with waiting. He immediately turned for the back of the house and walked out the servants' entrance, which had yet to be used since his taking up residence, as he had yet to hire any actual servants. He might not know much about this finer part of London yet, but he certainly knew how much time it would take him to walk to Bond Street.

Leisurely, it would take between six and seven minutes. At this pace… If he took much longer than four, he would wash his hands of ever participating in anything remotely related to covert operations, no matter which country asked him.

Yet he could not look as though he was intentionally making haste. He could not run all the way to Bond Street in the middle of the day in a fine corner of London. He'd already risked attracting attention by not appearing in finery, but it was early in the day, and he did not look like a beggar. Surely the London League would not have asked them to arrive in plain clothing if it would draw attention to themselves.

It was curious, Teo thought as he hastily—yet not hastily— walked toward his destination, but there seemed to be a greater number of people out than usual at this time of day and in this area, particularly those of unremarkable attire. Sturdy dark coats, dark hats, and collections of both trousers and breeches, depending on the gentleman in question. A few had walking sticks, some had nothing, but there certainly had something occurring in the vicinity to draw such attraction. And to raise voices to such a hum.

Had this all been set up specifically to aid them in their task today? Or was this part of the enemy's plot to murder their designated victims?

Whichever it was, the crowd and noise was making Teo's heart race, and he found himself even more invested in finding Emmeline quickly, let alone getting them both to Gent.

If she were alone, as he suspected she would be, she would be vulnerable in a crowd of invigorated men. Her disguise might not pass muster in the light of day, and if any of the men circling about had been imbibing early…

He lengthened his strides, his eyes constantly moving about his surroundings in search of her. Hartley's, Rook had said, and, for a moment, Teo could not recall where on Bond Street that shop resided. He needn't have worried; it was the third shop in from Piccadilly, and just outside, holding up news sheets, was his Emmeline.

Well, she was actually Ears today, if her disguise was any indication. Either way, his chest heaved with relief at seeing her and how much attention she was *not* attracting.

Her eyes met his and her smile spread wide. He slowed his step, aiming to appear casual as he reached her, but there was nothing casual in the way he surreptitiously took her hand for a brief moment, nor the way she clung to his for those few heartbeats.

She set the papers down beside the stoop and turned with him to continue up Bond Street. "Where are we going?" she whispered, her voice carefully lowered as though she were an adolescent boy. "All I was told was to come in disguise and meet you outside of Hartley's."

"We are meeting Gent at the corner of Burlington Gardens," Teo told her, forcing his expression to be as impassive as any Londoner out for a stroll. "That is the extent of what I know."

"All of those meetings," Emmeline hissed, her arm brushing his as they walked, "and we don't know the plan?"

He could only shrug.

"I think I need to have a very serious conversation with Fritz when all this is over," she muttered darkly.

"You intend to join them?" Teo asked, giving her a sidelong look.

Her eyes were quick to meet his. "Do you?"

For a moment, they only stared, waiting for what the other would say.

"Yes," they said together, grinning at hearing an echo of their own response.

"I won't be an operative, strictly speaking," Teo told her, his thumb grazing her hand. "But Diehle House would host a great many from time to time, and I would certainly be able to participate where needed. Rafa has volunteered to be the eyes and ears in all of our ports, so it seems…"

Emmeline shook her head, still smiling. "I love it. Utterly. I don't quite know what my function will be, but Fritz assures me that I will have one. Perhaps when all this is done, we might know."

Teo's mouth curved. "I won't like having you in danger, *cariño*, but so long as they provide training—"

"And you think I'll like having you in danger?" she overrode. "But we were putting ourselves in danger before we met, you recall?"

"I do." He grinned swiftly. "My daring *Orejitas*."

Emmeline laughed a little. "What does that mean anyway? I know it's not Ears."

"But it is!" he protested. "It means 'little ears', actually. Not that you are little, but in my culture, anything precious can be translated into little with a small change. Ears is *orejas*, and *orejitas* is little ears. You are too precious to me to only be *Orejas*. Thus, I called you *Orejitas*."

"Even then?"

He nodded, wishing they were alone so he could kiss her. "*Sí*."

Her look of adoration was a kiss in itself, and he could almost believe they were alone. But a sharp, piercing whistle broke them from their spell, and Teo was once again on the alert. They were nearing Burlington Gardens, but with all of the men about, finding Gent in the midst could prove challenging.

He had only really seen the man by the dark of night, as he had not been in the same meetings Teo and Emmeline had attended. But from what Teo had heard, it was difficult to reconcile the man on the streets with the peer he allegedly was in reality. That had to be the charm of his position, then, or the skill he possessed. He could blend in anywhere and be somehow unremarkable anywhere he went. Rather useful for a spy.

Reaching the corner, Teo continued to look but tugged Emmeline along with him as he crossed. "Don't stop," he murmured to her. "We mustn't behave differently from the rest."

She nodded, moving closer. "How will we find him?"

"He'll find you," a new voice said, falling into step on her other side.

Teo glanced over, nodding as Gent smiled at them both.

"Good day, lads. Ears, pleased to finally meet you."

"Likewise," Emmeline managed, though her eyes widened as she did so.

"What is this?" Teo asked him, using his eyes to motion around them.

"Phaeton race," came the easy reply. "Mr. Perry-Whitcomb's son Edward challenged Randall Quincey after hearing him boast about his new phaeton and its speed, and the challenge gained some significant wagers. Some of the members of Parliament thought it a way to draw support from each side, and as Mr. Perry-Whitcomb and Mr. Quincey are on opposite sides of the House..." He shrugged, eyes now focused ahead. "The majority of our targets will be here, and, as we discussed yesterday, we cannot disrupt activities so much that it becomes noticeable, or they will simply try again another day."

Teo nodded, seeing the wisdom in the plan, despite the risk he also saw in it. "So the crowds?"

"Our foreign friends needed to hide their plan in plain sight," Gent replied simply. "Eager crowds work well. Who would suspect murder in this setting?"

"Genius," Emmeline grumbled, shaking her head. "Maddeningly genius."

"Welcome to my world." Gent chuckled, though Teo heard a note of darkness in it. "The three of us are responsible for Gregory Lambeth. Arguably the loudest voice against the bill our friends are so eager to see pass."

"Why would they want stricter sanctions?" Teo asked quickly, eying the wall of people ahead.

"Greater control," Gent answered. "The appearance of progress while enslaving freedoms. Perhaps they have a player in power over in customs or with the gaugers. Any number of possibilities, and all have the potential to do great damage."

"This is a *coup d'état*," Emmeline suddenly breathed, gripping Teo's arm with a cold hand. "Slowly, which is unusual, but they are grabbing for power without the trouble of war." She looked up at Gent in shock. "They have members in Parliament."

Gent nodded, no hint of amusement in his tone. "Yes, and who knows where else. The bill is so cleverly written and has been promoted by the dullest speaker on either side of the House. It is an attack that no one will see coming, and it will take years to fully realize. That is the most dangerous of all."

Emmeline looked up at Teo now, and he saw the same grave horror reflected back at him. But there was no time for thoughts or words as a shot rang out, making them both jump.

"The race," Gent assured them quickly. "They started on Regent Street, and they'll come down Piccadilly Circus, onto Piccadilly Street, and end at Albany. Come on, let's find Lambeth."

Would he even be in their area of the route? Teo shook his head as they hurried toward the onlookers, wondering how many pieces to this counterplan there truly were. He knew so little, and yet there were eight targets all in the same situation and requiring the same intervention. Those watching the race with genuine interest would almost number as many tasked with saving those victims.

"Got him," Gent grunted, indicating with his chin. "Clever chap, he's wearing a plum-colored coat. Easy to notice, but hardly *outré*. You two flank him. I'll handle the rear."

With a brief squeeze, Emmeline released Teo's arm, both of them moving to approach on either side, Gent coming up the middle. They didn't say a word as they reached him, but Teo felt a distinct shift as they stopped, his shoulder brushing the gentleman's own easily.

"Took your time," Mr. Lambeth hissed, his face a little pale.

"The race is on."

Well, it appeared the man did know he was a target for murder. No wonder he looked so drawn.

"Not a bother, guv'nor," Gent quipped in a thick accent. "We're 'ere now."

Lambeth nodded, releasing a shaking breath. "What do I do?"

"Cheer," Teo suggested before whistling in encouragement at the approaching phaetons. "Take part."

"Leave the watching to us," Gent suggested. "We know what we're about."

Teo bit the inside of his cheek, biting back a humorless laugh. One of them knew what they were about, and it was the one speaking. The other two were only following instructions. Was that good enough?

The crowd roared as the phaetons reached them and whipped past, several going up on their toes and craning their necks to see the race continue. All would be distracted now, which would mean the time could be right... Yet there was nothing. The rumble of the phaeton wheels could be heard in the distance, but they grew fainter. Then there was a roar of cheering again, rolling over the crowd like a wave.

"That'll be a sharp turn at the Circus," Gent murmured, as though mapping the route in his mind. "Seems they both made it."

Teo nodded as though he cared, though, he would admit, the image of phaetons racing and then enduring a turn of such a degree...

"Guh!" Emmeline suddenly grunted, jostling Lambeth into Teo with such force they nearly stumbled.

Teo braced himself and caught Mr. Lambeth, eyes immediately darting about. No one around them had noticed, all focused on the race ahead and jostling each other for better position anyway. But someone had... something had...

His throat burned, pulsed with his heartbeat, gripping Lambeth as protectively as he could without being blatant, and feeling Gent do the same behind them. Then Teo caught sight of Emmeline or, more importantly, the man directly in front of Emmeline.

His hands were over his nose as blood dripped down his face and through his fingers, his eyes squeezed shut. Emmeline still kept her back to Teo and Lambeth, facing the bleeding assailant as he towered over her amid the tightly packed crowd, her hands held tightly in front of her as if preparing to strike again.

Cielos. How had she managed such a blow with this many people about them?

Gent suddenly whistled three notes in an almost musical cadence, striking abruptly at a man to his left that Teo hadn't noticed. Three children darted into view in an instant, catching the legs of the bleeding man as they came between him and Emmeline and sending him dropping to the ground as they scampered out of sight again.

"That'll do," Gent muttered very low, looping the arm of the unconscious man he'd struck. "Teo, grab the other one. Follow me. Ears, take Lambeth. Get out. Don't make more of a scene."

"Right," Emmeline said at once, coming to Teo and nodding at Lambeth. "Come with me, sir. I know a shortcut to Albany."

Lambeth, shaking and brushing at his sleeves, nodded. "Th-thank you, lad. I would like to see the finish." Without meeting the eyes of the others, he started out of the crowd, Emmeline hot on his heels.

There wasn't time to worry, only to act. Teo scooped up the groaning, woozy man the children had tumbled, his nose still bleeding freely, turning them both to wade back the way they had come through the crowd.

And just like that, simple and clean, their task was done.

But they were only one piece, Teo reminded himself. There were seven others out there, and he had no idea how they'd turn out.

"Dreadful blow you took, sir," Gent was saying to Teo's man, keeping his accent coarse. "Me and Ted here saw the whole thing. Lad popped up right in your face, straight up like aiming for your brain. Dreadful thing. We know a good pub, sir, where you might take your ease. Cost ye a farthing to get bes' directions."

The man mumbled something, his words slurring, his weight growing heavier on Teo as they staggered away from the crowd of the race.

"Wonder who taught the lad to strike like that," Gent murmured, giving Teo a quick grin. "Never seen anything like it myself."

It was all Teo could do not to beam with pride and delight, even as they carried the assailants away from their scene. At least one of the victims had been spared that day. He could only pray the others had been successful as well.

They walked only a block or two before both men were unconscious, and Gent ordered Teo to deposit his man toward Regent Street while he'd find a separate place for his own. They'd meet up with Ears at Albany, provided Lambeth hadn't requested her to escort him home. After all, Gent had said with a laugh, Mr. Lambeth had no idea that Ears wasn't just a feisty boy of thirteen with an excellent punch.

Finding his way toward Albany, his sleeping companion now alone in an alley, Teo still felt his pulse thudding in twelve different places. Where were the other targets? Had the operatives gotten to them in time? Had they managed to avoid much detection in the crowd? Had Emmeline managed as well on her own as she was capable of?

She had the advantage in London at night, there was no question, but this was London during the day with a great many obstacles, not to mention actual murderers. How would any of this play out for them?

He reached Albany shortly, the race over, the crowds beginning to disperse. Gent appeared from behind him, nudging his arm.

Teo barely acknowledged him. "Any word?" he asked as he continued to look for Emmeline.

"Not yet. Rendezvous at Weaver's house at ten. Ears knows the way."

It belatedly occurred to him that Weaver was the code name for Fritz, Emmeline's cousin, and he nodded. "Disguise or polite?"

"Does it matter?" Gent nudged his arm again, turning away.

"Aren't you going to wait for Ears?" Teo bit out, glancing over his shoulder, stung that their operative companion would leave so soon.

"I did," Gent replied, still walking away. "Look to your two o'clock."

The reference gave Teo pause, but he did as he was told, scanning his way around the courtyard to the position indicated. Walking toward him, grinning freely, was a familiar figure in a padded jacket and cap, stray curls flying at her brow. He waited for her to reach him, his heart thundering as much as it had in the crowd, unable to look anywhere else.

Emmeline sighed as she reached him, swallowing. "Right. Now what?"

Teo laughed and draped his arm around her shoulder, as he might have done to a lad he was steward over, and steered her from the courtyard, back toward the streets. "Now, *Orejitas*, I hold you for a very long time while we wait to report back in."

"Well, my aunt is away for the day, thanks to my cousin's very clever and cunning plans," she told him, shoving her hands into the pockets of her jacket. "So I really have no demands upon my time."

"Yes, you do, *cariño*," he assured her very seriously, pulling her more tightly into his side. "You're coming home with me. I demand your time."

"*Sí, Capitán*," she replied, her accent nearly perfect. "Whatever you say."

Chapter Twenty-Three

$\mathscr{I}$t was dark before Emmeline, Teo, and Rafa left the house in St. James's Square, walking quietly toward Fritz's house. They'd not said much as they waited for time to pass, for all the other operatives to endure their own attacks and succeed or fail in the rescue of their target. It had been too much to contemplate, particularly once the excitement of the moment had worn off.

Emmeline had needed Teo to hold her for a while, her body shaking slightly in the quiet of his house. It hadn't made sense to her at the time, given how long after the attack the shaking had begun, but once she'd considered it in retrospect… well, she'd never really endured something like that.

Yes, she'd been chased throughout London. Yes, she had been in dangerous situations. Yes, she had overheard a plot to assassinate significant members in Parliament and reported the plot to a band of operatives, which had then drawn her in.

But she had never endured a physical altercation like that and never on behalf of someone else. She had never been part of saving someone's life and been so directly faced with the threat. She had spent all her investigations trying to avoid detection and stay away from confrontation, yet today, she had stood and faced it. Had thrust the heel of her hand into it, just as Santiago had taught her.

The blow hadn't stopped the man entirely, but it had given Gent's children enough time to upend him in a way that could never be blamed on her alone. Simple actions that would all appear to be the results of an overworked crowd, yet it had been so coordinated and so effective.

When Rafa returned to the house after his task, he had joined them in the sitting room and relayed his experience with Rook. Their target had also been made aware of his danger and advised to continue with his chosen course. They'd been right at the curve of Piccadilly Circus, which had made the situation more precarious and more crowded. The assailants had not been so easily deterred as Emmeline's and Teo's, nor were the surroundings such that Rafa and Rook had the room to maneuver well. But Rafa had thrown a punch at a surly onlooker, which had earned him a blow himself, and soon there had been a near brawl, which had allowed Rook to ferret their target away from the crowds and out of sight.

Rafa's bruises would be unsightly for some time, and his lip was badly cut, but he repeatedly insisted he had no regrets. He'd also said something about a good fight being worth the punches, but Teo had been laughing too much for Emmeline to trust the translation entirely.

And then they had waited. Waiting had never been among Emmeline's better utilized virtues.

Juan had cooked a meal for the household, though whether it was intended to be a late luncheon or an early dinner was up for discussion. It was simple fare, but none of them seemed particularly hungry, nor particularly interested in what it was they were eating.

For part of the time, Emmeline had asked Teo to show her the house. They'd walked the corridors hand in hand, studied portraits and antiquities, even played a few notes on the dust-laden pianoforte, though neither of them could play well. It had been in the study, though, that the revelations had come.

Teo explained he hadn't spent much time in there yet as he sat behind the desk, feeling some distance from his grandfather since the discoveries at Diehle House. But, Emmeline had reminded him, they could not let ghosts of the past come between them and their future. She had not yet told him what she pictured that future to be, but she would soon enough.

She'd been lost in Teo's smile for several moments before she realized a box sat on the shelf alongside some books behind him. He'd turned to it after she'd indicated the thing, and once opened, his expression sent her around the desk to kneel at his side.

Contained in the box were letters addressed to Teo's father. All unopened, and all returned. There were several years' worth of them, and some were quite thick. Teo had not opened them then, and Emmeline could not blame him for that. But he had asked that she be present when he did do so, to which she had assured him she would be. Hell itself could not have kept her away.

It had been a strange thing, seeing this house that belonged to him and yet was not his. The building existed, and that might have been all. There was nothing of Teo's taste or manner in the house, no light in any corner, no cheer or sense of adventure or comfortable situation. That would all come in time, of course, as he settled in and began to make changes, but seeing what had been before Teo... well, it had made her appreciation for Teo something even more significant.

Her life had been fair and full before Teo had come into it. She'd had no complaints, apart from her aunt's insistence that she continue to participate in Society despite her lack of enjoyment there. Even then, the insistence was well-meant and full of good intentions. Emmeline had taken matters into her own hands and began her wandering about London, which had given her a secret passion and joy for her life and her situation she might not have found elsewhere.

Somehow, Teo compounded everything she thought she'd had and made it feel so much more complete. Nothing had been missing in her life, yet Teo made it whole. How could something be made whole that was never quite lacking?

But that's how it felt. That was how *she* felt. Whole. Complete. Full. True.

Without ever being incomplete or empty or wanting on her own, and despite being perfectly content with what she had achieved for herself and where she was, she now felt the most honest, truest version of herself that she could have been.

Teo made her even more herself. Her love for Teo made her better. His light made her shine. How could she ever go another day without embracing such beauty and goodness?

"Why is it," Emmeline mused aloud now, her hand in his, "that walking with you at night feels the most perfect?"

Teo exhaled at the question, a sweet sound of satisfaction despite the tension in the air. "Sometimes, it is the simplest things in life, not the finest, that can mean the most."

She smiled at that. "Like a marzipan horse."

He gave her a strange look. "*¿Qué?*"

Astonishing how some words needed no translation.

"Amy," she explained, her fingers brushing against his hand as he held them. "The day after we found her, I brought an entire basket of food to her and Suds simply because I was going mad with wondering. Of all the things I brought, what she loved most was a marzipan horse."

"*Preciosa niña*," he laughed softly, shaking his head. "Simplicity is taken for granted. Look at Rafa." He pointed at his friend, walking far enough ahead of them to be nearly out of earshot.

Emmeline did so, then back at Teo. "What about him?"

"If he were to smile a little," Teo pointed out, "no one would think him so angry all the time."

"I am angry all the time, *camarada*," Rafa called back, sounding amused. "I live with you. What else could I be?"

"*Largarse*," Teo laughed, waving him away.

Emmeline loved the banter between them, the brotherhood they shared and the understanding. "You two are more like brothers than friends."

Still laughing, Teo looked at her. "Is that a question?"

"No. Simply an observation." She shrugged, smiling fondly at him. "I have no siblings, and no friend as close as having one. I like seeing it."

"Well, Rafa has half-brothers," Teo told her, looking mischievous, "but I have it on very good authority that his mother likes me the best."

"*Cállate lunático*," came Rafa's growling voice once more.

Emmeline clamped down on her lips as a giggle escaped. "No translation needed on that one."

"Rafa does not usually require translations," he whispered. "Only apologies."

"We need to find him a wife," Emmeline suggested lightly. "That might soften him."

Teo grinned. "Oh, he has one. Well, he has a woman he loves

and plans to marry. We're rather alike in that respect." He trailed off, letting the silence speak for itself.

Emmeline caught her breath, the opening too perfect to rush into, too important to let pass. It was now or never.

"I cannot speak for Rafa's lady," Emmeline said slowly, her heart somehow beating at the base of her throat, "but I would like to hear more about those plans. Yours, to be specific."

Teo stopped in his tracks, tugging at her arm when she continued to walk. She turned, looking at him as though his halting was a surprise, but said nothing.

His eyes were wide, searching hers. "*¿Qué dijiste?*"

Emmeline felt her lips quirk, though she didn't dare smile yet. "You plan to marry. I would like to know more."

"*Por favor, no me tomes el pelo,*" he rambled, his grip on her hand clenching now. "*No puedo soportarlo sí no estás serio.*"

Though she had no idea what he was saying, she laughed and came to him, laying a hand alongside his cheek. "When you are no longer overwhelmed or frightened or whatever it is you are feeling, I would like to say yes to a certain question, Teo. But you will need to ask it before I can."

"Marry me," he breathed, reaching up to cover her hand against his face.

"Still not a question," she pointed out, tapping his cheek.

He swallowed once. "*¿Por favor?*"

Somehow, that was the most beautiful, tender, adorable way she could ever have been asked, and nothing could have been more perfect.

"Yes," she whispered as she touched her brow to his, her eyes fluttering shut. "I love you."

His lips brushed across hers, just once. "*Yo también te amo.*"

Emmeline hummed a soft laugh, nuzzling her nose against his. "I know, love. Believe me, I know."

Teo chuckled breathlessly. "What a moment to choose, Emmeline. I have nothing to signify this. But perhaps…" He reached into the pocket of his plain weskit, something mischievous entering his eyes. Then he held up a small coin, grinning wildly.

She squinted at it. "A ha'penny? Why would that mean

anything?"

"It was yours, *Orejitas*. You dropped it the night we met. The very first night when you crashed into me. I picked it up, and I kept it for luck. Had I known what it would truly mean…" He shook his head, laughing again. "Perhaps I should have my signet ring made from it."

"You've kept that worthless coin in your pocket all this time?" Emmeline asked, her voice going hoarse. "From the beginning?"

Teo kissed her softly, slowly, tenderly. "*Sí, mi amada*. From the beginning."

Emmeline sighed against his mouth, stroking his jaw. "I adore you, Teo."

A faint throat clearing disturbed the night, and Teo sighed, kissing her palm quickly. "I suppose anything else must wait," he grumbled, glaring up at Rafa as they started walking again.

"Threats against the nation," Emmeline mused, making a face. "Mass assassinations. Foreign sympathizers and spies in the houses of government. Perhaps I did pick a poor time to force a proposal."

"It wasn't forced," Teo insisted. "And there would be no bad time."

Emmeline hissed and shook her head. "Fritz wouldn't agree. If we're tardy, he'll have my head."

"Will he give permission, though?" Teo asked as he swung their hands like a child. "He is your guardian."

The thought made Emmeline frown. "He'd better."

A few moments more, and they were at their destination, being led in by Fritz's presently solemn butler who privately winked at Emmeline as she entered.

They were led to the large drawing room, where several others, both men and women, waited. A few of the faces were familiar, but most were people Emmeline had not met. Perhaps one or two had been in the meetings she'd joined in the day before, but there had been so much going on, so much information to absorb, that individuals did not stand out to her.

She caught sight of Gent by the fire, and he smiled grimly, nodding in greeting.

At least she'd finally met the most elusive man in London. The day could at least be counted for that. And she had just gotten engaged. Did the fate of their mission mean more than that?

Fritz entered the room then, followed by a few others, one of whom she recognized as Sir Robert Peel, the home secretary. High governmental offices indeed. To Emmeline's surprise, Fritz did not address the group. An older gentleman with bushy brows and a slight smile did so.

"I would like to congratulate all of you," the man began. "Because of your efforts, quick thinking, and brilliant strategies, we have successfully saved all eight of the intended targets of today's attacks."

It was as if the room heaved a sigh of relief, and a few of the men clapped each other on the back. Yet the senior men in the room did not. Emmeline's stomach sank.

"We did, however," the older gentleman said, "have a casualty. Mr. Hubert was stabbed in his office while we saved the others."

"Hubert?" someone repeated in disbelief. "He wasn't on the list."

"Why would they target him?" someone else chimed in. "He's one of theirs."

"Actually," Fritz broke in, "he's one of ours. He's been feeding us information for three years."

That sobered the entire group.

"How did they know?" one of the ladies asked, her voice hard. "How did the devils know about him if none of us did?"

"We don't know that yet," Sir Robert told her, his tone saddened, if not concerned. "I've just received word from the prime minister that the bill perpetuating the increased statutes on shipping into England has failed in the House, so we must consider that a success."

One of the other senior gentlemen stepped forward. "We can assure you that all of our offices and departments will be working together to gather all of the intelligence and information available to us. You may be assigned to work with new operatives as we pick up leads. And do not be surprised if you are arrested during the upcoming missions. We will do what we can to preserve the mission, even at the risk of your assumed identities. If anyone doubts us, just ask Sparrow. Her first mission, we had to arrange an arrest to save her. Speaking of the Convent agents... ladies, Milliner has said she will be in touch. And Ears, where is Ears?"

Stunned at being called out, Emmeline raised her hand. "Here, sir."

All eyes turned to her, making her face flush and her throat tighten.

But the man only smiled. "It is thanks to you, Ears, that any of today's actions were made possible. While we may never be able to grant you the full accolades and honors such a service deserves, know that you have the gratitude of the entire government, and from His Majesty, who has been debriefed as to the situation."

Emmeline blinked at the words, not entirely comprehending as her mind repeated them. "Thank you, sir," she managed to say, unsure how else to proceed.

Fritz stepped forward then, grinning proudly. "And just so it's clear, Ears, Milliner will also be in touch with you to explain everything."

That made no sense whatsoever, as she had no idea who or what Milliner was, but as it would not do to question her cousin in front of a room of spies whom he had some authority over, she only nodded.

"Congratulations, *Orejitas*," Teo murmured beside her as other conversations began and orders were handed out.

"I don't know what any of that means, apart from 'His Majesty,'" she admitted in a hoarse whisper, giggling slightly. "I suppose it must be good, right?"

"Seemed to be," Rafa agreed from her other side. "Gratitude is always a good word to hear from higher authority. *Felicitaciones, hermanita.*"

Teo's eyes widened even as he grinned, and Emmeline sensed that Rafa had just paid her some great honor, even if only in his own estimation.

"*Gracias, Rafa,*" she replied, smiling as well. "I think we're going to be great friends."

Rafa raised a brow. "I would only be so fortunate, Emmeline, if you can bear my *mal humor.*"

Her eyes narrowed as she tried her best to translate without help. "I've never minded a sour temper, so long as I was not the cause or the target."

The tall Spaniard smiled at her, which she had never yet seen him fully do. *"Muy bien, hermanita. Te haremos española todavía."*

She huffed playfully at that, propping her hands on her hip. "It's no use complimenting me if I can't understand it, Rafa. For pity's sake!"

Teo and Rafa laughed as Fritz appeared at the edge of their group, smiling slightly. "Cheery bunch, I must say. Cousin."

Emmeline nodded. "Fritz. Teo asked me to marry him, and I've said yes."

Teo made a strange yelping sound from beside her, but she kept her expression clear as she stared at her cousin expectantly.

"Very good," he replied without concern. "I'll have the banns read and spin a marvelous tale for Aunt Hermione. Let me know where you would like the wedding to be, and I will arrange everything. May I walk you down the aisle?"

Emmeline stepped forward and kissed her cousin lightly on the cheek. "As if anyone else could."

"I don't know about that," Fritz mused thoughtfully. "Suds might have liked to."

Before she could reply to that, he turned to Rafa, surprising them all. "Rafa, I've been tied up with the details of this mission, but I feel an overdue explanation is owed to you. May we speak privately?"

Rafa's brows rose, and he looked at Teo before saying, "I have no secrets from Teo. You may speak freely."

Emmeline ducked her chin and moved to leave, but Rafa put out an arm to stop her.

"Stay, *hermanita*," he insisted gently. "Whatever he has to say, you may hear also."

Touched, Emmeline blinked away surprised tears and returned to Teo's side, clasping his hand in hers.

"Your father," Fritz began, his voice very low, almost imperceptible, "was not captured and sold into slavery. He was in France doing business in 1792 when the prison massacres took place, and he became trapped there until after the execution of Louis XVI. He stowed away on a ship headed for Brittany, then paid a local to ferry him across the channel to England. He came to find a friend of his, someone he knew well from other business ventures in France, someone who might be able to join him in fighting the wrongs he had seen there."

Rafa's eyes were round as Fritz spoke. "But… I was born in early 1799, sir."

Fritz nodded, smiling. "We learned of that much later. You see, my associate introduced Marco to us right away. We all had a vested interest in the Revolution and in the fallout for Europe. He joined us, Rafa. Unconventional for a man of Spanish nationality to join the British in covert operations, but he was firm. He continued his career in business as an excellent tradesman, and he made sure to return to Spain often enough to call it home, but he was always focused on his next mission and how many lives he could save. I was very young at the time, fresh in my career as an operative, still very much learning the trade, but Marco was a natural."

Emmeline watched Rafa as he listened, looking very much like a young boy rather than the surly man he always appeared to be.

"The British defeat of the French navy by Admiral Nelson was a direct result of Marco's work," Fritz insisted, his eyes bright. "Astounding information he was able to obtain. He was in Cairo, helping them rise up against the French in rebellion in October 1798 and was killed in the ensuing battle when the rebellion was suppressed."

Rafa swallowed hard, fumbling for something to latch onto. Emmeline reached out a hand, and he gripped it hard. "Why weren't we told, sir?"

"We didn't know he'd married your mother," Fritz admitted softly, sounding a little choked himself. "Marco was very private about his personal life. We didn't know your mother existed, and we had no idea she was carrying you. We don't even know if your father knew. He'd been passing as a Frenchman for so long as an operative, we couldn't claim him as a British asset until the trouble with Bonaparte was over and done. Had we known, Rafa, I swear to you that we would have found and protected you both. You would have known of your father's courage and bravery and of his sacrifice."

"Why the rumors?" Teo asked him, sounding as awed as Rafa by all of this.

Fritz smiled sadly. "I can't even tell you that for sure. Marco thought some of his friends knew he was dealing with the British more than he said, so when he disappeared, they presumed... Well, it wasn't possible to correct them, and we felt deserving of some guilt for leaving him in Cairo after his death." He looked at Rafa again, reaching out a hand. "Should you ever have an interest, Rafa, I will take you to Cairo myself and show you where he died, where he is buried, and the memorial that some of us who were his friends have set up over the years as we've been permitted to enter Egypt."

Emmeline held her breath, wondering how Rafa would feel about all of this, how he would react, what he would say.

What could any of them say?

Rafa exhaled slowly, then grasped Fritz's hand, shaking hard. "I would like that very much, Weaver. And, if you'll allow it, I would like to follow in my father's footsteps. I would like to become an asset for you."

Fritz nodded, looking almost proud. "You are the spitting image of him, you know. It's only fitting you should have his heart as well. We'll talk in the coming weeks, Rafa. Perhaps after your wedding." He shook his hand again, winked at Emmeline, and strode away.

Rafa stared after him in shock, then looked at Emmeline and Teo. "How does he know about that? I haven't even asked Maria yet."

"He's always been interfering," Emmeline assured him, glaring at her cousin's back. "Now that I know he's a spy, it makes so much more sense." She looked up at Rafa, wincing. "How are you feeling?"

His brow furrowed in thought. "Lighter. Relieved. *Confundido. Firme.*" He looked at Teo again, his brow clearing. "*Entiendo ahora, Teo. Entiendo.*" He nodded at them both, then walked away, still looking dazed.

"What did he say?" Emmeline asked as Teo steered her toward the window.

"He understands now," Teo told her. "That's all."

"Understands what?"

Teo touched her cheek gently, smiling. "Why I was so driven for answers for so long. Why I chose to come to England. Why I'll stay in England."

"And why will you stay in England, Sir Teo?" Emmeline inquired, leaning into his touch, her eyes fluttering as his thumb touched her bottom lip.

He laughed softly. "Because I found the answers to every question. Even the ones I didn't know to ask. I found myself in England when I found you."

Emmeline sighed, her mouth finding his in an instant. "*Te amo, Teo*," she murmured against his lips.

His shiver of delight made her smile. "*Te amo más querida. Siempre te amaré.*"

Epilogue

"*A*nd you are certain she wanted to see me as well?"

"Yes, Teo, she specifically asked for us both."

"But this is your school, and I don't have anything to do with this."

"You are my husband now. Perhaps that is enough."

Teo did not look convinced, but Emmeline was certain of it. The spring fête of the school had taken place the day before, and she and Teo had opted to remain in the area afterward for a few days rather than proceed immediately to Diehle House.

In the six weeks or so since their first mission, they had both been involved in training and meetings, learning just how far back the trouble from the Faction went, and all that had been accomplished to stop them at this point.

She had received several letters from the one called Milliner, though she had yet to meet her. She would be brought into the fold of the Agents of the Convent, she had been told, but no one had made it particularly clear what that meant or what would be involved. She must allow for secrecy in communication, she supposed, but it was most disconcerting.

Being brought into the operative world at all had made her head spin, and she had been so grateful to have Teo beside her throughout the process. He made sense of the world when she struggled to, reminded her of the good, and always found a way to make her smile.

Fritz had been good to his word when it came to their wedding. The banns had been read straightaway, and, as soon as custom permitted, they married in the lovely St. Martin-in-the-Fields chapel with Fritz leading her down the aisle. Aunt Hermione, of course, had wanted it at St. George's in Hanover Square, but Fritz had managed to convince her that St. Martin's was more aligned with Emmeline's tastes.

Aunt Hermione was beside herself with joy over the union and with adoration for her new nephew-in-law. Nothing Teo could or would do in the future would ever be able to diminish his luster in her sight, and she was anything but shy when it came to letting Emmeline know about it. Emmeline didn't mind. Teo would never diminish in her sight, either.

Marriage to Teo was a dream, though there had only been a few weeks of it so far. He was adoring and charming, deliciously affectionate, and masterfully witty. She had laughed so much in the days of being his wife, she wondered if she ever had a moment of seriousness in his presence. How had she ever resisted this idea?

She had finished the coursework for her students at the Miss Masters's school just before the wedding, though the term itself had not ended until last week. Much as she hated it, there would be no possibility of her continuing her teaching while she was the wife of Sir Teodoro de Vickers y Mendoza. In portioning her time between their house in London for the Season and at Diehle House in Lincolnshire for the remainder, taking time to live alone in Kent simply wasn't feasible. And the wife of a baronet certainly could not be a teacher at a girls' school. Or so Emmeline continued to tell herself.

Besides, she had it on very good authority that Lucy Allred had been offered a teaching position at the school for the coming term, which was exactly as Emmeline had hoped. It also made her wish even more fervently that she could teach just one more term, even as Lady Vickers, just to share some time on the faculty together.

If she managed not to beg Miss Bradford to make an exception for her when they met with her in the next few minutes, it would be a miracle.

The note had come this morning to them at the inn, asking them to meet Miss Bradford in her office at the school shortly after luncheon. It was likely a formality, given the years that Emmeline had taught there, and perhaps even a personal congratulations on their wedding. Miss Bradford had been unable to attend, given the continuation of the school term and taking over in teaching for Emmeline in her absence. She had always been a fair woman, caring about her students and her teachers, and generous in her attentions there.

Emmeline still could not manage to call her Pippa, but perhaps that would come with time.

"Are you certain this is the way, *cariño?*" Teo asked in a low voice, which somehow still echoed in the grand corridors.

"Yes, Teo, I'm certain," she replied with a laugh. "I've been to her office on several occasions. You went to university. Could you not still find your way there?"

"The University of Salamanca is not quite the same as this place," Teo informed her, shaking his head. "This is *imponente y aterradora.*"

Emmeline sighed and looped her hand through her husband's arm, pulling him close. She had not learned much more of the Spanish language since marrying the man, but she knew full well that he reverted back to his natural tongue when he struggled to express himself in English. It was an adorable trait that she secretly hoped would never fade.

"There is nothing to be nervous about, *cariño,*" she soothed as she rubbed his arm with her free hand. "Miss Bradford has always been very kind to me and very understanding when I could not stay here to teach all term. It was never difficult to return to London when I needed to."

Teo gave her a look. "She thought you were tending to an ailing relative, Emmeline. You were not. She was understanding about a lie."

He had a point there.

The faintest nudge of discomfort tugged at her stomach. "True… but I am no longer a teacher here. Now I am Lady Vickers, am I not?"

As she hoped, the use of her new name made him smile, his usual light reentering his eyes. "*Sí, esposa mía, ciertamente lo eres.*"

She leaned in and kissed his cheek gently, winking with the promise of further interesting discussions as to their married state at a more appropriate time and place.

His quick rising of a brow told her he caught her meaning with exactness. The soles of her feet caught fire at once.

This meeting had better be short.

They reached the headmistress's office then, and Emmeline, suddenly filled with nerves, rapped on the door.

"Come in," Miss Bradford's voice called from within.

With an anxious look at Teo, Emmeline pushed into the office, pausing inside with a polite smile and a quick curtsey. "Miss Bradford."

"Lady Vickers, surely it is I who curtsey to you," Miss Bradford said from where she stood beside her desk. She did so, her smile as warm as ever. "My warmest felicitations on your marriage. I've been told it was quite lovely."

"Yes, we were pleased with it," Emmeline told her in an oddly formal tone she could not seem to shake. "Miss Bradford, may I present my husband, Sir Teodoro de Vickers y Mendoza?"

Teo stepped forward and bowed with perfection. "A pleasure, Miss Bradford."

"*El placer es mío, Sir Teodoro,*" Miss Bradford replied warmly, lacing her fingers before her and nodding. "*Bienvenido a nuestra escuela.*"

Emmeline's jaw dropped as she stared at the headmistress.

Teo cleared his throat. "*¿Habla español, señorita?*"

"*Un poco. No lo suficiente para ser hábil.*" She grinned then, laughing at herself. "And certainly not enough to continue this conversation in it, if you'll permit me."

"Of course." Teo grinned at Emmeline with adorable excitement, then returned his attention to Miss Bradford. "Your accent is very good."

"*Gracias,*" she returned before gesturing to a pair of chairs before her desk. "Please, won't you sit?"

They did so, and Emmeline felt her heart racing with renewed anxiety. She was desperate to ask questions but bit them back in an attempt at patience.

Miss Bradford smiled at her then, as though she knew. "Did you both enjoy the fête yesterday? Sir Teo, you would not have been before, but I have heard from the villagers it was our best one in years."

"It was wonderful, Miss Bradford," Teo assured her, taking Emmeline's hand. "The young ladies were most accomplished and very impressive. I hope you were pleased."

"Thank you, I was." Her smile spread for just a moment. "Lady Vickers will, no doubt, assure you that the maypole remaining upright was a wonderful change from the year before."

Emmeline snickered at the memory. "It was a relief. I won't pretend otherwise."

"Yes, Mr. Fairfax and Mr. Quinn thought so as well." Miss Bradford sobered a little and looked between the two of them. "Well, you can probably ascertain that I did not request to meet with you both purely to offer my good wishes and have a polite chat, though I certainly do mean both."

"We were a little curious," Emmeline ventured, smiling slightly. "But I would never presume to judge."

Miss Bradford nodded at that. "I believe you, Emmeline, if I may still call you such."

Emmeline returned her nod. "Please do."

"Thank you." She paused, wetting her lips. "There is never a simple way to say this, and I trust you will appreciate my frankness when I tell you that your response to my letters has been everything I hoped."

"Letters?" Emmeline looked at Teo in bewilderment, then back at the headmistress. "I received no letters from you."

"But you did," Miss Bradford assured her. "And you've started your training, just as I had asked. Weaver has been very detailed in his reports to me, and I have every expectation that you will continue to excel as you progress. Given your past as Ears in London, I have no doubt you will." She smiled just a little. "Have you guessed it yet?"

Emmeline hadn't been aware her jaw had dropped until she'd had to close her mouth to swallow. "You're Milliner," she finally managed.

"I am." Miss Bradford leaned forward, resting her arms on the desk. "And this school is no mere finishing school, although it does function properly as such. It is also a training academy for the finest female spies in England, Scotland, and Ireland. Next term, we will even add a few Welsh girls to our numbers."

A breeze could have knocked Emmeline over with the shock of the revelation. She slumped back against her chair, completely foregoing posture.

"Training spies," Emmeline said slowly, thinking back on all the students she had known over the years, wondering which of the girls were spies and which were not, and who were even now working as operatives across the country.

"Yes," Miss Bradford said simply. "We wanted to bring you into the program while you were a student here, but your cousin preferred otherwise. Under usual circumstances, guardians are not so well informed... But you got to us in the end, didn't you?"

Emmeline swallowed with some difficulty again, shaking her head. "I never knew. I never expected to hear that from this place."

"That is the point," Miss Bradford assured her. "If it was obvious, we would not be doing our task well. This place is known in our world as the Convent, which is why the female spies under my care are known as Agents of the Convent. You have agreed to be one of us. Are you still willing to join the ranks?"

Teo squeezed Emmeline's hand, and she looked at him, her heart pounding unsteadily as her lungs struggled to keep up. His smile was as warm and gentle as the dawn, his expression one of complete trust and support. He nodded a little, his thumb brushing against her hand.

Emmeline nodded in return. "Yes, Milliner. I am willing."

He squeezed her hand again, winking.

"Then we must plan your training here," Milliner said briskly, bringing Emmeline's head back around. "Fists and Thistle will start your fight training tomorrow, if you both can be spared to linger in Kent a while longer. We'll say you are preparing affairs for the teacher taking your place. Sir Teo, if you would also like some fight training, we are more than happy to oblige. Weaver has claimed you as an asset, but one day, you may be asked to do more."

Milliner continued to instruct them, scheduling various meetings and trainings with code names Emmeline did not recognize, and she simply nodded through it all, clinging to the warmth of the hand beside her and feeling a new pride pulsing through her veins.

Everything she had done, everything she had endured in her life, had brought her to this moment. Had prepared her for this. Had led her along perfectly. How could she have ever suspected that?

"Right, that should do for now," Milliner said, smiling brightly. "It does get easier to take in, I promise. Would you like to walk about the grounds? Show your husband about? There are no students now, other than the academy girls, so you are free to do so. We'll meet again tomorrow; shall we say at noon?"

At their nods, she rose, coming around the desk. "I am so pleased to have you both with us. Truly. And if either of you have any questions, at any time, please ask. I am always available. Understand?"

"Thank you, Miss… I mean, Milliner." Emmeline blushed at her own correction.

Milliner, however, only grinned. "You'll get used to it, Ears. I promise." She gestured for the door, and they turned, heading out of the office.

"Oh, would you send Miss Dalton in on your way out?" Milliner called. "She should be waiting."

They moved into the corridor, Emmeline feeling almost light-headed.

Minerva Dalton stood patiently in the hall, brightening as she saw them, though not seeming entirely surprised. "Well, if it isn't the newlyweds! How nice to see you both again so soon!"

Suspicious now, Emmeline returned her smile. "Miss Bradford said you may go on in, Minerva. Perhaps we might chat tomorrow?"

"I'd like that very much." Minerva placed a hand on her arm, squeezing gently, before moving past them for the office.

"Do you think she…" Teo whispered, watching her go.

"It would not surprise me a jot," Emmeline replied with a nod. Then she shook her head. "Oh, Teo, I will never look at this place the same way again."

He put a hand at her back, starting them down the corridor. "Good? Bad? Somewhere in between?"

"Good, I think." She inhaled deeply, then exhaled as well. "I always thought of this place as another home. Now I may understand why."

"You'll be brilliant, *mi dulce amor*," he told her softly, his hand stroking at her back. "I have no doubt."

Emmeline shook her head. "I couldn't do it without you, my love. It won't work unless you're with me."

"I always will be, *cariño. Siempre.*"

"*Siempre,*" she repeated as she took his hand, holding tightly. "Always."

Coming Soon

Of Mist and Mirrors

Agents of the Convent
Book Three

"The better part in spying is discretion."

by

Rebecca Connolly

About the Author

Growing up, Rebecca Connolly wanted to be Elizabeth Bennett, Mary Poppins, or British royalty, so it came as a great shock when she discovered she was an American girl from the Midwest. She started making up stories when she was young, and thanks to a rampant imagination and a fairly consistent stream of hot chocolate, ice cream, and cookie dough, she's kept at it. She loves a good love story, and a good swoon, and tries to share that with her readers. She still lives in the Midwest, has two degrees in non-writing fields, and dreams of one day having a cottage of her own in her beloved British Isles.

Rebecca is a huge fan of period dramas and currently writes in the Regency era, though she refuses to rule any other time period out. You just never know where the imagination will take you, and she'll write whatever story comes to her whenever it's set! There is always a story to tell, and she wants to tell them all!

You can find out more at www.rebeccaconnolly.com.

Lightning Source UK Ltd.
Milton Keynes UK
UKHW022228041222
413345UK00011B/1540